Blooms of War

Suzanne Tierney

DEDICATION

To Maria and David—
Whose love story is for the ages

ACKNOWLEDGEMENTS

With heartfelt appreciation to the frontline medical care workers on the battlefield of war and in the war against diseases. Your courage and sacrifice keep our communities healthy and safe.

Thank you to: Kristina Kairn, who always demands more fight scenes; Colette Dixon who always requests more love scenes; RickRack books for keeping me historically accurate and making sure this book is readable; Jannie Mitzeiko Harvey for making order out of chaos; the Persisters whose talent and support inspire me; the Rebelles whose collective wisdom and humor bring magic to my every day; my in-laws and parents for babysitting; my husband for brewing coffee; my children for turning every day into an adventure (even if it's just finding the match to that sock) . . .

And YOU, you lovely, lovely readers, who choose to go on heart-wrenching, joyous journeys with my characters. I hope Vera and Nick make you laugh a little and love a lot.

PART I

You have dancing shoes with nimble soles.
I have a soul of lead.
—William Shakespeare,
The Merchant of Venice

CHAPTER ONE

Halsop House, May 1, 1919

Everyone has one defining sentence, the grammar precise, the words impersonal, the tone officious. The sentence designed with the flatness of a telegram to inform you your life is irrevocably altered. In the blood-soaked muck of France, it was the drawn medical officer rubbing his weathered cheek, glancing at his watch, and declaring *time of death* even though the bullet-ridden boy who lay in the worn stretcher had taken his last breath hours before. A man wasn't dead until the doctor said he was.

In the breakfast room of Halsop House, I tamp down my nausea and focus on the William Morris wallpaper, the sunflower motif as familiar to me as a nursery rhyme. I grew up in this house. I am home again. I wasn't even supposed to have been in Northern France. My family still doesn't know I was. We are six months after Armistice. We are at peace. So I do not let my hand tremble when I pour myself a cup of tea and pass my older sister the basket of croissants and hand Papa his newspaper. I push away the stench of the tent hospital where, for four years, I served as a nurse, cleaning out rotted flesh and bandaging wounds that would never heal. I buried all those *times of death*, so many earnest faces, some so young they'd yet to shave, now tiny gravestones in my heart.

The tea I'm drinking is hot, earl gray. I note the fact, but I don't feel the heat, I don't smell the smoky bergamot. It's merely liquid that slides down my throat. *Swallow*, I have to remind myself. *Swallow*. It's what the living do.

Beside me, Papa is humming and running his forefinger down a column of numbers in *The Financial Times*, a paper he never read before 1914. His breakfast of eggs and bacon, orange juice fresh pressed, coffee piping hot, loads and loads of toast will grow cold before he finishes savoring the profit reports. Where the rest of England is straining under rations, Papa can let things go to waste. Others might have been broken by *It is my painful duty to inform you*; *No peace till victory*; *Men being mowed down like grass*. But all those sentences meant only one thing for Papa. For the medical supply business his earldom had so distastefully absorbed by marrying merchant-class Mama—*gross profits were up*. It was war, after all. I suppose someone had to win. Why not Papa? At least he didn't manufacture bullets.

The sun has rolled out across the Surrey countryside, focusing its morning rays on the garden where Mama spent the three decades of her marriage cultivating roses. It takes me a moment to remember to squint. The light is bright, almost harsh, each ray pointing an accusatory finger at the once lush garden where Mama had turned earth and nurtured saplings, tamed branches and bred hearty blooms to perfume the hot summer air. Now the bushes lay scraggly and unkempt, blooms wilted, petals browned, branches choking round themselves. Papa will not let the gardeners save it. It serves more of a tomb than my mother's gravestone marked with the perfunctory *loving mother and wife*.

It's influenza. That had been Mama's sentence, a diagnosis she knew she would not survive. I came home too late to save the woman who had given me life and kissed away my hurts and sent me on my disastrous path into the arms of war. I never got to tell her, *I'm sorry*. I never got to say, *I forgive you*.

Across the table, my nephew Matty giggles and I smile at the cherubic three-year-old, the movement of my mouth following distant muscle memory. My sister Gwendolyn wipes a spot of orange marmalade from his cheek. "You have the manners of a monkey," she chides him.

"Mama's monkey," he answers back.

She tickles his belly and he laughs, trying to wriggle out of her arms. She tightens her hold with a selfishness I admire. It doesn't matter that the day is early or that we will have no visitors, Gwendolyn has swept her blond hair into a French knot, dressed in a periwinkle shirt dress, dabbed her neck and wrists in lavender water, and set her lipstick. She flicks a glance across the table at my hair, brown and bobbed, not in the dangerous Marcel wave of flappers and movie stars, but dull and practical. My sweater is overbig and grey, a shroud hanging over my shoulders. Her disapproval registers just above my left temple, like a headache I'm so used to, I've almost forgotten it hurts.

Most people would assume Gwendolyn's sentence would be *I do.* She abandoned her hard-won place at Cambridge to marry Jerome, from whom Matty gets his chestnut curls and thick lashes. She gave up the chance to rival Marie Curie for the prospect of becoming a marchioness. Why wouldn't she have? Even I wanted to marry lighthearted, not-a-worry Jerome, who never stopped smiling and treated you like you were worth his affection. Besides, I had met him first.

If not *I do,* then perhaps Gwendolyn might have wept over the letter from the army chaplain in Rouen, *And a cross now marks his place.* Thousands of families received similar letters. Whether she cried or bit back her tears, I know Jerome's death saddened, but did not break her. She's not sentimental and doesn't even wear her wedding ring. What broke her were the words *You have a son.* Matty is the one person who doesn't care if Gwendolyn is beautiful or brilliant or perfect. She is merely *Mummy.* He has reduced her to human.

Matty reaches a sticky hand across the table and says to me, "Comics please."

"No comics today, love. Just black and white print."

Matty sticks out his bottom lip. "Yuck."

"Yuck," I agree, ignoring one particular black and white headline.

"How goes the news of the world, Margaret?" Papa at last acknowledges the congealing feast of eggs and bacon on his plate and wrinkles his aristocratic nose. He'll have the housekeeper, who lost her son in Egypt and her daughter to pneumonia, set it out for the dogs. Papa lathers his toast in heaps of rich, creamy butter.

I press my fingers to my head. The sharp, greedy scrape of Papa's butter knife against the toast jumbles with the memories—the not-so-long ago screech of convoy trucks bearing the wounded, the sharpness of the wind against my cheek as I stood on the shores of Wimereux, the sweet taste of cinnamon from an unexpected kiss. I rub my lips and glance down at *The Times*, at the tiny article pushed to the back pages, as if the story was an obligatory piece of politeness, like an obituary.

The old Margaret, feisty and passionate and undirected, a person I barely remember but my family insists I still am, she would have launched herself from the breakfast table and made some kind of scene—shredded the newspaper, pounded her fists, smashed the tea cup against the window where beyond lies Mama's dying garden.

I am not the energetic, whirling dervish Margaret from before the War. For the past four years, no one even called me Margaret. I answered to *nurse* or *sister* or a cry of panic in the dark of night when a boy who could have been my younger brother awoke from surgery to find he had no leg. The name I was born with feels vague and foreign to my ears, like a refrain from a half-forgotten song. I can't quite remember the tune.

I fold the paper neatly, block out the headline, though the words still pound against my aching head. "The usual," I tell Papa. "Nothing much."

Papa studies me, trying to hide his concern. He is not used to this new Margaret. Neither am I. I am a ghost of my old self, and a stranger to my new self. The one thing I know about this Margaret, formed by four years of war and six months of peace is my sentence. It drives a knife through my numb heart and shocks me back to life. My sentence is an omen made of three words.

Doctor To Hang.

CHAPTER TWO

Lady Sullivan's Ambulance Hospital, Ypres, France, May 1, 1918.

The halo is an omen.

Outside, amidst the roar of a truck grinding its wheels through mud and the now needless warning call of the bugle, Lady Sullivan is directing orderlies where to deliver the wounded. Inside my ward, the acute injury ward, but also where we treat the soldier who has a seventy percent chance of dying but we should—*we must*—try, I prep my heartier patients for the operating theatre. I have seven so far, all boys so young I doubt they've yet to have their first kiss. The orderlies bear them in on dirty stretchers, and transfer their broken bodies onto trestle tables, careful not to disrupt the slapdash, blood-soaked bandages. Mud cakes the boys' boots, their clothes, their eyes, their mouths. It isn't even raining, but the French soil is invasive.

Back in England, people imagine tent hospitals this close to the front as a scene of panic, of bitter and harried nurses, of screaming bullets and endless gunfire, of men writhing in agony. They don't realize our chaos has an order. Triage hemorrhages, chest, and head cases first. Then limbs and sepsis. And always, be alert for our ever-present enemy, gas gangrene. Our patients are usually calm, often apologetic. *Sorry for the mess, Sister,* the soldiers often say. Or, *Don't worry about me, it's me mate that needs you.* Adrenaline and shock and stubborn will provide a veneer of civilized structure. The rat-tat-tat of gunfire is nothing but background noise. Sometimes, I forget to hear it.

Instead, there is humming. We are down two nurses, but the Padre, with his thick gloss of white hair and reassuring country vicar's smile is bustling about, singing a hymn. "Abide With Me." He rinses the soldiers' faces and holds their hands and spreads the last of his faith.

I check the tag on my next patient and greet him with a line I have repeated every day for four years, sometimes six times a day, sometimes sixty. It's so ingrained in me, it defines me, even if it is not true. "Private Flaherty, I'm Nurse Betts and I'm going to be taking care of you."

Beside me, my most reliable (except when he's seducing French girls) medical orderly, McMannis, asks in his too-big-for-any room Scottish brogue, "Back for more of our hospitality, are you, lad? Notta worry. You'll be awricht ance the pain has gone." McMannis has thickened his accent to incomprehensible, a little joke.

The boy smiles weakly. His pupils are constricted, his body sluggish, his heart rate tripping alarmingly high. I bite back my lip. The medical officer on the battlefield hands out morphia like it's an act of mercy, without regard to long-term consequences like addiction. That's the irony of battle; when you're trying to save a life, you don't think about the future.

According to the tag, Flaherty took two bullets to his shoulder and the scapula is broken. Given the nature of war, his injuries are mild. The bullets exited as they entered. His dressings are clean, the craters of exposed skin tissue are dark and crusting, no longer bleeding. But something is not right. Flaherty is perspiring. The beads of sweat run down his face. His back is soaked. My fingers against his pulse are burning up. His skin is too hot. Even without my thermometer, I know his temperature is soaring past 103.

"Private Flaherty, can you tell me where else you're hurt?" I press my hands against his temples, along his jaw, the tendons of his neck.

"No *welcome back*, Sister?" Flaherty's voice is raspy, his words slurred. When he was here three months ago, he was an ambulatory patient, earnest and energetic as a clumsy puppy. Newly arrived to the trenches, he kept apologizing to his mates for having been shot so soon. The other nurses made him a favorite, fattening him up with cream puddings and his first taste of champagne, letting him bang jolly tunes out on the Padre's piano. McMannis taught him a few Scottish dirges and a rather shocking French ditty. Flaherty's voice then had been clear and lively, though it did at times squeak, a boy whose larynx hasn't yet grown into manhood.

McMannis raises Flaherty's head and helps him swallow water from a tin cup. "Aye, you know better than to flirt with Sister Betts, don't you lad? She hides her heart beneath her sleeve. The less she smiles at you, the more she loves you."

I trail my hands down the rest of his body, putting pressure onto his muscles and joints to remind him he has them, to make him feel them, in hopes he will at least wince. I need to find the injury. Everywhere, he is too hot. Nothing so far suggests an external cut or internal hemorrhaging. At the base of his knee, his right calf feels swollen. The body is fighting infection. Trench foot, perhaps. It's common enough. I can treat it.

"Private Flaherty, I'm going to remove your boots."

He blinks at the electric bulb swaying above our heads. Faintly, he says, "You read me *The Count of Monte Cristo*."

McMannis shoots an odd look, one of surprise. I am not known to be sentimental. I *tsk* him.

When I crossed the English Channel, I did not pack a single book, much less a luxury like *The Count of Monte Cristo*. I didn't need to. I know it by heart. I used to read and reread the adventures of Edmond Dantès to my younger brother Tad, who could not read. The words on a page always jumped out of order and played tricks on his eyes.

Flaherty is the same age as my brother. Too young.

I unlace his left boot. The sole is worn through, the foot within it swollen. When I remove the boot and his sodden sock, the scent of sweat mixed with moldy wool and damp earth hits my nostrils. His toes are red and chapped, mud sits between them, and one of his nails is black. I dip linen into a basin of lukewarm water and antiseptic, and scrub his foot clean.

Flaherty sighs. "I know your voice, Sister. You read to me in my sleep."

My voice. Before I could even read, my mother stood me by the piano and taught me to sing. I spent pitch perfect afternoons hitting the high notes of "Somewhere a Voice is Calling" and "Woodman Spare That Tree." *Parlor songs*, Papa would sniff. But all that mattered to me was when I sang, Mama glowed and I was not a disappointment. Somewhere between the Battles of the Marne and the Somme, in all the shouting to be heard above the blast of bombs and flashing gunfire, I damaged my vocal cords. I sound like I have a permanent sore throat. If she heard me today, Mama wouldn't recognize me. Perhaps that's the point. I ran away to hurt her because in the epic tug-of-war for her love, in the end she sided with Gwendolyn. At least in this battlefield, I am useful, if not entirely loveable.

I turn to Flaherty's right boot, pulling the laces undone. The leather is sealed to his skin. Blood can act like a glue, his foot must be damaged, something the field medic didn't bother to notice. I slice through the leather. Flaherty jerks his knee, kicking my chest and I fall onto my bottom. The boot flies off, arcing in the air. A sweetly putrid scent hits me hard. The boot lands squarely in my lap, the stub of Flaherty's severed foot within it.

That's when I see the halo.

A man pushes aside the canvas flap of my tent and strides in. His gait is easy, but purposeful. Not the walk of a military man, despite the khaki uniform, which is so crisp and clean you can hear the stiffness of the fabric. There's too much athleticism in the bend of his knee, in the fluid way he swings his arms, in the flow of motion from straight back to striking heel. He has a rhythm. He takes off his cap, it's marked with the Rod of Asclepius and the motto *In Arduis Fidelis, Faithful in Adversity*. A doctor, then, though he moves more like a dancer than a surgeon.

Cap in hand, he directs two orderlies I don't recognize to deliver a patient to one of my trestle tables. The gesture is open and direct, a quick wave and nod of the head, a polite thank you. The bulb sputtering above my head stills for a single moment, shorter than a breath, shorter than a heartbeat. He looks at me. Perhaps I am staring. Electricity whips through my body. Even my fingertips tingle. The light strikes the burnished gold of his hair, casting a glow someone else might have called angelic. Not me. There is something untrustworthy about a man who the war has not robbed of hope.

In the distance, the train carrying the wounded to the base hospitals whistles, a high-pitched, urgent shriek and the bulb goes back to its scattered, unreliable work, casting shadows when I need to see.

Flaherty's boot is still in my lap. The detached foot stares up at me; a piece of human detritus. The ankle bone must have broken first. Bacteria ate through his flesh. All the while, blood soaked through the wool of his sock and sealed him to the boot, so he looked whole, when he wasn't. I cut through the pant leg and am confronted by a stump covered in purple, necrotic blisters. Sepsis.

A short fuse of fury spikes through me. How long did Flaherty lay in the mud, bacteria burrowing into his skin, eating his flesh, destroying his muscles, before the medics brought him to me? No matter how bad the mutilation, I could have saved Flaherty had he come to me in time. He could live without a foot. Countless men do. But once gas gangrene sets, you have thirty-six hours to treat it. A simple bandage soaked in picric acid is all the frontline medic needs to stave off infection. Every soldier carries one in his kit. Every medic has them.

They are marked Blackpond, issued by the British Army, manufactured by my family.

I set the boot down on the floor, beneath the table. McMannis is a strapping six-foot-five of muscle. He's picked up human intestines with his bare hands and fitted them back into a man, but even he is green. He swallows hard and turns his head away.

"We'll irrigate the leg," I tell him.

His thick, reddish-brown brows knit together with a touch of sympathy, a touch of reprimand, like I'm a naïve nurse who doesn't understand the rules of war. I click my jaw. This is my ward. I make the rules. Lady Sullivan is no longer directing the orderlies, no more injured are coming into my tent. Of the seven patients I have, I've already seen to three. Only four left, not including the patient being carried in. Not so many I have to sacrifice the dying to save the living.

"Get the Carrel-Dakin kit," I say. They are precious, these kits. A new way of treating gangrene, supplied by Johnson & Johnson, they go to the American and French hospitals, not our privately funded, semi-governed by the British Royal Red Cross, operation. I cannot begin to imagine what Lady Sullivan bartered or promised or blackmailed to get a case.

McMannis doesn't budge. "You know the policy." *Conserve the fighting force.* A bureaucratic euphuism to give up on the weak.

McMannis is a hulking man. I raise myself to my full height and barely meet his top rib. I have to lean back to look him in the eye, a precarious position. My toes curl up. For balance, I square my heels in my too-big boots. "It will take you two minutes to get to the surgical stock marquee and back."

"You've got a ward full of lads," he reminds me.

"All the more reason for you to hurry up."

"You've never done the Carrel-Dakin."

"That's not an excuse."

"The best you can do is make the lad comfortable."

"That is *never* the best. *I* can do better." I've jury-rigged railroad tracks for trestle tables, concocted poultices out of forest weeds, filched rubber tubes from bicycle tires. In fact, McMannis was by my side for most of these *necessity is the motherhood of invention* moments. I don't understand his sudden readiness to surrender.

"What's wrong with you? It's not like you to be hen-hearted." I stop to notice how much his brutish face has thinned out. Exhaustion drags down the brightness of his green eyes.

He's not even looking at me. I turn to follow his gaze, to the two orderlies we don't know and to the patient they are settling on the trestle table. Each of the patient's limbs is wrapped and splinted expertly. The splints follow the line of each thigh, the legs are raised and the feet attached to a suspension bar with a modified clove-hitch over each foot. He's cosseted with blankets and hot water bottles to keep him comfortable. The medical technique is modern, the Thomas Splint, but the patient is an anachronism, from a time before we were dragged into mud and a war of attrition.

The pristine patient is restless, thrashing on the table, muttering, "Trapped . . . trapped . . . trapped." The orderlies look about nervously. The doctor—a lieutenant colonel according to the insignia on his uniform—measures the man's pulse and gives him an injection.

McMannis cannot stop staring at the patient. The expression on his face is not one of recognition or attachment. It's the opposite. I yank at his sleeve, but cannot rouse him from his detachment. Next to me, Flaherty's breathing has become shallow. Each of his weak, short sips of air scrapes my ears. I am running out of time.

"Sister Betts," the Padre calls out, quickly grabbing a tin basin and helping a soldier turn on his side to vomit. My concussion case.

"Trapped . . . tra . . ." says the pristine patient, his tongue thickening beneath the sedative. He must itch in those splints.

"Sister Betts." The Padre is doing his best not to shout.

"Trapped," the two syllables come out warped and slow, like a funhouse mirror distorting an image.

I press my knuckles to my forehead. Private Flaherty's infected stump throbs and oozes, dark purple and pus-filled. "The Carrel-Dakin, McMannis."

He moves not at all. I contemplate shoving him.

"Sister Betts!" This time the Padre does shout.

"Ask him to recite the alphabet backward, Padre." I rub my tongue against the back of my teeth.

"Z . . . Y . . . X . . ." mumbles the concussion patient bravely.

I nod gratefully to him. To McMannis, I say, "The Car—"

"No." McMannis runs his big, rough hand gently across Flaherty's pale cheek. He avoids looking at the raw leg missing its foot. He should never have gotten attached to Flaherty. There's no room for affection when you're trying to save lives. "Have some mercy."

"The only mercy I know is the River Mersey." It runs along Widnes, where the Blackpond factory sits. "And if you should happen to slip in, you're sure to drown."

"We stitch them up and send them back for what?" McMannis asks. "We're as much the enemy as the Germans."

His despair sinks into me like a knife. I stare down at my hands, scrubbed, scrubbed, scrubbed and still beneath my cracked fingernails, there are red stains.

"I believe the Sister gave you an order."

The voice makes me half-jump out of my own skin. The depth of his tone resonates deep down in the hollow of me. He sounds, of all things, like a grand organ, the notes flooding a cathedral, rousing the congregation to stand. It's the kind of voice you want to sink your fingers into, to cling to. I squint above the doctor's head to make sure the halo is a mirage or trick of the light. It isn't.

He raises his eyes to the electric bulb, a line of curiosity crosses his otherwise smooth forehead, and he searches the canvas ceiling like he wants to help me find whatever it is I'm looking for. I feel oddly

15

young. Odd because despite the forged papers indicating I should be at least twenty-seven, the required age for frontline nursing, I am young. I will be twenty-two in a few days.

McMannis obeys the doctor and shuffles out of the tent. Lady Sullivan bustles in. Even after sixteen hours of organizing and commanding, debriding infected flesh and sewing up wounds, she is a whirl of energy. Like the wind, if she does not move, she fears she will no longer exist. When she sees the doctor staring up at the light and me squinting above his head, she bites back a laugh.

"Nick—Colonel Wallace," she says, her tone at once respectful and indulgent, "if your patient is stabilized, could we borrow you for the operating theatre?"

He places his cap back on his head like it's an unfamiliar object. "The trick to the Carrel-Dakin is there is no trick. The powders are pre-measured in ampoules, so there's no chance you can make a mistake. Dissolve them in the liter bottle that comes with the kit. Run the solution through the larger rubber tube, wind the smaller tubes around his leg so the solution will drip into the sores." He leans toward me and winks. "There's hope, Sister. There's always hope."

After I get my concussion patient settled, send my surgical patients off to the operating theatre, welcome them into the recovery ward by taking their temperature and checking their circulation and tucking them in for the night, my shift is at last over. My never-white-enough apron is stained with my night's work—pus, blood, vomit. Weariness batters my shoulders. Everywhere, my skin feels stretched, like it's splitting at the seams, like it can't fully cover me anymore.

At the far end of the row of beds, Private Flaherty lays in a half sleep. His fingers twitch. I go to his side, take his hand in mine and begin where we left off in Edmond Dantè's quest for revenge and redemption. I condense a few of the chapters, skipping over the sections my brother always found dull—the Count's manipulation of the bond market, his relationship with Mercedes, Andrea's tale—and finish with the final lines. *All human wisdom is contained in these two words—Wait and Hope.*

He squeezes my hand. His whole body contracts from the effort, the muscles on his young face tighten, but there is no strength in his touch. I squeeze back, lending him mine. Hand in hand, him laying down, me sitting up, we sleep.

Private Flaherty slips away at dawn.

CHAPTER THREE

Halsop House, May 2, 1919

I awake at dawn because I cannot bear the silence. I pour myself a glass of water from the pitcher on my bedtable and pull back the curtains. Fog rolls over the Surrey hills. Beneath the beat of the rising sun, the fog looks pink, like the strawberry meringues our cook whips up. When I unlatch the window, the air tastes sweet and innocent. We had days like this in France, mornings so fresh and beautiful it made me want to scream.

I almost cry in relief when I hear the patter of a child's feet, a boisterous "Ahoy Ahoy" breaking the silence apart.

"Shhh Shhh," Gwendolyn chastises. "The house is asleep."

Matty throws open the door and bounds into my room. "Auntie never sleeps!"

Gwendolyn trails behind him, her long hair braided loosely. She tightens the belt on her quilted robe. It's thick, indigo with a pattern of lush cherries. Her satin pajamas are cropped above her ankles, mandarin style, and trimmed with matching cherries. Even at dawn, my sister is impeccably dressed.

Matty hops onto my bed, rolls his hands like they're binoculars and peers through them, surveying his imaginary sea. I draw open the remaining curtains and greet him with "Good morning, captain."

At the foot of my bed, Gwendolyn notes the leather valise packed and ready to go. "So, you really are off to London."

I nod.

"Just for the night?"

"Short trip."

She unzips my bag and inspects the contents, sighing heavily at the flannel skirt and grey cardigan. "You might at least stop at Harvey Nichols. I hear this season's color is any shade other than morose." It's easy to forget Gwendolyn is brilliant, able to calculate an entire accounts book in her head. She hides her brain beneath her beauty. It gives the illusion of normalcy.

"I have a busy schedule."

She arches her blond eyebrows with sisterly doubt and sits down on the settee, tucking her feet beneath her. "Shopping. *Kissing Time* at the Winter Garden. Champagne at the Savoy. Do tell."

A court martial. An execution. "Yes. I'm on the morning train," I say flatly, hoping she won't invite herself along, though, to be fair, she's never sought my friendship. As children, she held herself apart while Tad and I climbed trees and splashed along the river, returning home wet, mucky and happy.

Matty leaps from my bed, landing like a cat on the plush Turkish carpet.

"Well done," I say.

"Beds are not for jumping," Gwendolyn tells him.

"One more time?" Matty presses his palms together.

"Just once," she replies. To me, she offers, "You could take the motorcar." She doesn't mean it. Five minutes after I leave, Gwendolyn will discover she needs to purchase yarn or drop in on a meeting with the gardening club, even though she doesn't knit and thinks the gardening ladies idiotic. "Why so early?"

According to the newspaper, Lieutenant Colonel Wallace will make an allocution for murder at noon. "Early bird, worm." I shrug my shoulders and zip my valise back up.

"What worm?" she asks.

"Why the Spanish Inquisition?"

"Why the Mata Hari act? I am making small talk, not trying to ferret out national secrets. I don't recall you ever being quite so surly. Difficult, yes. But surly, no. You have a new talent for turning teatime into a funeral."

"Auntie has to be." By this time, Matty is on his fifth jump of the morning. "We're to play pirates today. I say *Ahoy* and Auntie says *Aargh* and squints like she's real mean." He scrunches up his face and gives his best impression of *real mean*.

Gwendolyn unfolds her legs and rises from the settee. "I'll play with you, darling."

"No." Matty shakes his head and Gwendolyn pauses mid-step, unprepared for this flash of a child's independence. "Mummy, you are always the princess."

Same as when we were growing up.

"Your mummy has a particular expression, where she purses her lips and narrows her right eye." I mimic one of Gwendolyn's more disdainful expressions, the one she uses when she finds a hair out of place.

"Mummy can't say *aargh*." He adds an impressive amount of grist to the sound.

I laugh, but my sister is less appreciative, coming to sweep Matty up into her arms. He accepts a kiss on his head before kicking and squirming his way to the floor. He races back to the bed, climbs up, jumps down. "Auntie, Ahoy!"

"Aargh," I reply, the sound thick and rough, like the rusty gears of a truck maneuvering around potholes.

Gwendolyn winces. "What is wrong with your voice, Margaret? You used to sing so prettily."

My sister would have made an excellent sniper. She always hits her mark. "Smoking."

She studies me from head to foot. The inspection is not kind. It's rather like a champion boxer who was prepared to pummel her opponent, only for her opponent to forfeit. Victory has no pleasure without the bruises.

Finally, she says, "How disappointed Mama would be. You don't know how much she regretted letting you sail off to America for university. And then you not coming home the entire four years."

"I wrote every week."

"About the weather. *We are having an unusually wet spring. Summer has turned unusually warm.*" Gwendolyn rolls her eyes. "I suppose Bryn Mawr and the smoking and daughterly negligence can be attributed to cousin Kristina. She's always been a bad influence. Dropping out of finishing school. Such nonsense."

When she was sixteen, cousin Kristina announced she was finished with finishing school (*It near finished me, kiddo*), packed her trunks and sailed to New York to seek her fortune (though she's already a Blackpond heiress). Ten years later, when I was sixteen, I only got as far as the school gate before Papa, waiting in the motorcar, caught me by the scruff of my neck and hauled me off to the Blackpond factory for a *proper lesson in life.*

Kristina was essential the second time I ran away, the time I succeeded. While everyone else was celebrating Gwendolyn's happy union to Jerome and thought I was sulking away at Bryn Mawr, Kristina routed my tuition fees to support Lady Sullivan's Ambulance Hospital, and played post mistress, repackaging my letters home with an American postal stamp, sending Mama's letters on to me. Gwendolyn never wrote.

"I ran away because I was desperately unhappy," I say.

"Well, you've certainly copied her flair for hyperbole," Gwendolyn snaps back. "Investigative journalist, my foot. More like dramatist. And not a good one."

"She did marry well," I remind my sister.

"To an American."

"A Du Pont."

"Twenty years her senior!"

"Kristina says he is a magnificent lover." Her letters provide the play-by-play details.

Gwendolyn pinches her brow. "Mama's only solace was you skipped the war. Not all of us were so lucky." She flicks a glance at her buffed nails.

When I glance down at my own nails, they still bear the stains of dying boys. I sit down on the window bench, the same one where I used to read to my brother on rainy days. How I miss him. The rising sun is bright today. It will be hot. Outside, Gardener Jack is talking to his father, Old Jack. The two are having an animated discussion. Gardener Jack's hands dance through the air, pointing to a folly, drawing a line to a cluster of yews, wiping the trees away with a swipe of his palm. Old Jack's hands are up in a *no no no*. It's the ancient struggle between a father's wisdom and a young man's vision. Old Jack pats his son's shoulder. At least between them, there is affection. Something Gwendolyn and I have never shared.

Gwendolyn stops along the row of windows too and watches the men outside. Gardener Jack bears most of his weight on his right leg, occasionally shifting his hips to lean on his left, but he's uncomfortable doing so. He always puts out a hand, as if to break a fall. His sleeves are rolled up, exposing muscled forearms and skin tanned by the years he spent fighting in Egypt. Gwendolyn sinks her top teeth into her bottom lip, like she is imagining the taste of something she can never have.

I hear a muffled thunk and my head snaps up. My shoulders tense, adrenaline hits my heart. My brain trips, confused as to why the ceiling is made of plaster, not canvas. Where is the scent of blood and antiseptic? I catch sight of a child's foot. Matty, who is pushing open the window and now leaning dangerously over the ledge. I know where

I am, and yet I search for my nurse's basket of bandages and can think of nothing other than *Triage hemorrhages, chest, and head cases first.*

"Matty, Matty, Matty," Gwendolyn cries, racing toward him.

"Gar'ner Jack! Gar'ner Jack!" Matty calls. He has not yet learned how to roll his soft *rrrs* against hard *ddds.*

Gardener Jack doffs the straw hat shading him, turns to the house, looks up and says one word. I don't think he shouts, but his command carries along the breeze and through the window. "In."

Matty immediately obeys.

Gwendolyn grips Matty. Her face is flushed and she's blinking rapidly. Matty kisses her cheek. "Princess Mummy," he says and scampers over to me, where I stand, trying to set my brain back to rights. *No convoy. No convoy. I am home.* The words swirl, devoid of meaning, into the pit of my stomach.

"Gar'ner Jack cut off his foot," says Matty. He points to his own. "He cut it off with his poffettknife and threw it straight into a German trench. Boom boom." Matty flashes his hands like explosions. "The stink killed them all." He giggles, a child's laugh.

Gwendolyn rubs her brow. "Really, Matty, you shouldn't be listening to Gardener Jack's tales. His job is to clip hedges, not terrify children." Matty is hardly terrified and the way she says *clip hedges,* as if by reducing Jack to physical labor she can right a world that's blown itself apart, nags like an open sore.

"Guns are democratic," I say. "They aim to kill, no matter whose son you are."

"Learned that studying art history in America, did you?"

"I highly doubt Gardener Jack used a pocketknife."

Matty looks up at me, his eyes round and his attention whole.

Gwendolyn shoots me a warning, but my darkness is unmoored, flailing in search of a port.

"The foot has two arteries," I explain to Matty, "so if you sever one of them, you'll die within the half hour." Matty holds up his foot and I kneel down into the plush carpet expecting it to suck me down like the mud of France did. I trace the arteries along his foot. He watches, mesmerized.

"Stop," Gwendolyn says quietly, with the menace of a mother.

"A pocketknife is far too dull to slice through skin, tendons, ligament and bone." I take Matty's soft hand, dimpled with baby fat, and show him on his own ankle. What kind of God would armor humans with flesh rather than iron? Even a single sheet of paper can slice us open.

"Margaret." Gwendolyn is sterner now.

"So it would have to be a very big knife. Or a bullet or a bomb. Most likely, though, it's gas gangrene. Bacteria sneaks into your wound, making gas bubbles, and poisons your blood." My pulse is pounding in my ears, trying to drum out a distant sound. Is someone humming? Private Flaherty's detached foot stares up at me.

"An axe!" Matty claps his hands so loud, my nerves jump and before I can understand what I'm doing, my arm raises and slams toward Matty's vulnerable ankle.

He glances up at me, his innocent face confused, not understanding if this is part of our game or if someone who loves him will hurt him. His eyes glisten, the color a warm chestnut. The shade and depth send my brain spinning. I spent enough time looking adoringly into his father, Jerome's face, to know they were blue. As are Gwendolyn's. My nephew's eyes make no sense.

The energy driving my hand toward Matty's ankle dissipates. My hand falls away, listless. I rub my knuckles on the carpet. "Why are your eyes brown?"

Gwendolyn grabs hold of my arm, jerking me back to standing. Digging her perfectly curved nails into my skin, she hisses, "You know perfectly well his father's eyes were hazel."

"Were they?" I blink rapidly and realize I cannot conjure up Jerome's face. A vague recollection of tawny hair—or was it dark copper?—a romanticized smile. But I do not remember if he parted his hair to the left or the right, if he had freckles, or what his laugh sounded like. The details are lost because my memory is caught in a loop still searching for a convoy.

My sister releases her hold on me and I stumble. Her nails have left marks on my arm. Neat little crescent moons.

"What is wrong with you," she demands.

So many things. Nightmares and cold sweats. An ever-present, numb ache. Guilt for all the boys I could not save. Guilt for having survived. And worst of all, a longing to return to the battlefield. Because at least then, I was alive and capable of love. "I am not fit for tea."

Her expression curls in on itself, as if I have wounded her. I ought to pity Gwendolyn. She does not live with her in-laws in the marquis-dom Matty will one day inherit. She's chosen to live here at home with her family. A sure sign of loneliness. But there are worse things than loneliness. There is love.

CHAPTER FOUR

Lady Sullivan's Ambulance Hospital, Ypres France, May 2, 1918

E ven in my thoughts, I am not alone.

In the cemetery, mist rises off the damp grass like ghosts searching for the white crosses marking their resting place. I place a handful of bright blue forget-me-nots on the grave of Gunner Gavin McAvoy, November 1, 1890—September 26, 1915. Septic influenza. Wood violets for Major Samuel Dennis, whose wife's name was Violet, June 1, 1881—December 6, 1916. Hypothermia. On and on. I know so many dead.

We are to think of them as medical failures, Lady Sullivan advised, trying to teach me detachment. But each medical failure left behind a sweetheart, a mother, a child, a sister. The grave diggers will be trudging up the hill in an hour to bury Private Flaherty in the French earth that demanded yet another boy. Will demand more today. Tomorrow. Forever, it seems. Pointless as it is, I pray my brother, who has just joined the war, is safe.

A murmur of voices slips through the woods. I am so bleary and tired, I assume it's the ghosts.

"Dammit all to bloody hell. I'm a surgeon, not a soldier."

Not a ghost. A doctor with an organ in a cathedral voice and a halo hanging above the burnished gold of his hair. Colonel Wallace.

"Your uniform suggests otherwise," comes a second voice, authoritative and irritated because every conversation to him is an argument. Papa uses the same tone with me.

I retreat behind a large oak with thick, spreading branches, and peek through the leaves.

Colonel Wallace and the other man stand at the edge of the grey, glistening lake. They are near identical in height and build, in dark-gold hair and olive-toned faces. The second man appears a few years older, a few years more jaded. He wears a black patch across his right eye.

Colonel Wallace's uniform is still crisp. He loosens the collar like he resents it. "First do no harm."

"For God's sake, you can't think in single lives. We are in a *world* war."

"My job is to preserve life, one by one," Colonel Wallace snaps back.

"Your job is to follow orders."

"Not when they don't make sense." Colonel Wallace bends and selects a stone, weighs it in his hand, sends it flying through the air. It hits the smooth water and skips, once, twice, thrice. "Why this order? Why not another one? What's the goal? Are we trying to end a war or wipe out humanity?"

"We're the left hand." The second man holds up his left palm. "Someone else is the right." He holds up his right. "Neither needs to know what the other is doing to function as a whole."

"When the two sides of the body aren't communicating, we diagnose hemispatial neglect, likely due to stroke."

The second man selects a stone and tosses it. It too skips three times across the lake. His movements, in the shift of the feet and arc of the arm mirror Colonel Wallace's. I cannot tell whose stone travelled farther. The way the two face each other, shoulders spread equally wide and confident, it's clear each thinks his was the better.

Colonel Wallace rubs his eyes. "You shot his knees out. They're going to heal. I can't keep a healthy man wrapped in bandages forever."

My skin prickles. His pristine patient. *Trapped…trapped…trapped.* When I left my ward this morning, he was laying in his cot, cut off from the other patients by a wall of privacy screens, and two supposed medical orderlies, who I realize now, were standing guard.

"Would you rather I had shattered his spine? Your specialty isn't it? Raising Lazarus."

Colonel Wallace responds with a dry frown.

The other man sighs. "If you want this war to end, you had better start acting like an officer." He draws a pack of cigarettes from his pocket. He lights one, inhales, and coughs.

"Smoking will blacken your lungs," says Colonel Wallace.

"To match the soul." The man drops the cigarette, grinds it out with his foot.

"*Me duleveis?*"

The hairs on the back of my neck stand on end.

Colonel Wallace's accent has changed. Not German. Having nursed Jerry prisoners of war, I know enough of the enemy's language to recognize it. This language feels far more dangerous. Colonel Wallace embraces the vowels, lingers comfortably on the consonants, as if it is native to him, as natural as breathing. Is he not English? Are those orderlies really orderlies? I did not see them perform a single medical task. Are we even on the same side?

The man answers Colonel Wallace in the same language, and the two carry on, too at ease in this foreign tongue. A creeping sense of danger edges along my sleep-deprived nerves. I should not be on this cemetery hill, eavesdropping on this conversation. Friend or enemy, I am not the left hand, nor the right. I am unimportant. They could make me disappear and no one would know where to find Sister Vera Betts, a woman who doesn't exist. Or Lady Margaret Halladay, a girl who is supposed to be at Bryn Mawr.

I rise, careful to weave through the cover of oaks, though there is no clear-cut path and the soil is damp. I pull down the hood of my sou'wester. I want to run, but can't. I suffer from a kind of hemispatial disorder of my own. When I am triaging a patient, my brain is sharp, my focus precise. But when I am not in crisis mode, I make stupid choices. My boots, for example. They are two sizes too big. I absent-mindedly grabbed the first pair I saw and was too tired to return them. Instead, I have learned to walk by curling my toes and gripping the insole.

The thirsty mud and I play tug of war. The soft, squelching earth sucks my foot down. It takes all the power in my thigh muscles to yank my foot back up. With each step, my knees crack. All the while my hands shake and my heart beats wildly, begging me to hurry toward safety. Safety—what a laugh. We are a mile from the battlefront. The trenches are waking up, the soldiers on both sides greasing their machine guns, loading their canons. A stray bullet here, an answering shot there. Soon the sounds will build to a crescendo, my wake-up song. I'd be safer bandaged in splints and sent off to sleep with morphia.

By the time I reach the bottom of the hill, my leg muscles are burning, and my knees are ready to shatter. I near slip before I secure my boots on the duckboards that cut a path above the soggy earth. I'm faster now, my steps banging along the wood, and I am running at last. I veer toward the supply marquees; we have three. They sit next to each other in a logical row. What better way to clear one's head after overhearing possible spies than by taking inventory? In my rush to get to the linen marquee, I collide into the Padre, almost knocking him down.

He grabs hold of my shoulders, steadies me. "Gracious, child. You're paler than mist." He studies my face for a moment, thoughtful and kind. "Private Flaherty?"

I nod my head and unclench my hand to find I have been clutching my morning's bouquet. The flowers are crushed and wilted, the violet petals stain my palm and spill through my fingers, falling to the ground like blood drops.

"Ahh," says the Padre. "I am on my way to the ward. I thought to check in on our boys, share a few prayers. I will write the break-the-news letter to his mother." He squints up at the lightening sky. "Blessed are the peacemakers—they will be called children of God."

The sun is settling on me like a headache. Not strong, not bright, but sharp and painful. "What does the line even mean, Padre? It sounds like a condemnation, not a benediction. Our patients are soldiers. They fight. They kill."

He says nothing, instead gripping my shoulders so tight, it feels like he means to fuse some message into the bones. I must have winced because he lets go and retreats a step. "You should get some sleep, my dear, before the shadows beneath your eyes overtake you."

I slip my arms into the sleeves of my coat and watch him amble to the wards, my head a jumble of thoughts. Why is the Padre awake at such an early hour? Most of the patients will still be asleep. Why is he unshaven, as if he never went to bed? Where is his bible? I chew the inside of my cheek. The specter of the conversation between two men I don't know has played havoc with my trust in the men I do.

In the distance, I spot McMannis, another man who, until last night, I entrusted with lives. He and Gaspar, our camp cook, are cutting across the row of supply marquees, sneaking back into camp. Gaspar is carrying an opened bottle of wine. McMannis is tucking in his shirt. His gait carries a hint of guilt. As it should. While I was whispering those last words to Private Flaherty, *wait and hope*, McMannis was no doubt lounging in the arms of a buxom French girl. Thirty-six hours, that's how much time we have between inception of gas gangrene and lost cause. How many minutes did he squander with his self-indulgent stonewalling? I outrank him. When I give an order, his job is to obey.

"McMannis," I shout across the path.

He freezes, caught out, exchanges a look with Gaspar, who scurries off to the mess tent.

I storm forward, pointing my finger at McMannis. "Funk my orders again and I'll have you digging latrines. If not graves."

"Sis—"

I don't hear the rest of what he has to say. His pathetic excuse or reasonable response or sincere apology. An explosion rocks the ground. The impact sends me flying off my feet. My head slams into the duckboard. A tinny bell rings in my ears. When I open my eyes, I see dots. Touching the back of my head, I find the rising swell of a lump. A weird pain travels through my chest and spreads through my arms. It's a struggle to stand. I raise myself up, joint by joint. First my knees, then my hips. My legs are shaking.

"Get down! Get down," warns McMannis. He's flat on his stomach, rolling toward a dugout. But there are no lizzies buzzing through the sky, dropping bombs. The drumfire did not come from above.

A fire rages a hundred yards to my left. The linen-supply marquee is burning to cinders. Gauze, cotton balls, poultice cloths, cradles, crutches, sheets, blankets, bandages, are all blackening into ash. I stuff my fist into my mouth and bite down on a sob. How are we going to restock?

A second blast hits. The earth vibrates with anger. I hunch down, drag my sou'wester over my head. This time it's the medicine marquee—aspirin, atropine, digitalin, pilocarpine, eserine. Everything we need to ease and treat and save.

Still dressed in nightgowns, two fellow nurses burst out of their tent, strapping their Tommy helmets to their chins. They are older than me, mid-thirties, legitimately trained and certified. They joined Lady Sullivan's hospital a few months ago, replacing a nurse who'd gotten married, another who slit her wrists. Both looking to escape the war.

"Is it an air raid?" asks one.

"Are we under attack?" asks the other.

"Get back into your tent," shouts McMannis from the safety of the ditch.

"Get to the wards," I counter. Our patients, trapped in beds, no guns by their sides, will be terrified. The nurses bob their heads between McMannis and me. One brackets her hands around her mouth as if she means to call out to me. I glare and she reconsiders. The two scurry to the wards.

Red flames engulf the buildings, wood splinters, glass shatters. Above the marquees, clouds of yellow smoke choke the air. The heat licks my face. Smoke bullies its way into my lungs. My eyes sting while I stare, transfixed, unable to move.

I have seen yellow smoke before.

When my father shipped me off for my *lesson in life*, it was to the Blackpond factory where I "volunteered" at the cottage hospital serving the workers and their families. He assumed changing bed pans would repulse me, not be my calling. At Blackpond one division manufactures bandages, another produces the picric acid used in the bandages. Picric acid has antiseptic properties; it's especially useful for burns. It also has explosive properties. It's used in ammunition, though Mama would never allow Blackpond to do so. One afternoon at Blackpond, the machine that grinds picric acid crystals into powder malfunctioned, causing a blast so big that even though we were a safe mile away, it ripped the roof right off the cottage hospital. It shattered almost every window nearby and killed a dozen workers. The bodies mutilated, families had to identify their loved ones by the contents of their pockets.

The sight of yellow smoke billowing above the flames slaps me awake. We have three medical supply marquees. Two are burning. The one left standing is stocked with liquid chemicals—nitrous oxide and oxygen for anesthesia, salicylic acid, the precious Carrel-Dakin kits. An explosion could create a gas cloud, poisoning us all.

I push myself forward, toward the marquee. All the aches and pains of nursing—so familiar I usually forget they exist—gather like gravity, elbowing me down. Bursitis in my left shoulder. A tangle of knots in my trapezius. The arches of my feet splitting. The new one, right above my heart, a stinging, burning pain. Probably a metaphor for the past twenty-four hours. I grimace at my black humor. The wind whips around me, pulling my coat open like it means to yank it off.

"Sister Betts!" McMannis is gesticulating wildly.

"Don't be a clodpole. If the surgical supply marquee catches fire, we will have a chemical explosion!" My nose stings from breathing.

At last, McMannis leaps out of the ditch and scrambles toward the water pump. "The hose! The hose!"

From behind the mess hall, Gaspar unrolls the hose. Two ambulatory patients toss the tubing on their shoulders and hustle forward.

"The surgical supply marquee!" I try to raise my right arm, to wave them toward the building, but my arm disobeys and refuses to move. We need to soak down the marquee. Water neutralizes picric acid. It is why we keep it stored in a slurry.

Me duleveis. The foreign syllables throb in my ears. *Your job is to follow orders.* Who orders an attack on a hospital?

"Sister Betts!" This time it's Lady Sullivan crying out my name, slamming her fist into her chest like she's trying to Morse code something across the chaos. Her nurse's apron flaps in the wind. The Padre struggles to draw her back, to keep her safe.

"The gas masks," I shout to her, my throat ragged from the fumes. We have only a handful, but if we fail, they will be our last resort. Who do you choose to save?

I keep running.

The camp is awake now. My fellow nurses are soaking linen in bowls of water and instructing the men to cover their mouths and nose. An alarm is clanging. The Houdan chickens Gaspar fusses over like they were the wife and children he lost, squawk and beat their wings. A patient hobbles out of the ward, raises his crutch. "Fuck the Jerries!"

The sounds hook through the air, hang suspended. Thick smoke curls across the sky. And all the while comes the cry of "Sister Betts!" "Sister Betts!"

Why the devil is everyone screaming my name? If I can find the source of the explosion, or smash up all the picric acid, or haul out the boxes containing chemicals . . . or . . . I slam into a wall of heat so thick, it knocks all the air out of my lungs, all the strength out of my bones.

I clutch my sou'wester close and something sharp cuts my hand—a jagged piece of metal, six inches long, is driving through my coat, through my uniform and straight into my chest. I cough in shock and inhale a cloud of fire. The flames march on, my knees buckle, I stumble to the ground, claw at the dirt. My stomach clenches and convulses. Like an egg that's been cracked, its yolk spilling and pooling in the mud, I retch and retch and retch. *Give up*, says the voice of reason in my head. But then who will take care of my patients?

Blindly, I struggle up from the dirt. I lift my left foot, stumble. My right foot next. Stumble. The heat feels like teeth, biting into me, chewing through ligament, breaking through bone. I am likely to die. I feel strangely alive. Through the haze of ash and fire, darkness and smoke, something glitters. A ray of light, tinged gold. A soot-stained face. A doctor I can't trust.

The world goes black and silent.

CHAPTER FIVE

London, May 2, 1919

The world is choking on sound.

In the cramped London omnibus, the windows rattle, the tires jostle, the engine grinds, and muttered conversations roll over the rows and rows of seats, gathering and building until they reach my ears, dulled and blunted.

I have not been to London since before the war, back when Gwendolyn was enthralling the young bucks with her London debut and my brother and I were still children, flying kites in Hyde Park. I do not recognize this beaten-down, hunched-shoulder city. We pass a construction site where a bombed-out building is being rebuilt. A poster affixed to the wooden fence reads, *These Premises Were Totally Destroyed by a Zeppelin Attack*. From my perch on the omnibus, the streets are so packed with grim coats and widows' weeds, the pedestrians meld into a collective shadow, a physical grief.

I take a strange sort of relief in the individuality of a man on crutches, his right leg amputated at the knee. He sideswipes a pedestrian who tries to pass him and I tap my finger against the window to cheer him on. *You've a perverse sense of justice*, the doctor with a halo, Colonel Wallace, once told me. *Never lose it.* I almost smile at the memory, though it hurts. We had been stretched across a blanket, laying beneath a sparkling night sky at the time, my emotions so intense, I finally understood the phrase *to die from happiness.*

At the sound of a child crying, I turn from the window and search the omnibus. Three rows in front of me, across the aisle, a boy, around the same age at Matty, sits on his sister's lap. She strokes his hair. Their mother, the half-moons beneath her eyes so deep they are permanent, reaches into her purse and pulls out a packet of gum, offering it to the children as a consolation to replace the wooden airplane that has snapped apart.

The boy is holding the pieces up. Tears stream down his face and his nose runs. His sister wipes it with her green coat sleeve. Their limbs are twined, their little feet in buckled leather shoes swing back and forth in unison. It is not maternal, the girl's affection. It is not meant to soothe. It is meant in empathy, the wordless, instinctual communication between siblings. Something my brother and I lost to the War.

I rise from my seat on the rumbling omnibus. The bus driver shouts at me to sit back down. I ignore him as I've ignored all the men who have tried to commandeer my life, beginning with Papa. Instead, I curl my toes into my shoes to steady my gait and shuffle forward to kneel down before the children. Holding out my hand, I ask, "Would you like me to fix your plane?"

They glance warily to their mother. She assesses me. My clothes may be colorless, but they are expensive. My coat is cashmere, my hat bespoke, the pin holding it in place twenty-four carat gold and deep-sea pearl. The mother nods her head.

"It's a Sopwith Camel," The boy says in a tone that doubts a lady in fancy togs could distinguish between a boat and a plane, much less a Sopwith Camel and a Sopwith Pup. As he should. Even I don't trust the woman I am, trussed up in all this finery, with shoes that fit.

I remove my hat, draw out the four hairpins keeping my thick bob from frizzing. "May I have your gum?" I ask the sister.

Her eyes go wide. I might as well have asked her to spit in church. Gingerly, she removes the chewed, saliva-soaked, grey gob from her mouth and places it in my hand.

"The trick to triage is there is no trick. You use what you have." I break up her gum, roll the bits into balls, flatten them against the points of my hairpins. "Now we've got supports for your wings." I nod my chin toward the plane and wait.

Unimpressed, the boy raises his own chin.

Fair enough. "The Sopwith Camel is the hardest plane to fly. Do you know why?"

"It took down the Red Baron," argues the boy.

"It did because it required the best fighter pilots. The Camel has trouble when it needs to turn left because of the torque of the rotary engine."

The boy turns over the broken body of his plane, squints at the bottom like he's imagining the rotary engine. Finally, he hands it to me. I show him the slow left. "But, the same torque is what gives it the speed to turn right faster than any other plane in a dogfight." I demonstrate.

He places the splintered wings and tail in my palm. I use the gum like it's a glue and cement the plane back together. When I place it in the boy's waiting hands, we inspect the gray seams together. Triage is never pretty.

"When you get home, you can touch it up with furniture glue." My stop is coming.

The boy looks up at his sister, a question forming on his furrowed brow. I want to run my thumb across the lines. He is too young to be so fretful. "The other boys will laugh," he says.

"Who wants a fancy plane," replies his sister, her voice as no-nonsense as a six-year-old's can be. "This Camel has been in a scrap and won." She runs her finger along the exposed gum lines. A strange itch burns along the scar running from my breastbone to my collar bone, a gift from my own scrap with exploding picric acid and a metal shard. "We'll have ourselves a Victory Medal."

My eyes stinging, I go back to my seat, grab my valise, and squash my hat back on top of my head. I'm about to jab my hat pin back in place, but pause. The pin was a gift from my brother on my sixteenth birthday. Tad pinched it from one of the fox-furred great aunts who sipped their tea and looked down their aristocratic, in-bred noses at my bourgeois mother, whose money kept them in fox-fur. Cheeky-grinned and cat-limbed, my brother could leap and run and steal hat pins without stirring so much as a whisper. Though in the end, even he couldn't outrace German bullets. The *Maschinengewehr 08* always gets its man.

The omnibus jerks to a stop. I clutch the pin in my hand and drag my valise down the aisle. The children smile up at me. I feel the way you do when you've woken up from surgery and the anesthetic has worn off. Nauseous and helpless.

I don't know where the children are going, whether it's home or to a shop or to a hospital or a cemetery. There is no guarantee the plane will make it off the bus, much less home without falling apart again. I will never know how the story of this brother-sister pair and their plane ends.

I drop the hat pin into the little girl's lap. "Your Victory Medal," I say and rush off.

❧

The Court Martial chamber is silent and near empty. Lugging my valise down the aisle, I have the sense I've entered the cavernous lungs of a slumbering beast. You know it's alive, and yet there is no sign of life. The only two spectators in the gallery are a man, his cheeks so round and flushed and earnest, you know he never donned khakis, and a woman dressed in black silk, the bell sleeves trimmed with fur, the broad brim of her velvet hat displaying, rather than hiding, her *This is why we fight for England* face. That's all the interest England can muster up for a war crime. As if war itself wasn't a crime.

At the bench, the Judge Advocate presides, imparting seriousness and wisdom (whether he has them or not) in a bench wig, black robes and red sash. When he swallows, he licks his fat bottom lip like a man searching for his scotch. Flanking the Judge Advocate on either side is a row of men in uniform—the board—who are supposed to deliberate the facts and render a verdict and suggest a sentence. The officers wear matching expressions—efficient, impatient, a *let's get on with it* set of the jaw. No worries. The defendant is confessing. They should be home in time for tea.

Before the bench sit two tables, the prosecution to the right, the defense to the left. The prosecution team consists of one wet-behind the ears attorney. A mere formality. The defense consists of no one besides the defendant. A spinal surgeon-cum-solider-cum-confessed murderer. I swallow something ragged. I think it may be a scream.

I should not recognize this hollowed-out man. His golden hair has faded to a dulled metal. The locks are cut unevenly, like someone used a blunt knife rather than a pair of shears. His shoulders are still broad, but do not fill out the uniform. His bones work like a hanger to hold the jacket in place. And he stands military-issue rifle straight, not like a dancer, but a soldier, which he never was.

And yet, I more than recognize him, I *know* him. The salty taste of his skin. The scent of coffee and cinnamon and antiseptic clinging to him. The touch of his calloused fingers across the scar running from my breastbone to collarbone. The sound of his laugh, which has the strength to reverberate through my body and draw out my own laugh, even when I am angry. Staring at his back now, the blood in my feet surges, follows the forgotten trail of veins to reach my heart. It pumps, slow and heavy as an ache.

"The Court Martial has received notice that the defendant Lieutenant Colonel Nicholas Wallace wishes to enter a plea of guilty," declares the Judge Advocate. Like Papa, his voice carries the bored,

Etonian-Oxford authority of all men of his age and class, the age that didn't see trench warfare, the class where women were designed to be delightful and decorative, their voices light, their hands lily white, not drenched by the spurting artery of a hemorrhaging soldier.

I stand frozen in the aisle and the widow raises her gaze, appraising me beneath her overlarge black hat. A tense, *friend or foe* challenge plays on her lips. *Bride or Groom? Guilty or innocent?* I don't care. Were the Germans the only ones guilty of murder? I treated many a POW. They were just boys wanting to return home as badly as my English patients did. And we, the nurses and doctors who put soldiers back together, were we really innocent? We all committed atrocities, physical and emotional. There is no such thing as guilt or innocence. This confession is an injustice. Colonel Wallace's victim deserved no mercy.

"You continue to refuse counsel," says the Judge Advocate.

"That is correct, Your Honor."

Colonel Wallace's words sink into the pit of my stomach. How defeated he sounds, as if he has lost the very thing he taught me: *There's always hope.* I want to stab the person who has robbed him of it, but that man is already dead. If one can die of happiness, one can also kill for it.

I select the bench with the doe-eyed boy. He greets me with a friendly smile and leans over to shake my hand. "James Stahler. *The Times*," he says enthusiastically. There's a Jersey thickness to his accent, a boy who grew up on an island now seeking his fortune in the larger world. He would be the type who is sorry to have missed the war. Had he gone, he would be the type to die first.

The Judge Advocate glances at me, noting the gallery now consists of three. "Though it is not required in cases of a guilty plea, the Court Martial finds an allocution not only appropriate, but necessary. Let it not be said we rushed to judgment or condemned a man who was awarded the Victoria Cross, our nation's highest honor, for his work in saving the lives of the gravely injured. We have received unsolicited letters attesting to your character from your prison chaplain and fellow prisoners."

The widow taps her black-gloved fingers on the railing.

"Objection?" the prosecutor suggests meekly. "The victim, Major Carburry, was also awarded the Victoria Cross."

The Judge Advocate nods to the widow. "Of course, one must question the merit of a character reference made by men guilty of high crimes against the Crown. Nonetheless, they were submitted as testimony and the Court Martial acknowledges them. Colonel Wallace, do you understand that you stand accused of murder? That on the thirteen of August 1918, you did rob of breath and life Major Guy Harrison Carburry, the son of a national hero whose statue graces Westminster Abbey, and a hero himself, who weathered capture by the enemy, escaped by virtue of his English ingenuity, and sought to return home to his beloved wife and young son?"

On cue, the widow sniffles.

"Are you prepared to make an allocution to such a heinous crime?" asks the Judge Advocate.

"I am, Your Honor," says Colonel Wallace, his voice steady and dry, "but wish to make a clarification for the record."

The reporter, Master James (he is too fresh-faced and earnest for me to think of him as a *Mr. Stahler*) leans forward. The widow slaps her black gloves together. I bite my lip.

The Judge Advocate rolls his hand. "You may proceed."

"Your Honor, the letters submitted were not meant as character references, but rather to inform you of the abysmal living conditions of the prison. It is not merely the lack of proper nutrition and clean water. The cells are damp, crowded, and unsanitary, a breeding ground for disease. I entreat you to make changes before an outbreak of a contagious airborne disease decimates the population. The conditions are unimaginable and inhumane. They put—"

"Your fellow prisoners have betrayed Crown and country by engaging in acts of moral turpitude—theft, rape, murder. The conditions, I would say, are part of the punishment."

"Does committing a crime strip a man of his humanity? 'The degree of civilization in a society can be judged by entering its prisons.'"

"You're a philosopher now? Quoting Dostoyevsky," answers the Judge Advocate crossly.

"No, Your Honor. I am a physician," Colonel Wallace answers. "My purpose, no matter my mistakes, is to preserve life."

"Before this Court Martial, you are a soldier. Your actions are in contempt of our Sovereign Lord, the King and his laws, to the vile example of all others, and offending and contrary to the duty of the allegiance you have sworn as a soldier." The Judge Advocate radiates stern authority at Colonel Wallace.

"Very well," Colonel Wallace replies as if his confession is unimportant. "On the thirteenth of August, 1918, while in service of the Royal Army Medical Corps, I boarded a private commercial vessel flying under a Greek flag that was docked in East Sussex. On board was Major Guy Harrison Carburry."

The widow smirks. The Judge Advocate leans back in his seat and steeples his fingers, as if rendering not legal judgment, but God's. The board nod as if this case is closed. They are wrong. All of them. Each of them. Wrong. *I am a physician*, Colonel Wallace said, in the same organ-in-a-cathedral tenor he had the night we met. He is the same man he was nine months ago. The one who promised he would come find me. I was the one who lost faith, thinking he had abandoned me or died. But he is alive. Mercifully, blessedly alive. There is hope. It rises, sharp as a needle and lances through my chest.

I have to stop this confession. If he knows I'm here, will it be enough to give him pause? I knock my valise to the floor. Colonel Wallace tenses. Does he sense I am near? He must. Our bodies have always been acutely attuned to each other. So why then is he marching with renewed determination toward the Judge Advocate, not like a condemned man, but a man who seeks to be condemned? There's a limp to his left leg, caused by the man he is admitting to have murdered. Despite the limp, I recognize how dangerous this particular gait of Colonel Wallace is. It's the same gait with which he strides into an operating room.

It's not this trial I need to save Colonel Wallace from. It's himself. I have to find a way to interrupt the proceedings. I wish I were clever and eloquent and could stand up in court and convince the Court Martial they are wrong. But emotion always churns so violently through me, the right words lay forever beyond my grasp. The only thing I am good at, according to Papa, is making a scene.

So I feign a coughing fit. It starts slow, a catch in the throat, an *oh the tea is hot* gasp. I let it build, careful to keep it sounding dry lest it be mistaken for consumption or whooping cough, both contagious diseases for which I could be quarantined. No one in this room besides Colonel Wallace would know how to diagnose it, but it's important to be accurate. I end with a rattle, a suggestion of an inflamed airway. Master James searches his pockets for a handkerchief. I slap my hand against my chest, exhale roughly, and debate whether to froth at the mouth. Too unladylike? I unbutton my jacket. It helps that my blouse is made of the finest silk, it clings to my breasts. Gwendolyn would be proud. Master James is man enough to notice. The bored officer at the bench perks up as well.

Colonel Wallace refuses to stop. "Major Carburry was a decorated hero and had suffered grievous injury to both his legs. He was immobilized, vulnerable, and it was my duty as his physician to deliver him to England's shores alive and well. In this task, I failed."

"You did not fail, Colonel You deliberately—"

My coughs come faster and harder now, my breaths shorter. Lungs burning, eyes watering, cheeks red hot, but the color gives me a pretty blush. I knock my hat off and turn my face to the officer who looks most susceptible to a pretty face, the weak link sitting at the bench. He pours a glass of water from the pitcher and stands, the officer beside him yanks him back. I clutch my chest.

"Can you breathe?" Master James whispers.

I shake my head. Thanks to my recent triage of a toy plane, I'm missing a few hairpins, so my hair sticks to my flushed forehead. A nice effect.

"Are you choking?"

Asthma I mouth and gesture to Colonel Wallace and back to my lungs. The blood is leaving my head, tiny stars spot my vision. I rise to my feet and wobble.

Master James tries to take hold of my arm to steady me. I wave him away and point dramatically at Colonel Wallace.

Who ignores me. He doesn't move a single hair, so focused is he on the fate before him. As if he wants to avoid the fate hacking her way to a fainting spell behind him. Instead, he says, "At approximately seven p.m.—"

I double over, trill between hacking cough and wheezing breath. Even the widow looks concerned.

"The young lady needs a doctor," shouts Master James. "The defendant—Colonel Wallace, if you please, we have an emergency—"

The Judge Advocate bangs his gavel. "Sit down, young man or I will have the bailiffs remove you. Bailiff, please see to the young lady."

I scan the room for the best place to faint without getting bruised.

"With the intent of causing cardiac arrest to Major Carburry," says Colonel Wallace, his words coming faster, trying to beat me to the punch.

I suck in my last breath, savor it like a lozenge, and cast my damsel-in-distress gaze at the weak-link officer. I totter. I clutch a bit of my skirt to make sure I leave a healthy length of leg exposed when I hit the floor. Not one, but two officers at the bench leap to their feet. I start my descent.

The doors to the courtroom fly open. A voice calls, "Oi! You can't—"

Immediately, I grab the railing and straighten up. My asthma attack miraculously cured (to his credit Master James eyes my recovery suspiciously), I turn to take in the three men charging into the courtroom and the young officer running after them demanding they stop.

The first man is short and energetic and, despite his dour barrister's robe, carries himself with such robust confidence, he strikes me as handsome. He clutches his bench wig to keep it from sliding off and waves his fist in the air, shouting, "Objection. Objection. Pardon the interruption, Your Honor. Objection." Not an Eton-Oxford boy, his accent is the full cockney of a man who bare-knuckled his way to the Inns of Court.

Behind him two tall, grey-suited men follow. One sways under the weight of the tower of boxes he carries. The other strides down the aisle, determined, purposeful, arrogant. A patch covers his right eye.

"What is the meaning of this," shouts the Judge Advocate. His face is red, the fat bottom lip radiating displeasure. "This is a Court Martial, not a gin hall." Interesting choice of words. The man looks like he needs a drink.

"Apologies, my lord," says the lawyer, hopping the rail dividing the gallery from the defense table. "Nigel Higgenbotham, King's Court, at your service. Terribly sorry for the disruption. But such a serious, serious matter. Justice, you know." He shrugs, as if Lady Justice herself has dragged him into the courtroom.

The Judge Advocate points his finger at Mr. Higgenbotham. "You are out of order."

"Now, my lord, I cannot think one as lauded and noble as yourself would disparage a member of the King's Court for seeking a fair trial. All due respect and such." He bows.

"I did not give you leave to address this Court."

"We don't need leave," says the man with the eyepatch. "You don't have jurisdiction."

"And who do you think you are?" sputters the Judge Advocate.

"Who I am doesn't matter. Who I come on behalf of does."

"Oh for Christ's sake," says Colonel Wallace. "I object to this objection. These men are making a mockery of your Court. Bailiffs." He snaps his fingers. "Remove them."

The Judge Advocate slams his gavel. "The defendant shall stay silent."

"Then you are in agreement with the Home Secretary," says EyePatch. "The defendant was in his service at the time of this *alleged* incident."

"Carburry's death is not *alleged*," says Colonel Wallace. "It is a fact. I signed the death certificate."

EyePatch delivers a *shut-up before I wallop you* frown at Col Wallace.

"Ahem." Mr. Higgenbotham raises his index finger. "I have prepared for the Court a motion setting forth the reasons this military tribunal has no authority over *Doctor* Wallace. If I may?" Mr. Higgenbotham draws a sheaf of papers from his briefcase.

"What are all those boxes?" asks the Judge Advocate.

The widow whispers furiously to the prosecutor, who nods his head obediently and watches the unfolding scene like a child thrown off a boat and ordered to swim. The other grey-suited man, the younger one with the tower of boxes, approaches the bench. He hands one to the Judge Advocate who lifts the lid, pulls out a stack of documents and flips through them.

"Is this meant to be a joke?" he asks. "These documents are redacted. Besides the date and a few prepositions, they're meaningless."

"I counted at least eighteen definite and indefinite articles per a page," says EyePatch.

It's Colonel Wallace's turn to deliver a *shut-up before I wallop you* glare.

"National Security," explains Mr. Higgenbotham cheerfully. "Secrets of the Crown."

The widow shoves the prosecutor toward the bench. Mr. Higgenbotham hustles forward. They argue in low voices while the Judge Advocate glowers and the board at last takes an interest in the proceedings, passing the blacked-out sheets of papers between them, holding them up to the light to divine their secrets. EyePatch folds his arms across his chest, satisfied.

Colonel Wallace mutters to EyePatch, "You are making a dog's breakfast of this," and barrels forward. "Your Honor? My confession, if you please? Major Carburry, aged thirty-five, weighed 12.86 stone. In generally good health. Death came quickly and unnaturally—"

EyePatch elbows Colonel Wallace in the stomach.

The Colonel Wallace of nine months ago, athletic and confident, stubbornly optimistic despite the bombs and the boys with shredded limbs and severed spines, would have absorbed the blow lightly and marched on. He might even have chuckled. Not now. Gaunt and sallow, he collapses.

And my body, remembering at last how to obey my heart, crashes through the gate dividing the gallery from the defense table. I rush to Colonel Wallace's—Nick's—side, kneel, grab his wrist, and lay two fingers on his radial artery. I want to weep. I want to strangle him.

"After the ship docked in East Sussex, you were supposed to come find me. Not the gallows," I tell him.

Nick sighs, a slow exhalation that stretches the seconds to minutes. His breath is all-consuming, like he had been holding it for too long, probably from the moment I walked into this court room. His gaze takes me in small bits and all at once. Every hair on my head, each of my eyelashes, the pores on my skin, the cells of my body. He is the only person who has ever looked at me thus, like I matter more than water and air and sunlight.

The lines fanning out from his eyes are deeper. His cheekbones are sharper, more angular. Sweat beads along his forehead. I want to kiss each worry away. His gaze drops to my collarbone, as if he can see straight through my shirt to my flesh, deeper still, to the gravestones weighing down my heart, to all my wounds. The six-inch scar, running from my breastbone to collarbone, the one he stitched together, vibrates.

Eyepatch demands, "Who the devil are you?"

Nick shuts his eyes and shutters his expression. He tries to yank back his wrist. I hold on tight. "A ghost," he murmurs.

"In the flesh," I answer.

CHAPTER SIX

Lady Sullivan's Ambulance Hospital, Ypres, May 2, 1918

My limbs are weighted down, as if the blood coursing through me is molten lead. My tongue feels thick and swollen, my mouth dry. I can barely manage to open my eyes and when I do, the light burns so sharp, I shut them tight and seek relief in the aching darkness. Perhaps I am a ghost?

"In the flesh," comes a voice, deep, resonate and male.

I must have mumbled my thought aloud. My parched lips are cracked and I taste salt. "Colonel Wallace."

"So they keep telling me." He chuckles, but his humor can't hide the frustration beneath. *I'm a doctor, not a soldier.* "Mind if I look into your soul?"

My eyes flare open. Vision bursts in blurry white spots, I struggle to sit up. My body seems to have forgotten how. The muscles are so asleep they are near comatose.

Colonel Wallace places a hand on my shoulder, eases me back down to the cot. "Steady, now. Bad medical humor, I apologize. I meant I had to check your pupils."

The scent of ether lingers. The air tastes metallic. We must be in the surgical theatre. At last my eyes catch up to my senses. The room comes into focus. Colonel Wallace is sitting on a stool, wearing a doctor's coat and a bedside manner.

He holds up a small light and smiles. "See?" It's not a defense, nor is it an invitation. It's a challenge.

Despite the pounding in the back of my head, I sit up. "Pupils even in size? What about fundus of the eye? You'll want to examine the optic nerves, make sure there's no bleeding from the brain."

"And they say doctors make the worst patients," he mutters while he raises one finger and directs me to track it while he flashes the light and watches my pupils prove to him I am concussed but otherwise unharmed.

He switches off the light and puts it back in his coat pocket, picks up my wrist, and takes my pulse. My blood goes from molten lead to hot lava. He says, "I suppose it's not proper, me asking to look into the windows of your soul when we haven't even had a proper introduction. One forgets Mr. Hartley's *The Gentleman's Book of Etiquette and Manual of Politeness* still applies." He glances around at the bare, efficient surgical theatre. Three surgical tables, trays of instruments, a sink to scrub up and wipe away blood afterwards.

Turning back to me, he continues, "Though I did manage to carry you in my arms out of a blistering fire. And removed a sheet of metal from your sternum, stitched up a six-inch gouge."

His voice may be bedside manner casual, but I am suddenly, acutely aware that I am wearing a thin dressing gown, its bodice loose enough to reveal a square of linen bandage covering my chest and very little else. Someone cut through my sou'wester, my thick cotton nursing uniform, my undergarments. Sensation returns to my hands, I fist them.

"Don't worry. Amy—Lady Sullivan—undressed you and supervised like a proper chaperone. And I'm a professional, Dr. Nicholas Wallace at your service." He bows from his seat.

His voice sounds English enough, but even in my grogginess, I recall hearing his other accent. The foreign one. "Nicholas? Are you English?"

"Though my mother fervently denies it, she is Greek."

"Are we on the same side? I thought the Greeks were . . ." The only news I read comes from the articles written by my cousin Kristina and she is more dedicated to uncovering graft than the goings-on in the Mediterranean.

"Neutral until last summer. My mother led the negotiations. She represented England, of course."

"Of course," I repeat, not understanding why his tone takes on a heavy note.

He holds his hand out as if meaning to shake mine. "So to summarize, Nicholas Wallace, Greek mother, English father, physician, lastly of London. Currently of Wimereux."

"Do you speak Greek?"

"Fluently. And you?"

I wrinkle my forehead and give him a quizzical look. "I do not speak Greek."

He laughs. Not loudly, but with a quiet surprise, like he's forgotten surprises could be good. Golden stubble roughens his jawline. He has not shaved this morning, perhaps he never went to bed last night. He points to his hand still outstretched to shake mine, and gives me an amused smile, a touch mischievous.

I catch myself before I make the mistake of returning it. "Vera Betts." I do not shake his hand. I lay my head back down on the cot. I want to close my eyes. I want to sleep. For days and days and days. It's not the aftereffect of the anesthesia. It's a new sort of exhaustion, the kind that overtakes you when you make the mistake of lowering your defenses and admitting you could use a wee nap.

"Betts, you say. Would that be the Betts of Birmingham, Leicester or London? The way you were swearing the devil at McMannis, am I safe to assume you're a city Betts, not a bucolic country lass?"

"You clearly haven't spent time on a farm."

"Ahh, so a country Betts it is." He leans back and crosses his legs as if settling in for a leisurely chat, but there's a firmness in his tone, a sense of direction, an agenda. I need to corral my wits. "And your friends call you . . ."

The last person I counted as a friend ran off with my sister. And this man, this Greek doctor whose easy charm is a weapon, who I overhead conspiring with another Greek earlier this morning, is no friend. His questions are not innocuous, they're pointed. So why am I so inclined to trust him?

"Vera," he supplies. "From the Latin, *verus*, feminine *vera*, meaning true, real. Or from the Albanian, meaning summer? I suppose there's the ancient Greek *Saint Fides*, faith."

"You must be great craic at cocktail parties." Carefully, I slip in the Northern slang I learned at the cottage hospital.

"Forgive me. Force of habit. My father was a Cambridge Don. Linguistics. Dinner conversation tended to revolve around origin and meaning."

"Topping fun."

He nods like we're flirting at a cocktail party. "There never was a livelier night than when I brought up onomatopoeia."

"Your mother's Greek must have come in quite handy."

"Educated and clever too. I fear I'm about to get down on one knee and beg for your hand in marriage." He flashes a smile so bright and golden, so lighthearted and sincere, I almost believe we are in a swanky London salon, clinking high balls and smart barbs. But the noise in the background is gunfire, not jazz.

"I'm not interested in marriage," I manage to say.

"Dedicated to your career? It only makes me love you more. Where did you train?"

Nausea rolls through me and I have to swallow hard. It's the concussion and the anesthesia. It's the sense that this man who I do not know wants to know something about me that no one knows. And not trusting my strange desire to tell him.

"If you doubt my credentials, I suggest you take it up with Lady Sullivan," I answer. Who could not have cared less about the politics of paperwork. When she met me (more like found me), I had been waiting for the steamship bound for New York and sulking in a café when the tea cart crashed and spilled scalding water over the serving girl's arm. I was by her side in a trice, tearing through her sleeve, cooling down the skin with, of course, Blackpond bandages. I had been all of eighteen. A lifetime ago.

"Amy says you are all action. You never pause. Not even in the face of an explosion, which I myself witnessed this morning. Is that instinct, would you say, or training?"

"It's a gift," I reply drily. A gift from Dr. Bettany at the Blackpond cottage hospital, whom, with his stiff, arthritic hands had placed more and more responsibility in my eager-to-matter hands. Everyone at Blackpond called Dr. Bettany *Old Betts* and I was so often by his side, I came to be known as *Little Betts*. It was a name I had earned. Which was why it was the name I gave Lady Sullivan when she approached me in the cafe and asked, *Would you like an adventure?*

"Why did you choose medicine?" he asks.

Because I am wanted. I am useful. "Why are you asking me so many questions?"

He taps a finger to his forehead. "You've a concussion, remember? As your physician, I must check for neurological damage—memory, focus, your ability to recall facts."

Accurate enough. I do the same as a nurse. But the facts he wants are lies I have told. "Why are you a doctor?"

He studies his open palms. The hands are strong, the position vulnerable. "My younger brother drowned when he was two."

"And you blame yourself?" My voice is harsher than I mean it to be. I know what it is to love a brother. I refuse to imagine the pain of losing one.

"Hardly. I was six. Strong enough to pull him out of the bathtub, not old enough to know how to resuscitate him. I didn't have the skills then. I do now." He provides this deeply personal information like it's a fact, not a tragedy, but a fact to be respected, like gravity. A rule that determines life's outcome.

"So your career is an act of penance?"

"A crusade," he corrects. His conviction hits me hard in the chest.

Another wave of nausea courses through me. I'm dizzy, but I refuse to cave to the desire to vomit. Digging my hands into the sides of the cot, I close my eyes and will the sickness to pass. I have rounds tonight.

"Are you a crusader, Sister Betts?" His voice has a calming quality to it. When I inhale, there's a scent of cinnamon and coffee. "What sent you running to the fire?"

"The desire to put it out." I ease my head back onto the pillow. If I keep my eyes shut, maybe he will leave me alone. It's hard to balance a touch of the truth with a fog of lies when one's brain feels ready to burst.

"Without a water hose?"

"I wanted to remove the picric acid from the chemical storage." I'm struggling to make this sound rational.

"Picric acid is an odd thing for someone to be well-versed in."

Resentful, I sit up, set my feet on the rough, cold floor. My head spins in protest. "I went to primary school." *I was tutored at home.* "There were books." *That only Gwendolyn read.* "And everyone knows picric acid is volatile." *If your family happens to manufacture it.* "That's why it's used in bullets." *For which I am grateful my family doesn't.* "Emits a yellow discharge."

"Volatile is a nice word for its power to tear a man apart." The good doctor's face has hardened, like the cause of war is picric acid, not human nature. He catches himself. More gently he asks, "Did you see anyone near the supply marquees?"

McMannis. Gaspar. The Padre. "You."

He sits back, startled, and appraises me with an expression—not hostile—curious. I've surprised him again. I should not be so pleased.

"I was up on the hill by the lake this morning," I say, matter-of-fact.

"By the graveyard? Interesting choice of place to be."

"It's so quiet up there, sometimes I think I hear voices."

Is it guilt wrinkling his forehead? Is it shame drawing his gaze away from me and toward the one small and dusty window? He rises, runs his thumb along his stethoscope like he's trying to reassure himself he's still who he thinks he is. I'm not the only one in this room lying about their identity.

"Shall I have Lady Sullivan come sit with you?" he asks. "You should rest, but, no sleeping. Doctor's orders."

No sleep. But five minutes, just enough time to give in, at last, to the black shadow engulfing my head. I relax into the cot. In the darkness, I hear the rustle of military-starched fabric, the echo of polished boots, Colonel Wallace seems to be saying something. I do not turn my head. I'm not sure I can lift it.

"Vera."

The wind batters against the opened door, sending cold air into the theatre. I burrow deeper into the cot. It is always cold in France. Even when it is sweltering hot.

"Vera."

I wish I had a thick blanket. Perhaps my coverlet at Halsop House. Mama had embroidered the corners with yellow flowers and my initials. *Margaret Adelaide.* I carry my mother's name, a sign she treasured me, before she betrayed me.

"Vera."

Shhh Shhh, Mama used to whisper in my ear, stroking my hair. What was the perfume she wore? Bergamot mixed with vanilla. The smell of comfort.

"Sister Betts." Colonel Wallace's voice rises sharp in my ears. "You cannot fall asleep."

I flash an angry smirk toward the open door. The wind beats against his white coat, ruffles his hair. "I know how to treat a concussion." I lean up on my elbows. The effort makes me wince.

"Nevertheless, Sister Betts"—he adds a particular emphasis on *Betts*—"the next time someone addresses you by your given name, you should answer to it." He settles his military cap on top of his head. "And by the way, you're hired."

"I won't go."

I've rested a full twenty-four hours. Lady Sullivan had me moved to her private tent. I have taken my medicine, cleaned my wound, slept when told to, and am in fact sitting in a chair. Upright. With clear vision and no headache. I am in fine shape to determine the course of my own future. And my future does not include being dragged to Wimereux by Colonel Wallace who is guilty of something.

"You're concussed." Lady Sullivan hands me a glass of milk and under her vigilant eye, I drink. "You have stitches in your chest. You can't be on your feet. How are you supposed to triage? We'll need to watch you for infection."

"I can perform other tasks. No one folds linens faster than me." I place my empty glass on her wobbly camp table and nod my head eagerly.

She sets her jaw, like an indulgent nanny who is having to learn to be strict. "I have done my best to protect you from bureaucracy and the newsmongers' lust for heroes. But this time, in front of two generals, you ran *toward* a fire with shrapnel sticking out of your chest. Someone will send a dispatch. Someone will want to pin a medal over your heart. Which means more than one person will want to know . . ."

Who I really am. Something not even Lady Sullivan knows.

"You are to go to Wimereux. Military orders. Which, as an arm of the British Royal Red Cross, we must now follow." When we had arrived in France, we had been under the French Flag Nursing Corps. It was the only way we were allowed to operate so close to the battlefield. But as the war grew, so did the rules.

"I don't know Colonel Wallace." I sound petulant, which is at least a degree or two better than what I am. Petrified. The only world real to me is Lady Sullivan's Ambulance Hospital.

"He runs a hospital for spinal injuries," she says reasonably. "He performs miracles. Is that not enough?"

"Where does Colonel Wallace come from? What are his credentials? What is his character?" An odd thought strikes me. I already know the answers. He is a crusader. But for which side?

"I've known Nick since he was in short pants. *Not* that I am significantly older. I may even have been his first . . ." She coughs lightly and smiles naughtily.

If I am caught off guard, I cannot be blamed. We were a small band when we crossed the English Channel and we had one fully qualified nurse amongst us, QAIMNS Sister Agnes Reynolds. Sister Reynolds was everything Lady Sullivan is not—charmless, heavy set, dull hair, blunt. But she was also very precious to Lady Sullivan. They shared the same bed.

"I heard Colonel Wallace talking," I say cautiously.

She cuts in. "Our job is to heal, not hear things we will misunderstand. Whatever Nick does, you cannot doubt his moral compass. He will always do the right thing, no matter the cost. If only the rest of the world could be so absolute." She folds her hands across her lap. They must have been soft and delicate once, dedicated to the things ladies of our rank are supposed to do—embroider and arrange flowers and serve tea. The skin is cracked and callused now, the knuckles red. Too much carbolic acid, too much scrubbing. She has the most beautiful hands in the world.

"He has no right to reassign me from your hospital." I do my best not to stomp my foot.

"Don't be angry at Nick. I suggested you could be of help to him. Perhaps I bullied him. You are too young to be here. I worry that in plucking you from that café, I was selfish."

"Never. No." Lady Sullivan saved me. I ask, "What did you say to Col Wallace?

She smiles ruefully. "That no one is more honest a liar than you."

I raise my eyebrows. "You want me to trust a man who would hire me on such a recommendation?"

"Think of him as a friend. God knows, we are otherwise so very much alone."

She gazes at a silver-framed photo of her and Sister Reynolds. They're standing with their arms around each other, dressed in motorcycle gear—leather jackets, goggles, white scarfs—Ben Nevis in the distance. We each had our reasons for running away from England. And we each paid the price. Sister Reynolds with a stray bullet.

"What am I supposed to do at a fancy convalescent home in Wimereux? The nurses there do little more than flirt and plump pillows."

"You are supposed to rest."

"I am not tired."

"My dearest Betts, we are all tired." She sighs and rubs her eyes. The circles beneath her light brown eyes are dark, heavy, and permanent.

A glimmer of hope strikes me. "When the dispatches fade and the news moves on to someone else to convert to a hero, I will be able to come back—" I cut myself off before I say *home*. Lady Sullivan's Ambulance Hospital should be nobody's home. "I can return to my work?"

She cups my face. Even as I long for the maternal gesture, I flinch, unused to the tenderness. "Betts, you do realize, don't you, one day this war will end. It will," she insists when I start to shake my head. "What will become of you when we are at peace?"

CHAPTER SEVEN

London, May 2, 1919

In peace time, I have become a blackmailer.

His imperial majesty, the EyePatch, crosses his arms and glowers down at me, blocking entrance to the antechamber where Nick has been escorted while the Judge Advocate reviews sensitive documents from the Home Secretary. "I don't know who you think you are—"

"I'm a witness."

He curls his lip, a feral snarl. I wobble back. "More like a lonely heart who writes letters to condemned men. Schoolgirls and their perverse crushes. Go home to your nursery."

I run my tongue against the back of my teeth. "I have vital—"

"No press!" EyePatch points to Master James Stahler, the puppy/reporter trotting down the hall and trying to squeeze past the military guard. The intrepid journalist does not have my advantage, namely that I am female and impeccably dressed, my pristine lace gloves conveying class and money and authority, not the type of person a guard would expect to be breaking in to see a murderer. When I flashed past the guard a minute before, he hesitated. Not now. He puffs his chest and pushes himself in front of Master James, who jumps side-to-side and waves. Irritation ripples off of EyePatch so thick, I can bite into it.

And taste my advantage.

I wave back to Master James and smile broadly. Poor Master James. His smile is automatic and trusting. It withers the moment Eyepatch narrows his one amber eye and says to him, "Take another step and I'll have you arrested."

"I *am* a witness," I tell Eyepatch, my voice all sugar and spice. "I saw you."

"At the fish and chip shop?" His sarcasm suggests he has never stepped foot inside a chippie.

"At Lady Sullivan's Ambulance Hospital. Ypres, May 2, 1918."

"To lovelorn schoolgirl, I should add fantasist," replies EyePatch. He's lowered his voice, though, and is checking to be sure the guard is keeping Master James at bay.

"Left hand." I hold up mine. "Right hand." I hold it up. "Neither needs to know what the other is doing to function as a whole—your words. What did the Home Secretary have to say about the neck? Did no one consider that it might meet the hangman's noose?"

EyePatch leans against the door, hooks his thumbs on his pockets. Despite the façade of calm, his fingers twitch like he needs a cigarette. With his full looming height, his shadow alone could swallow me whole.

"Still doubt me?" I raise my voice, glance back at Master James, who is listening attentively even while the guard is ordering him to turn 'round. "In Ypres, at Lady Sullivan's Ambulance Hospital, you were by the lake, next to the cemetery. *Conspiring.*"

"I have never been to *Wipers.*" His mispronunciation sounds deliberate.

"I heard you speaking Greek. About a man you shot. In the—"

EyePatch grabs me by the shoulders and shoves me into the antechamber and slams the door behind us.

"I don't know who the hell you work for –" he starts, but we both stop short at the sight of Nick, staring at a glass of water, sliding his finger along the table edge like he's drawing a barbed wire fence between it and him.

"Nick." My voice is so quiet it might be a whisper.

"Can't you let a man hang in peace?" A frightening energy buzzes off his shoulders. Someone who did not know Nick well would call it anger. It is deeper than anger. More raw.

"Why?" I ask.

"Because I am guilty." The words are dull, flat. He's excised all emotion out of them, the way he would cancer cells.

"Jesus, Nick." EyePatch comes to the table and leans across it to face him. "Just because you're guilty doesn't mean you should hang."

"Words to live by," he says drily.

I am frightened for this Nick, this thinned-out, pale version of the man who fused spines together and taught broken men how to hope again, even if they could not walk.

"You've gone from crusader to martyr," I say.

"There's a difference?" Drops of water have condensed on the outside of his glass. He draws his forefinger back and forth, back and forth across the edge of the table.

I take a step closer to him. "You're the son of a linguist. You should know."

EyePatch studies Nick, swivels his gaze to me and back again. "How do you know each other?" It's phrased as a question, but Eyepatch isn't the type to ask, he demands information like he's ordering off a menu. "Who are you?"

"No one who matters," Nick says so quickly my pulse jumps. Only he would understand how to wield that sentence like a knife. A protective one, but I don't need protection. I need Nick. Whatever fear is driving him, I will rescue him from it.

"We were lovers," I tell EyePatch.

"Passing fancy," Nick says to the glass of water. "You know how it is in hospitals, in between the cardiac arrests and surgeries are long expanses of utter boredom." He feigns a yawn.

"Your passing fancy claims she saw me in Ypres."

"She saw nothing. She knows nothing. She is no one." Back and forth, back and forth, Nick's finger draws that barbed wire fence.

"I did," I insist. "And I knew Major Carburry. I knew the . . ." I can't make myself utter the word *victim*. It feels like a betrayal to Nick. "I was his nurse."

EyePatch studies me. "Your name?"

The tip of my tongue catches at the top of my teeth. My real name, the one printed on the calling cards Gwendolyn insists a lady of our rank carries, bears no weight in this room. Who is Margaret Halladay other than an undutiful daughter packed off to Bryn Mawr to sit out the war?

Nick supplies the answer. "Vera Betts."

EyePatch crosses his legs, settles back in the stiff wooden chair, and tips the front legs off the floor. A balancing act. "And what could you testify to, Sister Betts?"

"Forged credentials," says Nick, crossing his right leg over his left. "Claiming to be a qualified nurse, serving England's injured soldiers, sewing up wounds, administering medications, participating in surgeries. A serious crime. Though I doubt the Crown would want to prosecute such a lovely young thing. Imagine all the bad press. Speaking of bad press, how's your wife?" Nick tips his own chair back, shifts the balance of his weight and the two men stare at each other like schoolboys daring the other to blink first.

EyePatch blinks first, slamming his chair back to the floor. "Jesus, Nicky. Two days ago, I didn't know whether you were rotting away in some godforsaken POW camp or buried beneath the mud with a bullet between the eyes. Do you know what it took to find you and have your trial moved to London? We are supposed to watch out for each other. At the very least, you could have scratched out an S.O.S. I am your brother."

"Brother," I repeat. It makes sense. Even in Ypres, I noticed the matching hair color, the long, sharp noses, the mirrored stances, the competitive nature.

Nick shrugs.

"Lucky for you someone in the Home Secretary's Office cares." Eyepatch invokes the Home Secretary with such conviction, he sounds like a religious convert. But there's something about the way he runs his thumb over his finger pads, a weariness masking a sadness. He's a man who thought the best way to beat the odds was to play for the house. It's the safe bet. You don't win, but you survive.

"After your Essex prison cell, London must feel like the Savoy. I'm told you even had a meal." EyePatch puts a strange emphasis on *meal*, it's both ironic and a reprimand.

Nick gives EyePatch a pitying look. "You're not saving the world, Alex. You are playing cricket. Victory only lasts as long as the time in between this match and the next. Five minutes tops. Last year it was the Germans. This year the Russians. Carburry was right. I'm just another ball to crack against your bat."

"This is not a game," says Eyepatch.

"What's your barrister doing with his blacked-out reams of paper?" Nick asks.

"Buying us a few days."

"And then?"

"We challenge jurisdiction," says EyePatch.

"For what purpose?"

EyePatch answers between clenched teeth. "Time, obviously."

"And when you lose that motion?"

"Move for a trial. Drop an air raid's worth of motions on the Court Martial. Appeal each decision. Stack the deck so the Judge Advocate will have to declare a mistrial. The Home Secretary will eventually remove you to his custody. From there . . . a new identity." EyePatch keeps a level, authoritative tone, but Papa has made me an expert at sussing out the fissures. When Eyepatch notes my skeptical expression, he tries to cover with, "I should stick you in a cave in Greece. The mouth of Hades would be fitting."

Nick runs his hands through his hair. "No games. No delay. I want to be finished. I am pleading guilty."

EyePatch looks ready to punch Nick. "For once in your life, you are going to shut your big, fat, self-righteous mouth."

"What does one life matter?" Nick bites back.

My stomach convulses. I press my hands hard into the wooden table to make sure the world is still solid. What has thrust Nick into despair? What does nine months in prison do to a soul? Was it worse than what Carburry did to us?

"Every life matters," I insist. "That's what you said in Wimereux. When Corporal Langdon tried to throw himself from the balcony? You stopped him. You told him his legs didn't define him, his child did, and she did not deserve to be orphaned. When the MPs brought German patients and the nurses revolted, still you operated, because even the enemy is human. When—"

Nick digs his palms into his eyes. "Enough."

Eyepatch searches his pockets, looking for his cigarettes. "And Derrick? Did he die for nothing?"

The unexpected scratch of emotion sneaking through Eyepatch's glacial veneer makes me ask, "Who is Derrick?"

"Our younger brother." Nick rubs his jaw and exhales.

"A pilot," I remember.

"Once we were four." Nick holds up four fingers. Folds down his pinky and ring finger. "Now we are two."

"I won't let you reduce us to one." Eyepatch tugs at the cuff of his grey coat sleeve.

"Alex," Nick says gently. "You don't have the power to stop me."

Silence falls thick as a fist to the mouth. A lock of my hair is plastered to my forehead. I am heavy-limbed, sinking, like I'm wading through a marsh full of corpses. Nick is back to drawing the imaginary fence between him and the water. I want to pick up that stupid glass and thrust the water down Nick's parched throat till the water flushes out the filth contaminating him.

"We are done." Nick nods toward the door, exhausted.

"No." I slam my gloved hand into the dark table. My palm will bruise from the force. "No."

The change in Nick is minute, near imperceptible, seismic. A slight parting of the lips. A pause in the incessant running of his forefinger along the table. A tiny sip, not of the water, but of me. A reluctant easing of his jaw. The expression is bittersweet, like I am both the ill and the cure.

EyePatch raises an eyebrow. "Miss Betts," he says, suddenly collegial, "please tell me more about your service in Wimereux."

Nick tenses and mutters to his brother in Greek.

"What interesting terms." EyePatch forgets me and focuses on Nick.

Nick answers, again in Greek, and the two argue back and forth with the speed of card sharps who know each other's every move. Thick syllables and meaningless sounds fly by. I don't know how to distinguish a word from a sentence from a decision.

Finally, Nick says, "You win, Alex." He imitates a ball being tossed in the air, a cricket bat swinging.

Eyepatch rises. A smile—not cruel, but not warm—touches his angular face. It looks almost like relief. "I thank you, Miss Betts. Let me see you to the door."

My knees are shaking. I plant my feet onto this impersonal floor, the wood scratched and faded from the pacing of those who have stood before me, maneuvering and strategizing, out-gaming. Whatever happened in the brothers' negotiations, Nick has rendered me helpless, useless. He thinks he is safe. More fool him. It's his determination to push me away that spurs me on.

I dig into my purse. "I insist upon you taking my card." I hold my calling card between my fingers and Nick reaches for the glass, except instead of taking hold of it, it seems to slip from his grasp and slide across the table, tumbling off the edge, spilling water on EyePatch, and smashing to the floor.

EyePatch jumps back, draws a handkerchief, and dabs at his pant leg. "*Malakas*. Wanker."

Nick ignores him and is by my side so quickly my heart spins dizzy and drunk. He no longer smells like cinnamon or coffee or the fresh air of Wimereux. He smells of sweat, of dank quarters, of rough lye soap. He presses his hand into the small of my back. There's a pause, a faint flutter, as if I am too precious to touch. His hand is trembling.

I love Nick's fingers. Long and firm, they belong to a spinal surgeon, someone who must move with precision lest he sever a nerve or cut a vein. Clumsiness is antithetical to him, which is why, a moment ago when he knocked over the water glass, I stifled a sob. Hollowed out, worn to the bone, the man I love is disintegrating. But there is still life. It thrums in the fingertips running along my spine.

His lips hover just above my ear. Every pore in my body blooms under the heat of his breath. "Vera-not-Vera," he whispers, his name for me even before we were lovers, even before we were friends. "You cannot save me. Let go." He thrusts me into the corridor and shuts the door against me.

Outside the Royal Courts of Justice, I'm holding my creased and bent calling card between my thumb and index finger, pondering whether to track down the omnibus to Mayfair or hail a cab. Both ridiculous options. As the calling card indicates, I am the daughter of the Earl of Halsop. All I need do is ring the London house and our butler will send the chauffer. I shake my head. I'm not used to these choices, small, incidental, meaningless. A man's life does not hang on my choice of transport. And so I do not know how to choose.

"I knew there was a story," comes a young voice from behind me.

I stuff the card into my purse and turn to acknowledge Master James. Above him, the Victorian-Gothic spires of the Royal Courts prick the grey and dusty sky. How do those spires manage to stand so straight? My own shoulders are sagging.

"Pardon?"

"How's your asthma?" he asks, sly and yet respectful. "All better?"

"Infinitely." I readjust my hat, fiddle with my gloves, and reassess Master James. It was his name on the byline *Doctor To Hang*. "What makes you think there is a story?"

"I have an instinct. My editor told me not to bother, said no one wants to read about another military murder. Dead heroes don't sell papers. People need cheering up. Assigned me to the St. Pancreas Pound Cake competition."

"Pound cake," I repeat, trying to make sense of the way my stomach stretches in yearning, even though my tongue lays heavy and numb. When I was a child and could not sleep, Mama used to cut me a slice of pound cake and dunk it in sherry. The sticky sweetness would coat my tongue and cling to my teeth, settle in my stomach like warm milk, and I would nestle deep into the curve of my mother's body, her arms tight around me. Cook baked her famous pound cake the other day. It tasted like everything else does now, a memory covered in dust.

Master James leans forward, conspiratorial. "You know who proclaims their innocence the loudest?"

"The innocent," I suggest.

With a narrow-eye and a *tsk*, he warns me not to patronize him. "The guilty. A guilty man fights the noose even once he's dangling."

I think of Nick denying himself even a sip of water. "Unless he's a martyr."

"For a cause? You don't hide. You draw attention. But even on his hunger strike, the only thing Colonel Wallace spoke of was the prison conditions. Not himself."

"Hunger strike?" The thought of Nick starving hurts my ribs. EyePatch's *I'm told you even had a meal*, rings in my ears.

"Colonel Wallace has been refusing food for months. Last night, he had to be strapped down while a medic shoved ox broth down his throat."

I can see Nick, worn through and yet righteous, bucking against the straps, the fabric rubbing against his thin flesh, leaving burns. He's not a shouter. He would not yell, he would rail against the cramped prison quarters, the filthy water, the vermin spreading disease. Stripped of everything, he would hang on to the last ounce of what defines him—his need to make things better.

"A medic?" I ask.

"Yes?" Master James is unsure of my question. He doesn't understand the significance.

"He's not being housed in a jail? He's in an infirmary?" I'm not charming or clever enough to steal into a prison cell, but a medical ward? That's another matter entirely. "How do you know?"

"I have my sources."

"Who?"

"I'm a journalist. I have a code of ethics." Master James smiles a little, boyish and young. He's probably at least a year or two older than me. Beside him, I feel brittle and ancient.

"The man from the Home Secretary's Office," I say slowly, feeding the greedy journalist within Master James. "His name is Alex Wallace."

"Related?"

"Brothers."

"He's important, Colonel Wallace. He's connected." Master James mulls this over, chewing on his bottom lip. "Why didn't Mr. Wallace step in sooner?"

"Apparently, he didn't know until the other day his brother was in prison."

"The day of my news article? A coincidence? It's odd, isn't it? Really odd. Like someone was hiding him."

"Or Colonel Wallace didn't want to be found. I gave you Alex Wallace. Your turn. How do you know about the ox broth?"

Mr. James glances down at his feet, a bit sheepish. "My cousin's sweetheart's uncle works in the infirmary where Colonel Wallace is being held."

"You have good instincts. Even before I walked into the Court Martial, even before the Home Secretary's team came barging in with an air raid of motions, you sensed a story. You might be the only person who can save Colonel Wallace."

"So you think he's innocent too? You know it." Master James' face is bright and earnest, eager and full of faith.

I look away. Even though we are far from the East Sussex seaport, I taste salt air and a touch of bile, and see Nick's anguished face as Carburry slammed into his hip bone.

When I don't answer, Master James asks, "Do you think Major Carburry deserved to die?" His tone is darker now, less trusting of me.

"I think Colonel Wallace doesn't deserve to hang for him."

"Are you looking for justice?"

Justice. Peace. Victory. They all seem to be excuses for the opposite. "I don't know if I believe in justice."

Master James recoils. He's mistaken me for someone cynical. "Then what do you believe in?"

I think of the oversweet pound cake and the way it felt to be held by my mother. I think of the way Nick used to draw water from the well in Wimereux and drink it in long, slow takes; of the brother sister pair on the omnibus and how their legs kicked in rhythm to each other. I think of all the names carved into white wooden crosses dotting the hills in Ypres. I hold up my palms, helpless. I don't have the words.

Instead, I ask, "What do you need for your story?"

"The facts. Who, what, where, when, why."

My shoulder muscle spasms, a reminder of EyePatch's firm hand shoving me out of hearing distance of the press, a warning to tread carefully. My right hand is interlaced with my left. I almost laugh at the irony. "I don't have most of the facts. And even if I did, I doubt the Home Secretary will let you print them. What do you really need?"

Master James taps his foot against the step, considers. "To know more about Colonel Wallace."

"Colonel Wallace headed a small hospital for spinal injuries just outside of Wimereux. Thanks to him, men like General Hardy and the Earl of Whisham are able to walk."

Master James frowns. "They're toffs. People expect men with rank and money to get the best of everything."

He's not wrong. Where RAMC hospitals usually separated officers from enlisted men, Nick's hospital didn't. All patients were men, equally deserving of respect and care. I try again. "Lance Corporal Joseph Langdon. He had an abscess in his spinal cord. He also tried to commit suicide. Colonel Wallace brought Langdon's six-year-old daughter to stay by his side. She attended a Catholic primary school. I remember because a nun accompanied her across the Channel. In Camden, I think?"

"Sounds like St. Dominic's."

Why, my puppy is an English pointer, a hunting dog. I smile at him and rack my brain for more patients, the ones who should be easy to find or close by. "Private Alan Green. Vertebrae broken in three places. His father was a grocer in Dagenham. Sergeant Frederick Dawson came in with seven bullets along his spine. No one thought they could be removed. Colonel Wallace was in the operating theatre for almost ten hours. Do you think you can find these men?"

Master James' pencil has been flying across his scratchpad. He stops and winks. "I'm sure I've got a cousin who's got a sweetheart who's got an uncle."

He closes his notebook and stuffs his tools of the trade into the inner pocket of his black coat pocket. I lick my lips. I've got a story of my own to uncover. To save his brother, EyePatch will make him disappear, to the mouth of Hades, he'd suggested. More likely to South America. I need bargaining power. Or blackmail material. So far, I am sure of two things. First, the explosions at Lady Sullivan's Ambulance hospital were designed to destroy but not kill. Second, it was he who shot Major Carburry's legs out from under him. Whatever EyePatch is hiding, I am going to find it and use it—Nick is not disappearing again, not without me.

"One more name." I swallow hard and force my throat to stay open. "Arthur McMannis. He was an orderly with Lady Sullivan's Ambulance Hospital in Ypres."

"McMannis? What's his relation to Colonel Wallace?"

"I'm not going to tell you the truth. But I've been told by more than one person, I am an honest liar. You're going to have to trust me."

He taps his index finger against his thumb, the beat as even as a metronome. "All right." He holds out his hand like we are reintroducing ourselves, this time not as spectators to a trial, but partners. "James Stahler." He waits for me to answer.

In the pause, my mind goes to the calling card I meant to hand to EyePatch, to the water glass sliding across the table, shattering on the floor. I had attributed the accident to Nick's exhaustion, but now I recall the arc of his arm, the curve of his knuckles, the grace of the motion. He'd calculated the trajectory with precision. For a reason.

I shake Master James' hand. "Vera Betts."

At the door to our London townhouse, the butler studies me from head to foot for several minutes before he bows. "Forgive me for not recognizing you, Lady Margaret. It has been some time."

"Five years," I reply. A thousand lifetimes.

"Halsop House informed us you were coming. I hope you'll find everything in finest order."

I thank him, decline a meal, and make for my bedroom, exhausted. On my way up, I encounter a crew of upstairs maids pretending to busy themselves, likely curious to catch sight of me. They are all new, country girls who left their villages when their sweethearts failed to return from the war. There are only a handful of young men in the household. The rest lay buried in foreign lands.

My bedroom belongs to a girl I never was. The coverlet is a candy pink, the canopy trimmed with lace. A doll house sits empty, waiting for furnishings and a family. I poke through the wardrobe. Where are my muddy high boots, my kite, the parasol I used against my brother for sword fighting? Instead I am faced with gingham dresses decorated with bows. I can imagine the girl who should belong in this room pulling out her first ball gown, a lavender off-the-shoulder confection, her first taste of adulthood. I danced with Jerome in that dress. It might still fit. I'm the same height I was at fifteen, but I have shrunk. My bones are sharper.

In my haste to come up to London, I forgot to pack a sleeping gown. I wander to Mama's bedchamber. I open her door and pad across the thick carpet in my bare feet just as I did so often as a child, when I had a bad dream or wanted an excuse to be near her. I half expect to see her now, sitting in bed, reading, pulling down the covers to let me climb in next to her.

The air in her room is dead still. No one has slept here since the influenza hit London and my family fled to Halsop House. And still didn't escape. I crack open the window that looks over her garden. She was always trying to tame the earth, my mother. A faint scent of roses billows up. Like the garden at Halsop House, this too has been neglected, but still the roses climb their trellises and continue to bloom.

I wander over to her bureau. A bottle of her *society* perfume, she called it, Creed's *Jasmin Imperatrice Eugene* sits atop. My hand hovers over the handle of a drawer. There is nothing frightening laying inside. Cotton night dresses, crisply ironed and neatly folded, untouched for almost a year. They are plain, generic, they could belong to anyone. Perhaps that's why I can't touch them.

I turn instead to Mama's wardrobe. It smells of cedarwood, a practical solution to the problem of moths. Inside is a treasure trove of memories. Here is the blue shirt dress she wore when we went to see an exhibition of Raphael's works at the National Gallery. Here is her cream suit, trimmed at the cuffs and collar with mink. Her *good luck* suit she called it, though I never knew why she needed the luck.

I pull out her favorite dress. Or maybe it was mine. It is yellow, patterned with tiny white flowers. She wore it when she gardened, when we were home and not expecting guests, when I cried bitterly because once again Gwendolyn was gifted something I had asked for. I can't remember what—a pony or a trip to Paris or a music box I had seen on Oxford Street. Draped in her yellow dress, Mama lifted my chin to her face, her faded blue eyes matching my own. *Yes, Gwendolyn gets everything. But I gave you my name, Margaret.*

Why, I had asked, rubbing my sleeve against my nose.

Because we are alike. We are the least loved.

I crumple the dress against my chest and bury my face in its faded collar. The cotton has thinned at the elbows. There's a grass stain along where she kneeled to garden. It does not smell of Mama. It is not fleshed out by her. I lay it across the bed on the side where she slept, curl up next to it, bury my head in the flat shoulder and sleep . . .

My dream is a familiar one. I'm surrounded by blank white walls, tucked beneath white sheets and a heavy coverlet, my head rests against a white down pillow. Maybe I am a child, maybe I am an adult, I can never quite tell. I hear my door crack open, the quiet fall of gentle footsteps, a smooth hand strokes my cheek. *Shhh.*

Mama.

In my dream, I sigh.

A finger traces the curve of my lips, settles on the center. Taps once, twice. *Shhh.* Grateful I do not have to speak, my eyes grow heavy and I sink deeper into my pillow, into the cloud of white. Cocooned in silence, I inhale through my nose, searching for the scents of my mother—sweet grass, earthy loam, and roses. But this time, she is wearing her society perfume, bergamot, vanilla, a hint of amber. I do not like this fragrance. The finger is smoother than I remember, no calluses. Mama always had calluses from her garden.

The dream is not quite right.

The finger taps again. The hand spreads across my mouth, not a caress, a push. The air changes, thins, and tastes of cigarettes and almonds. Harder now, the hand presses down, covers my nose. The thumbs squeeze my cheekbones. A man's hand, smooth, but cruel. I cannot open my lips. I cannot unlock my jaw. I try to lift my head, but the hand is too strong. It bears down on me. The whiteness surrounding me will swallow me. I choke on my own scream.

The hand bears a gold wedding ring.

CHAPTER EIGHT

Wimereux, May 15, 1918

Sunlight glints upon the gold wedding band adorning the ring finger of Major Carbury. He strokes the smooth marble black knight before he moves it diagonally across the chessboard, into white's half. He sits back in his wheelchair and glances down at the two legs cast in plaster as if they're strangers. It's hard to believe this man is a soldier. His hands are so pristine they look like carved ivory. I cannot imagine him absorbing the recoil of a shot rifle, or crawling through mud, or living in the filth of trenches.

On the other side of the chessboard, Colonel Wallace drums his fingers along the wicker lawn table. His hands have sliced open the bodies of men and dug through bone and tendon and muscle to retrieve shrapnel, to fuse vertebrae. He has slipped closed the eyes of soldiers and pronounced time of death. And all the while, that halo clings desperately to him, like it refuses to let him go. Even now, in this summer sun beaming down on us as the two men play a gentleman's board game in a manicured garden of a former French chateau, the halo hangs on like a warning.

I cross one ankle over the other, re-cross in the opposite direction, shoo a buzzing fly, consider standing on my head and belting out a dance hall tune. I cannot understand how Lady Sullivan would think I would be a good fit for a place such as this. I am made of listless limbs and a swirling energy that only chaos can contain. I resent the solid walls of this yellow chateau, its pipes delivering water cold or hot on the turn of a tap. But for the rattle of wheelchairs, the trays bearing needles and amber jars of medicine, and the occasional sob, you would not know this was a hospital. A place of last hope for shattered men.

Colonel Wallace moves his white bishop to face Major Carburry's black knight.

I mutter, "Checkmate."

Both men look up. Colonel Wallace's expression is open, one of surprise and a touch of doubt. Major Carburry's is different, unsettling. It's one of alarm. He covers it quickly, and instead offers the kind of smile one does when entering a jewelry store to purchase a gift for a mistress. "So the pretty Nurse Betts speaks."

Nurse. I have been demoted from Sister to VAD. Paperwork. Policy. Bureaucracy. At Lady Sullivan's Ambulance Hospital, we never had to comply with codes and rank. Here, Sister Rosling (Matron if one is being technical) with her QAIMS red stripe, was determined to put me in my place.

Colonel Wallace goes back to studying the chessboard, focuses on his white pawn, then his rook. I can practically see him plotting out the next moves. He shakes his head at me. "The Major is nowhere near my king."

Major Carburry shifts in his wheelchair. He too senses Colonel Wallace's mistake. He covers his anticipation with, "Nurse Betts?"

I rise and adjust the pillows supporting his back. He tries to stroke my hand with his ring finger, the one with the gleaming gold wedding band. I snatch mine away and move to the chessboard.

To Colonel Wallace, I say, "You are minutes away from being checkmated. You think Major Carburry's black knight is overextended and so you will capture it and then the pawn." I walk my fingers across the chessboard and remove the two pieces. "But it's a trap. In two moves, you are going to castle on the king's side." I slide the pieces.

"Then you're going to get greedy and take Major Carburry's other black knight. Fatal. He will slide his pawn here and open an attack line for his rook to your king. No matter where you go, you've got no more than three turns till checkmate."

"A master champion in nurse's clothing," Major Carburry purrs and waits for me to feel flattered.

Even as I speak, I know I'm making a mistake. "I've seen this chess play before." It's Gwendolyn's signature strategy.

Major Carburry, who has been rolling his black bishop across his palms, pauses and studies me behind half-lidded eyes. "Do we know each other?" I can see him scrolling through his memories to match my face to a moment.

"I'm your nurse. I fluff your pillows and feed you beef tongue sandwiches. When you are surly, I give you aspirin. Safe pair of hands, I am." I add the latter with a sprinkle of a Manchester accent. Not too much, only enough to hint it is an essential part of me, faded by my years in France.

He is not convinced. "From before the war. Surrey?"

Halsop House is in Surrey. It's such a pointed question. "I'm from the North." I gesture in the general direction of a distant England.

"You look quite familiar," he insists. "I'm sure we've met."

I pick up a red plaid blanket thrown across one of the wicker chairs and fold it, neat and square. "I'm standard-issue English." Brown hair that is neither chestnut nor auburn nor any shade beyond wet sand. Eyes the color of washed-out denim. Though my nose rounds a bit too much at the tip, "I look like every other English girl."

"Hardly," mutters Colonel Wallace.

I blush despite knowing better.

"I was, in fact, going to checkmate you, Wallace." Major Carburry sets down his black bishop. "Where in the North?"

"Where my business is none of yours. This is a professional relationship, Major Carburry. I'm not one of your flirtations."

He chuckles. "*Au contraire,* as our French allies like to say. If you are a woman under fifty, you are by God's design, my flirtation."

"Have you had a bowel movement today?" I ask. "Or shall I fetch the enema kit?"

Colonel Wallace makes a choking sound and buries his laugh in the crook of his elbow. Again, I shouldn't blush.

"Perhaps you should loan your Florence Nightingale to the Germans," mutters Major Carburry. "A week under her care and they'd surrender."

Colonel Wallace's laugh dies away. "I suppose that's one way to conclude a stalemate."

"Stalemate? Don't be such a cynic, Wallace. To save lives, you have to sacrifice them. A hundred men today for a thousand tomorrow." For a man who lost his entire regiment in the Battle of Saint Quentin, Major Carburry sounds positively lighthearted.

Colonel Wallace makes to answer, but pauses as the sound of a child singing trickles across the lawn. The singer is a little girl, Lucy Langdon, who is tossing flowers in the air while she skips in circles around her crippled father. The night I arrived, the father had tried to throw himself from a balcony. Now, he is joining in his daughter's song.

"More bodies?" Colonel Wallace contorts his face with a mixture of disgust and sorrow. I feel nauseous myself. "Death is a consequence of, not a means to ending, war."

"You don't achieve peace without one side admitting defeat," Major Carburry says, his tone tipping on indulgent. It strikes me this is not the first time the two men have argued on the subject. "Don't mistake me for a warmonger, Wallace. In the end, we both want the same thing. But you have to accept that for peace to be possible, victory must be absolute."

"Otherwise?" Colonel Wallace asks.

"A stalemate. A forever war." Carburry shrugs his shoulders as if the notion were not repulsive.

"Said like a man whose worst fear is peace," I snap. I've met soldiers like him before. They thrive on bloodlust, not courage. "Who would you be outside of your uniform?"

"Who would you be," he shoots back.

I clamp down on my tongue before I confess. *No one.*

Colonel Wallace answers for himself. "I would be what I already am. A doctor."

I cannot help but admire his answer. It rings so true, it strikes a chord within me and when I peek up at Colonel Wallace, he catches me and smiles back.

Major Carburry yawns. "God, between the two of you, I shall die of boredom before I die of a bullet." He frowns at me dolefully. "I was shot by a sniper. Rather unsporting, don't you think?"

"I think I've made clear: War is not a sport." I begin packing away the chess game.

He sighs up at the cloudless blue sky. "Such a serious creature." He relaxes his shoulders, a change of posture, and a change in tactic. False charm and false camaraderie. "I say, Wallace, do you think Nurse Betts might treat me to a bed exercise or two?"

Colonel Wallace has developed a series of exercises the men perform lying in bed, to strengthen their muscles and prevent atrophy. The moves are akin to ballet, but performed on one's back.

"Contrology," Colonel Wallace and I say at the exact same moment. We glance at each other, surprised by our timing. Butterflies come to life in my stomach.

"Call it what you wish," says Major Carburry. "When Matron lays her hands on me, I hear angels sing and devils cheer."

"I'm not trained." I hear the note of resentment in my voice.

Colonel Wallace hears it too. He nods, like he means to override Matron Rosling of the scarlet stripe and legitimate qualifications.

"The least you could do is prescribe a swim in that indoor pool of yours. Such a luxury." Major Carbury stretches his arms and imitates diving. "The last time I swam, it was at a weekend party with the Duke of Derweld. Raging cold outside, but he converted one of his barns into an indoor pool." Now Major Carbury narrows his eyes and smiles at me the same way he smiled when he moved his black bishop. "Ever attend a bathing party at Derweld Castle?"

I don't bother to point out his casts cannot get wet. "La-di-da. Princess Mary and I took a dip after a game of *hitchy-dabbor*—hopscotch," I translate, "but before the sailing regatta." The mention of a regatta is deliberate. Derweld Castle is landlocked and the Duke prone to seasickness.

"You're no fun." The Major juts out his bottom lip.

Up on the veranda, one of the VADs rings the luncheon bell. Tables are set with white linen cloths and flowers cut from the garden. The patients, some in wheelchairs, some on crutches, two taking slow steps as they learn to walk again, spill out of the house or crunch up the gravel path.

In the garden one of the walkers, Private Green, bends slowly, tentatively from his waist, to pluck a yellow rose dangling from a bush. He's using a walker and wearing a back brace. Matron stands beside him, smiling like a movie poster heroine, but also positioned to catch him should he lose his balance. To a stranger's eyes, his movement is awkward, painful. To mine, it's a miracle. His vertebrae had been broken in three places. No one thought he would ever walk again. No one, except Colonel Wallace. It is hard not to admire a man who can mold hope out of despair. But that does not mean I should develop a schoolgirl's crush. Surely, I'm more sensible than that.

"Private Green is doing quite well," I say quietly.

"Do you think so?" A quick smile lightens Colonel Wallace's tired face. Private Green has given the rose to Matron, who tucks it into her white veil. "He's unbreakable, that boy. All spirit."

I take hold of the handles on Major Carbury's wheelchair and start to push him up the path.

"I'm not a complete cripple." He shoves my hands away, grips the wheels and steers himself toward the veranda's ramp.

I am left walking side by side with Colonel Wallace and caught off guard by the quickening pace of my pulse. Our steps match each other's, our arms swing in an unintended unison. When I inhale the summer air, I catch the scent of cinnamon. I've seen him sprinkle the spice into his black coffee, which he drinks around the clock.

He leans conspiratorially close. His breath rustles the wisps of hair beneath my veil. "Was I really going to lose at chess?"

"Without a doubt."

He pauses to take a deep, rehabilitating breath of the vibrant summer air, and stretches his arms above his head. "I'm terrible at games," he says, his relief palpable.

Colonel Wallace may be terrible at games, but he is still playing one. His lack of skill only means he's more likely to lose.

⁂

"You have a letter." Matron, she of the hands that make angels sing and devils cheer, waves a thick envelope bearing American stamps. It must be from my cousin Kristina. Between the logistics of sailing ships and battleships, I haven't had a letter since I left Lady Sullivan's. I'm desperate to tear open the envelope and devour the pages. I wait for Matron to pass it to me.

"New York? How exotic." She studies the envelope, puckering her plush lips. Far too sensuous for a nurse. Then again, she tends to position her starched veil so her black curls frame her face, drawing one's attention to the velvet darkness of her cat eyes. She's used to being the most beautiful woman in a room, not a hard feat at a hospital, but were she at the London Savoy or the Paris Opera House, she'd still draw all eyes to her. So it makes no sense she has taken a distinct dislike to me. I am no threat.

I set my coffee cup back on its saucer, keep my palms open, my fingers stretched, and attempt a placid smile. If I've successfully placated an irate Papa with a bland and docile expression, then I can fool Matron.

"Have you been wandering about the wards off duty?" Her voice is so soft and lilting, one could mistake it for caring. "At night?"

"Nurse Betts reads to the men in Ward One," offers Nurse Fukimoto, a Japanese Red Cross nurse whose English comes from growing up the daughter of a diplomat. "*The Count of Monte Cristo.* Edmond Dantès is ever so dashing."

Matron delivers a how-enchanting smile, but her lips are curled at the edges, a painting beginning to warp. Beautiful she may be, but her youth is fading. Perhaps that is the source of her animus. "Do you prefer to walk the night, Betts?"

I ignore the snide inference. "I'm not a sound sleeper. And the men need to be turned often." Soldiers don't die from broken legs and shattered spines, they die from lying in bed. The pressure creates sores that turn into weeping, open wounds, their damaged bladders cause urinary tract infections, their bodies devolve into sepsis. Even in this gilt chateau, there is no turning back from sepsis.

Matron taps the corner of my precious envelope against her palm. "I do appreciate your heroics." This is said not as a compliment, but as if I am a spoiled child. "Lady Churchill's articles about Lady Sullivan . . ." Her resentment reveals itself like the glint of metal off a hidden knife each time she says *Lady*. "Your dear little ambulance hospital and the brave nurses at the warfront are an inspiration to us all. But we cannot let a bit of fame color our duties, nor our humility. We are here for the wounded, not our glory. We complete our shifts, no less"—she pauses to frown—"but no more."

Fukimoto spears a tomato and whispers something in Japanese. The words are beyond me, but the meaning is precise.

Matron tilts her head as if she's charmed. "Sister Fukimoto, we have a new patient, a German." She makes a sour expression. "He is to be kept quarantined from our soldiers. You shall have day duty with him." She leaves the implications and insults unsaid—the German is our enemy and does not belong here, Fukimoto is foreign and does not belong here. The two deserve to be isolated.

"Delighted," replies Fukimoto. Brave soul.

Matron keeps tapping my envelope against her palm, holding the letter, waiting for me to bow my head. I'm more likely to cut hers off. The patients in Ward One are our most desperate. More than bedridden, they're helpless—we've cut holes into their mattresses so they can defecate into a bucket. The humiliation is worse than the stench. The least I can do on a sleepless night is look in on them.

I run my tongue against the back of my teeth to keep from lashing out. "I'm not being heroic. I'm reading a book. Whether I do it in my room or in Ward One should make no difference."

"Healing requires order," she retorts.

"And a book is disorderly?"

"You are disturbing the men, who should be sleeping."

"If they were able to sleep," I reason, "they would not ask me to read aloud."

Matron pauses, smooths down her skirts, and reconsiders her tactics. "It's important you be well-rested. Poor sleep habits take their toll on the mind. How am I to train you in Contrology, if you cannot focus?" She furrows her brow for added affect. How did this woman end up in nursing? She should be treading the boards at the Lyceum.

"If my *years* at the front have taught me anything, I assure you, it is to manage more than one thing at a time. I can read *The Count of Monte Cristo* and learn Contrology."

"If you insist on wandering about at night, then I have no choice but to assign you to the night shift." She rolls out a heavy sigh.

"And Major Carbury?" He comprises part of my day shift duties.

"I shall see to him myself." She glances down at her palm, where my letter sits hostage, and I realize I've been outmaneuvered.

If we weren't at war, I'd be overdressed for an afternoon at the beach. But the ocean is dotted with warships, not sailboats, and beneath the glistening turquoise waters of the Channel lie telegraph wires bearing battle orders.

I trek through the sand while a gusty breeze tugs insistently at my hat. At an outcropping of rocks, I unlace my boots and roll down my stockings, removing them to dip my toes in the chilly water. There's a dull ache in my shoulders and a crick in my neck. I stretch to relieve them and unfold my cousin Kristina's letter anticipating the delicious play-by-play of her marriage bed.

There I was, clack, clack, clacking away at the typewriter, when my darling cake-eater knelt right between my thighs, stroking me with his thumb and hitting all sixes, if you know what I mean. And his tongue. Oh kiddo, his wicked, wicked tongue! I'm knee to over-active-imagination deep in her description—when I spy the tanned, golden figure of a man sluicing through the water. He keeps his head low, torso and arms work together, left elbow pulling back, then the right, and left again, synchronized. The body moving as one.

I lick my parched lips. They taste like salt from the sea spray. Colonel Wallace would taste the same. I close my eyes to imagine a little more and when I open them, he is rising from the sea, standing. His hips move in a rhythm, absorbing the resistance of the water, which seems reluctant to give him up. He rubs his eyes and runs his hands through his wet hair and I realize he hasn't yet recognized the woman on the shore, gaping. I should grab my boots and skedaddle. Instead, I bite down on my bottom lip, draw out the salt. I have never encountered a man like him. He strides through the water with the same sense of purpose as he does hospital corridors.

No, that's not right. It's the opposite. He moves on land like he is in water. He is a creature of the sea. Instinctual, but also intentional, measuring the power and direction of the current, rolling and adapting to the wave and chop, adjusting his tempo to take advantage of a swell. He takes no step for granted.

When he reaches the shore, several feet to the left of me, he collects a rucksack, pulls out a towel, and dries his hair. The armholes of his navy bathing costume are cut large so the tank exposes his tanned, muscled shoulders, the flex and curve of his biceps. He tosses the towel across his shoulder and waves. I pretend I am so focused on my letter I can barely manage to wiggle three fingers in response.

A few quick, easy steps and he is by my side. "Hullo."

I greet him with, "Swimming, I see."

"Reading, I see."

"A letter from my cousin."

Out of the gate, this conversation is already proving to be inane. I half open my mouth, trying to formulate a coherent sentence about the weather, but my stomach distracts me with tiny backflips and somersaults. Colonel Wallace smiles shyly, making his eyes crinkle. His hair is tousled. A few strands stand straight up, out of alignment, like rebellious toy soldiers and I'm tempted to lick my finger and comb them down.

I joggle my toes in the shallow, foamy water. His smile deepens, the crinkle of his eyes slides into something more sly. Dressed as he is in a bathing costume clinging to every muscle and sinew of his body, I'm not the one who should feel naked. I am merely barefoot. Still, the heat of Colonel Wallace's gaze burns straight into all twenty-six bones of each foot.

"Good swim?" Trying not to sound addled, I add, "Training for the Olympics?"

"Don't you think I'm a bit overdressed for an ancient Olympian?"

I turn pink, which is what he wanted, and my chest heats. Attraction is a daft, stupid thing. I should gather up my things and prepare for my duties as night nurse. "Doesn't the word *gymnasium* mean naked?"

It's his turn, not to blush exactly, but to warm. "It's derived from the Greek word for naked, γυμνός."

Opening his khaki, RAMC rucksack, Colonel Wallace digs out a chrome canteen, lifts off the nesting cup, and unscrews the lid. The sea air between us takes on additional scents—coffee and cinnamon. He pours the hot black liquid into the cup, offers it to me. I tuck my letter into my pocket, take the cup in both hands, savor the heat radiating off the metal, and sip.

He says, "In ancient Greece, nudity was a form of civil protest. Thucydides—do you know him?"

I roll my eyes.

"Fifth Century historian—BC that is. According to Thucydides, the Persians found public nudity disgraceful, so the Greeks, being Greek, stripped off their clothing for sporting events. An excellent thumb in the eye, don't you think?" His tone is equal parts informative and envious. We both cannot stop ourselves from looking out toward the Channel.

The sky may be a never-ending, untroubled stretch of blue, but grey naval ships heave, bearing the brunt of the choppy waters. Deeper still lay the cadavers of sunken ships and drowned sailors. The ocean floor is a cemetery. Swimming in this sea is an act of protest.

"Is there an eye you would like to thumb?" I ask.

"Does my hospital not speak for itself?" His laugh is weighted, grave. "We take patients so weak they barely survive the hospital train. They lie in Ward One, near death, and within the year, most—not all—have moved through the wards, from surgery to Contrology to sitting up to physical and occupational therapy, to writing, to swimming and occasionally, even to walking. The men in Ward Eight are a beacon to the men in Ward One—a promise of healing. And the men in Ward One remind the men in Ward Eight how far they have come, how much they've conquered. To stay strong, because all we have is courage."

On the other side of the Channel sits England. It would have been easier for him to stay home. There would have been more resources. "Why France?"

"You know it will take at least six months for recovery. And we need specialists—surgeons and osteopaths and neurologists, staff experienced in different medical arts. Fukimoto with her acupuncture. Matron Rosling—"

I must have made a sour face because he chuckles. "Naturally, you two would be rivals."

"Naturally?"

"This is not Matron's first war. Nor will it be her last. She's toiled and sacrificed for her authority. Whereas you're so young, one suspects you were born into your confidence."

"I've earned my place."

"Of that, I have not doubt. I've seen you in action."

I bend my head and drink my coffee to hide my pleasure. "Your hospital requires a specific infrastructure. You're close to the base hospitals in Wimereux, but far enough away you're not tied to military protocol." I consider the logistics until it dawns on me. "To get your hospital, you *had* to join the RAMC."

He finishes his coffee. The grinds must be bitter. His frown is tight. "That's one arm of the bargain." He shrugs like it shouldn't matter. "What about you? Couldn't you have stayed back in . . . Was it the North?" He asks this with such obvious doubt, I smile guiltily.

The easy answer is I came out of love. Or anger. Because Jerome threw me over for Gwendolyn. Because Mama was the one to deliver the news, wrapped in a mink stole, her diamond earrings sharp, her Creed perfume suffocating. She had been the only person I trusted with my jumping, beating, coltish heart. And there she was, in my tiny bedroom at the cottage hospital with its big window overlooking the laundry line, the battered white fence leading out to the hills, beyond where Jerome's family's hunting lodge sat. I can still feel the impersonal touch of her leather gloves, the pinch of her forefinger and thumb against my quivering chin, the hollowness where maternal comfort should have been. *Put yourself together, Margaret, we don't all get to love who we want.*

But these answers are too easy. Between love and anger, there was Dr. Bettany, slicing open a woman's abdomen, ordering me to *step up, dammit* and pull a screaming, purple baby from the womb, directing me to snip the umbilical cord, chuckling when he caught me furtively kissing the top of the infant's bald, sticky head. Despite what my family believes, I am not the sum of my emotions. Or, as Old Betts said after I strapped a raging drunk to the bed so he couldn't hit his wife, I am a safe pair of hands.

Colonel Wallace fills the silence with an "Ahh."

I challenge him with an *I dare you* narrowing of the eyes.

"You're the kind of lass who runs toward a fire."

It's wrong that I sigh. It's wrong that between us flares a low-banked fire of connection. In each other, we recognize ourselves.

The wind picks up, making mischief with my hat. When I stretch up to catch it, Kristina's letter spills out of my pocket, the pages scatter, and the wind swoops them up. I let out a small cry, let go of my hat, which tumbles off and into the water, and race after my letter.

Colonel Wallace gives chase to a page nosediving toward the sea, catches it between forefinger and thumb. "Fifteen love," he calls out.

I jump and capture one between my two palms. "Fifteen even."

The pages fly through the air like wings without bodies and the two of us crisscross the beach, helter-skelter, grasping at air and declaring our points. We are made of athletic limbs and determined spirit. I imagine we both played thus as children. Free, unfettered.

Unafraid to be silly. How long has it been since either of us moved for the sheer joy of it? Centuries, I think.

The final uncaught page of my letter seems ready to concede, descending gracefully toward the sand. Colonel Wallace and I face off, each with a glint in our eye. A challenge. I sprint forward, he pivots to cut me off. The wind, however, has a mind of its own, sweeping through with a gust that sends the paper flying again. He and I kick up our pace. My skirt shortens the length of my stride. I grab a handful of fabric, bunch it above my knees.

"No fair," decries Colonel Wallace, giving my legs an exaggerated ogle.

We keep running and both leap, trying to grasp the stubbornly airborne page, and end up colliding into each other. Midair, his arm goes around my waist, my arms around his neck, and when we tumble, we do so like lovers falling from the sky. We land, a soft thud on soft sand, and he's careful to release me, letting me roll off of his arm like I am too precious to tether. I lay back, squint up at the baby blue sky. Something vibrant and alive forms a ball in my stomach, flares through me and bursts out.

Laughter.

I cannot stop. My shoulders shake. Wet tears roll down my face. My stomach muscles tighten and release. I grab salty sea air as if I had locked my lungs away in a basement and starved them for years. Beside me, laying beneath a semi-warm sun, atop the semi-damp sand, Colonel Wallace joins me, his baritone acting as the bass rhythm for my wild, improvised notes.

Eventually, when my lungs are at last satiated, I sit up and lean back against my arms. "I win."

Not at all true, but even as a child on her very best behavior, I was a notorious cheat. For my victory lap, I toss him my conqueror's smile. One part sweetness, two parts insouciant. A splash of wicked. His response is as automatic as a fish finding water. He dives in without thought, returning my cheekiness with one of his own. It crests across his golden face, as breathtaking as dawn.

"I won," he corrects. Rolling up to a seated position, he holds out four pages to me. He hands them over one by one, counting up his points before he comes to the last. A passage catches his attention. His eyes go wide, leaving no doubt as to which passage. "Match point," he murmurs, all admiration and inspired lust.

I snatch it back quick as I can and he murmurs, surprised, "She dances like a Bomb."

I raise a questioning look up to him.

"It's from a poem. Emily Dickinson."

"Not much of a reader," I reply.

"Me neither, unless its Pythagoras. My brother, however." The playfulness of his smile slips away.

I already know he has a brother who drowned as a baby. "How many brothers do you have?" I ask.

It takes him a moment too long, as if he has to recount and sub-tract. "One."

In his answer I feel his loneliness and know I am in danger. "Me too," I say. "I have one."

Above us, two Sopwith Camels roar through the sky like they in-tend to tear the air apart. Perhaps they do. Or just did, somewhere closer to the North Sea, where German battleships rattle off machine fire. We are far enough not to hear it, but never far enough to forget. He squints at them and his jaw ticks with unmistakable anger. But at least they are on our side, I want to say. Unless we are not on the same side.

Shuffling Kristina's letter back into my pocket, I still. Colonel Wallace's hospital should be proof enough his halo is real, but the sabotage at Lady Sullivan's leaves doubts. "My cousin is a journalist. She was telling me of an explosion on Black Tom Island, in New Jersey—"

"As opposed to Old Jersey." Already he is rising, brushing sand off his back.

I follow his lead, hopping back up on my feet. "Black Tom is—or was—a center for munitions. And two years ago, when America was neutral—"

"Ancient history."

I push forward, hurrying my words. "An explosion with the force of a 5.5 magnitude earthquake—"

"In Greek mythology earthquakes are caused by Poseidon striking his trident—

"—destroyed the island. It was so powerful, a baby in Jersey City was thrown out of his crib and slammed against a wall. The Brooklyn Bridge . . ."

He makes as if to speak, but before he can slip another syllable through his grit teeth, I ask, "Are you trying to distract me, Colonel Wallace? You won't succeed. The explosion was caused by a picric acid bomb." I wait for him to react—to interrupt or step back or, I don't know, confess. Instead, he is nonplussed. I tell him, "It was an act of German sabotage."

"Have they caught the perpetrators?" He asks this in a reasonable tone, like he is a medical professor and I've made the wrong diagnosis.

"No."

He strides back toward the other end of the beach, to the rock where we left his coffee and my boots. "You are assuming your saboteur is German. He could be an Irish nationalist or an Italian fascist. He could have no loyalty at all—a saboteur who acts out of greed. Or he could be an idealistic Englishman." Is he confessing something?

I do my best to keep up with his brisk pace, but my feet sink in the ever-shifting sand. "Why would England destroy the munitions factory supplying it?"

"You've been in France long enough. Don't you know better than to assume war to be logical? Left is right. Right is wrong. Brothers are enemies and enemies are allies."

"And what are we, Colonel Wallace?"

My own question stops me in my tracks. What is wrong with me? *We? We?* There should be no *we*. I had meant to say—what? My brain is caught on a gear and instead of words, sensations come to me—the wind whipping through my hair, the burn of sunlight on my cheeks, a hollowed-out leaping of my stomach when a pair of powerful arms pull me into a damp, solid chest that smells of the sea, of coffee, of cinnamon.

Do my lips reach his first? Or his mine? Does it matter? We mold ourselves to each other so our tongues can meet, drifting and sliding, touching and tangling in the chop and wave of desire. I flick my tongue to the silver-white scar above his mouth. It's in the wounds that one divines a man's secrets. It's in my sigh that I confess mine.

With the water lapping at our ankles, time is suspended. Sopwith Camels and white crosses and war be damned. There is a *we*. Only us two, searching and finding room to breathe, a place beyond the floating death cans and drowned sailors, beyond the pockmarks of the scarred sea.

CHAPTER NINE

London, May 3, 1919

The buildings on this crammed Silvertown street are pockmarked by the scars of the 1917 TNT factory explosion. I trip on a gouge in the sidewalk. The crowd is so thick, my fall is caught by the backs of the people in front of me and mistaken for a shove. A squat man turns to snap at me, but the throng pushes us forward, his curse swallowed up in the bustle and chatter around us. The dock bell clangs and is answered by the caw of seagulls, the shrill factory whistles, the creak of ships docked along the River Lea.

I do not know this part of London, so busy there is no room to pause. I recheck the address on the scrap of paper in my hand. I got it from Master James. This morning I rang my spry reporter, who had slept not a wink, *banging out an ace interview with Corporal Langdon.* His editor gave him a full column on page three.

I take a deep breath. The air, despite the smokestacks and gut-spinners and fertilizer-makers, carries the scent of sugar. Above me a sign reads, James Kellier & Sons. Mixed in with the hard industry of Silvertown is a marmalade factory. I elbow my way to the left and turn onto a no-less busy street, where a throng of factory workers are queued outside a canteen.

Heading to the front doors, a hand reaches out to grab my arm. "No cuts," says a sharp-eyed, narrow faced woman.

"I'm not here for lunch."

"Oy, too 'igh class for the likes of us is ya?"

"Back 'a the line," says another woman, younger and plumper, but equally hostile.

The crowd is at least fifty people deep and I don't have time to dawdle. "I'm seeing to a friend," I say.

"'Er ladyship's come fer tea, 'as she," cackles a third woman.

The three of them rake me over. The crowd is growing restless, more and more people darting annoyed glances and mumbling insults at *'er ladyship*. My walking suit is a practical grey-striped cotton denim, dull and plain. But surrounded as I am by men and women in folded caps and baggy overalls, with their boots and cotton clothing and hair and lungs covered in dust, I'm overdressed, out of place.

"I just need to—"

"Give over, lady," mutters a jowly man.

"We're on a punch clock," explains a red-cheeked girl.

"But *dahling*," trills my narrow-eyed nemesis. She can't be much older than me, but her shoulders stoop. "'Er ladyship's got ta rabbit with a pole."

I'm not going spar in cockney rhyme. I'd lose even before I could translate it, but Mama taught me how to use every part of my body, my bones, my cartilage, even my teeth, to not just sing an aria, but to magnify it. So I dig my expensive spat boots into the grit of this industrial street, fist my hands, fill my diaphragm full of air, and belt out my *Triage hemorrhages, chest, and head cases* voice, "MMMCCCCCmannis!"

I sound rather operatic. Perhaps I should take a bow.

One of the men wipes his brow with his cap. "Girl's mad as a hatter."

"A lot of inbreeding amongst the gentry," explains my original nemesis.

"MMMCCCCcmannis! Arthur MMMMCCC—"

A side door bursts open and out lumbers a blur of a giant Scotsman. "Why stone the crows, if it isn't Sister Betts." McMannis lifts me in the air and spins me around, his hold tight and reassuring.

When he sets me down, I shoot my nemesis a petty, *we ken ruf and tumble' wit' the toughest of youse* grin. She nods me the win. McMannis leads me through the side door and into a large kitchen full of pots on the boil and fish on the fry. A trio of men are washing dishes, singing "Sister Susie's Sewing Shirts for Soldiers." A scent hovers in the air, strangely familiar, though it makes no sense. My mind is bending time, the sight of McMannis bringing back the memory of vegetable ragout.

From the kitchen, McMannis plays the tour guide, taking me through a hallway stacked with brown sacks of rice and corn, and out into a large vegetable and herb patch where a crew wield shovels and clippers and wheelbarrows. Here, the rosemary bushes are near out of control, their pine and lemon scent prickles the air. In Ypres, when we were low on antiseptics, we ground the needles into powders and oils. When we were lucky, Gaspar, our French cook, baked the herb into soft bread.

McMannis gestures to a sunny bench and we settle, me easily, he more slowly, grabbing the back of the bench to support his weight and bending at the hips gingerly. "Me knees aren't what they once were." He winces. "Damp's getting to 'em."

He was always a bulwark, McMannis. Strong enough to carry men across his broad back. Nimble enough to scramble up muddy hills with medical equipment. It's hard to watch him struggle with the simple act of sitting.

When he settles, he stretches out his long legs and takes me in like he's missed me. "How've you been keeping, Sister Betts?"

"Well enough."

"We wondered after you in Wimereux. Not easy, a spinal hospital. The patients stay for long spells. Harder to stay distant, I expect. You always kept yourself together in Ypres, efficient and no-nonsense.

Everyone else blethering about anything and everything. Not you. You were like a factory manager, you were."

Was that how I managed? "I wrote to Lady Sullivan. She never answered."

"Did you not get our news?"

I wrinkle my brow, shake my head.

"They dismantled us. Can't say I was disappointed." McMannis rubs his beard and lowers his voice. "Scottish as I am, even I couldn't bear up anymore. Felt like we weren't doing any good. Felt like we were making things worse."

"We were saving lives." My tone is sharp, insistent. We were nursing, not overseeing a factory line of bodies.

"So Britain could throw our lads right back into the trenches?"

"So they could come home."

"To an England that does nae want them." He juts his chin toward the garden, to the crew harvesting vegetables. His Scottish brogue is harsher, grating, angry. "Open your eyes, Sister Betts. Do you not see how people slide away from the men with missing limbs? Or worse, the ones who lost their faces? The streets are littered with beggars who were once soldiers. And the addicts. Jesus, God. All those patients we shot up with morphia. We injected the Devil straight into their bodies like we were inviting him in for Christmas dinner."

From across the garden, a dozen men pour out of a red brick, dormitory-style building. They stand at attention before someone calls out a command, and they leap into calisthenics. Jumping jacks, squats, push-ups, repeat. They are, all of them, woefully thin, the belts buckled so tight their ill-fitting shirts blouse over. Closer by, one of the gardeners digging at potatoes drops his spade. When he stretches to retrieve it, his body moves jerkily. His hands are shaking.

"What is this place, McMannis?" When McMannis had walked me through the kitchen to the garden, the workers had all greeted him with respect, some with reverence, as if he were father confessor. "It's not a canteen. Or not only a canteen."

He unwinds tensed shoulders, stretching his arms across the back of the bench. "It's a sanctuary for addicts. The National Food Committee was running it as a National Kitchen, but they planned to close it down after the Armistice. A group of us—never underestimate the power of the housewife—convinced the Committee to let us operate it as a clinic. The one thing that beats back the Devil is busy hands."

I'm nervous, hopeful, when I ask, "Who comes to you?"

"We won't take anyone who doesn't want to be here."

I swallow and taste the dregs of hope sinking down my throat. Between the lure of a drug-induced numbness and the digging of a potato, only the most determined of men would choose the potato. Instead, I say, "I had to riot to get past your line. You serve a good meal."

The smile cresting his face is wide and tender. "And wouldn't you know it, our most popular dish is vegetable ragout. I've had more than one lady in her finery try to buy the recipe out from under us. But you know the French. Gaspar wouldn't so much as share how to boil an egg proper. He'll be sorry to have missed you—out shopping for spices."

"Gaspar? Gaspar is here?" Our French cook was McMannis' drinking and poker and chasing ladies partner. Who else did McMannis bring with him from France? A breeze shakes the thick green leaves of the climbing French beans, a shimmering, flowing movement and I find myself searching for a glimpse of a tall figure in white. "Where is Lady Sullivan?" I half rise.

McMannis draws my elbow down, a warning. "We all have our breaking point, don't we? Losing the hospital was hers. It had been her mission, hers and Sister Reynolds and as long as she had it, Sister Reynolds wasn't quite dead. But the day we got our orders, we loaded up onto a transport train. Not Lady Sullivan. She got on her motorbike and disappeared. To a POW camp or behind German lines, I doubt we'll ever know."

He leaves the rest unsaid. I don't want to think of a world in which I won't find Lady Sullivan plucking lost souls from shipyard cafes and fitting them to a purpose. I am losing more people in peace than I did in war. I unpin my felt, bowler-style hat, and bend its flat brim, back and forth.

McMannis juts his thumb toward my hat. "But for your voice, sister, I would nae have recognized you. Never took you for a Bond Street *elegante*."

He means it as a joke. It sets me off kilter. Out of uniform, I feel like an imposter. Ironic, considering I was never qualified to be in uniform. "When was the hospital dismantled?"

"Right after you left for Wimereux."

"Right after the medical marquee explosions." I bite down on my bottom lip. I remember how devastated McMannis was the night Flaherty came in. How he seemed to quit right there and then. How he was lurking about the medical marquees the next morning. But how do I ask this bold, burly man who has built a refuge to heal drug addicts if he sabotaged our hospital? If, in a moment of weakness and despair, he destroyed the very thing he stands for? As he said, we all have our breaking point.

"I'm in love." I make this confession more to my hat than to McMannis.

He sits up, no doubt meaning to tease me. One look at my miserable, defeated face, and his cheeky grin evaporates. "Ah, lass. It's a lang road that's no goat a turnin.'"

"With a man on trial for murder," I add as an afterthought.

He stifles a choke, of shock or laughter, I cannot tell. "Only you," he shakes his head. "Only our Betts."

"Do you remember the night . . ." I stop myself just as I'm about to mention Flaherty. His name haunts us both. Instead, I move straight to my enemy. "Remember the night Major Carburry came into our ward? He had two broken legs."

"Pray to God, Sister Betts, that's nae the man whose taken your heart."

"No. He's the murder victim." I wrinkle my brow, wondering at his dislike for Carburry. When he'd seen the Major trussed up in blinding white bandages, McMannis had reacted strangely. Like he'd lost his nerve. "Did you know him?"

"Not from Beelzebub. But, I have a sense." He points to his nose.

"What triggered it?"

"The Padre. He looked afeared."

"Of Major Carburry?" I don't remember the Padre being anything other than worried about a concussed patient.

"Nay, the other one. The doctor."

"Colonel Wallace? Why would he be scared of him?"

"Because he had the face of an angel. Not one of those pretty ones who flutter about. More like an archangel. When he walked in, I near crossed myself."

I cannot help it. I smile, a stupid, schoolgirl sort of blushing grin, because Nick does have a certain effect on people.

"So it's the archangel Colonel Wallace who opened up your shuttered heart."

"War makes strange bedfellows of us all." I try to be blithe.

"War makes us honest in ways we don't want to be."

There are layers to McMannis' sentence, notes of regret and wisdom, pain and humiliation, a scarring over, a healing. That I recognize them all makes me cringe, makes me want to shrink back from my own skin. Because I realize now what I didn't understand in war. McMannis is dear to me, more so than my whole family combined. And I am about to accuse him of treachery.

I force myself to plunge forward. "You wouldn't bring me the Carrel-Dakin kit for Flaherty."

He turns to me, startled. "The lad was dead."

"He was still breathing."

"There was no point. There was no point anymore." Despair drags his voice down to a whisper.

"Is that why the medical marquees were destroyed?"

McMannis is slow to stand. On his feet, he crosses his arms. The shadow he casts across me makes me shiver. "Are you asking me something else, Sister Betts? Because it seems to me your phrasing is lacking the proper words. Try *McMannis, did ye set fire to the medical marquees.*"

"They didn't burn down." I pick at the grey ribbon on my hat, pulling at the threads. In a moment, I will have ruined it. "They were bombed."

"So I'm a bomb maker, am I? If I recall correctly, 'twas you who was always clever with the jury-rigging. Knew an awful lot about explosives, you did. Picric acid and such. Convenient for you to disappear right before the hospital was shut down."

"You said yourself you were done in."

"And so I would sabotage our hospital for a wee rest?"

"Or hate. Or revenge. Or political protest. Madness. Exhaustion. Despair."

"Who am I that you should know me so little?"

"You refused to save Flaherty!"

The memory of Flaherty, the ghost dividing us, pushes all the air and anger out of McMannis. His chest deflates and he sinks back onto the bench. "Flaherty" He rests his head on his hands, hangs his elbows from his thighs. He swallows hard, several times, and I realize he is holding back tears.

"Aye. The first time the lad came to Lady Sullivan's, it was like seeing me younger self in him. Messed with my heart, the second time, finding his foot in his boot, gnawed off."

Inch for inch, I cannot think of two more different people than brawny McMannis and soft-hearted, full-of-song Flaherty. But I cannot deny McMannis was generous to him, as protective and doting as a mother hen.

"I'll confess to losing me faith, Sister Betts. I may be twice your size, but I haven't got half your strength. Still, I would'na leave so much as a scratch on Lady Sullivan's hospital. I'd more likely put a bullet through my head."

I shudder. More than one person we knew did just that. McMannis and I mopped the brains off the stained floor.

"I'm sorry." It's all I can think to say. At the moment, it's all I feel. Sorry I doubted McMannis. Sorry I did not seek him out sooner. When I was entombed in Halsop House, I should have been breaking through lunch lines in Silversmith. McMannis has found a new purpose. He is doing good again.

"I misjudge everyone I'm close to." The grey ribbon at last slips off my hat and floats to the sandy path. "I thought Colonel Wallace had either abandoned me or died. It turns out, he was in prison. I should have faith in people. And yet I seem to assume the worst. That they give up on me." I manage to utter the last over the small lump rising in my throat.

McMannis picks up my ribbon and threads it through his large fingers like he's contemplating a mistake and already knows he will regret it. "There was someone else at our camp. Man claiming to be from the Home Secretary's office."

"Tall. Smug. Wears an eyepatch."

A slight catch in his throat, followed by a resigned, "Aye. He said for me to keep my nose to the ground for an incoming patient."

"Said, not asked?"

"Not the asking kind."

"What did you do?"

"I went and got blootered with Gaspar."

I tap my finger against the brim of my hat. "EyePatch denies he was in Ypres. He's hiding something. But you saw him. You talked to him. And I know a reporter—"

"I would nae tangle with that scorpion."

"I wouldn't expose him. Just threaten him a little." Whatever deal Nick struck with EyePatch, it involved removing me. Having at last found Nick again, I won't lose him. And the one thing EyePatch loathes is the press. I can use it against him so that when he disappears Nick, he disappears me with him. "I need leverage, someone else who saw him in Ypres besides me. For some reason, it's information he's closely guarding. Maybe for the Home Secretary."

Next to me, McMannis coils up tight, the ribbon drawn taut between his thumb and index like it's a tourniquet. Eventually, he asks, "Out of everyone at Lady Sullivan's, how is it, do you think, I was the one he picked?"

I send him a questioning glance.

"He saw me and Gaspar."

"Even better! Eyepatch may have the Home Secretary behind him, but even he cannot fight three witnesses and my erstwhile reporter.

"You're not understanding me, lass." His broad shoulders creak, as if the canteen and garden and dormitory and the recovery of all these too-thin men weigh on his shoulders. "Me and Gaspar were . . . are . . . like Lady Sullivan and Sister Reynolds."

"McM . . ." My heart squeezes so tight around his name, I cannot breathe. In war, institutions are too busy battling chaos to bother with arbitrary rules. But in peace, society tends to enforce its rules with a vengeance. McMannis and Gaspar could go to prison. Mama's last lesson to me takes on new meaning and new consequences: *We don't all get to love who we want.* I never thought to ask her why not. McMannis wiped the blood and vomit and urine off dying men, giving them back their dignity so they could appear fresh and clean before God. He risked the firing squad to usher Flaherty through his own confusion to self-acceptance. If anyone deserves to love who he loves, is it not a man like McMannis?

"I knew you had a soft spot for the French." I link my arm through his. In all those years on the battle front, this is the first time I've ever touched him.

He squeezes my hand. The pressure is gentle, cautious, half apologetic, half protective. "Rotten luck, isn't it? Falling in love."

I pull the ribbon from him, pinch a sprig of rosemary and tie the ribbon around the stem "Remind Gaspar to use a light hand with the salt. It's not good for your blood pressure."

"You might try the Padre. One of the lads, who was it, Dixon, that's who. Dixon come in and he mentioned seeing the Padre up at St. Pancras. It's a home for the injuries you can't see." McMannis taps his temple.

"Doing his part."

"Self-righteous toad. Preached with the Bible in one hand, hogged the lemon curd with the other."

We laugh together and rise. I secure my hat on my head. "I'll get what I need from the Padre. I've always been his favorite."

He places his wide palm on my shoulder, the weight of him heavy, reassuring, like he means to pin me to this earth, like he means not to lose me again. "You know what happens to people in over their head?"

"They develop a thick skull?"

"They drown."

∼✦∼

At St. Pancras House, I follow a young woman through the lemon scented halls of what once was a wealthy man's vanity. It's now a retreat for soldiers suffering shell shock. An expensive one, with leather chairs and its own library, and a garden with a tinkling fountain. She walks quietly, her footsteps barely more than a whisper against the shiny wood floors.

She says, "He's such a gentle soul, Rev. Barnes. Always humming a tune. I think his vicar's collar brings a bit of ease to the men."

The sound of a muted piano spills down the hall. I would recognize the Padre's playing anywhere, the march of his fingers across the keys steady and faithful. She opens a pair of oak double doors. "A visitor."

The piano music stops. An orderly looks up from a complacent game of checkers. His patient, dressed in grey pajamas, cheats a jump across the board. Another patient stands at the window drawing imaginary patterns along the rain-splattered glass. He has no left hand. Both patients are so young, the sight of them is a needle to my lungs. They went from home to war to madness.

I step past the nurse, nodding my thanks. "Hello, Padre."

He adjusts his collar and studies my face for a long minute, taking inventory of my eyes, my nose, the shape of my mouth, like he's putting together the pieces of a memory. Finally, he breaks out into a smile. "Come and give an old man a hug, child. It's like sunshine, seeing you." He keys the first few notes of a hymn, "Beautiful Beams of Sunshine." One of my favorites.

I join him at the piano bench. "Beau-ti-ful beams of sun-shine, Scat-tered o'er all the earth," I sing, the notes rolling thick in my throat like stones on a muddy road. His fingers are light on the piano. It's a joyous song, but we are cautious not to be too loud, not to rattle the frayed nerves around us.

When we're finished, he interlaces his fingers and stretches them back. "You were always a good girl, never missed a Sunday. Even with my eyes closed, I could pinpoint your voice."

"Bit creaky, I'm afraid. At least this piano is in tune. Not like the one in Ypres." Not wanting to upset the patients, I whisper the last.

He taps a key on the piano, High A sharp, repeatedly like he's trying to dislodge something. "My sons all died in France."

The patient at the window covers his left ear with the stump of his wrist.

I place my hand over the Padre's, slide it away from the piano. "I'm sorry. I remember."

"They went over together, the three of them, believing as long as they were side by side, they'd be all right. I prayed for them. Every night. Every morning. To be kept safe from dysentery and canons and bullets." He rubs his cheek. There are razor cuts and patches the blade missed. "But I forgot to pray against flame throwers. My mistake. All three at once. March 21. Battle of St. Quentin. I should have asked God to make them prisoners of war."

Over six-thousand Brits died that day. And there was a story in the papers, of troops losing all their ammunition but refusing to cede to the enemy. Divisions fighting to the last man. One man in particular, who lost every single soldier under his command, who was taken prisoner by the Germans, who managed to escape. A hero, the papers called him. Despite the death toll.

"Padre, remind me again, where was your parish?"

"I wish you'd call me father. Saffron Walden, dearest. South of Cambridgeshire."

Where a square is named for the Carburry family.

"Shall we sing another song? 'Abide With Me'?" It was the hymn the Padre was humming the night Major Carbury came into my ward. What was the Padre doing that night? Tending to a concussed patient. At the time, he had seemed over-concerned for the boy. Nothing out of sorts. Not then. It was later, the next morning. *Blessed are the peacemakers*, he'd said when I told him Flaherty had died. *Flaherty was a soldier, not a peacemaker*, I'd said and he'd squeezed my shoulders like a punishment.

"We should pray for your brother's soul."

Confusion makes a knot of my thoughts. He cannot know what happened to my brother. He cannot even know I have one. I never talked of my family at Lady Sullivan's. How could I? I was someone else.

"Clasp your hands." He grabs my wrists and forces my palms together, sealing them in prayer. His jagged fingernails dig into the skin above my gloves.

"I'd rather sing." I try to wriggle out of his grasp. His nails cut, cut, cut.

"The trouble with young people today is they think they know better than their elders." His bloodshot eyes take on a wild, nervous tilt. His eyelids are purple, like he's rubbed them raw. Like he's seen too much.

I remember now, the concussed patient was relatively well, and the Padre did not shout for my attention until Major Carburry began moaning . . . *trapped* . . . *trapped* . . . *trapped*. Or had it been, *trap*? Was he sending the Padre a message? Is that why the Padre had tried to distract me? To cover a trail? Of what?

"Do as your father asks."

A bared electric wire sizzles through my brain. I could not have heard him correctly. "Do you remember the morning . . . at Lady Sullivan's . . . there was an explosion?" He'd told me he had been headed to the wards. But he hadn't been carrying his bible. He hadn't been wearing his collar. And he'd been walking from the medical marquees. The earth above his sons' graves was still fresh.

I do not want to accuse him of anything. I want to understand. Careful to keep my tone level, I ask, "Padre?"

"Father."

"Father—"

"Pray for your brothers, Chloe."

"Who is Chloe?" I use my nurse's voice, the one reserved to tell patients we must amputate, but it's more to calm my rising panic.

"You are."

"No. I'm . . ."

The orderly is watching us, his muscles poised to move fast. We're upsetting the patients.

"Why have you not come before? I did not kill your brothers. I righted the wrong of war. 'Onward Christian Soldiers," he sings, releasing my wrists to pump his fist.

"I only learned where you were today—" I catch the last of his words, tamp down the queasiness. "How did you right it? What did you do?"

"Don't lie. Proverbs 12:22?"

"I-I-I don't . . ." Confusion makes the blood in my ears pound.

The orderly rises. His footfall is silent.

"Say it with me. 'The Lord detests lying lips.'"

"The Lord . . . I'm not Chloe."

"What mischief is this? Do you mean to deny me? No matter what I did, I did it for you. My sins in exchange for my daughter's soul."

The electric wire in my brain sparks. The Padre has no daughter.

He's not here as a priest. He's here as a patient.

❧

I stride into Nick's room at the prison infirmary and am greeted by, "What the hell is this?" Nick waves *The Times* at me. The thin sheets flap against the tense air.

"It's a newspaper. Into which goes the news—information, facts, reports. Fascinating stuff." I take a seat on the ledge of the dusty window, lean my back into the worn wooden frame.

"It's crap." Nick tosses the paper to the side. I don't miss what the effort of sitting up in his infirmary bed costs him. Without his military uniform to cloak his body, he cannot hide the sharp angles of his too-bony shoulders, the wan, wiped-out exhaustion of his pasty skin. His legs, those long, muscular limbs that once sluiced through riptides, lay bony and restless beneath the rough fabric of his prison garb.

"Crap it may be," I say. "And yet it is not untrue."

He flashes an *I'll wring your neck* smile.

I smile back. It feels good to fight with Nick. The energy crackling between us may be the only thing keeping me from slumping to the floor. I'm so tired. Not the *up all night* hospital kind of tired, but the *worm eating out your heart* kind. Lady Sullivan is likely dead. The Padre is mad. McMannis could be imprisoned for loving who he loves. I cannot bear the weight of loss, this airless blackness feasting off my flesh.

Nick turns to my new partner in crime (I seem to be collecting a motley crew), cub reporter James' cousin's sweetheart's uncle, the infirmary orderly. "What the devil is she doing here?"

The orderly, Wilson, shrugs his shoulders and opens a hypodermoclysis kit and pretends to be absorbed in attaching needle to tube. "She offered me five quid."

"And the guards?"

"Smoking French cigarettes. *Ooh la la*," I add, to rankle him, because a rankled Nick is an alive Nick.

"Throw her out." He shuts his eyes as if the thin skin of his eyelids has the power to block me. Does he think I'm blind to the way his body is pitched, tight as a tuning fork, toward me? Does he think I don't see him inhaling the scent of me in this otherwise sterile, ammonia-drenched room? He keeps stroking the edge of the bedsheet with his thumb the way he once stroked my cheek. The memory of the touch hangs heavy between us, a storm threatening to burst. What I wouldn't do to taste a single drop of rain.

I point to the wall clock. "I bought five minutes." I glance out beyond my perch. Three floors below, just outside the gate, Master James is holding court on the sidewalk. He can only distract EyePatch for so long before the man picks him up by the scruff of the neck and tosses him into oncoming traffic.

Nick kicks the blanket away. "You wasted your money." Even his feet are gaunt, the skin sallow.

"I consider it an act of charity." I sweep my hand dramatically toward Wilson, who is arranging needle, tube, and saline solution on a metal tray. Nick still refuses to eat. The saline will at least rehydrate him. "Do you really want Wilson to insert the needle or shall I?

"I'd take the lady up on her offer," warns Wilson. "My thumbs can be thick."

"I'll do it myself." When Wilson comes to his bedside, Nick grabs the tray. The needle clinks against the metal, the tinny sound so familiar, the muscles in my arms flex with anticipation, near jealous.

"I'll just pop out for a smoke, shall I?" Wilson opens the door and glances back. "Mind the time," he says, patting his chest pocket, where sit five fat quid and a packet of French fags.

"Toodle-oo." I wave.

Nick ignores us, pulling up his shirt to reveal a hollowed out stomach. He tries to pinch an inch of flesh, but there's not enough fat. Fumbling with the needle, he asks, "How'd *The Times* know to interview Langdon?"

Master James' article surprised even me. It was not a hard-hitting piece on the burdens of war, but rather a celebration of a wheelchair bound man's resilience. Langdon is a teacher now, a choir director for his church, a father who treasures every moment with his daughter, a grateful patient who believes Nick saved more than his life. The optimism reminded me of the Nick I love. Stubborn. Unconquerable.

"A source?" My tone is cloyingly sweet.

Nick knows this tone. I thrill at his irritated expression. "You. You gave his name."

"I have a great many names."

Needle in, Nick uses his teeth to tear a strip of adhesive plaster (Blackpond—is there no branch of English government safe from Papa's enterprising greed?) and secures the tubing around his emaciated waist. He throws me a smirk, one meant to communicate *I know what I'm doing*. "It won't make a difference."

"Why not?"

"I killed Carburry."

"Yes. I've read all about it. In the papers," I add with a healthy dose of sarcasm.

Nick sinks into his pillows. His jaw becomes slack, his eyelids grow heavy. Were we in Wimereux and he my patient, this would be the moment I would take out *The Count of Monte Cristo* and ease him into sleep. But he is a prisoner and this is an infirmary. There is no time for rest.

"Earlier today I went to visit an old friend at St. Pancras House."

Nick flashes a guarded, warning look. *Go away*, it says. *Stay away.* No, that's not right. He is not shutting me out in anger. It's something else. There's a tenderness in his eyes. *Save yourself.* But without Nick, what is there to save myself for?

"And it was the oddest thing. The oddest thing really," I soldier on. "But when I asked the chatty nurse how a mad vicar with no living family could afford a private facility, do you know what she said?"

Nick turns his head away. The hair of his once golden head is matted and greasy. It strikes me only now, when he inserted the needle into his stomach, he did not flinch. As if he could not even feel it. My stomach muscles clench.

I continue, "She said the Padre's fees were paid for out of a trust set up by . . . let me think now, her exact words . . . the *ever-so-handsome* Greek doctor who brought him. In May of 1918." My tone turns sharp. "When you were supposedly off collecting a spinal patient from the front, you were actually moving the Padre to London. Why?"

When he says nothing, I try to bait him. "As long as you're so quick to confess to murder, you might as well offer up the rest of your crimes." If he killed Carburry, he had a reason. One I can use to save him. "What are you playing at?"

"I don't play games."

"You do," I snap, coming away from the drafty window. Eyepatch has at last sidestepped Master James. He will be pounding up the stairs and bursting through the door in a minute. "You're just terrible at them."

He mumbles something. At first, I can't make out the rasped syllables. It comes to me a moment later, the sound of lungs exhaling over closed vocal cords. He is laughing. Reluctant, begrudging, defeated, nevertheless he is laughing.

And I am helpless, tumbling deeper into love with a man who is starving himself to make a point that will be lost on everyone. Except me. Because I understand him. I know him. This is my Nick.

"The Padre . . . you cannot blame him," he says, careful not to turn to me, careful to keep as much of himself locked away as he can. "He was suffering shell shock long before the marquees. I would not have him punished for a crime he was exploited to commit."

The irony is obvious, but it is a thing to be avoided. "I don't think I'm angry. More confused."

"He must have been pleased to see you."

I pick up my felt hat, which feels more like mine now that I've tugged off the ribbon and ruined it. "He mistook me for a daughter he never had. Even McMannis, who is sane, said he didn't recognize me today. Am I so altered?"

Nick stills. There's a heavy sigh, signaling that he will unlock the window just this once. But no more. "When I am dead and buried . . ." Anticipating my protest, he raises his hand to stop me, the gesture as firm as the snap of a neck in a hangman's noose. "When I am dead and buried six feet below a frozen earth, I will know the moment you walk by. You have a way about you. You change the very air."

I am on the verge of tears in a body too tired to cry.

I come to the edge of his narrow hospital bed and sink into the thin mattress. Back turned or no, I long to curl up next to him, to bury my head against his neck, to drape my arms around the too-thin shell of his body, to feel the fall and rise of each of his breaths. But even in Wimereux, we never had such luxuries. Time was against us.

"Everyone has a breaking point, Nick. What was yours?"

He says not a word. He moves not a single muscle. If he's breathing, his body does not betray it. The answer vibrates off his skin, echoes in the gaping, yearning, awful chasm between us. In his silence, he confesses everything.

Despite my exhaustion, the tears slip free.

I am his breaking point.

CHAPTER TEN

Wimereux, June 1918

A kiss is not going to break me. I am not lonely, I inform my heart. I am bored. It's three a.m. My patients in Ward One are sleeping. I have checked their temperatures and written down their vitals on form sheets clipped to the foots of their beds. With nothing left to do, I busy myself by organizing the amber medicine bottles alphabetically, from vitamin A to zinc oxide.

I have not seen Colonel Wallace since our ill-fated, rapturous encounter on the beach. He left two weeks ago to collect a patient from the front. The staff have observed he is usually not away this long and worry after his well-being, speculating the fighting has made travel intractable. At breakfast each morning and dinner each evening the patients ask whether there has been word from him. The answer is always a forced smile and a *not yet*. I wake up each day fighting how hard a hold *not yet* has on me. How many times do I need to remind myself, there is no room for love in war?

Finished with the medicine bottles, my fingers plunk along the edge of table searching for a purpose. The ward is stuffy, the stench of body fluids dropped in buckets beneath the beds threatens to suffocate the room. The solution, Old Betts taught me, is fresh air. The memory of his tired feet shuffling through the hall to call up to me, "Arise, lass, there's a bairn to be born," makes me smile, but leaves me lonely. I miss him and worry for him, now that he has joined his daughter in Canada, where the bracing cold must make his arthritic joints ache.

I unlatch a window, inviting a lazy summer breeze and the scent of the garden below to clear the air. With nothing to do, I sit on the ledge and go over the Contrology exercises I have learned. Matron has trained me, though she won't yet let me practice on a patient. On this, I surprise myself by agreeing with her. Our patients are fragile, their bodies twisted and dismantled in ways no one is meant to survive. Upstart I may be, still I would never risk injuring the men.

Above me, across the night sky, the Milky Way is dancing. I find Bootes the herdsman with his spear in hand. In lieu of a live body, I trace the air, drawing out how to support Bootes' leg so he may stretch it to Virgo, bend his knee up to Izar. Lost in thought, I sense rather than hear someone lifting a chair, setting it down on the far end of the ward, and taking a seat. When I turn, I find Colonel Wallace. My heart disobeys my brain. It leaps.

Seated beside a patient whose body will fail him before the end of the month, Colonel Wallace has taken out a black, hardbound notebook. The pencil in his hand moves in long strokes. Not writing words, then, but sketching. His cheeks are rough, as if he has not shaved in days and his shoulders hang straight, but rigid, like they are obeying the strength of his command rather than holding up on their own. He looks haggard.

I want to kiss him.

Instead, hidden as I am by the large, wooden frame of the window, I allow myself the pleasure of watching Colonel Wallace. The lamp is set low and spreads a dim, yellow patch across his notebook, just enough for him to see. The position of his seat, the advantage he takes of the light, the determined posture of his body tell me he has sat like this before, sketching at the side of a dying man. Probably too many times. I struggle to tamp down a rising, lump-in-throat understanding. We are not so different, Colonel Wallace and me. He has his sketchbook. I have my *Count of Monte Cristo*.

He closes his book, raises his head, and pinpoints his gaze directly at me. The smile that curves across his face is reluctant, a thing he cannot fight, though he knows better. It matches mine. His footfall across the wooden planks is quiet. He must know well where the cracks and squeaks of the floorboards lay. He sidesteps them all, arriving by my side like a shadow. My stomach quivers and my blood thrums at the nearness of him.

"Bootes," I say, gesturing to the sky.

"He is chasing Ursa Major." He indicates a distant star.

"He must be very tired, forever running and yet standing in place."

"But what would happen if he caught the bear? Would he find happiness? Or would he throw the world off balance? Perhaps it's the act of running, knowing you will never reach your destination, that keeps the stars in place."

"The world has already fallen apart."

"No. It's turned ugly and brutal, but it's still whole." He takes a seat on the ledge. His uniform is wrinkled, the way khaki sometimes is when one has been caught in the rain or the damp and has no time to brush and dry it. I trace his jawline. The grist along his rough cheeks feels like salt. A distant scent of sea spray and smokestacks wafts between us, reminding me of Calais, where warships dock and sail away. He has been somewhere dangerous, but not where he's claimed to be.

"My father was a pacifist," he says and in the *was* I hear the finality and feel the loss.

"Before the war began, but well after the politicians committed to it, my father was asked to write a code."

"Because he was a linguist," I say, understanding already.

"It took him a year. Obsessive, exact, he went near mad drafting and tearing apart, and building this code until he designed a work of beauty, a complex structure of patterns housed under a simple shell. A code breaker would be fooled into thinking it was child's play, and translate the wrong message. A red herring." He rubs the heel of his palm against his forehead.

One of the patients stirs, a small groan, but does not wake.

"The code was my father's greatest intellectual achievement. And his undoing."

Not unlike this hospital. "His code became a weapon," I say.

"How many men, do you think, died because the message was decoded wrong and the red herring believed? How many more when the correct message was received?"

It's an impossible question. More so because the real question is who of our crippled patients here are among those men?

"For his magnum opus, my father was offered a knighthood. But he couldn't bear the guilt of his intellectual vanity being used against his pacifist principles. He swam out to sea. His body washed up on Smallmouth beach."

I suppress the shiver running down my spine. A baby brother drowned in the bathtub. A father drowned at sea. Water destroys his family and yet he brazenly swims each morning, defying the riptides and yet part of them too.

The ward is eerily peaceful. A patient sighs in his sleep. Another snores. They are tucked up in this chateau, with a summer breeze slipping in to clear the stench. It's a false calm. Beneath the sleep the men suffer, not just from their injuries, but their memories. The gruesome ones—of running a knife through an enemy and hearing his all too human cry—and the happier ones—of once being able to walk, to run, to move with ease.

Colonel Wallace leans his forehead against mine. "What would you do to stop this brutality?" he asks. "Would you compromise?"

"Yes," I whisper.

"Would you deceive?"

"Yes."

"Would you destroy the very thing that defines you?"

"Yes."

Our foreheads pressed together, our lips a single, silvery breath apart, we look into one another's eyes, communicating things that have no words, without spilling a single secret—who I really am, where he really was, what he's done, what he's willing to do to keep humanity from tearing itself to pieces, how deep my faith runs.

In this silence, tenderness wells and weaves a spell of dark of night and summer breeze, of instinctive trust and yearning. I murmur, "I will not love you."

He chuckles, his warm breath teases my parted lips. "Promise me you won't."

The spell between us does not break. Will not break. You cannot fight intangible forces—air, gravity, whatever it is that holds constellations in their place. We do our best. Pore by pore, inch by inch, we part, turning away from each other and toward the sky. I point to a row of stars. "Big dipper."

He gestures to a distant, but bright, orange light. "Arcturis."

Star by star, we map out the Milky Way. Far safer than mapping out the tumult of our hearts.

The sun has been up for a good three hours. I've served breakfast, hand feeding some of the patients, performed blanket baths for others, read aloud the comics, winked, cosseted, and no-nonsensed aplenty. Just when my duties were getting started, my shift is over. I climb the stairs to the room I share with Fukimoto, wondering at the odd stillness that has come over me. Odd because it sank into my pores the moment Colonel Wallace returned and has not left me. I am no longer listless. I am . . . I shake my head at the idiocy of the notion. I am comfortable in my own skin. I fit into myself again.

I meet Fukimoto yawning and stretching her arms as she crosses the second-floor landing, coming from the isolated wing where the Jerry POW is confined. She too must have had a long night. My cheeks warm, as if I've been caught out, which makes no sense. I am guilty of nothing. Colonel Wallace and I sat a respectable distance of at least three inches and talked of astronomy for a modest thirty minutes.

Fukimoto and I exchange cautious, guarded nods. Though I am not tired, I rub my eyes for fear of betraying anything other than a healthy sense of a job well done. "Night shift," I mumble.

"'Orbed is the moon and bright, And the stars they glisten, glisten,'" she replies.

I wrinkle my forehead.

"Do you not know your own Keats?" she asks. "I thought you to be a great reader."

I shrug my shoulders. "Poetry was never my forte. I tend toward shipwrecks and prison escapes."

"An adventuress." She chuffs, pleased, like she's found a kindred spirit. "You must have a brother."

My beloved brother's name plays across my lips. I force them shut. From Mama's last letter, I know his regiment is engaged in the Battle of Belleau Wood. I scour the dead and injured lists near daily. To Fukimoto, I skirt her observation with an indifferent shrug of the left shoulder and say, "Tomboy."

"I have four." She rubs the mahogany railing, seeming to note its smoothness and evaluating the curve of the banister, making a mental calculation. "Were Matron pleasantly detained, I would venture to slide down."

"I'd be happy to tie her to a chair for you."

Her laugh is light, pretty. "Coming for breakfast? I think I'm acclimatizing to your English way of things—baked beans and toast. Not the blood pudding, though." She wrinkles her nose, stops to consider something. "*Acclimatizing*—is this the right word? I usually ask

Colonel Wallace during his rounds. But he has been away and I keep playing with the word, wanting to exercise it."

I open my mouth to tell her Colonel Wallace is back, but the heat in my cheeks stops me. The fact I know of his return would lead to the obvious question of *how I know.* "I think it means to adapt to one's environment. So yes, one acclimatizes to baked beans. But there is no need to acclimatize to blood pudding. I find it horrid."

She leans over the bannister, double-checking no one is nearby to eavesdrop. "As long as we are making confession, I find your English way of tea barbaric. In Japan, we have a formal ceremony, a show of grace and art. Here, you have"—she purses her lips left to right before deciding on—"crumpets?"

"And strawberry meringues."

"Too sweet."

"I suppose each country has its own tradition." This may be the most civilized conversation I've had in months, if not years. A slow, pleasant chat about the quirks of how we take our tea, illuminating both how alike we humans are, and how complicated. Our differences are subtle. And yet we exploit them when convenient—to divide, to fight.

"In East Frisia they brew their tea very bitter, and then drop sugar rocks and heavy cream into it." Fukimoto stiffens, covers her mouth with her hand, her eyes wide and wary.

East Frisia is in Germany. The information could only have come from the Jerry POW. But who am I to judge? Colonel Wallace welcomed the man into his hospital, arguing with an incensed Matron, *We do not deny men because of the make and mode of their uniform.* Matron had shot back, *Why should we save the life of a man who has killed hundreds of ours?* And Colonel Wallace had replied, placing a soldiering hand on her shaking-with fury-shoulders, *If that is how you feel, Rosling, you've chosen the wrong profession. Which I know you haven't.* Beneath his faith in her, she'd calmed.

"Does he speak Japanese?" I ask, because I do not want to be like Matron.

Fukimoto's body softens, she blinks. "No, educated in your country. Cambridge."

The irony of war. The divides are artificial.

"Breakfast?" She gestures downstairs and toward the dining hall.

I shake my head. "Night shift, remember?" I point upstairs to the room we share, two narrow iron beds, two matching nightstands, two lamps, the occasional spray of wildflowers Fukimoto arranges. After Lady Sullivan's, the room is equivalent to the Palace of Versailles.

"'To sleep, perchance to dream.'"

"Keats again?" I ask.

She groans and tosses me a pitying look. "Shakespeare."

I leave her laughing, and lug myself two steps at a time up to the third floor, to our bedchamber, where I draw the curtains and wash my face and change out of my uniform and collapse into bed. It is only once my head has hit the pillow that my sleep-clouded brain forms around a vague, troubling thought. Fukimoto does not have the night shift. She should not have been coming from the German's room.

I am on my way to Ward One when the sound of a crash, a cry of pain and a guttural expletive send me racing down the far hall, into the private room of Major Carburry. He lies twisted, his plaster-cast legs tangled in the traction ropes, his hands splayed on the floor, catching his fall. Bitterness vibrates across his impotent body.

I kneel. "Did you hit your head? Are you hurt?"

"According to your colonel-in-a-white coat, would I feel if I were?" He is panting.

"You would." I run my dry, chapped hands over him, checking for winces and breaks. He smells of bergamot mixed with something heavier, sweeter. The scent reminds me of my mother. Which makes no sense. Nurses aren't allowed to wear perfume and where would a crippled war hero procure an expensive bottle of Creed?

"At last, I get to enjoy the feel of your hands on my poor, beleaguered body."

I grant him the requisite no-flirting nurse's frown. Tucking my shoulder beneath his, my arm goes around his back. "Let's get you up to bed."

"Surely you can't support me?" He raises his brown-as-English-oak eyes to me. They are shaded to convey trustworthiness, reliability, but a primal heat rises from them, purely sexual. He has not shown this face to me before. Unnerved, I swallow and focus on my duties.

"You'd be surprised." I ease him onto the mattress, rearrange and elevate his limbs, straightening out the traction ropes. He must have jerked his body rather violently to have fallen so. On purpose? By accident? "I'm stronger than I look."

"No wonder the boys are all agog."

"How would you know?" My index and forefinger to his wrist, I track his pulse, counting the beats against the breast watch pinned to my uniform, its face upside down so I can read it. "You don't talk to them."

"But what big ears I have." He grins wolfishly. "All the better to listen."

He reaches across and flips my watch, examines the back, where the initials V.B. are engraved. *Victor Bettany.* Dozens of patients have toyed with the watch, either out of curiosity, or to flirt. Occasionally to grab my breast. Innocuous gestures. Except this time, my stomach tenses. Like I am frightened of his sexual energy. Perhaps I should be. He has been caged, not neutered.

When I speak, I'm relieved by the steadiness of my humorless nurse's voice. "Next time, Major, if you need your brow wiped, rather than throwing yourself to the floor, ring the annunciator."

He crosses the brows in question and I point to the brass button on the wall beside his bed, well within reach and in working order. The orderlies manning the call box downstairs have complained of the Major's constant demands—fresher water, hotter tea, an open window, an extra blanket, a second shave.

"Where have you been, Nurse Betts? I've missed your version of bedside manner."

"You're Matron's patient now."

"Don't be jealous, sweetheart. Rosling is a sight to behold"—he sketches a curvy figure, exuberant breasts, undulating hips—"but she hasn't your sharp tongue. Better than an apple a day. Quick now, threaten me with something awful." He winks, but the shadows along the sharp lines of his high cheekbones deepen with world-weariness. He is a soldier. He lost his entire regiment in a single battle. What is wrong with me that I can't be sympathetic?

I tap my pencil against his medical chart. "Will a barium swallow do?"

"There's the spirit." A quick grin, a flash of triumph. "How young you look Betts, when you're not glowering. How is it this war has yet to corrupt you?"

"Trick of the light," I say, lightly, because he cannot begin to guess how, whenever I turn a corner in this gleaming mansion, I brace for the blast of canon fire, the piercing screams of men with guts spilling out of shredded flesh, the things familiar to me. The quiet hum of this hospital throws me off balance. I set the chart down and make my way to the door.

"Wait, don't go yet."

"I have rounds."

"Just another minute. It's . . . isolating in this room." The turn of his mouth reminds me that he spent months trapped behind barbed wire, likely starved, likely beaten. It's not unnatural for him to want a few moments of friendly conversation. It's practically my moral and patriotic duty to provide it.

"I'll pour you a glass of water." I turn back, head to the table where a pitcher and glass sit. My foot catches on a gold-plated pen poking out from beneath the bed. When I bend to retrieve it, I again catch the scent of bergamot mixed with vanilla and a hint of amber. I wonder if years of breathing antiseptic can have the same destructive effect as a bomb does on hearing. My sense of smell is broken.

"Were you writing a letter?" When I hold the pen up, the Major pales and sits up so straight, so quickly, so guiltily, I stop to study it. It's plain and heavy, no initials or engravings, no telltale inscription. The gold is dull. Nothing special.

"It's not mine. Wallace must have left it." He gestures for me to bring it to him and when he plucks it from my hand, he does so gingerly, like he's worried it will leak ink across his white sheets. "Is it true there's a German roaming the halls?"

"This is a hospital for spinal injuries. No one roams."

"Has there not been an uprising amongst the nurses and patients?"

"General Hildebrand is kept separated." I pour water into the glass.

"Wallace is a better man than me." The Major takes a reluctant drink, the squint of his eyes and narrowing of his nostrils communicating he would prefer a far stronger beverage. "I suppose to him a Hun is just another stone to the knee on the path to sainthood." He hands the glass back to me. "How do the two communicate? The German and your pacifist."

"General Hildebrand went to Cambridge."

"Who didn't? St. Catherine's for me."

I try not to get caught in the loops tangling in my head, of the Major and Colonel Wallace and General Hildebrand all attending the same university. Cambridge graduates thousands a year. It's a coincidence, not a pattern. "Did you study linguistics?"

He bursts out laughing. "Why in God's name would anyone study something so orphic?"

"*Orphic* is a rather obscure word for one who didn't."

"Perhaps you should embark on a course of linguistics. Cambridge lets women in now. Somewhere." He shrugs his shoulders like he's trying to recall a mad experiment.

"Girton." Which, until my sister transferred her ambition from chemistry to Jerome, had been Gwendolyn's alpha and omega. "I can't think of anything more boring. I'm a nurse, not an intellectual."

"Is that all you are?"

"It's all I want to be."

He turns his head to contemplate me, his dark eyes skimming across the starch of my veil, my pristine and practical apron, my thick cotton blouse and skirt. His perusal leaves me both hot and cold. The sensation is not unpleasant, but it is unwanted. I did not invite it. I am a little afraid of it.

"I've been thinking of who you remind me of," he says.

"A housemaid who thwarted your advances?"

He chuckles. "A naughty nanny. Wouldn't you be just the thing? I'd ask if you've ever ridden a hobby horse and—" When I cross my arms and turn on my heel to leave, he calls out hurriedly, "No, no. nothing like that. Do come back, Nurse Betts. I promise to behave. I realized the person you most remind me of is . . ." He pauses as if he can't quite fathom the answer himself. "Me."

"You?"

"We're both military. We're made for war."

I should be repulsed. "War doesn't make people."

"Doesn't it? My father's a statue in Westminster. I'm sure you've read of his bravery and ingenuity and whatnot in your primary school book. But me? Before this war, who was I? Nothing but a legend's son. Forgettable."

Isn't this how the Devil seduces? By preying upon one's weaknesses? Drawn to him, trancelike, I come to the edge of the Major's bedside, curl my fingers. The scent of bergamot and vanilla, so like

Creed, my mother's perfume, overtakes my senses.

"War changes the playing field," he says. "There are certain people—you, me—who thrive in a crisis. Who prefer disruption and chaos, and yes, even violence." He holds up his hand to stop me from arguing, but I have not so much as exhaled. "You miss the front. It's your place, isn't it? It did not escape my notice that you lit up at the sight of me crashing to the floor."

"I take no pleasure in your pain."

"No, of course you don't. But you find *purpose* in it. Don't be ashamed. I'm not. I'm a hero. I walked out of that hellhole on two sturdy legs." The glance he casts at his limbs is pure fury. "At least I have something to hand down to my son."

"A son," I repeat. My fingers wander across the sheets, coming so close to his, I near feel the wisps of hair on his knuckles.

"And then there is Saint Wallace. Peace by any means necessary." The Major's jaw tightens and the side of his mouth curls. "That's why the German's here. Wallace may be a doctor, but he is no angel of mercy."

Through the fug of heavy perfume and the clouded judgment of my war-damaged brain, I manage to say, "He's a crusader."

"All the more dangerous."

"Tilting at windmills?"

"Choosing the wrong battle. One does things"—up and down, he strokes the shaft of gold pen—"not understanding the consequences."

I am mesmerized by the long fingers toying with the dull gold. Controlled, calculating, yet sensuous. "Right hand, left hand?"

"My game is chess, sweetheart. I always know which hand to play."

Chess. A game of strategy. Without heart.

"You've forgotten, Major. I've watched you play. I know your moves."

He casts a sidelong glance. A *show me.* A seduction.

I hike up my skirts, raise my left knee, crawl onto the bed. The springs squeak beneath me. The Major's eyes flare: desire, anticipation, disbelief. Careful not to disturb his tractioned legs, I lever my body over his, our faces inches apart. Perspiration beads along his forehead. I smell the sour, salty tang of a man who has lain in bed for weeks. Beneath it lingers the fading musk of an earlier sexual encounter. My head is not broken. Someone in this hospital dips her pulse points in Creed.

"You are a hero." I lick my thumb and run it against his wet, hungry lips. He reaches for my breast. I pin his arms down. My voice, when I speak, is low and husky, poison sweetened with honey. "But the only man you saved was yourself. In your place, Colonel Wallace would have sacrificed himself so his regiment might live."

The Major squirms, tries to pull away. But he is trapped . . . trapped . . . trapped.

"Harm my crusader and I will kill you."

The hospital is awash in the snap and crackle of new energy. The windows are thrown open, the sun streams cheerfully in to light up the pale-yellow walls, and I am racing up the stairs, my boots clattering joyfully against the wood floors. Below me, from the library, I catch snippets of men joking and challenging each other to a game of cards. The patients from Wards Three and Four are playing poker with their newfound currency, Juicy Fruit gum. My cousin Kristina, never one to abide small gestures, sent a case—a full case!

Outside, the sing-song voice of a little girl is insisting, "Banana, banana, banana."

"Peach," replies Corporal Langdon to his daughter.

They are arguing over which fruit flavors the gum.

Laughter follows their argument, a clear, crystal sound so musical, I stop to savor the note before I realize the laugh belongs to Matron.

When I poke my head out the window, I see the little girl wiggling onto Matron's lap. "What fruit do you think it is?"

Matron pulls a ribbon from her apron, plaits it through the child's corn silk hair. "Something exotic," she teases, her tone affectionate, maternal, a hint of longing for the bairns she's never had. "Papaya."

The child giggles.

There's a sweetness to the day, a hard-won humanity. We are far from the front, but the patients here left blood and limbs and friends in the mud. None of us takes the simplicity of a stick of gum for granted.

Down the west wing I run, past the isolated room of the German patient, General Hildebrand, further still to a turret where my favorite perch awaits—a window seat that looks out on a wild tangle of garden and a fresh water well. I plop down lazily, pull up my feet, and draw out Kristina's letter. My heart is pounding from the pleasure of running, from the mischief of having a secret place to sit and hide, from the anticipation of who I will be able to watch from a safe distance when he comes to draw water from the well and drink it straight from the bucket.

The first letter in Kristina's packet is unusual, written on cardstock, the handwriting made of letters so square they look like numbers. More surprising, the note is from Papa and near affectionate – *Wire if in need of funds*. I laugh aloud.

Mama's letter is peppered with talk of baby Matthew, how he sucks his fingers, how he toddles, how his smile eases her anxiety. *You will adore him*, she assures me, and for the first time since I came to France, I do not seize, I do not close up. He is a child, not a reminder that I am unlovable.

I glance at the well and bite my lip. I wonder where the Colonel is. He is late. Usually he comes to the well after he's finished in the operating theatre. He'll have cast his surgeon's whites aside, his button-down too, the cotton fabric of his undershirt will cling to the sinews of muscle across his hard chest. Above the collar, I have glimpsed a patch of golden curls. I check my watch, impatient.

When I flip to the pages of Kristina's letter, I can practically hear the whirr and clack of her typewriter, the ding of the return bell. Her reporter's nose smells a story, a big one, involving a series of small and not so innocent events.

> *Conspiracies abound, Kiddo! Dinner at Delmonico's with that square-faced doer of good things, Police Commissioner Arthur Woods (politics being what they are, he's on his way out, alas. How I hate the loss of a good source) and over roast canvas-back duck and a bottle (or three) of Chateau Haut Brion, we got to talking of none other than the Black Tom Island explosion and Arthur's unwavering belief it is the work of German spies.*
>
> *And not their only work! He suspects a network has been setting fires to ships at sea and goes so far as to think the fire that destroyed the Canadian Parliament House was an act of sabotage. Juicy, juicy. Spies among our mists. But how have these nefarious agents escaped detection? The theory . . . timed bombs! What a clever, cruel invention. The perpetrator plants the bomb, slips back into the disguise of an ordinary citizen, and BOOM havoc and destruction ensue.*

So absorbed am I in reaching the next page, I almost miss the sight of Colonel Wallace in the garden. I bite my lip and my heart surges forward so quickly, I have to clamp my teeth together to keep it from leaping out of my throat. I force myself to breathe through my nose, inhale, exhale, and calm my pulse.

Something is wrong. He is standing at a distance from the well, holding himself back as if he doesn't deserve something as simple as water. His hands are fisted. He forces open his right hand, stares at the object sitting in his palm. A pen, of all things. Fat, the size of a cigar, similar if not identical to the one in Carburry's room. He does not go to the well. He picks up a shovel and heads toward the woods at a purposeful pace.

What is he digging? Or burying? My neck tightens. Sensation, like a witch's finger, skitters down my spine. I get up, planning to follow him, and pull open a heavy, seldom-used door leading to a set of exterior stairs. Three steps down and I bang straight into Fukimoto, near knocking her over the railing.

"Oh," she exhales nervously.

I notice the bouquet of wildflowers in her hand, recall the location of General Hildebrand's room. Her twitching fingers and nervous smile are guilt writ large.

We do not all get to love who we want. I've always been a fast learner. Mama's lesson has so shaped me that even as I am flying down a set of neglected stairs to catch Colonel Wallace, I have guarded myself well enough not to risk loving him. Love is not a gift. It is a punishment. I should impart this lesson on Fukimoto. I should warn her, *wall your heart.*

Instead, from the pocket of my apron, I pull out a green and white packet, labeled Wrigley's Juicy Fruit Chewing Gum, nudge my head in the direction of Fukimoto's destination. "Something to help General Hildebrand stave off a blue funk."

Fukimoto takes the gum and smiles, wide, relieved, naive. A pang of jealousy skims across my chest. I wish I could be like her. She says, "Do you know Oscar Wilde? 'True friends stab you in the heart.'"

The pain in my chest is sharp, but the knife does not pierce. A flesh wound, nothing more. I move to the side so she can step around me on the narrow stairs. She takes a step, pauses, wraps her small hand around my arm, squeezes. When I raise mine to cover hers, it is shaking. We stand in silent communication, perhaps camaraderie. I have never seen eyes like hers before, turned down at the inner corners, the dark color smooth, like liquid stone, reflecting depths, radiating light, full of earnest hope.

After she has yanked open the large, creaking door to the west wing, I break into a run. There is no joy in it. My feet pound against compacted earth, kicking up dust. The dirt is centuries old. I stomp on pinecones, crushing them into dry bits. A sense of urgency, of destruction drives me. My legs feel clumsy, my lungs burn. At the edge of the woods, unsure of which direction Colonel Wallace disappeared to, I trust instinct, and barrel toward the open meadow a distance away.

But I am too late.

From a mile away, possibly two, comes the sound of smothered thunder, as if the cause of the explosion had been deliberately buried. A plume of thin yellow smoke rises above the treetops. Grey clouds follow.

Kristina's letter echoes in my head:

> *How would one go about hiding and triggering a timed bomb? The device would have to be able to contain two liquids, a volatile acid and an incendiary. And it would need to be small, innocuous, something everyday.*

Like a pen.

CHAPTER ELEVEN

London, May 5, 1919

Leaning backward in his chair, head turned away from the machinations of the trying-to-out-barrister each other barristers, Nick strategically bypasses me, levels his gaze on Master James and asks in an angelic voice, "Lend a condemned man a pen?"

Master James' ears turn bright red. "Are you . . . are you talking to me?"

Nick tosses me a deceptive devil-may-care glance. I recognize it for what it is—a wall. "James Stahler. *The Times.* Fantastic article on the drug sanctuary in Silvertown. Good work being done."

"Y-y-es. Thank you."

"Why do you need a pen?" My voice is sharp.

"To write something," says Nick, feigning innocence, the one thing he has not bothered to do while on trial for murder.

Master James reaches into his coat pocket.

"Don't give him that pen," I order with so much authority even the Judge Advocate sets his hands down.

Nick tips his chair back far enough so he can rest his elbows on the wooden railing dividing the gallery from the proceedings. "You would deny me something as simple as a writing instrument?"

"Why don't you ask your barrister for one?" I indicate his black-robed advocate, who is shaking his finger at the prosecution with such righteous fury, the prosecutor looks likely to drown in his own spittle. This morning's proceedings involve a flurry of technical motions regarding evidence, jurisdiction, and applicable statutes. Nothing I, nor any other mere mortal, can understand.

"By order of the high command, his Majesty the Imperial Home Secretary, my barrister is instructed to refuse me any and all requests," says Nick. "At the rate he is going, I am more likely to die from papercuts than hang."

"A girl can always dream."

He's clean-shaven today and looks like he's slept for the first time in months, and also like he resents being rested. I'm almost grateful to EyePatch for the ruse of the infirmary. Which leaves me wondering where he is this morning. His absence makes me nervous. And explains Nick's request for the pen. His brother isn't here to sucker punch him into compliance.

Master James draws the pen out of his pocket. I shoot out my hand and knock it to the ground. He scrambles to pick it up. I kick it behind me. He rolls his eyes as if I've insulted his profession. Drawing another pen from his coat pocket, he holds it in his left hand, at a distance, and asks Nick, "Would you consent to an interview?"

"A kingdom for a horse? You're a wily one, Mr. Stahler. What if, you loan me your pen and I write you my confession? You can print it in the evening edition."

"You'd be printing a pack of lies," I cut in. "Probably committing treason. I'm sure Colonel Wallace's brother is, at this very moment, sharpening his steel blades against the treacherous press."

"I'm a fast writer," Nick assures him.

Master James straightens his coat, gives me a committed man-of-the-press tug of his forelock. "I'm sorry, Miss Betts. I'm a reporter. Colonel Wallace is offering—"

"I can top his story."

Master James' expression is half doubt, half pity. Handwritten confessions from war criminals are not an everyday occurrence and he may be a Jersey Island boy, but he's got enough street sense to know I'm grasping.

"Nobody but a handful of people care about this trial," I say. "Look around you. Even after your beautiful interview with Corporal Langdon, there are no new observers. People were moved, but they don't care. Because the defendant isn't your story."

"As the defendant in question, I beg to differ." Nick has the decency to sound affronted, but sarcasm does not come naturally to him.

"Colonel Wallace isn't well-known; he doesn't move people." I ignore Nick's attempt at puffed outrage. "He hasn't captured the nation's attention. You're working the wrong angle."

Master James shakes his head at me. "Was it not the very angle you recommended?"

"Where's your reporter's instinct?" I ask.

"Questioning why I should trust you."

"Because I have all the facts." But don't understand the story.

Nick has set down his chair and dropped the cavalier façade. Gently, he warns me, "Don't be foolish."

My heart thrills a little, because only Nick understands me well enough to know what I'm about to do even before I am sure myself. His warning becomes my commitment. "Wouldn't you like to know more about the victim, Major Carburry?"

"I think all that there is to say about the great hero has already been said." Master James sounds near-bored.

"What if I told you England's hero was no hero at all. That he was nothing but a fraud."

"Don't," comes Nick's second warning.

"I was his nurse," I continue, emboldened. "I have *intimate* knowledge. Of the blackness of his character."

"Stop." Nick says.

"The weakness of his soul."

"I don't believe you." Master James has drawn away from me. Seduction is never pretty when the seducer is panicked.

"Stop." Nick's warning comes with more urgency.

"We could start with his—"

A hand grips my shoulder. Black gloves. Fur trimmed. The Furies had a grip such as this. My muscles spasm.

"Miss Betts, I take it?"

I look up at the woman digging her fingers into my shoulder. Large black hat. Auburn hair coiled and pinned, wisps falling along her heart-shaped face. An English rose. The kind of woman men went to war for. Men fought to come home for. Or so the war posters told us. "Mrs. Carburry."

Her smile is small, tense, a flash of grit white teeth. "I wonder if you might join me for tea." She has a gin and tonic sort of voice, dry, bitter, intoxicating.

"Now?" I gesture to the court proceedings. Nick's barrister is waving his hands so aggressively, I can't tell if he's emphasizing a point or pantomiming the Battle of Agincourt.

"Why not? It seems the men will accomplish very little today—yet again." On the last note, she adds a twist of lemon to her gin and tonic voice. "Better for the two of us to move on to brass tacks."

"Brass tacks?"

"Military phrase. Something I assume you're not well-versed in."

"I served as a nurse in France."

"Noble, I'm sure. But medicine is not military, is it?" She directs the words to me, but her gaze, furious and pained, accusatory and sorrowful, is focused entirely on Nick. An unnerving energy sizzles so intensely between them, the air hisses. But not with animosity. There's something intimate in the way Nick shakes his head to her. There's something tender in the way she responds with a nod. There's a history between them. And the tension scorching the air is not the accusation of murder. It's far more subtle. It is of a promise broken.

With its faded pink rose patterned china and chipped wooden chairs, the café Mrs. Carburry has directed me to has the feel of old warm charm, a place that existed before war, when the world was gentle, now worn and tired. It is also, notably, the most expensive café within a five-block radius of the court.

We take our seats and make our orders. Gentlewomen to the core, we each peel off our gloves and place them to the side, making quiet study of one another, bare knuckled. Papa has a set of strict social rules, useful for hostile teas. But I was a terrible pupil and cannot remember whether I am supposed to discuss the weather or muse on the hunting season. Mrs. Carburry breaks off a piece of scone, slathers it in clotted cream, and devours it with a rapaciousness that is near wolfish.

"I like your charm," I try, indicating the gold and enamel case jewel dangling from her throat. Papa would know whether it came from Bond Street or Petticoat Lane. He has an eye for the petty.

"It's a locket," comes her reply, before she breaks off another chunk of scone.

"Are they not one and the same?"

"A locket is a subset of a pendant.," she says. "It goes around the neck. A charm is smaller. It goes on a bracelet. It's important to be precise."

"With jewelry?"

"With language. Lest there be any misunderstanding." She runs her thumb along the edge of her locket, like it's the most precious thing she owns, and like she's appraising its value as a bargaining chip. "You don't strike me as a nurse."

"I have a young face." I deliver a baby-cheeked smile to her.

"I don't doubt you're hovering close to thirty," she says drily. "It's your voice. Where are you from?"

"My Northern accent got lost in the war. Gun blast and lizzies." I twirl my finger in the air, as if the German bombers had been merely amusing, not deafening.

"You misunderstand. I was raised in India—my father was a Major General. We used to listen to records for the elocution of a proper lady. 'Oh what a to-do to die today/At a minute or two to two.'" She pauses and takes in my confused expression. "It's from *Merrie England*. The operetta?"

I shake my head.

"No, you wouldn't know it. Wouldn't need to, not you. Some people have to learn how to navigate the King's vowels. Some are born to it. North, South, Middlesex, doesn't matter. You've the voice for commanding a manor full of servants."

"I strike you as a housekeeper?" I ask, all too gleeful.

"Your turban is a bit dear for below stairs, isn't it?"

"It's a hat."

She selects a second scone and adds a healthy dollop of jam to her plate. "Continental shaped, blue velvet, no doubt one hundred percent silk. That pom-pom is mink, not rabbit. Not quite *au courant*, though. Selfridge's carried a similar style last spring."

"I've never been to Selfridge's." Papa is strictly Harvey Nichols, the one department store where he deems the number of stitches per an inch of hem worthy of his pounds. But I will give Mrs. Carburry her due, she has an eye for the trivial that rivals Papa. The hat is Gwendolyn's and is indeed last season's. It's why my sister didn't care when I pinched it.

Mrs. Carburry sets down her knife. "Do you know what you'd find if you opened to any page in *Burke's Peerage*?"

"A potential employer?"

Her laugh is tightly leashed. "You think yourself clever, don't you? Head girl at some posh finishing school. Snuck out a few windows, did you? Smoke a fag or two? Your rebellion doesn't make you special, it proves you're inconsequential, the girl your parents had along the way to begetting the proper heir and the hedge-your-bets spare. *Burke's* is littered with such daughters."

The facts are wrong, but the assessment isn't. I raise my teacup to her, a mocking toast.

"And then, hallelujah, along comes the War and suddenly you have a purpose, fluttering about like the lady with the lamp and thinking yourself to be one of those romanticized figures Lady Randolph Churchill so liked to write about."

"'The speaker was a young girl,'" I quote, "'and her outlook on life had assumed a new and marvelous focus.'"

"Every VAD from Northumberland to Lizard Point thinks that line describes her."

"Lady Randolph Churchill wrote it after visiting Lady Sullivan's ambulance hospital. Where I was a nurse."

Lady Carbury dismisses my pride with a smirk. "Soldiers get shot. It's part of their job. You weren't angels. You weren't healers. You were no better than a succubus, using another man's pain to make yourselves matter. But go ahead and congratulate yourself on your prowess for wiping brows."

"Arses too." My sarcasm is intact, but not my armor. The steam rising from my teacup smells not of Darjeeling, but of a necrotic, severed foot.

"The war is over. We won, as per."

"Order is restored?" Queasy, I swallow my tea and hope the hot liquid burns through the rot.

"Don't be ridiculous. Our army is two-hundred-and-sixty years old. What looks like chaos to a civilian is strategy to the soldier."

"'Theirs but to do and die.'"

"Aren't you chock full of quotes." There's something savage about the way Mrs. Carbury tears through her third scone. Perhaps she skipped breakfast.

"I know 'The Charge of the Light Brigade' because a fellow nurse, Fukimoto, recited it, while your husband invented a brutal lie that destroyed her."

"The rank and file may not understand the tactics, but they follow their duty. That is the way of things."

"Oh, did the Major write of his tactics in his many letters to you?" I take a mulish pleasure in seeing her clutch her locket. Major Carburry never wrote his wife. Treacly sweet, I ask, "Whose photo is in the locket?"

She snaps it open, daring me to look, likely praying I turn into a pillar of salt. I take in a tinctured photo of a toddler. Curly auburn hair, brown eyes, pink cheeks. She watches me the way Gwendolyn does when she talks of Matty, like I am supposed to be awestruck by the vision of a child who looks like any other child. Cherubic, healthy, distant.

"He's thirteen now," she says.

"Shouldn't you replace the baby photo?"

"You're obviously not a mother. People say my son favors me. Except for the eyes. That shade of brown is all his father's. Spirited and clever, he's passionate about history and cricket. And while he swears by his independence, he will occasionally send me a letter with a pressed flower inside."

In Mrs. Carburry's particular brand of motherhood, her son is both her love and her weapon. She wields him against me as if he makes her morally superior. "Away at school," I say.

"Duke of York. Where his father went. Where his father's father went."

"Tradition."

"Military," she corrects.

"I suppose he's lucky to come from a long line of heroes."

"It's not a matter of luck. It's a matter of lineage." She taps her polished nail against her glove, the black leather absorbing the *tap, tap* of her red lacquer and a realization, as pleasant as an electric shock, jolts me. I *am* my father's daughter. I too have an eye for the trivial. The black of her leather gloves bears the marks of a paintbrush; she's had to dye them, more than once. She doesn't have a healthy appetite. She's devouring her scones because she's foregone breakfast and lunch. When we leave this table, I will be the one to pay the bill. She's barely surviving on a widow's pension and her husband's legacy.

"As I was saying, Miss Betts, there is an order to things."

"Rank and file."

"Your doctor –"

"He's a lieutenant colonel. In the British Royal Army Medical Corps." A small jab. In military parlance, Nick outranks Carburry. I wait for her contemptuous response.

Instead, she nods her respect. "We each have our duty."

"And what is Colonel Wallace's? To have killed your husband or to hang for it? For that matter, what was Major Carburry's? To return from war or die a hero?"

With her forefinger, she chases a crumb along the flowered rim of her plate and exhales a smug, "Ah."

"Eureka," I snap back.

"You're rather like Colonel Wallace, aren't you? A crusader. The first time I saw him, standing in court, so handsome and straight-shouldered, so full of purpose, he reminded me of one of those Methodist ministers who trek off to Africa to convert the godless. Very brave. Full of integrity. Though, of course, it tends to end rather badly. One gets eaten by the natives."

"A hero's death?"

"Renegade's, more like."

"There's a difference?"

She lets out a puff of exasperation. "You really must attend to the nuances of our language. A hero is one who follows the rules to achieve a greater good."

139

"Like a commanding officer who loses every single one of his men in battle, but manages to survive?"

Her sigh is an untroubled *is that the best you can do?* "A renegade breaks the rules and suffers the consequences. Methodists shouldn't be traipsing through the savannah. Dr. Wallace himself would admit he had no right to be maneuvering outside of his operating theatre. He meant well. Crusaders always do. But one cannot subvert the regimental order of the British Royal Army. We are, none of us, more powerful than the whole."

"Why not?"

She blinks at me, baffled, as if I'd questioned God himself. Well, in her case, military.

Recovering, she asks, "What's one person?" She sweeps her hand across the café, gesturing to an old judge dunking his bread in his soup, the harried waitress wiping crumbs off a table.

All I see are fields and fields of mud, boy after boy falling to the ground, legs twitching even after the heart has stopped. So many. MacAvoy. Arthur. And always, always, Flaherty, his severed foot, and his too young voice, *You read to me.* I am not one person. An army of ghosts lives within me.

Would you rather they wander the earth restlessly? Nick asked me once. We were lovers by then, and we had just lost a patient, the one Nick had sketched the night we'd traced the cosmos. I had wept with unexpected fury. Gripped by grief for not any one death, but for the pointlessness of all of them. *Let them rest with you,* he'd said. *And you can rest with me. Together, we are never just one.*

I run the back of my hand against my cheek, surprised to find it's dry. "Do you know Colonel Wallace?"

"Obviously. He killed my husband."

"Before, I mean."

"Before he killed him?" She cannot hide the pleasure she takes in these small stabs. I can practically hear the extra splash of gin in her voice. "No. But after my husband died, you can say we struck up a . . . correspondence."

I focus on the scone I have not touched. A lump of flour, butter and sugar. "You wrote to him?"

"Don't be silly. He wrote to us."

"Us?"

A hesitation. She covers by taking a sip of tea. "My son."

"Ah," I say, "eureka," and swallow the bitter taste of understanding. Who other than Nick would murder a man and still do right by the man's son? No matter how evil, how corrupt the father, Nick, whose own father killed himself, would write to reassure the boy, full-knowing his act of honor would be used against him.

I feign a yawn. "No doubt he spoke of how nobly the Major comported himself in the face of his injuries. How inspiring he was to his fellow wounded soldiers. That kind of nonsense?"

Mrs. Carburry folds her hands together, a graceful motion, while she eyes the sugar glistening off my untouched scone.

To spite her, I crush it until it is nothing but a heap of dust. "Let me correct the misconception. I will skip over his pathetic whining, the way he sulked about and was inspiration to no man since nowhere in your definition of *hero* did you use the word *noble*. Instead, some blunt facts."

She squares her face, juts her chin out.

"Your husband introduced Colonel Wallace to picric acid bombs, timed devices that caused explosions. Some thought to use them to sabotage strategic sights, a weapon for victory. Others as a quixotic attempt to end the war—blow up the hospitals and Germany and England would see the pointlessness of war and lay down their arms. I'll let you pick which path Major Carburry chose. But either one makes him less a hero and more a...*renegade*. Do I have the word right?"

She sets down her cup with brittle force. "*Colonel* Wallace understands he is but one man and no man, not even parliament, can bring down the army."

"Is your child not merely one person?"

"He is the son, grandson, and great grandson of army men. He is the future."

"Rather a narrow view."

"How arrogant you are, in your youth—"

"You thought me well close to thirty—"

"—I almost pity you."

"I fully pity you."

Her face contorts, the façade of the brave, grieving, widow collapses, to reveal the starving, wounded animal she is. But she is not broken. Far from it. She uses the pain as a source of strength. When she smiles at me, she bares her fangs.

"Ask yourself, child, where is Colonel Wallace's brother today?" Her voice is deceptively calm, near maternal. I can imagine her tucking me back into bed after a nightmare, kissing my forehead. *There are no big bad wolves*, she would coo. Before biting into my throat.

She says, "Who could be so influential, so powerful, that he could remove the Home Secretary's right-hand man from the proceedings? No one man. Rather, an institution. A Court Martial is separate from the civil and criminal courts because it is army. The jury is all men of the army. The board knows when it is obligated to convict. They may not individually know the greater good, but the army does. There will be no more machinations from the Home Secretary's Office. There will be no more indulgent evenings resting in the infirmary. Your physician will be where he belongs, in prison, by the afternoon. Because that is what the army requires. And he will not fight it. He hasn't fought a single step of this process, because he understands what you fail to. The army is right. Always. He is following his duty."

She sits back in her chair. The façade has returned. Her plump red lips are arranged in a maternal pout. She holds her head and shoulders as if she survives on dignity alone. And I have been a stupid, arrogant, bloody damned fool. She lured me to tea to remove me from the Court Martial. To leave Nick on his own, to do what he thinks is right, no matter how wrong he is.

I jerk up from the table, toss down a handful of coins. "Those are for the waitress, not you," I warn, and rush out of the restaurant. She doesn't follow me, but as I pound up the sidewalk, cut across the street, dodge between speeding motor cars and a honking omnibus, and push through the black-coated crowds to the Royal Courts of Justice, I can hear her laughing at me.

Once inside, my heart is beating fast and my legs are primed to run, but my brain tells me to be still, to pace myself on the slippery floors of the marbled halls of justice. I open the heavy wooden doors of the Court Martial quietly, to not draw attention. The air I draw through my lungs is tense and dry, no oxygen. The Judge Advocate has left the bench, the board is filing out.

Master James grabs me at the elbow. "This Court Martial is a stitch up." He curves his mouth, cynicism chasing away his youth. "I suspect you already knew that. Why is this trial being held *ad hoc* in London in the first place? Why the Royal Crown Court? Criminal proceedings take place at the Old Bailey."

"I don't know," I answer flatly.

"He fired his barrister," says Master James, allowing the accusation to bubble up from under his Jersey Island accent. *You shouldn't have gone to tea.* As if tea were a simple affair, not an act of aggression. "He wrote his confession."

"Did I not tell you to withhold your pen?"

"He made a motion to be granted one. The Judge Advocate was so punched pleased, he loaned him his personal gold-plated from the house of Parker. They're taking him to prison. He *requested* he be confined in HMP Brixton." He studies me. "Do you understand what

Brixton is?"

Never one to shirk the gruesome, I shake my head.

"A death sentence. There's an influenza epidemic."

Nick is standing between two guards, his shoulders squared, his hands cuffed, and walking toward the side exit with purpose, not a man marching to the gallows. Someone who didn't know him would say was accepting the vagaries of fate. Except Nick doesn't believe in fate. He believes in the individual. And his gait is one of triumph, like he's reclaimed his halo.

"Not a death sentence. A last grasp at his humanity," I say bitterly. "He will play the physician in his prison stripes." My eyes sting. I can barely watch Nick, and yet I cannot stop. How stupidly I lost. To Mrs. Carburry. To her precious Royal Army. To institutions older than my paltry life experience. "Well, I suppose you have your front-page headline."

"Hardly. He wrote a one sentence allocution: On the thirteenth of August 1918, I Nicholas Wallace, physician and lieutenant colonel in the British Royal Army, injected Major Guy Harrison Carburry with a lethal dose of morphia."

"Morphia?" A strange seasickness takes over me. My feet grip the floor as if I'm trying to keep my balance on a rocking ship in the middle of a storm, rain slamming against the windows, salt air stinging my nostrils. I am back on board the ship docking into East Sussex, fighting off Major Carburry. His gold wedding ring sparks beneath the tinny electric lights. I wince from the sharpness of the light. From the feel of his hand crushing my mouth.

Shhh. Shhh.

I touch my cheek. Is it bruised?

"You lied to me, Miss Betts. This story isn't about Colonel Wallace and it's not about Major Carburry. They're bit players. This story is about war."

Shhh. Shhh.

Dare I speak? What will I destroy? Is there anything left to destroy? So much. Despite the irritation in James' voice, his face is baby smooth, still a child's.

"War is easy." My tongue moves slowly, reluctant and unsure. "Peace is hard. Go back to Silvertown and ask McMannis about an explosion at Lady Sullivan's Ambulance Hospital. Look for records on a German POW who attended Cambridge, Hildebrand from East Frisia. Dig through old news reports regarding explosions and fires— accidental or not so accidental. Look at libraries, civil building, hospitals. Especially hospitals. Educate yourself on timed picric acid bombs."

"Are you mad? You're suggesting a plot to sabotage medical facilities? For the sake of peace?"

"You haven't been to battle. You don't know the sound of grown men, screaming for their missing foot, their lost hand. Crying for their mam. Or the stench. Do you know what we did with all those severed limbs? We burned them. Cheap incinerator. The wind would blow the smoke straight into our lungs."

Master James pales and draws away from me. My memory turns his stomach. Lucky him. At least he did not live it. Nick did. And across the stifling heat of this courtroom, he must feel my shiver for he pauses just before he exits and turns to me, his expression so gentle, so full of love, so infinitely him, the finality of it tears through me.

In the stretch of space between us—a hundred feet? A thousand miles—memory pulls me back to the ship heading toward East Sussex. I taste the damp, salt air, suffocate beneath the weight of Major Carburry as he bears down on me, recall the flash of metal. A hypodermic needle, sharp, rolling off the silver tray, hitting the floor, skittering into a corner. Not morphia.

Relief from seasickness. That's what I promised Carburry. A sedative.

But there was no sedating the beast. He was wild, clawing. He'd found his legs.

I clutch my face, trying to pry fingers from my mouth, though the man suffocating me is a figment of my memory and dead. My hands shake, like they did that night. When I loaded the needle.

What had I said when Nick burst into the room and wrenched the Major off of me, commanding me to grab my valise and go ashore? My lip was bleeding, my cheek was bruised, I put the needle back on its silver tray, the liquid clear and comforting. Not morphia. A lethal dose of potassium chloride.

I said nothing.

The papers didn't report how the Major died. I thought, prayed, that Nick had strangled him. Slit his throat, something violent and out of character. At least then I could save Nick. But how can I save the man I love when he thinks he is saving me?

Nick. His name is barely an exhalation over the broken sob lodged in my throat. I can't release the single syllable.

He answers me, mouthing the words he whispered into my ear before he shoved identity papers into my hand that held my real name and thrust me back onto English soil, into the safety of my family's coat of arms. Then, I thought his words a romantic turn of phrase, that he would be lost without me, that he would find me. Now, I understand what the words truly mean. I throw my arms up to cover my face. *Don't look at me.* I am nothing more than the daughter my parents had between their perfect Gwendolyn and their heir. I'm not worth his sacrifice.

"*Je suis perdu,*" he promises.

CHAPTER TWELVE

Wimereux, June 1918

The moon is rising above the pine trees, a pregnant, glowing yellow. When I break into the clearing, Colonel Wallace does not turn. He skips a stone across the smooth surface of the small lake. *"Vous êtes perdu, mademoiselle?"* His question rolls out on a low, seductive laugh.

"Of course I'm not lost," I say huffily. I followed him deliberately. To know where he was going in the middle of the night. To stop him or help him or understand him, or perhaps just to see him.

He stoops to select another stone and gives me a sidelong glance before he tosses it, curving his arm as if he is measuring the resistance of the air. Even out of water, he moves like a swimmer. "The proper response is *Je ne suis pas perdu.* Weren't you given the military-issue French phrase book whilst crossing the Channel?"

"What is the point of asking a question in French if you can't understand the answer?" I come to stand beside him. The breeze across the lake is gentle, whispering of summer. "I will ask *Où suis-je?* But when a Frenchman responds *Mouquet Farm,* I'll search the map for *Moo Cow Farm.*"

He laughs again, an easy, tired, bittersweet sound. "I doubt you are ever lost, Vera-not-Vera. You may not know where you are going, but you certainly know where you are. Whereas I fear I am becoming more and more lost." He steals a too-long glance at me, smiles down at his boots. "Except when you are near."

Despite the knocking of my knees, I make a valiant attempt to be no-nonsense. "Were you not issued a map when you crossed the Channel?"

"One needs to recognize a landmark to know where he is on a map. And I recognize very little these days." He runs his hand across his face, as if even his own skin is unfamiliar. "Besides, we're at war. The map lines keep changing hands—Passchendaele is lost to the Germans. No it's won back by the Brits."

"One doesn't need a map for this war, one needs a ruler to measure the incremental one inch forward two inches backward of Flanders Field."

"No Man's Land grows larger by the day," he agrees.

"It shall swallow us whole."

"Not on my watch." He speaks quietly, almost nonchalantly, but the force of his conviction makes me shudder. He is mad. He is a fool. No one can stop the insanity of nations. Not even the nations themselves. Rather than argue, we watch the moon, which may wane, but will return always to wax. It casts its bright and cheery light against the gloom of the darkening wood.

"No maps and no French phrases book, then," I say. "I had a Spanish dance master who insisted we navigate the ballroom blindfolded."

"I did not realize Spaniards would travel so far *North*." The right corner of his lip turns up. He is teasing me. "And how did you fare with your waltz?"

"I don't know. I have only danced once." With Jerome at my parents' annual London ball. "And I was an awkward limbed girl of fifteen."

Despite my black boots, sensible stockings and the thick cotton of my skirt, he follows the line of my legs from ankle to hip. His gaze is slow, steady, heated. My belly goes warm, soft.

He says, "There is nothing awkward about your limbs."

I give him a proper-maiden's snort.

"Truly. I have never known a creature to move like you. As if you only have two speeds. Full-tilt run and absolute stillness." He bows to me, a gallant gentleman in coattails kind of dip. "I should like to know, Miss Vera-not-Vera, do you have any other speeds?"

According to the beat of my heart, I do not. "We have no music."

"We have the moon."

His answer makes no sense. The moon does not have a bow and strings. It makes no sound that reaches the ears of mere mortals. And yet, my stiff hips loosen and sway. His right hand comes across my left shoulder, my right hand falls into his left. In his hold, in the rhythm of his box step, I am not awkward and clumsy. I am fluid, as if I were in water. A sense of ownership comes over me—my body is both my own and connected to his. Each pore is vibrant and aware of the cool night air enveloping us, the sharp scent of pine blending with the musk of earthy loam and fallen leaves. The thick callus of his finger pad against mine are a match, lighting a growing fire within me. My skin is alive, these woods and this man a sea I am diving into. Deeper and deeper. I need never break through the surface. The cinnamon warmth of his exhalation is my oxygen. Beneath this musical moon full of possibilities, I know exactly where I am.

In over my head.

He releases my shoulder, but not my hand. Our fingers stay intertwined. The moon reflects our connected shadows across the lake. A breeze rustles through the trees. We stand drinking one another in, our eyes locked. A distant clock strikes the half hour, a warning. The rest of the world may be falling into bed, but midnight is coming and with it my shift.

"Best lead me back," he says.

Hand in hand, we walk along the overgrown path. An owl hoots. As if in answer, a family of rabbits scamper through the brush. Our boots crunch along the forest floor, drumming a quiet beat. We are part of the night's song. We do not speak. Words would fail us.

From a forgotten well within me, a primal emotion overtakes me, familiar in the way dreams are familiar and yet distant. Something I have longed for, but have never until this moment held. I tighten my hold on Colonel Wallace's hand. He presses his fingers against me, the shock and thrill of the strength within his surgeon's hands electric. His touch travels from my fingertips, up my arms, spills down my spine, pools in my belly, in the places where I am most feminine.

We are careful to keep walking. Not to stop. Not to give in to the myth of moon song, the all too human need for touch, for connection. Like Bootes forever chasing Ursa Major across the Milky Way, we know better than to cross the lines on the map we've drawn. Safer to stay in place, leave the cosmos as is.

Danger creeps through in the snap of a fallen branch. The forest seizes. Colonel Wallace stiffens. We step apart. I too smell tobacco.

A voice, low and rough, utters harsh, foreign syllables. They sound like a command. They sound like *halt*.

No. Not *halt*.

Hallo.

A greeting.

In German.

Colonel Wallace whispers into my ear—*run*—and whips around on his heel. I stand as if pinned in place. A man breaks out of the thicket. Stocky, thick muscled, no uniform to mark which side of the war he's on. Mud tracks along the hem of his pants. He's walked miles, crossed map lines.

Colonel Wallace shifts his stance, positions himself like he means to block me from view. Or block the man from mine. The man raises his hand. To strike? To shake hands? It is impossible to tell because despite the tension radiating off of Colonel Wallace's shoulders, despite the way he curls and uncurls his fists, his stance is not that of a man

150

caught off guard. It is almost as if he had been expecting him.

The man eyes me. His first expression seems to be one of amusement, a quirk of an eyebrow, like he's stumbled across a lover's tryst. Something innocent. He tugs the shoulder strap of his leather satchel, thoughtfully. Colonel Wallace splays his feet, and the man's expression slides into a grin—smug, threatening. He has assessed me. I am leverage.

What is in the satchel?

Again comes Colonel Wallace's low, urgent voice, "Run."

I stand frozen. A rabbit caught in the lamplight. A woman trapped—not by love, I am too jaded for sentiment—but a halo. I can't move.

A pair of hands grasp my shoulders, spin me fast to face the ornate, yellow-stoned chateau. Commands me, "Go."

The German lunges forward. Nick grabs him by the arm and I hear the sickening crack of human bone. The German screams. My stomach curdles.

"Run, dammit. Run."

And I race.

✺

I am bleary eyed, climbing the steps. My uniform is soaked with sweat—mine—and vomit. One of the patients in Ward One suffered a seizure in the night. I had to awaken Dr. Jonna as Colonel Wallace could not be found. How could he be? I left him in the woods, breaking the arm of a German. With his bare hands. Even now, I want to be sick.

I yank off my apron, crumple it in a ball. I reach for the bannister to drag my exhausted body up the third flight.

Lazy as a fat cat, a patient in a wheelchair suns himself by a window on the second floor. He rotates his wheelchair around and greets me. "Well good morning, Nurse Betts. You look as if you haven't slept a wink."

"Major Carburry, as you well know, I have the night shift."

"But not with me." He pouts and rolls his chair forward. "Don't be a spoilsport, Nurse Betts, and begrudge me a cheery morning chat." He stretches his arms. "Last night's full moon was magic, was it not? The thing love stories are made of!"

"Reading Shakespeare?"

He chuckles. "Don't be silly. Neither you nor I are readers. We're people of action."

I glance meaningfully at his immobilized legs. It's a cruel thing to do. I should regret my pettiness.

"That delicious cherry bonbon, Rosling—"

"Matron—"

"—assures me I'll find my legs. And just you wait, missy, for when I do, I will delight in giving you a chase."

I take another step up the stairs.

He calls out. "Though you are, I shall confess, a remarkable runner. A sight to behold. Especially at night. Beneath the full moon."

I'm smart enough not to stumble, but I'm so tired my legs want to buckle. I hitch my hip to the bannister, adopting a nonchalant pose.

"Do you know my bedroom window overlooks the treelined path? I am told it leads to a darling little lake. Ahh the romance of an evening stroll. Night air. The scent of the woods. Jasmine and whatnot." He sighs dramatically.

"I thought you more of a Creed man."

With a thoughtful lowering of his heavy lids, he reappraises me. It seems the cat forgot that his mouse has claws of her own. "I must confess to a certain level of heightened concern, Nurse Betts, as I witnessed you stumbling out from the woods as if you'd experienced an unpleasant encounter. Tell me, did Saint Wallace turn out to be the devil? Shall I challenge him to a duel? My legs may be indisposed, but my aim is still deadly."

I furrow my brows and ask, "Why would Colonel Wallace be in the woods?"

"Why indeed? If not to have a romantic assignation with you, my virgin queen?"

"If, as you claim, you saw me exiting the woods, then you saw me doing so alone."

"Because you fought off your erstwhile paramour? Thwacked him with a tree branch, perhaps? Left him with a broken bone or two?"

Tossing out my very best doe-eyed-nurse look of concern, I say, "What a fevered imagination you have. I worry you may be fighting an infection. Shall we take a rectal temperature?"

The Major curls his lip, a snarled, but begrudging touché.

A yawn overcomes me. "You'll excuse me if I don't linger. The sun may mean the beginning of the day for you, but for me, it's the end."

"Night duty."

I am halfway through a nod before the Major cuts in with, "Where was Colonel Wallace during your shift?"

His question is a snare looping round my ankle. "According to you, he was thwacked by a virgin and left for dead."

From his wheelchair, Major Carburry contemplates the three oak steps separating us. He does not need legs to traverse the distance. "Let us put aside our spirited repartee, shall we? Last night, while you were on duty, did you not ring for Colonel Wallace? To attend to a patient? And did he not fail to appear? So that you were forced to wake Dr. Jonna? Who, by all accounts, is a rather difficult man to rouse."

Despite my stubborn bravado, exhaustion has left me threadbare, susceptible to innuendo and misgivings. What if Colonel Wallace had been waiting to meet the German? Why? "I do not keep Colonel Wallace's diary."

"Lucky for you, I am a stickler for record keeping." Major Carburry rifles through a canvas bag hanging off the arm of his chair and pulls out a notebook. He holds it up to me, the pages open. "Note the dates? They mark each time Colonel Wallace has disappeared from his precious hospital, allegedly to retrieve a spinal patient. Within the exact same period there happens to occur a report of a mysterious explosion. Always at a medical facility." He taps at his notebook.

"Perhaps you should put your little gold pen to better use with the crossword. The other patients have been complaining you get most of the answers wrong."

"A puzzle indeed. Bombs go off, facilities burn down, and yet not a single injury. What kind of saboteur ensures there is no loss of life?"

I shrug my shoulders to disguise a nod. I cannot permit myself to agree with Major Carburry. Even if he is right.

"I have traced these occurrences back to Lady Sullivan's Hospital. Wallace was there when the marquees exploded."

"As were you."

"How I do appreciate your overestimation of my skills. I was crippled. And drugged."

"Major Carburry, you are talking nonsense. Which I will attribute to the effect of the narcotics on your brain. You cannot go about Colonel Wallace's hospital bandying the idea that he is a nefarious operative secretly destroying the very institutions he upholds. He'd more likely sever his own spine than betray the Hippocratic Oath."

"Even I have a soft spot for Saint Wallace, as he has rebuilt my knees. However, he is on a fool's errand. His father was a pacifist. He must be on some mad path to accomplish what his father could not."

"And you think this a weakness?"

"Peace is not within our nature. Humans are designed to fight."

"For what outcome?"

Like a disappointed teacher, he casts me a resigned shake of the head. "We don't dance because there is a purpose. We dance because the orchestra has struck up a minuet."

I imitate a marionette on a string, moving my limbs to the imaginary sound of a shrill violin. My head hurts so much I almost see starbursts.

I am saved by Fukimoto, who hurries up to the stairs, her cheeks flushed pink from the exertion. "You have a telegram. From New York. It must be urgent."

She hands me the envelope and casts a sidelong glance at Major Carburry. Her dislike of him is so sharp, it changes the tang of the air. She asks him, "Shall I squire you back to your solitude?"

"It's the German, Hildebrand, who is isolated." He matches her acid tone. "I am free to wander as I please."

I turn my back to both of them, and rip open the telegram. It is from my cousin Kristina:

Tad. 7 bullets. Wimereux Base Hospital 1.

My brother is dying.

✦

When I leave Fukimoto and Major Carburry on the landing, I am numb. I cannot parse out the waves of emotion rolling through me. The sound of cracking bone echoes in my ears, tips me off my balance. As does a pain, sharp and barbed. My mischievous, joyful brother is barely eighteen, too gangly and young to survive seven bullets.

Unable to think, no music to follow, I obey my feet, which drive me not to my room but to Col Wallace's office. I am done playing with insinuations. If he is a traitor, I need to know. If he is as good as I believe him to be, I need proof. The sick, purposeful cruelty of this war is ripping my heart out. I cannot hang on any longer without a hand I can trust.

At his office door, I pull a hairpin from my cap and pick the lock. Child's play. The office and his bedchamber beyond are empty. The fire is banked. The window open. My footfall against the woven carpet echoes against the walls. Books are stacked next to the fireplace.

Across one wall hangs a long chalkboard. He has listed patients' names, their ward number, and drawn diagrams of spines, pinpointing the injuries. Dotted lines map surgeries he is planning, how to reconnect nerves. Beside these diagrams are percentages, the odds the surgery will be a success. Sixty percent; forty-five; thirty. Nowhere is Major Carbury's treatment plan listed.

His desk sits tidy, organized, even the pens are separated by color. I pull the drawers open, one by one. None are locked. This office is open and trusting, it is where he wears his physician's coat, where he is the man he wants to be. It's his bedroom where he hides his secrets.

The bed has not been slept in. Already, evidence of guilt. I open his wardrobe, starched uniforms, crisp shirts, even his undershirts are ironed. His boots, three pairs, are polished. The drawer beneath holds neatly folded long johns. I rub the fabric between my thumb and forefinger. Practical wool. A little rough.

At his nightstand sits a glass of water and a photograph. I grab it, daring it to be a woman. It is of an empty beach cove, surrounded by pine trees. The colors may be cold, but the photographer infused warmth in the photo, sentiment. The heat of a summer's day touches my fingertips.

With no other drawers to open, I drop to the floor, pull up the coverlet and search beneath his bed. Underneath, it's too dark to separate shadow from discovery, so I thrust my arm through the empty space and know I will hit something because I do not run across cobwebs or dust. This dark space has been well-maintained. My palm hits upon something leather bound. A notebook. I drag it out from under the bed. It's his sketchbook.

A frisson of shock prickles me when I find a face I recognize. My own. The eyes are wideset, mischievous, world-wise. He's captured my nose, the long, straight bridge, the unexpected bulb that makes it too round to be aristocratic. Papa accused it of being Liverpudlian, a snide reference to Mama's Blackpond roots. The sketch is accurate, and yet there is more to the face than just me. There is an *us*. Or the hope of one. Each stroke of his pencil amounts to a caress.

I shut the cover, guilty. Why am I letting Major Carburry's words insinuate themselves into my tired brain? I should not be doubting Colonel Wallace. I shove the book back beneath his bed, and in doing so, hit the edge of something else. Stretching my arm till I think it may come off its tendons, I grab a corner of an open box and drag it into the light. Inside are letters addressed to people in England, but not yet sealed.

I open the first to find a sketch of one of the men in Ward Three. Sergeant Davey Parker, patient thirty-five percent. In the crinkle of the left eye and the curve of mouth, Colonel Wallace has captured the man's subversive sense of humor. Even in the haze of pain, Parker is always treating us to a bad pun, or as he likes to call them a *bed pun*. Another sketch is of patient twenty-two percent. The sleeping patient from the night the Colonel and I traced the cosmos. He looks out at the viewer with half-hooded eyes and gaunt cheeks that speak of suffering, but also resolve. I open envelope after envelope, and find sketch after sketch of men whose chances of surviving surgery are less than fifty percent. By the addresses on the envelopes, I know Colonel Wallace means to send these drawings to the men's loved ones. Despite the intricate surgical chart and treatment plan, Colonel Wallace is bracing himself for their deaths.

Grief spikes and pours forth in an ugly set of tears.

No one will draw my brother. The letter my mother receives will be earnest, but impersonal.

My Red Cross uniform makes me invisible. I am not a person who shouldn't be striding through the halls of Wimereux Base Hospital One. When I stop the ward matron to request an update on the status of Captain Halladay, she doesn't pause, reporting his vital signs, complaining about being understaffed, and commenting "Poor lad. He's lost so much blood, he won't make it through the night without a transfusion. And we've a shortage." She predicts my brother's death like she's noting an afternoon drizzle.

My brother's blood type is O Negative. Not the rarest, but rare. Papa takes a certain pride in the distinction, believing it to be biological proof of Halladay exceptionalism. Purple blood, if you will. Papa is not entirely wrong. Type O Negative is special. It is the most useful of bloods because it is universal. On the field, we use it to triage anyone regardless of individual blood type. At Lady Sullivan's, we always had a healthy supply. Because I am a Halladay. And my blood runs purple.

The ward my brother has been left to die in is full, but quiet. I find a meek looking VAD, a girl fresh off of a biscuit tin village existence, whose only medical experience is rolling bandages. So as not to betray my trembling fingers, I use my firmest voice, thoroughly devoid of emotion, and request a blood transfusion kit. The VAD nods and trots off to retrieve it, returning without so much as an ounce of doubt. What faith she has in me.

The kit is my first precarious step toward failure. It is not like the ones we used at Lady Sullivan's, where treatment required us to be single-handed miracle workers. This one is a luxury item, the kind where one has time to draw blood from a donor, use anti-coagulants to remove clogging, warm the blood to the right temperature, and then infuse it into the patient. To succeed, one must employ thought, not adrenaline. And at least two extra sets of hands.

My pulse pounds a slapdash, stuttered rhythm of panic. Above the thud, I instruct the VAD to set up a privacy screen around Captain Halladay's bed. The words—*captain* and *Halladay* are so foreign to me, so divided from the boy who splashed alongside me in the river by

Halsop House, the one who connected me to my family, I almost forget he is my brother.

My delivery of the strange words must have been convincing, though. The VAD eagerly jumps into action and when she naively turns her back, I pocket two hypodermic needles and a bottle of Novocain. The steps I take from her station desk to my brother's bed are excruciating. My boots seem weighted down by lead. No one at this hospital is going to save my brother. I, however, may end up killing him.

At his bedside, I nod a dismissal to the VAD and step behind the screen. My brother is not much beyond a grey face fading in and out life. Stitches and scars and open sores tell the story of bullets and infection. The pain would make a body scream in fury, but morphia has rendered Tad unconscious. He feels nothing. Not even sunlight. At least he breathes.

I hear the VAD talking to someone else, another woman, one whose voice carries more authority. Her firm footsteps act as effectively as gunfire. My nursing brain takes charge, sending my skittish nerves back to their station. I flick the tender skin on the inside of Tad's elbow and am rewarded with the blue outline of his median basilic vein.

I unpack the kit and lay it out on the standing metal tray: tubes, needles, glass flask. There is no other chair or worktable for this task. I am going to have to perform the transfusion one-handed, standing up, with gravity serving as both my friend and my enemy. Gravity will pull the blood from me to Tad quickly. A single slip and the equipment will crash to the floor.

Listening for the threat of a valid nurse poking her head behind the screen, I remove the cuff of my left sleeve, roll it up past my forearm, and load each of the hypodermic needles with a small amount of Novocain. I clean my brother's inner elbow. Then mine. Every hospital bed in a base hospital has a tourniquet belt. I pull the one beside Tad, wrap it tight around my left arm. Plunge the Novocain into my skin to numb the area. A slight pinch, it burns enough I bite my cheek.

I lance a needle into the cut, and my blood pours out through the rubber tube attached to the needle and collects in the Robinson flask. It sits on the wobbly metal tray table. My left arm immobile, I stretch out my right, and stab my brother with Novocain, to which he reacts not at all. With only the use of my right hand, I have to dissect out Tad's vein, insert the cannula into it so we are connected by tubes and blood.

There are steps I am missing. I should be sitting lest I become dizzy. I should ask for help. *For all your good intentions.* One of Gwendolyn's favorite phrases, when dressing me down for my various misdemeanors. Knocking a book off her desk, pinching one of her dresses only to tear it. Behind her, always, stood Papa. Wearing his disappointment like a coat of arms.

What neither understood was these petty crimes were not the result of good intentions. They were the antics of a child. Made with Tad by my side. We knocked Gwendolyn's book over because we were running through the house. We pinched Gwendolyn's dress because we meant to turn it into a kite. Now, however, my intentions are good. And Gwendolyn, who can predict the outcome of chemical combinations, has already prophesized the outcome. *You have a touch of the picric acid in you; you destroy things even when you don't mean to.*

How does one defy the laws of chemistry? Another voice comes to my head. Throaty, tired yet humored. *The trick is there is no trick.* Colonel Wallace's advice the night I tried to save Flaherty. I didn't save Flaherty. Given what I know now of Colonel Wallace, he'd already calculated the odds of Flaherty surviving as next to nil. But we both are incapable of capitulating to defeat. Here lies the root of our kinship. The reason I keep trusting him when I shouldn't. The laws of chemistry don't matter. Humanity does.

My knees begin to sink. I catch myself on Tad's bed before I fall to the floor. My blood draw has slowed to a trickle. How much did I transfuse? I forgot to mark the time. Given the murky lightness of my head, I suspect I should have stopped sooner. I disconnect the needles and pack away the kit for cleaning. Bending down to stroke my brother's cheek, I whisper a line from the only book we know, *The Count of Monte Cristo*, "It's necessary to have wished for death in order to know how good it is to live."

On my way out of the ward, I inform the VAD that Captain Halladay has received an emergency transfusion and instruct her to check his vital signs and monitor for signs of fever. She isn't even trained enough to ask where the blood came from. She writes down notes and sends me off with a cheery wave. Was I ever as ignorant as she? She likely doesn't even know the difference between systolic and diastolic blood pressure. So how is it that the imposter in the Red Cross uniform is me?

The road back to the spinal hospital is busy, hot and dusty. I am short of breath, hungry, thirsty, and dizzy. A passing ambulance stops and the driver, an American girl from St. Louis, offers me a lift. Like most Yanks, she's chatty and opinionated and when she's not stripping the gears, she sings "Over There" and "I'm Always Chasing Rainbows." Lightheaded, I lean my head against the window. The glass vibrating against my temples feels loud and violent, but works to keep me awake while I hold back roll after roll of rising nausea.

When we reach the driveway, the Yank whistles. "Are you sure this is a hospital? Looks more like Cinderella's hideout."

I should offer her a tour, but I can barely manage to open the door, so instead I thank her and invite her to sing at one of our Wednesday evening concerts. The gesture seems sufficient. She rips out of the driveway, gears clanking in protest, dust rising behind. I need to get myself to the kitchen. I need sugar. Juice will do the trick.

My walk up the steps and through the door is surreal. My body seems disconnected from itself. One by one, my organs feel as if they are detaching like parts of a watch being disassembled. My stomach has dropped somewhere below my knees. My liver is floating to the ground. I cannot focus. Furniture and walls blur. The cut pink roses standing in a vase grow gargantuan and bare fangs. I am hallucinating. I need to sit down. But the kitchen . . .

If I can count my steps. If I can ply my hands away from the chair I am gripping. If I can lean against the wall for support. If I . . . A figure looms before me. Female. *Friend*, I think. She is saying something, her words warbled and ghostly. I try to nod my head, to appear normal. My stomach tears its way up to my throat, pouring out acid and sick. I wave my hand to warn my friend, but when I release my hold on the chair I start to fall. Ahead of me, below me, the floor is a thousand feet away, a black abyss.

I awake in a room I should not find familiar. A low fire dances in the hearth. A man lies stretched across the floor before it, a damask pillow tucked under his head, one knee bent, the other leg crossed over it, as he turns a page in his book. "We ought to stop meeting like this."

Instinctively, I clutch my blouse, but of course I am not wearing a uniform stained with my own vomit and blood. Someone has dressed me in hospital issue men's pajamas.

"Fuki," Colonel Wallace assures me. He notes the page number of his book before he shuts it and I tuck away the fact that he is not one to dog-ear Pythagoras. "While she did need me to toss you over my shoulder and take you up the stairs, the nursing was all Fukimoto." He points to the bottle of Ringer solution, connected to a tube, piercing my right arm via a subcutaneous clysis, dripping sustenance back into my body. "The rumor swirling the dinner table is that you are either with child or have influenza. Fuki suggested you were suffering from exhaustion. One, far less generous soul, diagnosed you with the vapors."

"Happy to provide a bit of entertainment." I sit up gingerly.

"The median cubital vein of your left arm was heavily bruised." He ends his sentence on a pause, the way a priest in the confessional does, awaiting an outpouring of wrongdoings.

"I gave blood. The base hospitals were in need."

"There is a shortage of O Negative," he agrees acknowledging the technical truth.

"Of which I am."

"As am I." He pushes up his sleeve to show me the wad of cotton and strip of plaster wrapped around his elbow. "I spent the morning collecting donations from everyone here." Pleasant in tone, I do not trust this voice of his. Beneath the smooth surface the heat of anger simmers. "Had you wished to participate, you need merely have informed me."

"That would assume I could find you. Which I couldn't. Were you with a German friend? Or foe?"

"Is that a question or an accusation?"

"Would you answer if it were a question," I shoot back.

"You understand German, do you?"

"I understand *Hallo*."

"Blinder eifer ist feuer ohne licht."

From the concoction of foreign syllables, the only word I can extract is *horse*. But when have I ever let my own ignorance intimidate me? "I'm not going to take your insults lying down."

He is on his feet and by my side in a trice. His stride is whip fast, the hand he lays on my shoulder firm, like he means to tame a wild horse. My heart is an untamed beast, it kicks and jumps, even as I wrest my shoulder from his touch.

"I am trying to instill some wisdom in you," he says. "Simply because you *can* do something doesn't mean you *should*. Even on the battlefield, we won't survive merely on instinct. You must employ thought, Vera-not-Vera."

The bottle of Ringer solution is near done. My left arm still aches, but I will use it to yank the needle out of my right, not caring if I tear flesh. My clumsy fingers betray me. Colonel Wallace lifts my hand away, detaches me from the tubing and cleans the puncture wound with antiseptic. His movements are precise, synchronized. Almost a thing of beauty.

I should rip his hair out.

"You snapped a man's arm in two."

He doesn't so much as blink. Discarding the tubing, putting away the glass bottle, he says, "I did what was required."

The excuse of a solider. I won't accept it. Not from him. "First do no harm."

"Do I harm one to save a thousand? Or sacrifice a thousand so as not to harm one?" He's not hiding his temper anymore. It's broken through the surface, turned his golden cheeks red, locked his Greek, son of a pacifist, jaw.

"You do what's right."

"No matter what I do, there will be blood on my hands." He holds them up for my inspection, his expression one of restrained fury, and a challenge. "It is the nature of our profession."

I toss the chateau-issued blanket covering my lap to the floor. "Major Carburry's injures are to his knees, not his spine. And yet this is a spinal hospital."

Colonel Wallace bends to retrieve the blanket, folds it into a tight, neat square. "Correct."

"You have crippled him."

"I have temporarily disabled him."

"To what end?"

"So the world may begin again."

"Your sentence is as incomprehensible as your German." I launch off the cot and storm toward his chalkboard filled with names, injuries, treatments and odds of survival. "You speak of the *world*. The papers write of *troops*. Telegrams *break the news*. As if war is anonymous." I bang my fist against the board, dislodging a cloud of chalk dust. The detritus burns my eyes. "Sergeant Davey Parker scribbles limericks to his sister." I find another name. "Private Alan Green's father sent him currant jelly. He loathes currant jelly, but he ate every sticky drop for his 'da. War is personal."

Chalk dust and a shaking, frustrated sense of helplessness clog my throat, rendering me mute. The world, my tiny part of it, breezes into this room through the open window. From downstairs comes the sound of clanking pots being washed and the hum of the kitchen staff, singing yet another song of patriotism, "Sister Susie Sewing Shirts for Soldiers." The melody twists inside me, floods me with melancholy. The floorboards creak under the tread of wheelchairs. The scent of summer honeysuckle blurs with the burn of antiseptic.

In the silence between us, Colonel Wallace's eyes never leave my face. "And what is your name, Vera-not-Vera?"

Like music, his spin on my name runs circles round my head. Too intimate. It changes the current charging the air. What was once a chaotic, unnamed energy takes a shape, one both of us have been fighting to keep from becoming real. It is one thing to steal a waltz beneath the full moon. Another thing entirely to believe the moon's song.

"My name and your deception are not proportional. Mine is, at most, a white lie." I walk back to the cot to sit beside him. "Yours will get you killed."

"Says the woman who ran *toward* an exploding building." He takes my hand, turns my palm up, traces the callouses. My points of pride, they define me more than even my fingerprints. Back and forth, he rubs his rough thumb across them, drawing out sensation, awaking a flutter of nerves.

"I wasn't thinking."

"I am." He folds my hand into my other, sets the clasped pair in my lap, like he's returning a bird to its nest.

Beside me, the heat of his skin rises off his pores and sinks into mine. The smell of burning logs adds another layer to his sea and salt scent. Our lungs dance in time to the same rhythm. We sit mere inches apart. The space between us pulsates, a universe fraught with doubt battling desire, fear twining with wonder, the birth of a cosmos. If we let it.

Love is not inevitable. I have a choice. I can stand. I can walk away. Most likely, I should because if I choose Colonel Wallace, it will be irrevocable. Once lit, this is a fire nothing can quell. I will not belittle my zeal for Jerome, but I was young and our affair did not define me. Nor did its end break me. Colonel Wallace—Nick—is different. If I choose him, I will never love another. He will change the alchemy of me and I of him. Between us, there will be no lines on a map.

The sleeve of his shirt is still rolled up. The plaster covers the puncture left by his blood transfusion. He and I share one of the rarest of blood types, O Negative. Also the most useful. This is a matter of coincidence, not fate. His eyes, a golden brown, reflect the four elements of the earth. All that is true and essential. Still, I can resist the magnetic pull drawing my finger to the tender skin of his inner elbow. I don't have to tug the plaster away gently, to expose his wound. I do not have to stroke it, acknowledging his vulnerability, soothing it.

"You swore not to," he whispers, recalling my promise to not fall in love with him.

My laugh is low, wicked, the truest thing I have uttered in years. "I have rethought my lie."

I bend my head to the crook of his elbow, to the vein that gave the same blood as mine. And kiss it.

CHAPTER THIRTEEN

London, May 5, 1919

I could kiss the slip of paper the footman delivers. He brings it to me in the cavernous dining room of my family's London townhouse, where the cook and housekeeper have conspired to concoct a middling meal of cold roasted chicken and julienned vegetables, but to serve it on Spode china. The fork and knife don't match though. Has someone been pilfering the silver? Trivial issues. The congealed fat glistening off the bland meat makes me nauseous. I shove the plate away. So empty is this gilded room that the sound of plate against cloth and table bounces off the walls and pounds in my head.

I could not eat anyway. How could I? I killed Major Carburry and wrapped the rope around Nick's neck. After Nick strode off to Brixton Prison and an Influenza epidemic, I sent no less than sixteen telegrams to Kristina in New York City. Each time I assumed I'd written enough, another question flew into my panicked brain and I scribbled more. The clerk thought me a madwoman. If only the great engineers would hurry up laying the telephone cables beneath the Atlantic Ocean, I would have been able to call her. Oh to hear her odd combination of English-accented American slang, and cracking smart reporter's wisdom. Surely, she will know how to unknot the hangman's noose.

The erstwhile footman waits for instructions while I break open the envelope and anticipate whatever brilliant solution Kristina can squeeze into a single sheet. My desperation and fear, a lethal combination, focuses on the solid block letters splayed out in black typeset. Between telegrams fourteen and sixteen, I had wavered like a coward, unsure whether to confess to the needle filled with potassium chloride. Even now shame burns through me. I was a nurse. I abused my power. No matter how rotten the man, it was not my right to take his life. Even worse, though, I set the hypodermic needle on its tray without thought, leaving Nick to unwittingly commit my crime. I corrupted his principle that every life matters. And he will go to the grave to protect me. If Kristina cannot lead me out of this maze, losing Nick and hating myself will only be the beginning of my punishment.

I read her words twice. Three times. I don't understand.

Listen, Kiddo, the pickle is the truth will do no good.

Rip by rip, I shred the useless telegram. Kristina is a journalist. Her goal is the truth. She puts it above all else. The truth solves all. I scatter the pieces over the roasted chicken flesh, scrape back my chair, and push past the footman. He's trained to be silent, a shadow for us to ignore unless we need an errand run or a glass of wine refilled. In my furious, terrified state, he's a blur of young face and liveried uniform. He opens the door as I stumble out. My skin is prickling, the sensation akin to sharp needle after sharp needle piercing me.

He whispers something beneath his breath.

I stop, shocked. It is not a chill that runs down my spine. It's confusion. But also, a weird crystalline moment of solace. As if someone had taken a cool cloth and wiped my face clean.

"Wait and hope."

The last words to *The Count of Monte Cristo.*

I turn slowly back to him. He is young, but his grey eyes are old and familiar in the way a uniform is. They mark him as a soldier. He wears his livery with a certain sense of relief. Far easier to follow the inane rules of a household hierarchy than the mayhem of smoke and bullets.

His smile is small and nervous. "Sister Betts."

Astonishment reverberates in the space between us. All the time I was in France, I feared someone familiar would recognize me. And yet no one did. Not once did I treat a patient who asked if I were the Earl of Halsop's daughter. No one asked, "Are you not supposed to be at Bryn Mawr?" The only men who recognized me were from the Blackpond factory, and they already knew me as Little Betts. I did not expect, I never even thought, that once I returned to England someone would see me as anyone other than Margaret Halladay. I assumed everyone would be too busy forgetting the war to remember a nurse.

I answer the man before me. "Yes."

"Second Battle of Artois."

I close my eyes, mentally walking down a row of cots to match his face to my memory. "Knife wound to the quadricep tendon. Severe loss of blood. Two transfusions. Fever." I open my eyes to take in the healthy man standing on two strong legs before me. My father refers to any and all his footmen as James. It's not entirely out of indifference, aristocratic families have used the same name to label their servants for centuries. "Private Peters."

He salutes me. "Type A/B Negative. You connected a tube between my vein and yours and read to me."

I take Peters' hand and squeeze it. "It is good to see you well. How fares your sweetheart in Clerkenwell?"

"What a memory you have, Sister. Afraid she threw me over for a milliner's son." He leans forward, lowers his voice. "I've my heart set on Betsy. The upstairs maid." He twirls his finger, suggesting a set of corkscrew curls.

"I shall do my best to encourage her affections."

He grins, then bites his bottom lip like he's trying to hold back the obvious question.

"I ran away from home," I tell him. "I took up with Lady Sullivan. My skills from Blackpond cottage hospital were good enough to pass myself off."

"Even after we left hospital and were back on the field, we used to talk about you. The lads and I. The Sister of Monte Cristo, that was what we called you."

"It's the one book I know."

"Well, now I know it too. I never expected . . ." He furrows his brow. "Well, I never thought to find you hiding amongst the toffs, begging your pardon. Shouldn't you be running your own ward somewhere?"

"I'm not a properly trained sister," I confess. My face heats with shame.

He shrugs. "Who hasn't lied? I was sixteen when I enlisted. Told the captain I was eighteen. No one cares as long as you can march and manage a gun."

"Mine is still a crime." One of many I've committed.

"Makes no difference to us lads. There's the law and then there's what the captain used to call Rules for Survival. I'm alive. I can flirt with Betsy. One day, I'll read *The Count of Monte Cristo* to my children."

My throat is thick with emotion. "You're a good man, Peters. I hope you know that."

He bows to me. "At your service, Sister Betts."

And he means it. The rules of society, rank, and birth order mean nothing between us. What matters are kindness and loyalty, the things one earns when one is at their best. Though I meant to kill Major Carbury, I am not evil. I am flawed, broken, human. But I also saved men. Good men. I can do it again.

My sleep is heavy, but not peaceful. I struggle with the tangle of sheets and the odd sounds creeping into my dreams. Footsteps. A drawer being opened and shut. I pull my tired lids open. More footsteps. Heavy boots treading across the floorboards. Coming from Mama's bedroom. I throw on my wrapper and slip out into the hallway. Mama's bedroom door lays wide open. The electric lights burn bright. Whoever is trespassing is brazen. Do I need a weapon?

I brave it unarmed, thumping my fist against the open door as a warning, and step inside. The man rifling through my mother's jewel case turns to face me. He is wiry thin, worryingly so, his face so gaunt his cheekbones glint like razor blades. He blinks rapidly trying to put thoughts together and throws his arms wide open. "Sissy!"

I have not seen Tad since he and Papa had a row this past Christmas and he stormed out of Halsop House cursing at us all. Still, I cannot help myself. I embrace my brother even though he smells sour and unpleasant. I rub his greasy hair and he squeezes me hard. A gesture I take for affection. Maybe even relief. Thanks to my blood transfusion, he survived his seven gunshot wounds. The price of survival, though, the steady stream of painkillers, is marked in the bloodshot whites of his eyes, the tiny pupils unable to focus.

When he lets me go, he tucks something into his jacket pocket. We plop down on the edge of Mama's bed, much as we did as children. Except then we were little, our legs did not reach the floor. And Mama was alive.

"Apologies about Easter," he starts. "Another lecture from the Pater and I'd be driven to drink." His laugh is dry, cynical. Alcohol is the least of his vices.

Easter was just last month. I barely remember it. "Were we expecting you?"

"Someone is always expecting something from us. It's the nature of being a Halladay. Pater sets forth his edicts and awaits our spectacular failure."

When I say nothing, he provides the sentence I am supposed to, one of the ties that binds us. "Unless you're Princess Gwendolyn." He picks at a scab on his lips.

I brush his hand away. "You need an ointment."

He tips my chin. "Oh ho, what a severe face, Severity."

Severity is the nickname my brother gave me when we were children. Whenever Papa was disciplining us, he employed terms such as *consequences* and *severity*. So much so that Tad joked he was surprised it wasn't included on my birth certificate. And so Severity I became. Which then channeled itself to Vera. When Nick had asked, all those months ago whether I was the *Vera* of truth or summer, he had no idea I was actually a promise of punishment.

I do not smile at Tad.

"Come now, Severity. Easter could not have been all misery. I sent a chocolate bunny to Gwendolyn's sprog."

"Matthew."

Tad shrugs. "Poor sod. Her ladyship no doubt squeals in horror should a fleck of mud dare stain the bonnie prince."

"Spoils him."

Tad scrapes at his lip again. He will draw blood, a sight I cannot stomach. Not his O negative. "Switching sides?" he asks.

"Never!" I grip his arm. It is all bone. I force sisterly cheer into my tone. "Shall we raid the pantry? Rouse the cook?"

"Not hungry." Tad runs his knuckles along his torso. "Can't hold much down."

"You're ill. What you need is a good lie down and . . ." Intravenous fluids. Followed by ox broth. A hot bath to wash away the street grime. Antiseptic and a posit for the scabs and open sores hiding beneath his jacket. A safe place. "Are you still keeping rooms in Belgravia?"

"I'm a gypsy wanderer."

He must have been thrown out. Papa provides an allowance, so it's not lack of funds. More likely funds squandered elsewhere. "You could sleep here."

"I hate this place." He tosses it out as an accusation, directed at me.

I am betraying him by staying here. Our pact was to forever buck Papa's authority. Never mind that as the heir, he can rebel without consequences. Primogeniture ensures a roof over his head. Even Gwendolyn, by far the favorite, must curry favor. If she crossed Papa, she would have no home.

"Think of how it would aggravate Papa if you were to sleep in his bed," I suggest. "You could smoke cheap cigarettes and pinch one or two of his favorite suits."

"Hah." The idea seems to cheer Tad. "Leave the old boy a pair of filthy socks."

"I could have a tray sent up. A roast? Toast and jam? You could make a great mess of sticky crumbs in the sheets."

A spark of the old Tad, which is to say the young boy from my childhood, lightens the heaviness of his eyes. "Better yet, I shall order a whore."

I flinch.

"Just as I suspected," he says bitterly. "There's no teeth in your talk. You'll poke the old man, but you won't break with him. Recall the massive row we had on Boxing Day? Do you know why we fought?"

"Habit?"

"He encouraged me to find a Proper Job. At Blackpond of all places. He's gone full *cit*, the earl has. Between pride and money, he's chosen cold, hard gold."

"If you had a choice, Tad, what would you want?"

The weight of such a simple question seems to exhaust him. He lays back on the bed and closes his eyes. At this angle, I can see his ankles. He's not wearing socks. I sit on the edge of the bed, awaiting an answer. When none comes, when his breathing slows, I suspect he has fallen asleep. I stand, meaning to tuck him in. Let him sleep one night in a clean bed.

He grabs my wrist. His strength is the work of adrenalin, not muscle. The expression of his face is both hardened and haunted. "I would like to go back to being a boy without scars." He lifts his jacket, pulls up his shirt and exposes me to the thick network of mangled skin. They speak of pain, of scalpels and stitches. But they also speak of life. Dead skin does not heal.

"No pity, Severity? You're a cold one."

I push his sleeve up past his elbow. Tap each bruise left by a needle. His hands must be clumsy. "You could start by ending these."

"Something tidier? Like an opium ball?" He shakes his head. "My credit's no good in the dens anymore."

"I know a place . . ." I begin.

His sits up, eager. "Do you?"

"Where soldiers go."

"To smoke away their troubles?" He is near panting.

I struggle to hide my revulsion. This man, torn up and filthy, is nonetheless my brother. The playmate of my childhood. The one who scaled the trellis to sneak me biscuits when Papa had locked me in the nursery.

"To find solace from their nightmares." I swallow. "With the help of a good man. Actually, a great man. McMannis. He runs a clinic in Silvertown."

Tad tears up off the bed. "Why the fuck would I need *solace*?" He ends his sentence on a high-pitched mocking note, staring at me like I'm a black-clad moralist come to thump my Bible. "Do you have any idea what it's like to be me? Do you?" He shakes his head wildly. "There are nights I want to slice off my ears so I don't have to hear a single sound. No pitter-patter of rats scurrying across my legs. No random machine gun fire. But there's no point in cutting off my ears is there? Because the sounds not outside. It's in my brain." He bangs on his head with his fists.

I have triaged hemorrhages, chest and head cases enough to diagnose Tad's pain. But who of my dead patients would not happily trade places with him? All Flaherty wanted was to live. "Oh, I understand your self-pity." I circle my brother. "You, who have had everything handed to you. Wealth. Privilege. More than one roof over your head. You'd rather riddle your arm with needles than brave out a detoxification in Silvertown."

"The only reason I'm alive is because the painkillers *kill the pain*."

"No, they feed it."

"You're worse than Papa." He spits the sentence out.

Saliva lands on my cheek. I wipe it away. It's nothing compared to the fluid that has stained my nurse's apron. Including my own blood. Which I gave to Tad.

On her bureau, Mama's jewel case lies open. The real stones, sapphires and diamonds, are locked away in Papa's safe. But the costume knickknacks are still worth a few bob. And more. The cloisonné bumblebee pendant she wore every year on my birthday is missing. So too is her chrome-plated glass pin. She wore it to church on Sundays.

"I won't let you steal Mama's things."

"I'm not a thief. I strode into this house with my key. The butler addressed me as *Mi'lord*. This house and all of its contents, right down to whatever detritus sits in your little closet, will belong to me one day. What was Mama's is mine."

"Give it back." I lunge toward Tad.

He ducks. He has narcotics pumping through his veins. I have able-bodied strength and righteous fury. I kick him in the knee and he crumples to the floor.

"Bitch!"

Ignoring the insult, I bend to reach into his pocket. His arm comes up. A flash of chrome against the electric lights makes me squint. His arm comes down and with it Mama's favorite pin. He stabs my inner arm. The pin pierces my cephalic vein. I scream. I howl in pain. Blood spurts out, dripping to stain the Turkish rug. He scurries for the stairs. I follow, still bleeding, still screaming. At the bottom of the stairs he is met by Peters. Who decks him.

Tad lands in a heap on the marble floor. He points up at Peters. "Whoever the fuck you are, you're fired."

"You don't have the authority," I shout back. I've taken the belt off my robe and wrapped it around my arm. A makeshift tourniquet. "Enter this house uninvited and I will report you for thieving."

A crowd of servants has gathered. The humorless housekeeper jangles her keys. The butler opens his mouth to speak. I stare him mute. "Change all the locks," I order. "And if my brother returns, anyone who allows him entrance shall be dismissed without a reference."

Peters throws Tad over his shoulder. Betsy sighs in admiration.

"Where should I deposit him?" Peters asks.

"To Silvertown," I say.

"To Limehouse," Tad slurs, choosing London's drug and brothel district.

"Silvertown," I tell Peters. "Tell the cabbie to ask for McMannis."

With Tad slung across Peters' capable shoulders, the servants disperse. Betsy takes my arm and leads me to the kitchen. "I was a VAD," she says proudly, opening up a cabinet and retrieving a first aid kit. The antiseptic burns. She bandages my wound. "There!" She sits back admiring her handiwork, her expressive, milky white face radiating sweetness and trust.

I should gouge my eyes out. Kristina is right. The truth will do no good. I have banished Tad from his home, exposed him for a drug addict and a thief. Despite my orders, the cab will bear Tad where addiction dictates, because he has my mother's pin and the *Maschinengewehr 08* always gets its man. Who am I to interfere in the fate of men? That's God's job. Though what kind of God armors us in nothing but flesh? A cruel joke. My own brother called me a bitch. Even words cut.

PART II

She dances like a Bomb
—Emily Dickinson,
"The Soul Has Bandaged Moments"

CHAPTER FOURTEEN

Wimereux, July 1918

What a glorious organ is the skin. Porous, it gives us the gift of sensation. Against my lips, I taste the layers of Nick. The coffee and cinnamon, the salt beneath, deeper still a virile, heart-stopping masculinity. My naked foot rubs against the back of his calves—muscle sculpted by swimming, skin made rough by tiny blonde hairs. Even the place between my thighs, deep inside me, which clamps tight around him as he moves in and out, even that place is made of flesh. We do not consume through the mouth. We devour through the skin.

Nick and I are thieves, stealing time in the minutes between rounds and shifts, duties and favors. We come together in exhaustion. Sometimes without a word. Sometimes with too many. They burst out of me like water breaking through a dam. Without naming names, I tell him of my failed love affair with Jerome, of my admiration and resentment of Gwendolyn, of the growing affection I feel toward Matty through Mama's letters, and of my happiest moments of childhood, all of which involved misadventures with Tad.

Nick listens, his magical fingers rubbing out a war's worth of knots. I have never been so heard, so attended to. When we are apart, my lungs feel tight, like they're clinging onto the last taste of oxygen I shared with him. When we are together, my body rights itself. Lungs and heart work together. Spinal nerves telegraph messages to brain.

And skin. Love lives on my skin.

Tonight we have had the luxury of a full hour beneath the night sky. We were careful to take separate routes to the lake. Hidden beneath my coat, I carried a blanket. Nick brought a bottle of wine, bread, and cheese. Satiated, we lay stretched out, limbs intertwined, languorous and nude.

I trace the line of his sternum and the arch of his ribs, marveling how something so breakable is meant to protect things so vital—major blood vessels, lungs, heart. I bend to kiss the first costal notch of his sternum. A silly gesture, still I mean for it to protect him from harm. He responds by slapping my hip. Startled, I raise myself up.

"Mosquito," he explains, drawing his head down to the red mark on my hip. And bites into my skin. "I will not share you."

Once again, we twine ourselves around each other. Another kiss. His lips on mine, I run my tongue along the seam of his mouth, pausing at his cupid's bow to savor the way he inhales me as if I am breath itself. It is a tiny moment. A treasure. It completes me, even as I am greedy for more. But we cannot ignore the press of time. It edges around us. When we break the kiss, I flick a glance at the watch face sitting beside the blouse Nick near tore off me.

We begin the task of putting ourselves back into uniform. He shakes out my blouse and hands it to me. Noting my watch, he flips it around and observes the engraving on the back. "V.B? Is it possible you do exist, Vera-not-Vera?"

"Old Betts, Dr. Victor Bettany. I used to follow him everywhere, so much so that the patients started calling me *Little Betts*. He taught me how to take pulses with it." I pin it to my blouse. "Though honestly, I think it is the thing that keeps my own heartbeat steady." I have never confessed, not even to myself, how much this small token means to me. It has somehow come to define my true worth. I would be lost without it.

Nick slips on his shirt and I swallow a touch of jealousy toward the cotton and khaki that have the right to him. He laughs low and warm. "You truly are Vera-not-Vera."

Even before he came up with this nickname, long before we met, I was this person. I became her the day I crossed the English Channel with nothing but a valise and bravado. With Old Betts' training embedded in me, my nursing skills instinctual, Vera-not-Vera is my truest self. It took Nick to name me.

"Don't you have a talisman of some kind?" I ask. "A copper penny or, what is it Greek fisherman are always pictured with? A rosary? Worry beads?" I brush out my skirt.

"Not a talisman. A place." He sets his hands on my shoulders and straightens my blouse. Running his fingers through my hair he plucks out a twig, winks, and tucks it into his pocket.

Reluctantly we set out for the path returning us to the hospital. In a half mile, it splits in two directions. He will take the twisted, windy, one, the one on which he broke the German's arm. I will take the open route. It leads to the front of the chateau. Far out of sight of Major Carburry's window.

"What place?" I ask.

"Greece."

"The entire country?"

He chuckles at my teasing tone, acknowledges I know him well enough to know he is a man of specifics, not generalities. "Have I ever told you how I learned to swim?"

"I assumed you were born a fish."

"Hah. My *pappous*—grandfather—took me out to sea on a rowboat, threw me over, and rowed beside me till I made it to shore."

My mouth drops open. "How utterly barbaric."

Nick shrugs his shoulders affably. "Would I do the same to my own child? I doubt it. But the water was shallow enough and when you're five—"

"Five!—"

"—you're fearless."

"Or stupid," I shoot back, recalling too late that his younger brother drowned too young to have been taught to swim thus. I turn my guilty face up to him in an apology and am met with a bittersweet, tender half-smile. What is more terrifying? To share your wounds, or to be the safekeeper of someone else's? I would rather cut myself than hurt this man.

"Fear and stupidity are not mutually exclusive," he says in a tone that is equal parts Greek philosopher and mischievous boy. "In fact, one is likely the precursor to the other."

"Which comes first?"

Nick gestures with both his hands as if trying to balance a scale. "Chicken? Egg?"

I shake my head and raise a scolding finger at him. "You will teach my children in a proper pool. You will not leave their side."

He captures my finger, opens my hand and kisses the palm. "No, Vera-not-Vera. Not for even a moment." The night air is light, his voice is thick with promise. "I will take them to the sea and swim beside them. If a wave or a rip current so much as hints at danger, I will strike my trident to part the waters."

I should not take such relief in silly words. Nick is not a god and this War seems like it shall never end. We only have our tiny moments. I am starved for more, and yet filled by what little we can have.

Walking through the woods in the cool of night, we reach the point where our paths diverge. He lets go of my hand. The separation is physical, my skin turns inside out. "I can't."

"We can," he says roughly, swallowing to keep his own emotions in check. "Because one day, we will have Skopelos, that is the island where I learned to swim. In the Aegean Sea. My grandparents' house rests on a hillside. Their garden is filled with lemon trees, bearing fruit the size of a fist. I've cut a path through the kermes oaks to a secret, sandy cove where the water is warm and so blue, bluer even than your eyes, Vera-not-Vera. We will make love for hours beneath the hot sun. I will not neglect a single pore of your beautiful body. I will shelter you."

I close my eyes and try to imagine a world at peace, a place by a turquoise sea, the heat of the sun, and time, so much time, with this man. I cannot trust the vision. But I want it desperately. And who besides Nick could make it real?

"Promise," I say.

"On my life."

It is my turn to count linens. The pleasure Matron takes in assigning these pecuniary tasks to me and Fukimoto is near maniacal. Flanders Fields can't crush our spirits, but tracking down some missing Beecham's Patent Pills, *worth a guinea a box*, can dampen them. I tick off the items on my list and head to Matron's apartments. She keeps a set of rooms on the first floor and expects us to drop our reports into a cedar box by her door. I take enormous pleasure in rattling the door that opens into her wing and stomping my feet along the wooden floors. It's near four a.m. Hopefully, she is sleeping and I am invading her dreams.

I jiggle the lock on the cedar box. It's well oiled. Disappointing, that. And paper, no matter how aggressively shoved, makes little noise. I contemplate pounding on the lid when from beneath the door a woman's moan rolls out. Gasping breath follows. A second moan, higher pitched, like organs being squeezed. Something falls to the floor. I hear glass shattering.

I tiptoe backward. An inch away. A foot away. Three feet now and I'll be free. She did not call for help. I am not responsible for Matron. She might not be in pain. She may merely be drunk. Or enacting some witch's ritual. I'm farther away now, farther down the hall. At the door leading to my escape, my hand encircles the knob. She screams. The hairs on my arm stand on end. My feet, overtaken by my godforsaken nurse's instincts, change direction. I bully my way into her room and find her rolled up in a ball on the floor, one hand between her thighs. On the floor, blood pools.

I am not naive. Lady Sullivan performed such procedures on the French women who sought her out. She asked no questions. She involved no one else, though we all knew why she dug around the supply marquee for Pennyroyal Tea. Occasionally, Beecham's. We used the latter for stomach ailments, but it has other medicinal effects. The circular box I had been trying to track down earlier sits atop Matron's desk. The yellow pills are scattered across the floor. So too are shards of glass.

"Get out," she hisses.

I am loath to touch her. Her nightgown is stained with the sticky mess of a dead bairn. Matron clutches her stomach, a spasm wrenches through her so violently her eyes roll into the back of her head. I am grateful for Nick's insistence on French sheaths. Perhaps someone didn't give Matron the choice. Or perhaps Matron had dreamed a different outcome.

I am a nurse. My place and my purpose are to heal, not judge. Dislike Matron as much as I do, I owe it to her to help. Reluctantly, I force myself to tuck my shoulder beneath hers and lift. She shoves me, though I manage to keep hold of her. Together we trudge toward her bedroom. My boots crunch broken glass. Her bare feet are cut to pieces. I lay her down on the bed and strip off her filthy nightgown. Could I ring for Fukimoto? My apron is soaked. There is no chance of avoiding notice, whispers. Better not to involve anyone else. Matron will need antiseptic, paracetamol and sanitary pads. She must have given this situation some thought. Where are her supplies?

As if she's read my mind, she gestures weakly to the flame mahogany bureau. On top sits her toilette, a surprising collection of expensive lipsticks and perfumes. Even a charcoal pencil. Hints at a softer Matron, a woman. I search through the drawers and find what I am looking for in the bottom. Everything I need is laid out within it methodically. Between the white of the linens and the dark of the wood, it's like staring into a casket. One Matron prepped for herself.

I swallow my misgivings and gather up the standard nursing items—scissors, tweezers, bandages. Blackpond, as per. Returning to her bedside, I wipe the sick off her face and force her to swallow the painkiller tablets. She mutters curses. The first handful are meant for me. "Snooty." "Airified." The root of her antipathy seems to be my voice—"high toned and uppity." I reply with an ironic "thank you" to each insult. She may be in misery and I may be removing glass from her soles and bandaging her feet, but it does not make us friends.

Once the paracetamol takes effect, her mind wanders, worn out. "He thinks his confinement to a wheelchair is temporary. I'll make sure it's permanent." On this last note she sobs.

I don't know how long I sit beside Matron. A half hour, forty minutes? Eventually, her cramps ease. She falls into an unhappy sleep. Her hands cannot seem to stop from curving around her stomach to hold the child no longer there. In the corner, a mop and bucket cast a macabre shadow.

I collect them and return to her sitting room. A stench unfurls, a mixture of rotten blooms, of vanilla and amber snarled with the metallic tang of copper. I throw open the windows. Outside a dark, low dawn is cresting. It will storm today. I set to sweeping up the shattered glass strewn across the floor and toss the fragments in the trash.

Glass is easy. The other mess . . .

The child Matron extracted from her body is nothing but a mass of cells, an abandoned lump on a blood-soaked carpet. I do my best to scoop it up, hating that there is no place for it besides a cheap bucket. I mop the floor, wringing more blood, more cells into the metal can. My hands are stained, my fingers rubbed raw.

I'm sorry, baby. I'm sorry.

Not my words. Matron whispers them in her sleep.

I will not toss these cells in a bin. The hope they carried deserves better. I take the bucket, sneak out of Matron's rooms and head outside. I stop at the garden shed to grab a spade. For a moment, I think to walk to the woods, but realize there is a better place. A patch of soft, fertile earth beneath a Rowan tree. On my knees I dig and dig. Dirt soaks through my stockings. My shoulders ache from the strain. My eyes blur. I bury the bairn that never had a chance to grow so much as skin. Pat the dirt so it will cradle the babe.

Two stories up, a wide window overlooks this plot. It belongs to a man whose confinement to a wheelchair is temporary. In a few hours, Major Carburry will sit up in bed and admire his view, not realizing he watches over his dead child. The bottle Matron smashed was a bottle of Creed.

CHAPTER FIFTEEN

London, May 6, 1919

The bonnie blue-eyed lass who loops her arm through mine needs no cloying perfume. She smells of cut grass and spring rain. The freshness of scent against the grittiness of London overpowers me. She smiles, as easy as can be, and steers me away from the Royal Courts with its gothic spires. I follow her like an old friend. She is a complete stranger.

Confused, I tell her, "I have a trial to attend."

She furrows her dusty blond eyebrows. "Isn't the trial over?"

Which brings me to my senses. I try to wriggle out of her grasp. She clutches my upper arm, her lemon-yellow linen suit and jolly hat an odd contrast to the muscled steel of her hold. Yet her demeanor is not threatening, merely purposeful.

"Who are you?" I ask.

"Dorothea Charles. My friends call me Dovie." Noting the position of my feet and the way my body is angled to escape, she crinkles her eyes like she's perplexed. "Oh!" She pats my shoulder. "Mr. Wallace would like a word."

"Nick?" I spring on the balls of my feet, anticipating the drive to Brixton Prison. I do not know if I have the patience to wait thirty minutes, forty-five. Not when at last he's ready to talk. When he's *asking* for me. I will tell him everything. I will confess the potassium chloride. He will forgive me, he must, and we'll find a way out of the mess I created. Or I will break him out of prison and we will abscond to Skopelos Island without a trace. We can hide in his cove like the Count of Monte Cristo and never be found.

I near tear off the smooth metal handle of the motorcar door, barge in to the backseat, and open my mouth so my heart might speak. A beautiful, familiar golden head turns to appraise me. With an eyepatch.

Disappointment drains my blood. Only now does the meaning of *Mister* Wallace dawn. Bonnie blue Dovie Charles had not used *Colonel* or *Doctor* and I, in a brilliant display of my intrinsic idiocy, did not think. When she slides into the driver's seat, she shoots me an apologetic look. "I didn't intend to deceive you." She casts EyePatch a castigating frown. "You knew Miss Betts would misinterpret the meaning of *Mr. Wallace*, didn't you?"

"Charles," EyePatch drawls with the patience of an aggravated cat, "we are in the business of national security, not making friendsies at the vicar's tea party."

"My papa is a vicar," says Charles. With defiant cheer, she stretches her arm across the back to shake my hand. "I'm very sorry to meet thus."

"You are not meeting at all," corrects EyePatch. "Your task is to start the engine and drive through the streets of London in a pleasant and unobtrusive manner."

"Actually, my job is to serve as a silent witness should Miss Betts later report to her press friend some tale of your abuse that requires refuting." She starts the engine and pulls away from the curb, smoothly navigating between two lanes of speeding traffic. "Which I am happy to provide so long as you restrain yourself."

"A little discretion, Charles," EyePatch warns.

"Why? I'm not a spy. I'm a telegraph operator promoted to secretary." She gives the steering wheel a healthy slap. "And chauffer."

"Are *you* a spy?" I ask Eyepatch.

"Hardly. I'm merely discreet."

"Secretive," I counter.

He unfolds the morning paper and shoves the headline at me. *Sabotage for Peace!* Ace reporter Master James has drawn a line from Lady Sullivan's Ambulance Hospital to a shell-shocked padre to a question mark. *Was it the quixotic acts of one man, or a conspiracy? Does a German general who studied linguistics at Cambridge have ties to a certain physician whose murder trial has been shrouded in political deception? Or do his ties bypass the physician and run straight to the Home Secretary's Office? Where another Cambridge linguist serves at His Majesty's pleasure?*

I did not disclose to Master James the connection between General Hildebrand and EyePatch. So chuffed am I with the young reporter, I cackle. Or at least I start to, before the singular glare from EyePatch renders me silent.

He folds the paper and smacks it against his knee. "Explain." It's an interrogation, not a request.

"I'm trying to save Nick."

"With cooked-up conspiracy theories?"

"You forget, I was at Lady Sullivan's Hospital when you visited. I overheard you."

"We were speaking in Greek," he replies matter-of-factly. "It's just as likely my brother and I were chatting of the weather."

"If the weather involves three explosions and an honest man's guilty conscience."

From the driver's seat, Charles chuckles. "You're a bricky gal, Miss Betts."

EyePatch levels his sharp gaze at her. "For God's sake, Charles, watch the omnibus!"

In response, she accelerates, bringing us dangerously close to the black fumed tailpipe of the bus before bullying into the next lane, flying through the intersection and swerving to avoid a peddler pushing his cart through the street. All the while her head is turned, not frontwards to assess the road, but back to stare down Eyepatch. "Unlike you, I have peripheral vision."

We pass the British Museum. I did not grow up in London and so I do not have a good sense of the city's layout. Nonetheless, I know we are not moving toward Brixton Prison. We are driving in the opposite direction, away from the Thames. "Are we not going to see Nick?"

"Do I look like an orderly you can bribe?" EyePatch smirks.

"Shouldn't we be going back to the court?" I ignore the panic lancing through my nerves.

"Not in session today. Nor tomorrow. The Judge Advocate is . . . indisposed." Though he be golden-haired and amber-eyed like Nick, Eyepatch is a study in cool, distanced emotion. Very little breaks from the marble surface of his angular face. Which is why the near invisible tick of the upper left corner of his top lip shocks me. He almost looks mischief-making pleased.

Charles supplies the answer. "Slipped a diuretic in the Judge Advocate's morning coffee. He'll be feeling rather poorly." She grins winsomely at me and manages a left-hand turn against oncoming traffic.

EyePatch's groan of exasperation stretches a second too long. Beneath it is something more tender. A sigh.

I try to sound confident when I ask, "If neither Brixton nor court be on the agenda, then what is the purpose of our chinwag?"

"I am offering you a ride home."

I scoff. "Do you know my house?"

He gestures gallantly to Charles. "If you could provide my driver your address."

"You may drop me off at Eaton Square," I say. "The south garden."

"Ohh la la," chirps Charles. "Lyall Street or Elizabeth?"

In addition to telegraph operator, secretary, chauffer, and indiscreet-non-spy, Charles should add cartographer. "Elizabeth."

EyePatch relaxes into his seat as if he is finished with a conversation we never began.

I twist around to square off with him. "What are we going to do about Nick. His confession is on record. The Judge Advocate will recover from his . . . ahem . . . stomach ailment."

"I am not unsympathetic to your intentions, Miss Betts. But you are a civilian. These matters are beyond your grasp."

"You do not need to be vague with me."

"Don't I?" He taps the newspaper sitting between us.

"I am engaged in a campaign to save Nick. *Your brother*," I counter.

"You are swatting at imaginary monsters." He sounds like he's trying to placate a spoiled child.

I tilt my chin high. I won't be fooled by his denials. He was the one who shot out Carburry's knees. "Tell me where I should point my sword."

"Nowhere. Let the professionals handle the matter."

Oh the smugness of the man! I rub my tongue against the back of my teeth. "Think you've been doing a bang-up job, do you? Where were you yesterday when your brother confessed? Off on an errand for the Home Secretary? Chasing a red herring? You were outmaneuvered by a pretty widow and her single-minded determination to see Nick pay for a crime he didn't commit."

"So you know he's innocent." Is that relief in the easing of his jaw or suspicion?

"I wouldn't care if he were guilty. But yes, I know without a doubt he is innocent."

Confident as a church cat, he asks, "How?"

My moral conscience stumbles. I am not ready to say aloud to a man who reminds me of Nick, what I have done. I need Nick's forgiveness first.

"Woman's intuition?" Sarcasm rolls off Eyepatch's tongue like second nature.

"At least I have a plan," I snap. "What have you got in play? Bury Brixton in blacked-out documents? Engage in more, what are they called? Legal machinations?"

"Delay tactics," he replies coolly.

"At the rate you're moving, Nick will die in prison a *young* man."

"Don't underestimate my powers in inverse proportion to the overestimation of yours." EyePatch flexes his shoulders the way a predatory bird spreads it wings, to remind his prey of his superior strength. "If I can slip a diuretic into a Judge Advocate's drink, I can certainly sneak a man out of jail."

"With the Home Secretary's permission."

"Obviously. There is an order to things, Miss Betts. Neither you nor I have the full picture. We must engage strategy and nuance so as to unravel this situation brick by brick, without unintended consequences."

"Hang your unintended consequences!" I shout, loud enough to make EyePatch grimace. "What will become of Nick while you negotiate your steps? He is on a hunger strike. Amidst an influenza epidemic. Have you seen the way he winces when he moves his left leg? He needs medical care. He is not safe in prison."

"I can transfer him back to the infirmary."

"And Mrs. Carburry with her precious British Royal Army will toss him into another cell. Your brother is not a ping-pong."

EyePatch blinks once, as if the mention of ping-pong tugs at a memory, one that is painful because the event remembered was pleasant. "I don't play games. For one, I'm terrible at them. All the men in my family are." His *are* carries the same sound as a penny tossed into deep well. It's not the penny itself you notice, but the emptiness around it, the long, long minutes it takes for it to hit bottom. EyePatch and Nick *are* . . . for now. Their father and two brothers *were*.

We are not on opposite sides. We should be a team. I straighten my skirt and take a moment to rearrange my plan of attack. "Lady Carburry's weapon is her husband's legacy. With it, the British Royal Army will bend to her will. We need to destroy it."

"Why do I get the sense, Miss Betts, that you're the type to pull a stone out of a mountain wall, and shrug her shoulders when its removal causes an avalanche?"

"Because the goal is the avalanche?"

The shake of his head is not ill-humored. "If I am following you, your brilliant plot is to push out as truth an unformed theory regarding a saboteur ring bombing hospitals, and attack a beloved and, might I add, *fallen* national hero. To what aim?"

"Originally, I planned to blackmail you," I admit.

"How very noble." He almost laughs.

"But you're incorruptible. I see that now. You believe too hard in how little you matter. Right hand, not whole body. You'll never beat the likes of Lady Carburry."

Quick as a bullet, he sits up straight. "Lady Carburry is not our enemy. Nick is. Do you think I haven't offered to disappear him to Argentina or Greece? All it would take is some paperwork and we could say that for national security, the prisoner was removed to the custody of the Home Secretary. The reason the Court Martial continues is because Nick refuses to abandon his cause. Whatever that may be."

I shove any inkling of guilt aside. I can be as single-minded as Nick if need be. "Then we must exploit his weakness."

"Martyrdom?"

"Me."

EyePatch studies me anew and rubs his chin like he's discovered that the irritating thorn in his side might be used as a blade against someone else. "I'm listening, Miss Betts."

"You must inform Nick I intend to claim responsibility for Major Carbury's death. I was his nurse. I was on the ship with him." *I loaded the potassium chloride in the needle. I meant to kill him.*

"No one will believe you. They'll say you're a besotted nurse who will lie to save her lover."

Clearly, the man has never been in love. "The only person we need to believe me is Nick. You'll have to employ one of your legalistic machinations to reopen the trial or hold a hearing."

He says, "We can intercede before the sentencing." His tone is carefully neutral.

"And you will give Nick a choice. Either I testify or he agrees to your disappearance scheme."

Barely perceptible, Eyepatch's nod carries a hint of respect. He says, "I assume you'll expect new identity papers for yourself."

"I'd like to keep *Vera* if you please." I offer EyePatch my hand to shake. He pauses, assessing our truce, no doubt doubting the rationality of such a scheme. We do not know each other. We do not trust each other. But we both love Nick. Finally, he takes my outstretched hand. His fingers are long and elegant. A scar cuts across his index. I wonder how many wounds he's borne.

He still has my hand in his grasp when I look out the window to the white-faced stucco house my family has occupied for generations. "Here's home."

I reach for the door handle. Eyepatch tightens his hold, not painfully, and yet I'm aware how easily he could snap my bones. "This is the house of the Earl of Halsop," he says, startled and confused. "Are you a servant here?"

Oh. My pulse quickens. A tiny detail. It should not cause my stomach to clench. "Vera is not my real name. Nor is Betts."

EyePatch turns to take in the house, back to me, back to the house. His jaw tightens with each turn. The air in the car becomes stifling and tense. "You are the Earl of Halsop's *daughter?*"

The hostility in his voice, the derision and incredulity, make me shrink back into the seat. Unable to speak, I nod.

Eyepatch leans forward to raise the glass divider between the back seat and the driver. Charles thrusts her elbow through before it can close.

"Remove your arm," he commands.

"No," she replies.

And with the firmness of her refusal, for the first time, I realize, I am in danger. Real, physical danger. Near alone in a car with a man I don't know who has the power to poison judges and make people disappear. He drums his fingers against *The Times* in synch to his exhalation. He studies my throat like he intends to wring it. Oh I may be disappearing, all right, but not to Greece or Argentina. With the snap of his fingers, EyePatch could render me invisible right here.

"Get out," he says. His voice is carefully leashed, like he's trying to hold back the wrath of his disappointment. I had made a mistake. I had given him a sliver of hope. And then proved myself a sham. "Stay away. The more you try to help, the more impossible it will be for me to extricate him. Go near the Royal Court, go near my brother and I promise you, you'll find yourself someplace cold, dank and thoroughly unpleasant."

"I—I don't understand."

"Of course you don't." He glares at me with such heat, I'm shocked I'm not reduced to cinders. He says, "Think, for a moment. Timed picric acid bombs require what?"

"A spring-loaded device," I answer meekly.

"No, you idiot. They require *picric acid*."

He cannot be suggesting...no...never. I bite my lip, and argue faithfully, "Blackpond uses picric acid for medical purposes only." It was Mama's one hard rule. She understood the danger of picric acid and insisted Blackpond use it only for healing. And if Papa so much as suggested otherwise, she always reminded him she had the power to revoke his position. "We manufacture bandages."

"The Earl of Halsop is notoriously greedy. He sold excess picric acid to the War Office. Not for bandages. And some of his deliveries were short several ounces." The curve of Eyepatch's mouth borders on cruel. "For a master strategist willing to admit to murdering a national hero, you can be shockingly stupid."

My capacity for stupidity is boundless. Having been shoved from the motorcar and dragged by the elbow up the pathway and near tossed through my own front door by a furious EyePatch, I now stumble into the house and head straight to Papa's office. A rational person might ring up Papa at Halsop House or even drive to Surrey to confront him. I am too angry to be rational.

The door to his office is locked. I have no need for the housekeeper's keys. I use a hairpin to steal inside. The curtains are drawn, blocking the contents from the prying eyes of Eaton Square. I grab fistfuls of velvet and yank the drapes open. Sunlight, brutal in its sharpness, floods the room. Black ledgers line the bookcases. I drag each one off the shelf and thumb through the pages. Lines and lines of numbers, manufacturing orders, notes. So many supplies and contracts, but all for medical supplies, not chemicals.

His ledgers useless, I raid his desk. Stacks of papers, invitations, framed photos: Papa with Churchill, Papa with the King, several of Matty, a few stiffly posed family portraits with me staring out sullenly. The snapshot of Tad in uniform pinches my heart. He looks so frightened.

Never subtle, most of the photos are of Gwendolyn. Which is why the one tucked behind a practical shrine to my sister beckons like a message. It is of Mama and incongruous from the fur and diamond clad version of Mama that Papa prefers. Instead, her face is half-covered by a giant straw hat. In her hand she holds a spade. Behind her, her roses bloom. If I inhale, I will smell the richness of loam and summer, of flowers unfurling beneath the heat of the sun. Those same roses have been abandoned, left to twist and die at Halsop House.

Instinctually, I know the photo is a trick. I pick it up, remove it from the gilded silver frame, and turn it over. Numbers are written across the back. The combination to the safe. The handwriting belongs to Mama. Had she meant for someone to notice the picture, to intuit a secret? The only person who could have understood is me.

In search of the safe, I ransack the room, knocking over chairs, yanking down priceless paintings, pulling up the Aubusson carpet, rattling the bookshelves. God above, the location of the safe is more closely guarded than any contents in it. Perspiration runs down my back. A thick lock of hair is plastered to my forehead and my chest is heaving. I'm about to ring for Peters to bring a pickaxe so that we may rip apart the floor when the door swings open and I am greeted with, "What the hell has gotten into you, Margaret."

No one utters my name like Papa. On his lips, it is weighted with equal parts dissatisfaction and confusion, like he's spent a lifetime trying to make sense of me all the while knowing hurricanes have no logic.

His gaze sweeps the carnage I have made of his office. Anger blooms across his cheeks. "This is too much, even for you. First you throw your brother out of *my* house. Then you lay waste to *my* private study. What next?"

My laugh is high-pitched, near hysterical. What next indeed. Betraying national secrets? Springing my lover from jail? I say nothing.

"The severity of your recklessness calls for severe measures. I shall ring the physician. I suspect you are in need of a retirement to the country."

He means a madhouse. One covered with pretty wallpaper and shushed footsteps. No knitting needles or sharp objects allowed.

"In the meantime, you will collect yourself. And for God's sake, before I ring the servants to clean this disaster, fix your hair!"

Papa's obsession with the trivial acts like a balm. My breathing eases. My head clears. "First of all, Tad is stealing from *your* house. I caught him with his hand in Mama's jewel box." My voice is so even and calm, he takes a step backward and grabs hold of the only chair I did not overturn.

I hold up two fingers. "Second, the person you should be sending away is Tad. He is enslaved to narcotics and needs a clinic. There is one in Silvertown, but the addict has to be willing to go. While I have every faith in your powers of persuasion"—Papa's nostrils flare at my insolence—"should you fail to convince Tad, you will have to force him into a less desirable situation."

"How dare you," he sputters. "You are my daughter, God help me. If I require your opinion—"

"Third, you will show me where the safe is."

"What?" His eyes shift toward the paneled wall next to the bank of windows. No wonder he keeps the curtains drawn.

I march across the office, kicking aside ledgers and miscellaneous debris. When I reach the paneled wall, I run my hands along the seams. I need to find a spring mechanism.

"Papa," I say with such sweetness he shudders. "If you don't tell me where the safe is, I am going to ring for Peters."

"Who?"

"The footman. Not only will I ask him to take apart this sham of a wall, I will do so with my hair askew so that he will have not one, but two bits of gossip to take back to the servants. Three if you count Tad thieving. All of which will spill onto Eaton Square and spread like wildfire straight up to the House of Lords."

He crosses the room in furious strides and yanks my arm away from the wall. We come face-to-face, the royal blue of his Halladay eyes meet my faded indigo. His mouth is snarled, the pressure of his fingers on my arm sharp. He raises his other hand. I stare up, mesmerized by the sight of his palm suspended in midair. In all our years of shouting, my rebellion, his governing, Papa has cajoled and punished, but he has never struck me. His long fingers are braced, his palm wide and menacing. Fear makes me lightheaded, but I refuse to flinch.

"You have no right to question me, much less make demands." So tense is he that his hand vibrates as it begins its purposeful descent toward my cheek.

I almost want the strike to land, to feel the blow against my skin. My instincts, however, have other plans. Without thinking, I duck and twist out of his grip. With no target, his hand sweeps through the space between us with such force, the momentum makes him stumble. He near falls forward, but catches himself on the window ledge. His body slams against the glass. The windowpane rattles, shocking us both by its fragility. We stare at each other, out of breath, confused, and ashamed.

After a moment, he bends his forehead over his knees and rakes his hands through his carefully arranged salt and pepper hair, over and over. When he finally looks up at me, his eyes are damp, his skin grey and bloodless. "Why must you torment me, Margaret?"

"Human nature," I suggest.

He ignores me, still thinking aloud, perplexed by the child I was and the woman I've become. "You always wrestled out of your swaddling blanket. Refused the bottle. Walked without learning to crawl. I cannot recount the number of tumbles you took. You were always bruised. And for some reason, always angry with me, when all I have ever wanted for you is your safety."

"If by *safety*, you mean *obedience*, then perhaps I can agree."

Papa drags his hands through his hair so roughly, he reveals the bald spot he combs over. "No, it feels personal and unwarranted, the way you insist upon disobeying me."

"Does Tad not disobey you? Not just the thieving and the addiction, but before, when he was a child?"

"A father wants a bit of spirit in his son."

"But not in his daughter," I answer back.

"One would not mind it so, were it tempered with tenderness."

I would like to remind him that tenderness requires reciprocation to grow. But, strangely, this is the most Papa and I have talked since I returned from France and I am loath to return to our old father-daughter dance. I am tired of it. Perhaps he is too?

Instead I say, "I am not a tender soul."

"Not true. Not true at all."

The force of his statement startles me.

"It used to mortify me," he says ruefully, "how jealous I would become when observing you with Dr. Bettany. The two of you with your little medical adventures, finishing each other's sentences, laughing at things only the two of you understood. And the way you looked at him . . ." Papa's voice trails off like he's swallowing something unpleasant. "I, who provided you with the very best of everything was never afforded such respect. How is it a country surgeon, a man of little consequence, could bring out this . . . this light in you?"

The regret on Papa's face stings. He is not wrong. From the day I was born, energy pounded so erratically within me, I had to outrun it anyway I could to exhaust it. Not even Mama could diffuse me. And then Old Betts showed me how to harness it. He gave me purpose. He was more father to me than Papa ever was. But these are words I cannot say without betraying the very things Dr. Bettany taught me. *We are here to heal, lass, that is all, and it is everything.*

Papa drags a deep breath. His expression is uncomfortable, vulnerable. "You make it so hard to love you."

Though it's an admission wrapped in a recrimination, this is the closet Papa has ever come to expressing any fondness toward me.

"Exercising my only talent, I suppose." I offer him a joke in lieu of understanding.

He utters a reluctant, "hah," and sags deeper into the window frame. With his hair disheveled, the sun beats down on his usually combed-over bald spot, making it shine, like it's highlighting both his vanity and his fragility.

I sit next to him on the ledge. Overriding my stubborn-daughter heart, I admit, "I don't know how to talk to you."

"This modern age confounds me. Why do children want to converse with their parents? In my day, there was a natural order to things. Sons learned to run estates. Daughters brought comfort to parents."

"The world went to war, Papa. We smashed the natural order to bits and pieces."

"Christ." He rubs his eyes. "I knew I should never have allowed you to go to America after Dr. Bettany retired. This new wisdom of yours would have been put to better use rolling bandages."

I tamp down a snort. I can do far more than roll a bandage.

Realization dawns. A sentence flutters on my tongue. I could tell Papa about Lady Sullivan's. Of my work. Of the lives I saved. Tad's included. And he might . . . I hate the heated wash of hope rising through me . . . He might respect me. "I—"

"I'm too tired to argue, Margaret. Box up whatever barb you've got and save it for another day. My birthday, perhaps."

If I am disappointed, I won't admit it. "It will be a bang-up party. It's not every day an earl turns younger."

He chuckles and scans his office, a grand room filled with expensive leather chairs and masterworks, now scattered across the floor. He catches sight of the photo I'm holding. "You are hiding behind her skirts."

He taps on the barest outline of a shadow and only now do I note the way Mama's hand is curved protectively on what must be the top of my head. It seems she is trying to encourage me to peek out and I am steadfastly refusing. He picks up the picture, holds it up for closer inspection. Examining the back, his eyes flare, recognizing the set of numbers Mama penciled in. He spends what feels like an hour contemplating their significance, working his mouth left and right.

When he places the photo back in my waiting hands, he does so almost reverently, nodding his head as if agreeing to do the bidding of the ghost in this room. "I married your mother for money. Because it was my duty to replenish the coffers." The statement is matter-of-fact, without guilt. "I was not faithful to her. Nor was I particularly kind, though we had our moments. I exploited Blackpond. Gwendolyn and Tad will deny it, but you have never been fond of me. I can be honest and not fail your expectations."

I deliver an open-palmed half shrug.

He nods, seeming grateful for this opportunity to be honest. "I profited from the war. She did not approve. We fought fiercely over it. England needed so much, more bandages, new medical products, faster delivery. I ran the assembly line around the clock. One gets caught up in the flood of cash. One makes mistakes." He catches himself before he confesses more. Honesty has its limits.

"What kind of mistakes, Papa?"

"Nothing illegal." The lie is in his defensiveness.

"Picric acid is volatile," I begin.

"I manufactured no weapons."

"Merely sold the chemicals needed." I work hard to keep my voice level and neutral.

He clamps his jaw. Even he cannot bear to say the words. So I will have to. "With one hand you supplied medical aids for injured men, with the other you provided the ammunition that killed them." He must have hidden the sales of our excess picric acid. "You betrayed Mama."

A sound escapes him. Neither a gasp nor a cough, it rolls out heavy as stone. His shoulders tremble. He clutches his chest. "Oh Margaret, Margaret, Margaret." Papa is sobbing.

He is not calling out for me, but for my mother, whose name I carry, because she thought the two of us were the least loved. His breathing is ragged and I don't know what to do with the man crumbling beside me. Should I put my arm around him? Pat his back? Useless, I intertwine my fingers and remain still.

Removing a handkerchief from his coat pocket, he wipes his face and tries to compose himself back into the man I once knew, the imperious, authoritarian father. But when he speaks, his tone is earnest and filled with longing. "Your mother handed me my coffee, two sugars, every morning for nigh thirty years. Before her, I thought I preferred my coffee black. But I didn't. She understood people better than they understood themselves. Me especially. And now . . ." He weeps anew. "What becomes of a man who loves a woman only once he's buried her?"

It is a strange, awful thing to at last be able to share such frankness with Papa and learn that he is even more flawed and selfish than I had imagined. And to care for him. Perhaps that is the price of honesty. One can hate the acts, but not the actor.

Brushing away his tears, Papa rises. Against the wall, he pushes in a panel and it swings back, revealing the safe. He spins the nob and it springs open. Reaching in, he pulls out a white onyx box, its trim lined with lapis. He holds it out to me. "She left this."

I rub my thumb across the surface, as cool and smooth as a headstone. "What is it?"

Papa shakes his head. "She did not share it with me. This is solely for you."

Even as he places the box in my outstretched hands, he seems unable to let go of it. His palm rests on top. I place my own hand on top of his. We stand together for a moment, silent, connected by our grief.

"Papa?"

A sad smile crosses his face. It is likely the first time I have ever called for him without being angry.

"The picric acid was for bullets, right?" I ask. "Just bullets?"

Instead of answering, he shifts his eyes toward the collection of family photos on his desk and rests on the picture of the one person in our family who is still innocent, Matty. Papa takes a breath and leaves.

The worst part of a storm is not the gale force winds, the violent rain, the way it knocks you about so you don't know which side is up. It's the aftermath, when you are wrung out and empty. I sit amidst the destruction I wrought and cradle Mama's box. I am afraid to open it. It feels too much like an ending.

Finally, I lift the lid. Within lies my old copy of *The Count of Monte Cristo*, the leather cover stained by my little girl's damp fingerprints, my favorite pages dog-eared. Carefully I remove the book. It has been so long since I held the book, the weight of it fills my hands, not just with pages, but with memories. So many. Not all of them terrible. Mama read the book to me, night after night, her voice growing hoarse as I begged for one more chapter. In turn, I read the book to Tad. We would sit at the picture window, curled up together, us two against the hostile world of Halsop House.

I open the volume. A newspaper clipping slips out.

A flimsy sheet, it floats onto my lap. A line has been underlined in red pen: "The speaker was a young girl and her outlook on life had assumed a new and marvelous focus." Lady Randolph Churchill's article about Lady Sullivan's hospital. Though no one knew who I was, the quote refers to me.

Some hollow, unfulfilled cavern within me opens up. A yearning so tangible it makes my stomach clench takes over so I am near sick with hunger. If anyone were to ask me what I wanted from my mother, it would be that she acknowledged that it was her unkindness, not Jerome's rejection, not Gwendolyn's betrayal, that sent me flying into the arms of war. I wanted her to hurt, to feel the pain she caused me. And I wanted her to be proud. To see in me the woman I could be.

Not the reckless child she so often had to soothe.

But how did she know? Who gave her this article? And when? Would Kristina play the Judas and expose my scars? Did Lady Randolph Churchill recognize me? Or perhaps one of my patients? At Lady Sullivan's I treated several men from Blackpond. *Little Betts* they called me. Would they have written to Mama? More likely to their wives. Who Mama may have met? Throughout the war, she went to Blackpond to encourage the women who worked in the factory, and to make sure they were treated right.

So many questions. Not a single answer. Whatever Mama knew, she took with her to her grave. I bang about my memories trying to pull out lines from Mama's letters that might now have a different meaning. She wrote mostly of Matty, of her plans for her gardens, of a new rose hybrid. Thornless, she planned to name it *Gwendolyn*. She feared for Tad who she did not think had the temperament for war. She reminded me to wear my hat and gloves.

And yet when I saw the photo of her on Papa's desk, I understood she had a message for me. An apology. A mother's love. Imperfect as it was, it was still strong enough to connect us, even through death. *The Count of Monte Cristo* in my trembling hands, I open to the title page. With the same red pen she used to underline the news clipping, she has written an inscription from the book:

Return to the world still more brilliant because of your former sorrows.

CHAPTER SIXTEEN

Wimereux, August 1918

Have I returned to the world or am I merely entering it fully in my skin for the first time? Whatever the answer, I am reborn. On the verandah, the patients soak up the last of the day's sun as it sets where it's supposed to, in the west. Despite everything, the world has somehow managed to hold itself together.

Half-sitting on the balustrade, I try to hide my happiness beneath an officious scowl, pretending not to take pleasure in the hard-earned camaraderie the patients share as they fill in the day's crossword puzzle and discuss the mundane (cigarettes, cricket, which of the singing Farber Sisters is more kissable).

Nearby, Nick chats amiably with Corporal Langdon. Even as Nick talks of the weather, his voice carries the weight and depth of an organ filling the church rafters. "If this fine weather holds, we will be treated to a meteor shower. The Perseids will light the sky this week."

Perhaps I stare. Or even sigh. Nick lifts his head and tosses me a wink.

Who needs food or water or even oxygen when a man such as he loves me?

Corporal Langdon's daughter, Lucy, skips out from the kitchen, an apple in her hand. She has a particular talent for eluding the dour nun who is supposed to be chaperoning her. In this, the child has a formidable ally in Matron. Earlier, I passed the two of them conspiring in a corner of the library, the girl on Matron's lap, Matron plaiting her corn silk hair. When she had finished, little Lucy scampered off to go visit the barn animals. Matron stayed in the corner, staring at her empty lap.

"Do you hear that, Lulu?" Langdon asks. "We're to be treated to a meteor shower."

The girl reaches into her pinafore and pulls out a pocketknife. While one might question what a seven-year old is doing with a sharp blade of any kind, no one here does. She won it fair and square in a game of poker. She cuts a slice of apple and holds it out to her father, watchful until she's satisfied that he's eaten every bite.

She asks, "What is a meaty oar?"

What a haphazard education the child is getting. Knife skills, gambling, free reign in a spinal hospital, not a lick of maths or grammar. But she is not fatherless. And that is what matters.

"A meteor," I explain, "is what's left of a rock when it falls from space into earth's atmosphere. It bursts into flames."

To Nick, she asks, "Can a rock catch on fire?"

"If the friction is intense enough," Nick supplies. "Like flint and steel." He motions a rock striking metal. "And a meteor shower is like fireworks." He points to the last rays of the orange-tinged sunset and directs our attention to where the pale blue sky is fading into twilight. "Imagine streaks of lights shooting across the universe." With his fingers, he imitates tiny explosions and makes whooshing sounds. He pauses, startled by the motion of his hands and glances at the sky warily, perhaps recalling the fighter planes that sometimes soar above us, of the pilots who fail to return.

He shakes the melancholy away by picking up Lucy and tossing her into the air. "You are a meteor!"

So excited is Lucy, she clasps her cheeks and squeals. "Oh! We will have to have a party. A party. We must!"

Nick puts her down and frowns with a mock seriousness. "Unfortunately, the best time to witness the Perseids is late at night, long after we've all gone to bed."

Lucy chews on her bottom lip as she absorbs this news.

He taps his chin and sighs dramatically. The men watch him with looks of disappointment matching Lucy's.

It's unfair to tease them so.

"Unless," I say crisply.

"Unless?" Nick wrinkles his forehead as if he cannot think of a single solution to our terrible dilemma of curfew. I know that man's mouth, from lateral commissure to lateral commissure. He's biting his cupid's bow to hide his cheekiness.

"When I was a girl," I tell Lucy, "I was allowed to stay up well past midnight if I could prove myself useful." I tap my pencil against the clipboard and prepare to write. "Tell me, what are your talents."

One of the older patients, General Brunswick says, "I cannot imagine Nurse as a child. She is always so serious." He sucks in his cheeks and tenses his jaw to demonstrate.

Nick tosses me a furtive, *oh how you've fooled them* grin. "Come now, General. Who better than Betts to force castor oil down the throats of the razzle dazzle? Churchill himself would have invited her out of the nursery."

Brunswick chortles, but shakes his head.

Coming to my own defense, I say, "I made a terrific martini." I trill my *rrrrs* with the same self-important, spinsterly righteousness as my Halladay aunts, my imitation so accurate, I sneeze at the memory of their fusty scent—red wine, face powder, and cloying perfume.

General Brunswick spins his wheelchair around and stares at me, bewildered, as if he's just now realized the woman who shaves him each morning is an albino giraffe with two heads. "Did you . . . Did you?" He shakes his head in disbelief and turns to his comrades. "Did Nurse make a joke?"

Nick, he of the golden halo, doesn't have the common decency to disguise his amusement. I send him my best ipecac-and-enema scowl.

"No, I don't think so," says one of the patients.

"Isn't the sort to make merry," adds another.

"Once I saw her not frown," offers Langdon.

All of which makes Nick laugh harder.

I smack my hands reprovingly to hide my embarrassment. How must these men see me? I used to be funny, mimicking my snobbish aunts until tears streamed down my mother's face and Tad complained his tummy hurt. My old self, that lost girl Margaret, may have been elbows and knees and emotions run amok, but she was also fun.

With a repressive tone, I reply, "Of course I am not joking. How else does one dispense castor oil at a society crush?"

General Brunswick blinks rapidly. "By God! N-n-nurse is . . ." His shoulders shake and he doubles over. His fellow patients join him. "I'm sorry, old girl, I did not th-th-think"—the General cannot stop guffawing—"I never realized you could—"

"Is that a cough I hear coming on, General?" I flash him a mercenary grin and rifle through my mental list of medicines so bitter, seasoned soldiers have wept for their mam. "Hold a moment while I run and fetch Dr. Aubergier's wild lettuce syrup."

"Joke!" He shouts, pumping his first in triumph.

The patients join him, chanting "joke, joke, joke," with such fondness, I am rendered shy. I duck my head to hide my pleasure.

Amidst the shout of cheers, comes a quiet, "Worse." Nick's voice is a touch throaty, as if he's savoring something he never wants to let go. "A smile."

With me held in his gaze, with him held in mine, without so much as touching, we are lovers entwined, stretching and bending time to our will. We draw the seconds out so it feels like we have a full minute to be apart and yet connected, to be surrounded and yet completely and utterly together. Can no one else see how love blooms across my

SUZANNE TIERNEY

cheeks?

Not that the world around us fades away. Quite the opposite, each detail of it deepens. I can hear the crinkle of burning paper as General Brunswick smokes his cigarette, the sing-song pattern of affection between Lucy and her father, the muttered confusion between two patients discussing someone else's mistake on the crossword—"Who the devil answered HMS Minerve for Nelson's ship at the Battle of Trafalgar?" I smile. Even I know it was the HMS Victory. No, the world will not fall apart. Not with each of us doing our tiny part to keep it spinning.

Lucy pulls me out of my sentimental reverie by tugging at my arm. "Will you teach me to make a martini?"

"Castor oil or ipecac?" I ask.

"Betts!" Nick's tone is half amused, half horrified. He knows I would happily teach an innocent child how to mix gin, vermouth, ice and bitters. Plus a purgative. He indicates the child's father and wags his finger at me.

I give Lucy a helpless shrug of the shoulders and nudge my thumb toward Nick. "What a damper."

Lucy giggles, delighting in my insouciance.

"Is counting in French a skill?" she asks earnestly.

"Certainly not," I reply.

A far-too-sober frown comes over her young face. It is chased away by an impish smile. "Perhaps Sister Fukimoto can teach me how to make paper cranes. Then Colonel Wallace will have to let me stay up late!" She kisses her father's cheek and is about to race back into the chateau to find her.

But the sun has set, Fukimoto is not on duty, and I know where she is likely to be spending her evening. In the arms of a German prisoner of war. It would not do for a child to discover them. It would do even less if an adult were to find them. In the wrong set of eyes, Fukimoto's love would be mistaken for treason.

I press Lucy's shoulder. "You need to discuss cakes with Cook. Why don't I go up and ask Sister for you?"

Lucy pauses to consider the logistics. "I shall write a list of everyone's favorites first."

Leaving Lucy to her hostess duties, I trek into the hallway, planning to bustle up to our room to catch Fukimoto before she slips off to spend the evening with General Hildebrand.

"You really are made of two speeds, Vera-not-Vera."

I turn back to find Nick half-jogging to catch up with me. He is grinning. I am ecstatic.

"Where are you off to?" I ask sternly.

"Officially, to attend to the papers sitting on my desk. Unofficially, to admire the way you fly up the stairs like you're defying gravity."

I frown with professional concern. "I worry for your vision, Colonel Wallace. You seem to be seeing things."

"I pray to God you're not a mirage, Vera-not-Vera."

Flint strikes rock. The air between us crackles with electricity. My skin burns. What else is there to say? We don't need words. We merely need each other. The struggle not to touch Nick near consumes me. I concentrate on the forward march of my boots, the echo of his footfall keeping pace with mine, the smooth, masculine movement of his coordinated muscles, the scent of him. He swam this morning, I can tell from the faint hint of saltwater clinging to him. I wonder who envies the other more – me for the ocean's claim to him, or the ocean for mine. He may dip and sluice through its waters, he may be a creature of the sea, but he is entirely, body and soul, mine.

So focused am I on not touching Nick, that when his fingers graze my elbow, I let out a small screech.

"Hold," he says, not in the voice of a lover, but of a senior officer of the British Royal Army, which he joined so as to gain this hospital.

On guard, I follow his line of focus up to the landing where, head bent, Fukimoto stands between two uniformed military police. Her hands are shackled. All three are following Matron, who crosses the landing with pursed lips and a sense of triumph. The clomp of their collective boots sounds nameless, impersonal.

"What is this," Nick demands.

The younger MP, a lank and spotty boy who carries an air of importance he hasn't earned, answers, "We have a warrant."

"In which case you should be delivering it to me," Nick replies.

"We were met by Matron," explains the other MP. Older and more subdued, his tanned and wrinkled face tells of time spent in hot climates, of cynicism rather than wisdom.

"Who is under my command." Nick takes the stairs two at a time.

Matron fold her hands primly, her manner very much sister in charge, deferential to her superior, but not ceding ground. "I was bringing the prisoner to you."

"You were bringing Sister Fukimoto to me?" Tension vibrates off Nick's broad shoulders so violently, even the windows along the staircase shudder. "Well I am here now. She is brought."

"It's a serious matter, Colonel." The older MP spreads his legs into a wide, I've-handled-irate-COs before stance.

"Is it?" Nick asks, nonplussed. "I wouldn't have guessed by the warrant and your presence."

The younger MP squints his eyes in a subtle way to suggest that it is Fukimoto's foreignness, her Japanese origin, that makes the matter serious. "Fraternizing with the enemy."

In normal circumstances, this would be the moment Fukimoto would repeat the phrase, roll the syllables around with her tongue and try to divine its meaning. On the fields of No Man's Land in '14, English and German troops set down their weapons and climbed out of the trenches to greet each other on Christmas Day. The papers called it Fraternizing With the Enemy, but in a positive light. Fukimoto will not understand the darker use.

I half-open my mouth to explain to it her, but she will not lift her head to meet my eyes. She stares at the floor as if hypnotized by the random wood grain of hundred-year-old oak felled and transformed into dull plank.

Nick reaches the landing.

"We cannot be naive, Colonel," Matron warns. "Against my very clear objections, we have been housing a prisoner of war, a man responsible for the deaths of untold Englishmen."

"Which we did by special request of the Home Secretary. So if you are going to arrest Sister Fukimoto for doing her medical duty, you'd best cuff me as well." Nick holds out his wrists defiantly.

Matron has the good grace to draw back. "Her medical duty does not include passing letters on behalf of that German. Who knows what they contained? Coded messages? British intelligence? War plans?"

"Gained from hospital operations?" Nick asks mockingly.

Too mockingly. A premonition crawls, spider like, up my spine. Taking in General Hildebrand was an order. Maintaining the façade that Major Carbury's condition is severe enough that he cannot return to England was an order. Nick will not be able to save Fukimoto. Not if there are orders.

"Germans are bombing our medical facilities," Matron retorts. "Or have you forgotten about the sabotage at Lady Sullivan's? You've read about Cuperly? And the medical supply ship docked in Calais? Who is to say we aren't next? These explosions are moving closer to Wimereux and while the base hospitals are at least guarded, we are an unarmed chateau housing England's finest soldiers and officers. Even national heroes."

"They would not . . ." Nick stumbles. "Never harm the injured."

Beyond the landing, up the stairs to the left, I catch a shadow cast by steady electric light. Oblong, murky, I take note of the shape of a semicircle. A wheel. Which can only belong to a wheelchair. And there is only one patient who would skulk in the darkness to eavesdrop.

My heart goes numb as if stung. The poison spreads through my limbs. They grow heavy, dead-like.

What would you do to stop this brutality? Nick once asked me.

Would you compromise?

He has already done so.

Would you deceive?

Nick was at Lady Sullivan's when the medical marquees exploded. Nick was away from Wimereux, in places unknown, when the sabotage occurred in Cuperly and Calais.

Would you destroy the very thing that defines you?

My fingers curl so tightly, the bones might crack. That halo. That bloody halo. The weight of it is unbearable. Built on his faith in humanity and his drive to save lives, it will crush him. Is crushing him now.

"Nothing is above the Germans," Matron says. "They are a power-hungry race."

"German blood runs as red as ours," Nick snaps.

"And Fukimoto, you are . . ." She pauses almost like she regrets reporting Fukimoto, even as she believes herself right in doing so. "Are a foolish, sentimental idiot."

"Enough." Nick nods his head toward the older MP. "The warrant."

The older MP delivers it into Nick's waiting palm. As he reads it, his expression falls grim. He squeezes Fukimoto's shoulder. She shivers and bows her head even lower.

Matron says, "Your shame is too late. I know you have no loyalty to England. You are not one of us. Your patients, though? Do they mean nothing to you? General Brunswick, whose fever you worked so diligently to break? Private Green, whose fingers you have retrained to move? Shall I go on?"

"No," I exhale, barely a whisper.

Matron sweeps her gaze across the distance between us. Her smile hardens, becomes brittle.

On wobbly legs, I ascend the stairs. "All Fukimoto has done is show she has a heart."

"She failed in her job." Matron says matter-of-factly. She is nothing, if not her job. Whether war has made her so or she was made for war, I don't know. But I recognize something in her hunger for regulation, her near obsessive devotion to her patients. I recognize myself. Before nursing, she and I were unformed cells searching for definition.

"Fukimoto fell in love," I reason. "Perhaps she made a mistake. Have you never?" I let the question hang. Let Matron recall the other night. She sobbed for the child she will never have. Somewhere within that arch smugness lays a woman who is made of more than rules and medical swabs.

"Are you in all seriousness asking me, a twice decorated sister of the QAIMNS, if I've ever committed treason?" How pleased Matron looks as she delivers her line. By God, more than pleased. She is grinning from ear to ear. The source of her strength isn't her twice decorated QAIMNS status. It's other people's frailty.

Her hypocrisy, the antidote to my numbness, sets me surging forward. "You petty, dried up spinster."

Surprised, she wavers and takes a step back so that the window casement behind her frames her. Beyond her, the night is moonless and shapeless.

"I cleaned the sick off your face," I hiss.

She shrinks deeper into the darkness.

"I wiped the blood off your floor."

"Betts!" Nick warns. "Betts!"

I hear him. I do. In a crowd, in the rumble of thunder, in the chaos of No Man's Land, I will always be attuned to his organ-in-a-church voice. But he is helpless, constrained by a halo that bears down so hard on him it will snap his spine and still demand he crawl. I am free because I am not Vera. I am a pulsating, uncontained force, an energy I cannot exhaust.

Reaching Matron, our faces mere inches apart, I ask, "Is it so easy to forget your own ab—"

The crack across my cheek is so sharp, I do not even feel the sting.

"I'll see to it you're stripped of your nurse's uniform," Matron pants.

Something inside me snaps. I am nothing without my uniform. Neither is Matron. When faced with the choice of a baby she longed for and maintaining her position, she chose her position. And now will strip Fukimoto's of hers. My hands curled, my fingers stretched, I grab the collar of Matron's dress.

Nick releases Fukimoto and pulls me off Matron. Someone screams. Me? Matron? No, in the chaos, it is Fukimoto. She head butts the younger MP, shoves Matron out of her way, raises her boot, and smashes the window. Glass shatters, shards cascade into the empty night air and rain down on the innocuous rose bushes below. Voices rise from upstairs, in the wards, from below stairs, in the kitchen.

Fukimoto flies forward.

And is yanked back.

By Nick. Whose reflexes have been honed on riptides and waves. The air is nothing to him. He pulls her by the waist and cradles her in his chest as she wails, her tiny body shaking. She murmurs a line, over and over. "'Theirs not to reason why. Theirs but to do and die . . .'"

"Not like this, Fuki." Nick strokes her head.

Panting and horrified, knowing my temper added to Fukimoto's shame rather than protected her, I want to curl in on myself and disappear.

When the older MP moves as if to take control, Nick sends him such a look of reproach, the man jumps back and bows.

"Not like this," Nick repeats to Fukimoto. "There is still hope."

Fukimoto draws away from Nick. She lifts his hand to examine it like the nurse she is. "You are cut."

"Merely a scratch." He wipes the blood off on his doctor's coat. It leaves a dark stain. Nick wraps a protective arm around Fukimoto. "Matron, please see to the patients. The sound of shattered glass will have upset them. I would start with Ward One."

Pale and unnerved, Matron blinks at him. Somewhere within Nick, however, is either an innate understanding of what makes even a horrible person human or an untapped talent for manipulation. I wish it were the latter.

She brushes her skirts and readjusts her veil, reassembling herself into the dignified woman she wants to believe she is. "I shall summon the orderlies to address this mess."

Gently, he turns Fukimoto to face the long descent down the stair-case, out of the shelter of this hospital, to whatever the British Royal Army barracks hold. "I will go with you," he assures her. "I will not abandon you."

"There's an order to things," the lanky MP protests.

"Then you'd best follow my lead," Nick replies.

He turns to me. Not caring how much his touch reveals to the others, he cradles the side of my face Matron slapped. His palm means to offer warmth and comfort, but I am nothing but a storming mass of cells. They swirl and crash to give me physical shape. Inside I am hollowed out.

"You are better than this." He urges me, "This is not who you are."

CHAPTER SEVENTEEN

London, May 7, 1919

"I knew you were a fake." Matron waves my calling card between her thumb and forefinger, smirking at the gilded edges and the gold-lettered *Margaret Halladay*. "Not who you said you were at all."

Are any of us? The woman who once ran a state-of-the-art spinal hospital has been reduced to Ward Sister Rosling of the Ministry of Pensions Hospital in Hammersmith. She's thinned, her complexion has faded, and while my appearance has reinvigorated her, when she crosses the room, she is short of breath.

"I did not think you would agree to meet Vera Betts," I reply.

"But no one can deny *Lady* Margaret." From the way she takes in the understated luxury of the Committee Room, greedily soaking up the details of the intricate longcase mahogany clock and the tastefully faded Turkish carpet, it's clear she's never been in it. Nor have I, though I'm familiar with its contents. The cushioned clawfoot chair Matron settles into with mocking daintiness has a match collecting dust in the attic of Halsop House.

"With your oh-so-posh accent, I should have guessed you were some earl's daughter, run off for a lark." She studies the oil painting above my right shoulder, a portrait of one of this hospital's founding patrons. My mother.

Without a word, I pour her a cup of tea. No milk, no sugar. She raises the cup to her lips, lifting her pinky finger with exaggerated airs. "Tell me, did you enjoy France?"

"About as much as you did." I pinch the handle of my teacup between my thumb and index finger, no pinky.

She acknowledges my retort with a satisfied nod, an old gesture, reminiscent of the woman she was in Wimereux, a woman in charge. To save Nick, I need her to be that woman. I spent the better part of this morning slipping through dank alleyways to escape the sleek silver motorcar following me. I have no time to make missteps or guess my way through undoing Nick's confession. The Court Martial has concluded and I need more than a miracle to crack it open again. I need evidence of a war hero's treason.

"Let's be quick about this," Rosling says. "Unlike you, I have responsibilities and my matron has afforded me no more than five minutes for our idle chat. I am instructed to convey to you that we are ever so grateful for the supplies donated by Blackpond Manufacturing. Had I a forelock, I would tug it." She taps her forehead to demonstrate. "What do you want from me?"

"Your help."

She near recoils, splashing hot tea on her hands, and winces. "Why in God's name would I help you?"

"Not me. Colonel Wallace."

The hard angles of her hostile face soften with such tenderness, she is almost beautiful again. "I was my best at Wimereux. He made me so." She fidgets with her cap, pushing it down to hide the hair greying at her temples.

"He's going to hang."

"He confessed," she says, half-bewildered herself.

"Do you think him guilty?"

She considers the question. "He warned me about Major Carburry."

I lean forward, anticipating. "That he was treacherous?"

"That he was married," she answers drily.

Lord above! Not bothering to hide my impatience, I say, "Colonel Wallace did not keep Carburry in splints to prevent the man from engaging in extramarital affairs."

"What are you going on about? Major Carburry came to Wimereux with two shattered knees. Colonel Wallace performed surgery to reconstruct them. The Major was not a prisoner. He was a hero."

"Our hospital treated only the most serious cases. The ones who couldn't be transported for risk of death. Recall how fragile the men of Ward One were. So why was a man as robust as Carburry not being treated in England? Why was he in Wimereux?"

"For the weather? Or perhaps because we ran the finest hospital in all the War." There's a barely hidden smirk lurking behind her professional pride. Holding a secret restores her to her former glory, if only for a moment. She won't ever give it up. Not unless I can offer a new route to her old self.

I bite into a biscuit, thinking. How would Carburry have won her over? He had a particular talent for twisting one's strengths into weaknesses. Love of King. Love of Country. Can I inspire the same in her? It seems hardly likely considering how much we dislike each other.

"You opposed admitting General Hildebrand into our hospital," I start.

"He was German," she replies as if I cannot tell the difference between black and white.

"Was it your idea to isolate him, then, in the East Wing?"

"No one could expect our patients, noble though they were, to share cigarettes with the man who likely ordered the bullets in their spines."

"You selected Fukimoto to attend him." I lock the muscles in my foot to stop it from tapping anxiously. I have so little time, and yet I cannot rush Rosling.

"Fukimoto was foreign. She did not have the same aversion. *Obvi-*

ously."

"Yet General Hildebrand was not a stranger to England. In fact, he and Major Carburry attended Cambridge together."

"I walked up Du Cane Road this morning. Did you?" She pauses so I can nod. "And yet we did not cross paths? Shocking."

"What led you to believe Fukimoto had allied herself with General Hildebrand?"

Her eyes flare. "Do you think I took the task lightly? To accuse a fellow nurse, a good one too, of treason?"

"You had evidence?"

"I was matron. My job was to see all. And what I saw was this— once Hildebrand was admitted, Sister Fukimoto never once joined us for dinner. Where was she? She brought flowers to his room. Delivered books from the library. For God's sake, she helped him finish cross-word puzzles."

My instincts, always faster than my brain, set my fingertips tingling. "Crossword puzzles?"

"Rectangular grid, white boxes. You read a clue and fill in the letters." She imitates scribbling. "Does the House of Halsop not receive newspapers?"

"Do you know what I recall in particular about the crossword puzzles?"

Matron makes a show of relaxing into her seat and blows on her tea as if it is still hot when we both know it's lukewarm. "Enlighten me."

"Major Carburry oft started the puzzles, but never managed to finish. More than once a patient complained the answers he did supply were wrong."

"He was a man of action. Sedentary occupations bored him."

"There was a particular clue once, 'Nelson's winning ship—'"

"HMS Victory," she answers automatically.

"And yet Major Carburry, a career soldier, wrote 'HMS Minerve.' A French ship, twice captured by the English."

A line creases her forehead, but her voice doesn't falter when she demands, "What of it?"

"Newspapers were precious. We only received a handful of copies. You distributed them. You determined the order."

"How dare you." She rises to her feet, which I take as a good sign. Hostility is second nature to her, but the new color in her cheeks signals she's ready to do more than sulk.

"Did Major Carburry ever ask you for a favor?"

She cocks an eyebrow. "Is that a euphemism?"

"Perhaps you sent a letter on his behalf?" Like Fukimoto. "*Innocently.*"

"Did I ever play cloak and dagger? I suspect you're suffering the vapors, Lady Margaret. Major Carburry never sent so much as a postcard and while he was in Wimereux he received all of one package from his supposedly dutiful wife. With perfume, of all things."

"From his wife?" I ask incredulously. "Should it not be the reverse?"

"Who knows what goes on in another's marriage. Perfume, pens."

"Pens?" My pulse quickens.

"For his blessed crossword puzzles."

"Gold-plated?"

"Would you expect anything less of a man in his position?" She glances at the watch pinned to her chest and exhales gustily. "Really, Lady Margaret. Unlike you, I have to earn my seventeen pounds a year."

"Why did you think our hospital was vulnerable to sabotage?"

The change of subject startles her and I press my advantage. "It's why you reported Fukimoto, isn't it? In Wimereux, you spoke of the mysterious attacks on hospitals. I assume you read yesterday's paper. About the use of timed bombs."

Her shoulders defensive, she admits, "I caught a few snippets in between my rounds."

"To the ordinary eye, these bombs appeared to be nothing more than"—I swallow hard—"gold-plated pens."

Though she remains standing, she reaches back to steady herself on the arm of the chair. Her complexion drains to ashen. Thinking aloud, she reasons, "Major Carburry and General Hildebrand never traded so much as a sentence."

"Your whole career, you have been a military nurse. South Africa, France. You've treated untold injuries, stood vigil over many a deathbed. Did you not once consider how improbable it was that Major Carburry slipped out of a German prison camp without so much as a scratch? He had help."

"You distrusted him from the beginning."

"Call it instinct," I offer.

"Whereas the rest of us were blinded?"

"By . . . loyalty."

"Loyalty?" Her lips quiver and I don't know whether she is about to laugh hysterically or sob. "Oh that life were but a crossword puzzle, where even the most complicated clues could be fixed with easy words."

I cannot help it, like a child seeking comfort, I glance up at the portrait of my mother. She is but oil and canvas, no longer flesh and bone. No wisdom to dispense. "There is always a way to fix what's wrong."

Rosling retakes her seat and shakes her head. "How young you are," she replies gently. "How naïve. For some things, there is no solution. Only . . ." She shrugs, leaving off the answer.

"Only what?"

"What you're left with." She gestures halfheartedly to the interior of this room, and out the window, to the stone courtyard and rows of three-story red brick ward buildings beyond. "It's not much. But it's not nothing."

"Colonel Wallace would not have you settle for so little."

"Different time. Different place."

"No matter where you are," I remind her, "your job, your duty, is to save lives."

"You want me to waltz into the Court Martial and blather on about a suspect crossword puzzle and gold pens? Even if such speculation were enough, you think the prosecution wouldn't dig beneath the surface? *What was your relationship to the deceased? Did you bear him any hostility? Are you an adulteress scorned?* They stone women like me, Lady Margaret."

Her hands are shaking, the tremble so violent, it fills me with pity. And anger. "I expected more courage from our matron."

The clock chimes, a cheerful ringing of bells that I want to rip out like one would a tongue.

Matron dabs at the perspiration trickling down her forehead, rearranges her cap, and rises from her seat. She studies the wide stretch of carpet between us. The distance doesn't matter. Her helplessness is contagious. Even as I stand to meet her, my posture mimics hers, hunched shoulders, bowed head.

We do not shake hands. She walks to the door, opens it. With her back to me, she turns her head and says over her shoulder, "I understand why you care so much. Why you think there's hope when there is none."

"Do you?"

"Sometimes in the operating theatre or when he was tending to the wards at night, I thought I saw . . . I assumed it was a trick of the light. But ... I thought I saw a halo." Her smile is rueful, the act of remembering painful.

My eyes are burning. Tears form behind them. I won't be helpless. I refuse to be. So long as I can crawl, I can fight. Not a lesson Mama meant to teach me, but she never tried to temper me. She let me run wild and offered comfort when I returned home scraped and bleeding.

"You're wrong," I answer, my voice raspy. "There is hope. I will get up on the stand and admit to killing Carburry myself. Damn the consequences."

It's not the harshness of her laugh that undoes me. It's the near kindness of it, how maternal it sounds. "No one will believe you," she says. "Even if it is true."

My head aching, my stomach in knots, I wander out of the hospital to face the too-bright sun and am confronted for the second time today with, "You're not who you say you are." I adjust my hat and meet the accusatory glare of my cub reporter, Master James.

Who is sporting a black eye.

"What happened? Were you attacked?" I scan the road for would-be threats. "Let me take a look."

Master James dismisses the injury with a sardonic shrug. "I'm a reporter, not a toy poodle, Miss Betts. I've been asking a lot of questions, about Major Carburry and picric acid, and German generals and sabotage. But the answers, I suspect, are all sitting in the palm of your gloved hand. An expensive kid leather, by the way. As is your hat. And your accent."

For the second time today, it seems it's my voice that gives me away.

In the distance, I spot a sleek silver motor car, weaving through traffic with the confidence of one skilled telegraph operator cum chauffer/spy, Dorothea Charles. I imagine EyePatch is sitting in the back, cracking his knuckles and seething. He warned me to keep away. More than warned. Threatened.

"You throw in words like *bairn* and *bonny*," James continues, "but I don't know that I've met anyone who speaks as posh as you. You make King George sound like a cockney publican."

I search the streets for a hiding place to duck into. We're standing to the side of the hospital. Ahead of us is nothing but the broad, open fields of Wormwood Scrubs. Where is a urine-stained alley when you need it?

From one of the block wards of the hospital, a door cracks open and a nurse steps out. She stretches her arms to the sky and takes a deep breath. She must be coming off her shift. I loop my arm through James' and drag him toward her.

"I'm asking you a direct question, Miss Betts," he says aggravated. "I've provided every address you've asked for, including the whereabouts of Sister Rosling. And you've told me nothing of value."

"Not here," I warn.

At the door to the ward block, the nurse, a young friendly sort, inspects Master James. "You'll be wanting Urgent Care. Down the street, right on Du Cane."

"I don't need a physician," he replies starchily, but I can hear the roguish pride in his voice. He earned his black eye on the job.

"If you don't mind," I say to the nurse, rubbing the back of my neck as if EyePatch can see straight through car glass and brick buildings, "we've an appointment with the ward matron and we're terribly late. You know how matrons are. Live and die by the clock, they do." I toss out an easy smile.

"A minute late is a minute lost." She smiles back. "You'll need to check in with the front desk. It's around the corner. On Du Cane Road."

I dig into my purse and hand the nurse my card. "Lady Margaret Halladay. The Earl of Halsop is my father. We are patrons of this hospital."

The girl curtsies awkwardly. "Begging your pardon, Lady Margaret—"

"If you could let us pass. I left my—"

"—but without authorization, you cannot enter this ward." Her tone is polite, but firm.

Oh the irony. During the war, when I was a nobody nurse, I could slip in and out of hospitals with impunity. "Of course," I apologize. "We'll . . ."

She gestures again to her right and makes a circle motion. I peek to my left and think I catch the flash of EyePatch's motorcar. Is he going around the corner to the next street? Does he mean to stop in front of the hospital entrance?

Master James squints at me, the Cheshire grin of a reporter spreading across his face. "*Lady* Margaret?"

Before he can say anything smart, I press my hand against his back and shove him forward, guiding him left rather than toward the main entrance.

"How did you get here?" I ask him, not bothering to wonder why he is here.

"You may instruct your chauffer to drop me off back at Fleet Street," he retorts.

"Don't be ridiculous. I took the Piccadilly tube." I quicken my stride and try to retrace my morning route. Too late I remember the station is behind us, to the south. Where EyePatch's motorcar was headed. How did he know to follow me here?

"Are you going to explain whether you are Miss Vera Betts, formerly of the Red Cross, or Lady Margaret Halladay of Halsop House?" Master James pulls me back as I'm about to cross into oncoming traffic. A red motorcar speeds by, blaring its horn.

"Both," I answer, hurrying across the lane now that it is clear. A blister is developing on my heel. My spat boots are not made for escape. "I had a falling out with my parents and in a fit of pique ran away from home, met Lady Sullivan in Portsmouth, and joined her ambulance hospital."

Keeping pace with me, he whistles. "Now there's a story."

Was the station near the Imperial College? I did not pass it on my way here. I survey the buildings, trying to figure out our surroundings.

"Did you find any records of Sister Fukimoto?" I ask.

"Besides confirmation she was a member of the Japanese Red Cross, very little, unless you can read Kanji." He considers his own question. "Can you?" He sounds hopeful.

"What about General Hildebrand?" We cross another street. The trees lining the sidewalk seem somewhat familiar. Did I walk east or west from here?

"Nothing, besides a subtle message." He points to his eye. "Say, is there a reason we're ankling about in circles?"

I stop. Perhaps it's not me that's being followed. "Was it EyePatch?"

Master James crinkles his brows.

"The black eye. Did EyePatch—Mr. Wallace of the Home Office—threaten you?"

"Hardly. He's cool as a cucumber that one. When I barraged him with questions outside of the infirmary the other day, he merely lamented how poorly a pretty boy like me would fare in the Tower." James wipes his brow. "I was taken aside by a trio of naff gents who weren't gents at all. They shoved me up against a building and suggested that if I appreciated keeping my limbs, I should shut my mouth."

"English or German?"

"English," he answers. "With excellent posture. The kind you develop in basic training, if you know your onions."

"British Royal Army," I suggest.

"Disguised in civilian wear."

"Mrs. Carburry's people." I spot Wormwood Prison. I didn't pass by it earlier, but I remember seeing signs for it from the station. We trot down a narrow street whose line of brick walls provide cover from the main street running parallel and I pause, standing tiptoe to peer over the wall. No sign of the silver motorcar. I exhale.

"Lady Margaret? Miss Betts." Master James stops to scrape muck off the sole of his shoe. "Where are we going?"

"The tube station."

"Is that way." James rolls his eyes at me and gestures behind him. "How did you manage to navigate France?"

"The fields were marked by flags."

He nods his respect.

Together, we trudge down the narrow street, round the corner and directly into the path of an idling silver motor car. The driver's door swings open. A slim figure in a bright yellow coat slips out, her posture that of someone who is reluctantly following orders and hoping to fail in her mission.

She greets me with, "Good afternoon, Lady Margaret," and opens the back passenger door.

"Good afternoon, Miss Charles."

We English are nothing if not good mannered. I limp toward the open door.

"What's going on?" Master James asks, following on my blistered heels.

Charles holds her hand up to stop James from joining me. "I'm relieved those ruffians didn't thwart your courage. You may ride in front with me."

I slide into the back seat, expecting EyePatch's dour, one-eyed grimace, an insult, and quite possibly deportation papers. Instead, I am met with a figure far more frightening.

She's too tall for the contained space of a motorcar interior, this woman whose greying hair is bundled in a chignon without a single loose strand. Her diamond stud earrings glint like knives. Her suit, though elegantly cut to fit her figure, is standard issue black so that when she wishes, she can fade into any background.

She greets me, cool, efficient and to the point. "You are not supposed to exist, Vera Betts."

"Good afternoon, Dame Wallace."

CHAPTER EIGHTEEN

Wimereux, August 13, 1918

"Good afternoon, nurse." Major Carburry's silky greeting worms its way into my sluggish brain.

Ignoring him, I attend to one of the few menial tasks Matron still lets me perform. Besides emptying bedpans and mopping floors, I am charged with organizing the newspapers scattered across the library. I move slowly, distracted by thoughts that cannot settle. Major Carburry frowns as if my listlessness causes him concern. "Have you happened to see Sister Fukimoto?"

No one has seen her since she disappeared sixty-five hours ago into the cold of night with her hands cuffed. Nick beside her.

"She usually collects the crossword from me." He waves a sheet back and forth, taunting me.

I concentrate on stacking the newspapers into a tidy pile. They are too precious to be used for kindling. Perhaps I can read them aloud to the men in Ward One.

"I'm useless finishing these." The motion Major Carburry makes, gesturing to his lap where the crossword now sits, holds a sexual entendre.

This is the moment I should leave. No good can come from sparring with Carburry. Especially after the past sixty-five hours. I have been nothing but a thick, viscous pool of negative energy, my uniform the one thing containing me. Without it, who knows what level of damage I am capable?

Dusky ink collects on my fingers and I wipe it away on my apron. "I don't know why you bother starting the crossword puzzles when you can't even get the answers right."

Suddenly cheerful, the Major stretches him arms. "Taking an interest in me at last, Nurse Betts?"

"More like trying to prevent further waste." He is not the only one reinvigorated. We feed off of each other, he and I. We are two chemicals that should never be set side by side on a shelf. Dangerous enough alone, mixed together we become noxious. "Leave the puzzles to men who know what they're about. Nelson's ship at Trafalgar was the HMS Victory, not the HMS Minerve."

"What a clever little minx you are." He pats the seat of the chair next to him. "Do come sit beside your Uncle Carburry and help me muddle through sixteen down. *David Livingstone.* Do you suppose the answer is *missionary*? Such an interesting term, don't you . . ." Though he's lounging in his wheelchair before the French doors with the full light of a summer afternoon pouring down, he suddenly shudders as if a shadow has passed over him. More to himself than aloud, he says, "I think I shall very much miss the warmth of the Wimereux sun."

Beyond the glass doors, I spy the tall figure of a woman clad in black marching across the lawn. Lucy skips alongside her, stopping to pluck a daisy here and there. The sky is a cloudless bright blue. The lawn a verdant, manicured green. Against this backdrop, it is the woman in black who should appear colorless and drab. Not the world around her.

Curiosity bedevils me. I cross over to Carburry. "Planning a holiday?"

When I reach for the crossword puzzle, he runs his index finger along my inner wrist. "The tenderness of youth," he murmurs.

"Isn't yours." I snatch my wrist back, leaving the paper on his lap.

"Whose could it be?" he asks with false innocence. "The Archangel Colonel Wallace?"

My face betrays me. I flush.

"He seems to have disappeared with Sister Fukimoto. Who knew he had such a lusty and exotic appetite?" Enjoying his vulgarity, Carburry's mouth curls up.

"At least he has the power to indulge his appetite in any position he desires, missionary or otherwise," I retort.

Pleased with myself, I make the mistake of glancing back out through the doors, where Lucy has stopped mid-step, her innocent face wary. The plucked daisies slip from her hand. What does she see? I touch my fingertips to my lips. To my horror, I realize my expression mirrors Carburry's. Disgusted, I rub my fist across my face, trying to scrub myself clean.

The woman in black kneels and retrieves one of the daisies from the lawn, tucking it behind Lucy's ear. What does she say to the child? The innocence does not return, but Lucy shakes hands and scampers away with a new sense of purpose.

Major Carburry wheels himself backward, closer to the marble fireplace. Mesmerized, the two of us wait, watching the woman as she sweeps up the path, through the doors and into the library. Closer up, she's older than I had assumed. Her jet-colored hair is peppered silver, and soft lines bracket her mouth. She takes all of a cursory second to acknowledge me, and yet I cannot help but think it's all she needs to appraise me: height, weight, blood type.

Finger by finger, she pulls her black kid gloves off and settles onto the sofa, crossing her ankles. Even sitting, she dominates the room.

After a stretched silence, Major Carburry greets her heavily. "You were not the Greek I was expecting."

"Who were you hoping for?" she asks, folding her gloves into her leather satchel and pulling out a packet of Karelia cigarettes and a simple, silver lighter. "Pate, Momus, or Eris?"

Major Carburry shrugs his shoulders. "If you recall, I was never a good student."

"Deception, Blame, or Strife." Despite her formidable stature and severe clothes, when she speaks her voice is deeply feminine, low and so soft, the Major and I stretch forward to catch each syllable.

"To be so lucky." Major Carburry crumples the sheet of newspaper laying on his lap and tosses it into the soot-stained hearth. "I meant to send my regrets to you regarding Reims. Any news? One mustn't admit defeat, even if witnesses say his plane was engulfed in flames and splitting apart midair."

I lower my head. There are few, more brutal ways to die.

The woman in black responds by lighting the cigarette, her movements smooth and unruffled, her first puff relaxed and untroubled. "Do you need help packing your bags?" she asks Carburry.

"Being sent back to old Blighty, am I? Will it be a hero's welcome or am I to play the prodigal son?" He adds a particular emphasis on *son*, goading her still.

Her lips shaping an *ooo*, she exhales thick smoke rings. "I've not the talents of a gypsy fortune teller."

"Don't be so modest. As Deputy Chief of the Special Intelligence Services, you can do more than see into the future. You control it." With one hand fisted, Major Carburry imitates a globe spinning on its axis, with the other he flicks his thumb and forefinger, knocking the imaginary orb about.

"Very well, I predict we will hit a storm on the Channel. I suggest you bundle up." She lowers her lids, assessing his legs in casts. "Or ask for help."

He snaps back, "Nurse Betts can do my bidding."

The woman's attention swivels away from Carburry and directly to me. "Vera Betts?" she asks as if she's genuinely curious. "It seems I get both the bird in my hand and the two in the bush."

"I don't understand," I reply. Her intense focus makes me feel small and insignificant. "It's the Major being discharged."

He scoffs. "That's a nice word for it."

She sends him a moue of false pity and says to me, matter-of-factly, "I have papers for you as well."

"Pardon?" I ask stupidly.

"You're being reassigned to a convalescent home in England," she explains.

From his corner, Major Carburry offers up a handkerchief and points to my face. I must have ink splotches from where I rubbed it earlier. I wipe my cheeks and chin with my white sleeve. How petulant I must appear. I ask, "On whose authority?"

"I would not question Dame Wallace," Carburry warns.

"Wallace?" A coincidence?

"Forgive me," Carburry says. "I should have made the proper introductions. Dame Wallace, may I introduce to you your son's delightful pet?"

Not a coincidence. A chess match between Carburry and Dame Wallace where Nick may be the rook, but I am but a pawn. Expendable. "You can't just pack me off to England," I insist. "I'm needed here. We have a shortage of staff."

She studies my ink-stained apron and messy face with disapproval. "The sweet child I met earlier, Lucy? Such a smart little thing. She has taken it upon herself to welcome the five nurses I have brought over from England." She stubs her cigarette out in a cloisonné ashtray. "Not only are they QAIMNS, they are trained in spinal injuries. Are you?"

I jut my chin out. "I am useful."

"Your record of service has been duly noted."

"Matron—"

"Has threatened to file assault charges against you." Dame Wallace answers.

Major Carburry bounces up in his wheelchair. "I say, Nurse Betts, have you been a naughty girl?"

Dame Wallace checks the time on her wristwatch. "Your mantel clock is two minutes off, which means you have less than half an hour to retrieve your belongings and say your goodbyes. You're quite good with quick departures, are you not?" This she directs to Carburry.

"What if I refuse?" I ask.

The sparkle in her dark eyes suggests Dame Wallace might be charmed, the way the cat is by the mouse he bats between his paws. "It's not my order you're refusing. It's Colonel Wallace who requested your reassignment."

I reel back, pressing my damp hands behind me, against the wall. Nick? Why would Nick send me away? He, above all people, knows the woman I am exists only here. In England I am no one, most especially not a nurse.

"If N-N . . ." I pause to correct my ragged breath. "Why are you carrying out Colonel Wallace's request? Why isn't he here?"

From the disdain on Dame Wallace's face, it's clear I've failed a test. She replies, "Because the world doesn't revolve around you, child."

My humiliation gives Carburry heart. He tut-tuts. "I do hate to see a lover's tiff."

Dame Wallace rises and loops her satchel across her chest. "You weren't a terrible student, Carburry. Just a bore."

✧

The farewells I make are made in haste. Matron acknowledges my departure by watching my valise as its tossed into the transport truck, and turning her back to me, overjoyed that she will never have to lay eyes upon me again. Lucy, who has seen how ugly a human I can be, can barely muster a wave as she clings to the steady arm of her crippled father. And the patients, these men whose withered limbs I have washed, whose sunken cheeks I have shaved, express surprise at the abruptness of my leave, but no sentiment. They have learned well not to become too attached to any one person.

I should have learned the same. I am being banished from a place I have grown to love because I fell in love with Nick. Who has abandoned me. Why? Was I a trade, made to save Fukimoto? Did it run deeper? Nick, who works so hard to always do the right thing, damn the consequences, must have a reason. Am I the reason or the consequence?

What a selfish, stupid fool I am. He said it himself, the night we traced the stars. There was nothing he wouldn't betray in the name of peace. Not me. Not himself. And how can he be wrong? In a world where boys are blown to bits for an inch of No Man's Land, love cannot figure in the equation.

Still, the ache in my heart engulfs me. Even as I accompany Major Carburry in the ambulance to the Port of Calais, guide Dame Wallace's men in grey suits on how to load him onto the docked merchant ship, and settle him into the tiny sick bay, my head can't stop spinning. My organs twist and churn. I am seventeen again, a vulnerable colt of a girl, absorbing the pain of my mother admonishing me that we do not get to love who we want. Except I am a woman now. My love runs deeper, as do my scars.

We are sailing through a storm. The sea bucks and rolls beneath us, waves crash against the ship's sides, and water seeps in through the portholes. I cannot gain a foothold on the slippery floor. No matter how fiercely I cling to the bulkhead, I am thrown left to right and back again. In the passageway alcove, a young sailor retches into a bucket. To the Channel, eleven tons of pure steel is but a toy to toss and snap.

Through sheer dint of will, I reach the sick bay without dropping the canteen of broth I had filled in the kitchen. When I enter, the air is heavy with tobacco and the smoke stings my eyes. I seem to have caught Dame Wallace and Major Carburry in the midst of a fevered, furtive argument. She rises from the side of his cot, elegant and cool. Carburry smacks his lips loudly and draws on his cigarette greedily, which brings on a harsh cough.

"You might consider foregoing the Karelia," I suggest. He must be on his sixth already.

"Not a smoker yourself, Vera Betts?" It's strange how Dame Wallace over enunciates my name, as if determining its veracity by testing each letter.

"I have my doubts regarding its health effects," I answer like the medical professional my uniform suggests I am and gesture to Carburry, whose face has turned a bright cherry red from coughing.

"Calms the stomach," she answers. "Nevertheless, if the tobacco bothers you, do step out for some fresh air." She says this just as the ship lurches and sways. The motion rattles the metal cupboards and my teeth. I grasp the edge of the table, which is bolted down. Carburry clutches his sides and lets out a pained moan. Medical supplies crash to the floor and clatter about us. A tin bowl falls and spins haplessly toward my feet.

The ship, my nerves, the tin bowl, none have yet to settle, when Dame Wallace leaves her pack of cigarettes on the table and strides to the door, not so much as a hair out of place. "We should be coming into port inside the half hour." She inhales deeply. "Home sweet home, no?"

Neither Carburry nor I respond. The door clicks shut behind her. Carburry gags. I pick up the tin bowl and take it over to him. He leans across my lap and vomits into it. When he's finished, I wipe his face and rearrange him back into the cot, adding a stack of pillows to raise him to a sitting position.

"I don't think Dame Wallace is right about the stomach calming," he says wryly.

"Would you prefer a sedative?"

Embarrassed, he ducks his chin. "Yes."

"You'll have to take some broth first."

"A credit to your profession, you are," he says weakly.

I near feel sorry for him. All summer his legs have been trapped in casts, his body dependent on the care of others, but it's seasickness that has brought him low. "Come now, Major. We're well beyond compliments." I pour the broth from the canteen into a cup.

"I have always admired you." He takes mincing sips, struggling to swallow. "You have a rather singular devotion. It's unfortunate how misdirected it is, though. Like Fukimoto with her German general. Unfair isn't it? How it's always the woman who suffers for love. That damned Jerry is likely drinking tea in Wimereux and being fawned over by five new nurses while Fukimoto?" He holds his hands up in question. "We don't even know where she is."

Her name calls up the memory of a sweet, curious woman trying to throw herself to her death through a broken window. A horrible image, it has kept me awake and sleepless for days. I bite my inner cheek to chase it away.

"I don't understand why the poets rail against war," he adds philosophically. "All the nonsense about 'I think I shall never see/A poem lovely as a tree.' It's love that's cruel. Mothers should warn their daughters so."

"My mother did." I should not be confessing such things to Carburry, of all people. I do not trust his avuncular façade for a minute. But I hurt so much for missing Nick, if I do not keep talking, if I am left with my own emotions, I fear they will strangle me. "She told me we do not get to love who we want."

Carburry runs his thumb across his lips like he's trying to remember the song that goes with my mother's line. "But not its parallel? You do not get to stop loving simply because you want to."

I struggle not to recoil, discomfited by how soothing I find Carburry's insight. Even the sea seems to have calmed, at least temporarily. "And who broke your heart for you to learn such a lesson?" I take his empty cup and the sick bowl over to the basin and rinse them out.

"My downfall is my son." His sigh is tinged with resentment. "You hold your newborn in your arms and you can't help but promise him the world. Which dooms you to proving you can deliver. I'm no white knight. And yet he demands it of me." He studies his casts like they're to blame for his shortcomings as a parent. "Which is why I understand Dame Wallace."

"She strikes me as a chess master, not a fairy queen." Noting Carburry's too-bright face and the way he bows his shoulders, I suspect he is suffering another stomach cramp. I bring the tin bowl and a fresh linen back to him.

"You can't think SIS gives a toss about either of us." He eyes the bowl. "I'd prefer a cigarette."

I reach for the pack and pull one out. He takes it from my hand and dangles it between his teeth while I light it.

Drawing out the first taste, he says, "Dame Wallace is here to save her son. Nothing less. Nothing more."

"From what?"

"From sainthood," he laughs. "Like his father."

"The father who swam out to sea rather than accept how his vanity project became a weapon of war."

"Sins of the father." He twirls his cigarette. "The circle of life. Though I do find it amusing that it's the do-gooders who do the most damage, and their sons who pay the price. Road to hell, no?"

I dig my nails into my palm. As angry and hurt as I am by Nick using his mother to force me back to England, still I understand the wounds driving him. His insistence upon hope is born of grief. Nick must do more than take up his father's flag, he must prove he was not a failure.

"Damned idealists, the Wallace men." Carburry stops, overtaken by a fit of coughs. When he recovers, he spits dark phlegm into the sick bowl. "You and I, Betts, we're sewn from sturdier cloth. We're pragmatists. No matter how much you dislike me, and I assure you, I can feel every bitter ounce of your disdain boring through my pores"— he shudders to demonstrate—"we are people of action, not theorems."

Wiping the spittle from his mouth, I say, "I act to save lives."

"Some of us have a higher calling."

"Doing God's work?" I ask incredulously, riled by his arrogance and the hypocrisy powering it. "I must have missed your vicar's collar. Or is your calling card something more volatile? If I were to open your trunk, would I be more likely to find a gold pen or two or three or four? Which are not at all writing instruments but rather instruments of sabotage."

He chuckles, acknowledging me with a nod of respect that makes my toes curl. "You and I both know the fighting won't end because we are suddenly recalled to the ideals of fairness and goodness. It ends because one side is eviscerated."

"If you are attempting to recruit me, you are going to need a better speech."

"You know I was trained by the very best. Dame Wallace taught me how to assess people, their strengths, their weaknesses, what makes them biddable, what makes them breakable. And do you know what I observed during that bit of Shakespeare on the stairs when Fuki was arrested? Rosling, devoted to King and Country and blind to all else. Fuki silent and humiliated, touch of the martyr about her. Wallace tempering everyone with reason." He scoffs. "Everyone was so predictable. Except you, you never fail to surprise me. You have a violent streak. Had Wallace the Pacifist not stopped you, I think you would have dug your thumbs into Rosling's pretty eyes. You are *fascinating*."

Too late, I think to cross my arms. He's burrowed beneath my skin, dug out my vulnerabilities. What I have always feared most about myself is the volatile energy whipping through me. Isn't it why Mama thought I would be the least loved? Isn't it why Papa always fought me? I don't just stir up trouble. I make it. I am my own timed bomb. Except no one can predict when I explode. Not even me. No wonder Nick is sending me home.

Major Carburry tips my chin up to face him. "No, no, dear girl. Do not shrink from such strength. Wallace may have toddled off to mumsy to handle what he clearly cannot. But what I see in you is a woman to behold. To fear!"

I trace the edge of the watch pinned to my chest. The one I time my heart to so that I remain steady and true, the *safe pair of hands* Old Betts taught me to be. What if he was wrong? What if his watch masks rather than tames? Perhaps nursing was merely a route to satisfy something darker within me, a bloodlust.

Carburry stubs his cigarette out against the wall and flicks the butt onto the floor, all the while his posture relaxed and confident. He can taste my weakness, my belief in Vera Betts crumbling. "Once I am in England—"

"You'll be locked up."

"Is that the voice of hope or a mere assumption?"

"Women's intuition," I answer. "Mother or not, SIS does not send its Deputy Chief merely to discharge a patient, even one as ignoble as you."

"When we reach Blighty's shores," he says, "there will be a caravan of military officers prepared to throw a parade in my *noble* honor."

I cock my head to the left. "Is that the voice of delusion or men's intuition? I highly doubt Dame Wallace shared news of your impending arrival with the Royal Army. From what little I've observed, the different institutions devoted to our empire horde information."

"Silly Betts, you don't think I retreated to my room to pack, do you? I tasked Rosling with the sending of telegrams."

"Are you sure Matron is so spellbound she would obey your every order?"

"I'm hard to resist." He smiles smugly.

"And yet she aborted your child."

He shoots up to a soldier straight sitting position. The color drains from his face. "A baby," he whispers. Hand on his heart, he repeats, "My baby."

"He? She?" I hold open my palms in question and savor my cruelty. "We will never know. *Your* baby lays buried under the Rowan tree in the back garden. All those hours you spent spying on the world from your window, you never once sensed your dead bairn was right beneath your nose. Which makes me question the quality of your skills. Were you, as Dame Wallace says, little more than a bore?"

Carburry's Adam's apple bobs up and down. He is swallowing bile, fighting off another wave of nausea. He is no creature of the sea. "Scorned lover or no," he says, "Rosling's true fidelity is to England. She would walk barefoot through hellfire for our island empire. Even now the woman thinks it was her own observations, not my seductive whisperings that brought about Fuki's arrest. Oh she sent the telegrams all right. No doubt about it."

I lean over him, face to face. "You will hang."

He bursts out into loud, raucous laughter, repelling me backward. "It's Wallace whose fingerprints cover those golden pens, not mine. He was the one cavorting through France. I was recuperating. As you yourself can bear witness to. Where was the highly decorated Major Carburry when the cargo of medical supplies in Calais spontaneously combusted?" He mimics the voice of a prosecutor. "In bed with his legs in traction," he says, his answer high pitched to match a woman's.

"How pathetic does one have to be to have aligned one's goals with a pacifist?" I stand above him, my boots firmly planted and my knees locked. "No fatalities. Colonel Wallace undermined you far better than counterintelligence could. Your picric acid bombs are pointless." With my hands, I imitate a dramatic explosion, fist them again like a magician about to surprise a child with a penny from behind the ear, except when I uncurl my hands, all I present is empty palms to offer an empty victory.

"Wallace was merely my litmus test." Carburry punches the mattress. "He may have refused loss of life, but he proved how easy it is to slip in and out of hospitals. All it takes to plant a timed bomb is a surgeon's coat and a friendly wave. Both of which can be faked. The world is my proverbial oyster."

"Picric acid is not readily available. You need a supplier. It's volatile and difficult to transport."

"I have my sources." He puffs his chest. "And a network of like-minded men who have no compunction regarding death tolls. On my word, a single word, we'll eviscerate the Royal Army Medical Corps."

Through clenched jaw, I tell him, "You clearly do not understand human nature. If you raze medical facilities, you are murdering the innocent—men too injured to defend themselves and the people who care for them. England would rise up, one unbreakable force, and crush you."

"I don't need to understand human nature, Betts. I understand war. Don't believe me? In 1575, the English laid siege to Rathlin Castle. Do you know the story?" To my shake of the head, he smiles gleefully, a man sharpening his knives. "Rathlin was a refuge to civilians. Women, children, the elderly, the so-called innocent. All members of Clan MacDonnell, an enemy to Queen Elizabeth. The Earl of Essex blocked passage from the mainland so the clan leader, Sorley Boy MacDonnell couldn't reach Rathlin. And in the meanwhile, the English ran rabid on the island. Killed every last soul."

My mouth goes dry, my stomach convulses. "That is horrific."

"It is how victory is won," he replies, at ease in his savagery. "You know what Essex wrote to Queen Elizabeth's secretary? That Sorley Boy 'was likely to have run mad for sorrow.' It's a nice turn of phrase, is it not, for butchering a man's people? Fukimoto would have appreciated it."

"You would butcher England."

"Was it England that freed me?" he demands.

"Do you hate your own country that much?"

"Your notion of country is laughable." He takes a moment to cough. "National boundaries are nothing but barbed wire to pen in the sheep. I am no sheep."

"You're no wolf."

"Do you think Hildebrand and I collaborated because we both went to Cambridge? Or because we share an allegiance to Germany?" He speaks to me as if I'm a querulous child, not a woman who has witnessed four years of carnage. "We serve ourselves. What we want is power. If we weren't being paid to do otherwise, we would just as easily bomb every German hospital in sight."

"You have no loyalty," I say in horror.

"It's loyalty that leads countries into war, the very thing you abhor. My network knows no borders. German, English, French, American, Canadian. Swiss."

"The Swiss are neutral," I counter stupidly, refusing to believe that there could be something more evil than war, a league of saboteurs driven by greed.

"And yet it was a Swiss-German courier who came to visit me in Wimereux. To deliver a package." Carburry grins at me as if the anguish written across my face is his prize.

I recall the man Carburry speaks of. Nick snapped his arm in two. But he also set it. "What have you won if you've lost your humanity," I demand. "Nothing. And Nothing is the legacy you will leave your son." I rise and pace the cramped sick bay. The ship thrusts and heaves, as unsteady as I am.

"You disappoint me, Betts. I did not take you for a sentimental dullard."

"You think your son will view you as a white knight?" I clasp the edge of the table, pressing my flesh into its sharp, metal-trimmed edge. "No. He will witness the executioner put the rope around your neck. He'll see you writhe and jerk, watch how you claw at your throat as the noose tightens."

I return to Carburry, sit on the side of his cot and whisper sweet as poison, "He will smell the stink while you defecate yourself, the body's natural response to death. And he will *hate* you."

He rises up on his elbows and shakes his fist. "I am not bound by institutions and I am far more powerful than a hero. I am unstoppable." He digs his elbow into my torso and shoves me away. I stumble back and catch my fall.

His bravado fills my chest with the purest form of fire. Maybe I am not a safe pair of hands. Maybe I am untamable, difficult, wild, violent. But I can choose who to hate. I know how to destroy his arrogance. "Powerful? You can't even walk. You suffered nerve damage to your spine."

"My knees." He points downward.

"If you had even a fifty percent chance of ever walking again, you'd have been sent to England to recuperate in the pretty countryside, waited on hand and foot by a bevy of naïve VADS. Instead, you were held back in Wimereux, treated at an elite hospital dedicated to retraining severed-limbed bodies and snapped spines . . ."

Carburry's brain must be running like a rat through a dark alley, but my bloodlust has an appetite unsatisfied. It is not enough for him to be afraid. "You are helpless," I say. "Crippled." A condition my brave patients in Wimereux learned to accept because at least they were alive. Not Carburry. He is more vain than brave. "When the historians write of you, unlike the courage and acclaim they use to describe your father, they will speak of you in tragic tones. With *pity*."

Doubt and fear turn the color of his skin from red to sallow to red again. He labors to draw oxygen, chokes on the exhalation. Between the cigarettes and the heaving sea, he struggles to shout, but can barely expel the accusation. "Liar!"

Detached from my body, numb to my moral conscience, I smile while Carburry hyperventilates. If only he could suffocate on fear and humiliation alone. For suffocate he must. Otherwise, Carburry will have his Rathlin. The more innocent the soul, the more valuable his target. Not just women like Fukimoto, not just soldiers like Corporal Langdon, but the people who love them. Like Lucy.

I steel my nerves. "You seem overwrought, Major. Let me prepare your sedative."

"I don't need it." His body disobeys, wracking him with gasps and coughs.

"Nurse's orders," I reply in my best Florence Nightingale, a tone I have never once used. It bounces about the walls like a cheerful bell, and resonates false and ugly within me.

At the counter, I rifle through the glass vials, searching for something potent. Atropine? Morphine? Inspiration comes to me in the sound of Carburry dry-heaving. Potassium Chloride. We use it for patients who, due to nausea, have a potassium deficiency. Dr. Bettany taught me to administer it with caution. The wrong diagnosis or too high a dose, and a man's heart will seize within the minute.

Clicking the glass to ensure no air bubbles, loading the hypodermic needle, I expect my hands to shake. They are even-keeled, the violent streak Carburry identified is contained in my *safe pair of hands*. I stare down at them. Can I do this?

The ship staggers into the East Sussex port. I hear distant voices calling out commands, directing the berthing, shouting for the bollard to secure the vessel to the dock. I do not have much time. My vision tunnels, the needle in my hand guides me forward. The sick bay smells of tobacco and vomit, a pungent elixir.

Carburry sneers at me, confident in his power over me, over humanity. "Good little nurse." His use of the word *good* crawls over my skin. He means it dismissively. For him, good is a thing to be spat at.

He claims he acts for his son. His son is but an excuse for his evil. I smile down at my needle. Yes, I can do this.

I cross over to him. In my fevered state, a voice slips into the blackness of my tunneled mind. Nick. I recall the first time we met, when I was so desperate to save a man who died anyway. *The trick is there is no trick.* Always full of hope, my Nick.

What did he say to me the last time we spoke?

This is not who you are.

But I am, I am.

To destroy evil, one must become evil. A sin eater. This is the lesson Nick cannot learn. His goodness is his weakness. Carburry exploited it. But Carburry cannot exploit me for he and I are mirrors to each other. The same singular focus, but in reverse.

My vision clears. Carburry is watching me, his eyes red rimmed and worn through. He exhales and relaxes, fooled into believing I am following my nursing duty. I kneel at his cot and run my finger over the smooth skin of his inner elbow. Healthy veins. I pull out an elastic from my pocket and tie it around his arm to bring the vein to the surface. The electric light catches the color of his eyes, brown as the trunk of English oak trees, like the ones I used to climb as a child. The ones my mother wants me to teach my nephew to climb. My nephew who is fatherless.

I wonder, does Carburry's son have the same English oak eyes?

I shake my head to push away the thought. I've never met his child. It would be a blessing for the boy not to grow up with a father such as he. I tip the needle up so that when the potassium chloride is injected into his bloodstream, it will rush straight to his traitorous heart.

"What is your son's name?" I hear myself asking.

"Nicholas," he whispers with a mixture of fondness and regret.

My fingers tremble. What bizarre circle is this? The world spins round and round while men repeat the mistakes of their fathers and children suffer for their mistakes. For all the innocents who might be saved if Carburry were to die, there is the innocent who will suffer because of it, one who shares a name with the man I cannot stop loving.

The needle has pricked Carburry's skin. I merely need to plunge the liquid into his vein. Instead, I yank the needle out and drop it to the floor. It rolls beneath the bed and rolls out again, toward the table leg.

"Were you trying to poison me?" Carburry asks, but he is joking, amused.

"I don't need to." I am on my kneeling on the floor so the two of us are eye-level. With one hand, I cup Carburry's cheek, stroke it with my thumb. "Better for Nicholas to see you for what you are. A dog, not a man."

Carburry narrows his eyes at me.

"Woof," I answer. "Woof, woof."

"Shut-up." He grips my wrist.

"Woof."

"Shut-up."

"Woof."

He twists my arm behind my back, shoving me to the floor. I'd forgotten how strong he was. But for the casts, he is perfectly healthy and unrestrained. I can feel my rotator cuff tearing.

"Woof," I bark. "Woof."

When I lift my head, he grabs me by my hair and slams my jaw into the metal bedframe.

Saliva and blood trickle down my chin. I pull back, lick my lips, and prepare to bark again. He muzzles me, clamping down on my mouth so hard, his fingers drive into my jaw line. A wave hits the ship, giving him the momentum he needs to thrust his body out of bed push me flat to the floor. I thrash and kick, but am pinned beneath him. He will crush my bones.

"Shhh," Carburry whispers. "Shhh."

Sweat trickles off his forehead and spills onto my face. He is panting hard. My nose registers the scent of almonds off his breath, though he has eaten nothing but broth. I try to bite his hand, but cannot catch enough flesh. He spreads his palm to block my nostrils. No air. I close my eyes to shut out the sight of Carburry's snarling, heated face hovering over me. Where is the potassium chloride? Behind me, caught by the table leg. I stretch my fingers, trying to reach it, but it's too far away. My oxygen starved brain calls up the sound of Nick's voice, shouting. A memory? Or a dying wish? Sensation warps and blurs in my head. *Where?*, I think I hear him say. *Hold on.*

"You son of a bitch!"

My eyes spring open. That is not Carburry's voice. An arm comes around Carburry's neck and jerks him off of me.

"Nick!" I scramble onto my knees.

Using the added power of his plaster casts, Carburry swings his legs, smashing them against Nick's hip, knocking him into the door. Carburry keeps his legs angled up, blocking Nick from moving.

"Tourniquet," Nick shouts, nudging his chin toward the kit hanging off a hook, the large, heavy kind used when amputating limbs.

Sore and wheezing for air, I lunge toward it, take it off its hook.

"Come closer, Betts," Carburry warns, "and I will smash *his* knees."

We are not on a medical ship. The tourniquet is old-fashioned, the canvas rolled up, with a heavy metal screw and clasp. I unfurl it, wrap a stretch of it round my hand, and swing it like one does a fishing line. The metal clasp slashes the skin above Carburry's eye. He cries out, the sound one of frustration more than pain. Taking advantage of Carburry's supine position, Nick slams his body onto Carburry's torso, straddles his chest, and binds his wrists together. Carburry curses and howls the foulest words.

My head is buzzing. I am dizzy from the punishment I took from Carburry's attack. In a daze, I ask, "How are you here?"

Nick hauls Carburry back to the cot, and uses the last of the tourniquet canvas to secure him to the metal frame. "I accompanied Fukimoto to England and raced back to East Sussex to meet the ship. To get you off and home."

"How the fuck did I get trapped in your love story?" Carburry's laugh borders on hysterical.

Finished with him, Nick rises from the bed and searches the sick bay. "We have to hurry. Your bag? Your coat?"

I pull them out from a wardrobe. Nick makes to join me, but pauses at the table. Bending down, he picks up the hypodermic needle.

"Don't!" I screech.

"My bloody sedative," Carburry mutters.

Nick tosses the needle back onto the metal tray, swings my bag onto his shoulder and takes my hand. I squeeze his tightly, testing for the solidity of his bones, to be sure he is real and not a phantom.

Carburry rattles the cot and shakes the metal frame. "I thought you wanted to end this war, Wallace. I thought you were willing to do anything, even sabotage hospitals."

Nick stops at the door and turns back. "I told you then and I will tell you again, I will never take a single human life."

"Then why did you join my game?" Carburry asks, near sulky.

"Because my older brother asked for my help to deal with the man who ordered the bomb that killed our younger brother. You."

Nick slams the door behind us and guides me out of the sick bay and down the passageway. He means to move faster, but he's wincing, shifting his weight to the right to ease the burden on his injured hip. He drags his left leg, laboring to climb the stairs. At the top, we are met by Dame Wallace. Behind her, two hulking men in grey suits stand at attention. One reaches inside his jacket and I make out the shape of a gun resting in its shoulder holster. At Dame Wallace's signal, her men step back a respectful distance.

She furrows her brow, noting the way Nick stands heavily to compensate for his injury. "You are—"

"I told you, no," Nick says to her in a low, furious voice. "I specifically said not to involve Nurse Betts. And yet you did."

"We cannot constantly be making exceptions for your projects," she answers pragmatically. "You asked me to bring her home to the safety of England. I have. If along the Channel I requested that she attend to Carburry, she was doing her professional duty. She is medically qualified is she not? She comported herself proficiently enough."

I rub my face, bruised from Carburry.

Nonplussed, Dame Wallace ignores me and warns Nick, "The captain received a report from the port authorities. Carburry must have contacted the British Royal Army, who know nothing and will believe even less. This may be a private ship, the crew and captain work for me, but even I cannot prevent the Army from boarding and taking command."

"I passed a caravan of marked motorcars on my way here," Nick replies.

"We've set up two gangplanks. Naturally, the Army will embark via the bow. You take the stern. The porters are already unloading cargo and the crates will obscure you from view."

Nick juts his thumb behind him. "Carburry?"

"Is my problem. You need to get off this ship." Dame Wallace directs her command to me, leaving me uneasy.

Nick presses his hand into the small of my back and hustles me forward. Leaning his shoulder into the wind-battered door, he calls back, "Be careful, Mother. Even a cat only has nine lives."

Her smile, small as it is, is consumed by grief. Carburry's needling reference to a pilot burning to death over Reims comes back to me. This war has already robbed her of one son. What would it do to her to lose Nick? She blinks and the longing disappears, replaced by her cool, neutral veneer. She directs her men to accompany her down the stairs.

Nick thrusts open the door and we stumble out into the relentless rain. We need only pull up our collars and duck our heads, mind our step, keep a steady hold to the metal railing and cross the gangplank. On the other side lies England, the land of my birth, my home, whose soil I have not touched in four years. I might as well be lost at sea.

Sensing my trepidation, Nick wraps his arm around my shoulder. A blast of wind lashes through me, whipping at my skirts and pulling at my Red Cross cape, ripping the seams that keep me together. In the stinging cold, I feel myself unraveling. "We were supposed to see the Perseids tonight." My statement is an accusation. "A meteor shower, in this filthy storm."

"A mere storm over the Channel isn't going to alter the Earth's trajectory. Whether we see it or not, we're rotating through a thousand-year-old dust cloud." He offers me a small, tight smile and tries again to encourage me toward the gangplank.

"Right. Because we have no influence, no sway in this world." I shrink back and curl into the shadows of the ship's overhang. It offers no shelter from the wind and rain, but it wraps me in the safety of darkness. He shrugs out of his coat and throws it over me as if what terrifies me are the Earth's elements, not the journey home.

"What is it?" he asks, his tone so gentle and patient, I want to bite him out of spite. "Is it your papers? My mother has arranged your entry documents. You'll have no trouble."

"Your mother. Yes. Who you sent to collect me because you found me…you didn't want"—I hate myself for this bitterness, the effect of letting Carburry's taunts slip through my armor and play havoc with my equilibrium. "You said to me *this is not who you are.*"

"What are you going on about?" He sets his hands on my shoulders. "In what world would I leave you? Without you *je suis perdu.*"

"The real world," I shoot back. "The one where men like Carbury are heroes."

"There is no one in the world like you. No one," he says roughly, angry. "No one has your instincts."

"Right. The instinct behind every cut my mother had to bandage and every argument I started with my father. The instinct that led me to lie to Lady Sullivan and fake my nursing credentials and drives me to run toward burning buildings." The one where I loaded a death needle to inject into a man's veins.

"Exactly," he answers.

I snort and direct his attention to the port, where the motorcars he likely passed on the road are now collecting in a semicircle. Doors swing open. Men in uniform leap out and march urgently toward the ship.

Nick nudges me deeper into the shadows to hide us from view. "You're strong on instinct and weak on faith, Vera-not-Vera. You'd rather believe the worst of yourself than see you as you are. And that is an insult to me, to my love for you." He pounds his fist against his chest, the gesture powerful, the sound vulnerable. Just flesh and bone against flesh and bone.

My throat aches from the sob that wants to break free. I hunch my shoulders and press my forehead into the top brass buttons on his khaki tunic. The snake and rod emblem will leave an indentation on my skin. "I'm tired, Nick. I'm so tired. Of blood and broken bodies, of the smell of gun powder and antiseptic, of constantly running and yet not reaching any place, of waking up from nightmares where I can't remember the dream, of fighting, to be good when there is so much evil."

"Me too, darling. Me too." He seals me to him in a tight embrace, laying his stubbled cheek next to mine. His teeth are chattering. He'll catch pneumonia if we do not move along. I'm not ready to face home, but I have Nick.

In the distance, the Army officers pound up the bay side gangplank in formation, as if they mean to attack rather than board. Behind me, inside the ship, I can hear scuffling, the captain greeting the officers with an argument, raised voices. All these men, they're on the same side. How have they forgotten?

"Are we ever to have Greece?" I ask.

In answer, he kisses me. His chilled lips taste of rain. I deepen the kiss to lend him my warmth. We cling together. This kiss is not one of desire, but hope, the kind that starts deep within and builds and builds because despite the world tearing itself apart, we have found each other. No matter the madness around us, we can forge our own trajectory. And if we can do that, then there will be no Rathlin. We will find a way.

The sound of a gunshot shatters the moment. There's the frantic scurry of boots, collective shouting. I strain to hear if one of the voices belongs to Dame Wallace. Through the porthole, I can see the captain waving his arms, trying to calm everyone.

Someone—the sound seems to be coming from below deck—shouts, "Not breathing."

Another, "Bloody hell."

Still, I cannot hear Dame Wallace.

"Resuscitate!"

"We need a doctor."

Nick stills, his senses seem to sharpen. I wrap my arms tight around him, willing for him to ignore the pleas for help coming from the ship.

Someone demands, "Is there a doctor on this ship?"

We lock eyes. If I am built on instinct, he is built on duty. Even as I try to hold him in place, I know I have to let him go. "I can help," I say.

"I can't let you." He eases his precious hold on me.

"Why not?"

"My heart resides in yours." he says hoarsely. "And I need you to be safe."

The rain drips off his cap and streams down his face, following the contours of his high cheekbones, his solid jaw. I have never seen Nick so bereft. He must not have been able to save Fukimoto. He must be absorbing the death of his brother. The sharpness of his sorrow has teeth. It tears into me. I grab onto him, to hold him, to take as much of his pain into myself as I can. He sighs against me. My love is his relief.

Fumbling with the coat and cape covering me, I reach beneath the layers and unpin my watch, place it into his palm and fold his fingers over it. "My heart resides in yours."

From inside the ship voices continue to cry for a medic, for a doctor, for someone to save a life.

Nick spins me around and sends me down the gangplank.

"Vera-not-Vera," he calls out to me.

I turn. He has come out of the shelter of the overhang, his cap tucked under his arm. The wind beats at him. The rain pounds against him. Beneath a black and moonless sky, though the world bears down on him, he stands broad shouldered and straight backed. And so very much alone.

"We will have Greece," I shout up to him. Not a question. If he falls, if he loses his way, if his injured hip gives out and he is left for dead in a ditch, I will find him. I will pull him to his feet and share the burdens of his halo. I will keep him safe. No matter who I am, he is mine.

"Always." He secures his cap to his head, turns his back, and follows his duty, disappearing into the fray of the ship.

I tread carefully along the gangplank. Its ice cold metal railing burns through my thin gloves. I lift my knees high to keep my boots from sliding on the wet surface. My heart quivers with each inch forward. One step. Another step. Until at last I am swallowed up by the dark, gaping mouth that is England, Vera Betts no more.

PART III

LONDON

She dances like a life-boat,
though she carries flag and gun.
—Eliza Cook,
"The Fairy of the Sea"

CHAPTER NINETEEN

London, May 7, 1919

"All you had to do was continue not to exist, Vera Betts."

I watch transfixed by the imperial red of Dame Wallace's lips as she pops an almond into her mouth, rolling her tongue as she deskins the nut and savors the smooth nakedness of the white meat.

"You take more pleasure in almonds than cigarettes," I comment, wondering why the scent of almonds nags at the back of my head.

"If I recall correctly, you do not approve of smoking." She holds out her bag of almonds, offering me one.

I decline. "I'm surprised you recall me at all considering you ignored all my letters. And telephone calls, which were rerouted to the Library of Birmingham."

"And people accuse me of not having a sense of humor." Dame Wallace taps the window dividing the backseat from the driver's and wiggles her fingers at Charles, indicating unspoken directions.

Charles shifts gears and swerves into action. The speed of the car sends Master James' pencil flying onto the dashboard, rolling down and disappearing beneath his seat. Something I suspect Charles meant to do. She darts him a glance and pulls at her ear, advising him to listen and remember. Good reporters, like spies, are best unseen.

I square my shoulders. "You hid Nick from me."

Dame Wallace sucks on her almond. "Again, must I remind you, the world does not revolve around you, child."

"But I revolve around Nick. And he me." My tone is matter-of-fact because among all the things that define the world, sun and moon, gravity and buoyancy, surface field and pull field of a magnet, Bootes chasing Ursa Major through the night sky, Nick and I too are a fact.

"I underestimated the depth of his love for you." The admission of her own mistake costs her. She disguises her emotion by rolling up the paper bag of almonds and runs her lacquered thumbnail across the seam, back and forth, back and forth. "A miscalculation in an otherwise excellent strategy."

"We were pawns in your game?"

"Game?" She tightens her jaw and purses her lips. "Do you think we were playing lawn tennis? Do you know what it takes to make sure evil does not win? It is so much easier to cave to chaos rather than keep the pillars of civilization from crashing down on us."

I yank off my gloves and show her my cracked and callused hands. "My skin smells of antiseptic. No matter how much lavender soap I use, I cannot scrub out the mud of France. Nor the memories. Body after body. Boy after boy. Do you know who they call for, be they infantry or general? Be they German or Indian or Jamaican or English? They call for their mother."

"Why do you think I am here now," she shoots back.

"Because you regret your actions."

"To save my sons."

I bend my head, a touch cowed by this woman who bullied a neutral Greece into the War, who plots and strategizes and manipulates men and nations to fall into line with England. Beneath all this power, she too is a mother.

Dame Wallace leans back in her seat. "I gave life to four boys. One drowned as an infant. Negligence on the part of his nanny. I wasn't even in England at the time. Another died in the skies over Reims. He became a pilot not for me, but for his older brothers, Alexander and

Nicholas, who raised him far better than I could. They taught him Greek and music and astronomy and cricket."

A faint smile crosses her lips as if she is tracing a faded memory. Smoothing her features back to their distant veneer, she asks, "Do you know what tore my son's plane to pieces? A timed picric acid bomb, the kind Alexander was tracking down. Whether it was a coincidence or a threat, such a death feels personal. Alexander was getting too close to exposing the saboteur ring. So he recruited the person he trusts most, his last remaining brother. If Nicolas hangs, what will happen to Alexander? He has always suffered loss too deeply. I will be a woman who gave life to four sons and yet is a mother to no one."

Throughout her recitation of loss, of a baby choking and dying in mere inches of water, of a young man spiraling through the air and burning to death, of two surviving brothers taking up their mother's mission and trying to right the wrongs of the world, her voice does not so much as crack. It is as even and unaffected as a metronome. Which makes her pain devastating.

The motorcar slows as Charles too absorbs Dame Wallace's buried sorrow. "Alex—Mr. Wallace—he's made of sturdy stuff. The sturdiest," Charles says firmly.

I nod in agreement with her.

Dame Wallace's nostrils flare at our collective naivete. "Do you know how Alexander lost his eye? He was at the top of a church tower, chasing down a suspect, the one who planted the timed bomb in his brother's plane. They struggled. Alexander hit him, the suspect fell backward off the ledge, and my stupid boy reached out to catch him. Do you know how he was repaid for this act of humanity?"

I am holding my breath. Charles seems to be gripping the steering wheel. Master James drums his fingers nervously. We know the answer.

"He dug his thumb through Alexander's eye. And still Alexander did not let him drop to his death. He dragged the blackguard back to safety because the information the man held was more important than revenge. My son is blind."

"He's not blind." Charles slams her palm against the steering wheel.

"It sickens me," Master James says, his voice deepening several octaves, "how men like Carbury are heralded as heroes when it's the Wallace brothers whose stories we should tell."

"Write a single word of what is discussed in this car, and you'll find yourself nostalgic for those thugs who gave you the black eye." Dame Wallace grinds an almond between her molars. "I made it possible for you to discover this Court Martial. You wouldn't have what little you have of this story if I did not believe you could be useful."

"You control the free press?" Master James asks, rather bravely for a young cub reporter who's already been roughed up once this week. I flash him a note of rebellious encouragement.

"Institutions are easy to control," she replies dismissively. "They are dedicated to order." She gestures to the cityscape beyond the motor-car's windows, London's centuries old Neoclassic buildings and its long, straight streets.

"As opposed to people." I point to a group of boys whooping and hollering through the park. They could be reveling in the warmth of sunshine and youth. They could be hunting an innocent rabbit for sport. Impossible to tell. "We run on emotion."

"Chickens have more sense." Dame Wallace snaps open her purse and puts her almonds away. Possibly because I am human and nosy, I peek at the contents of her purse. She catches me, delivers a wry, almost-humored expression and says, "On the ship in East Sussex, all everyone had to do was follow the execution of my plan. But no. No sooner do I get you and Nicholas off than he comes running back."

"We heard a gunshot and cries for help," I explain. "More importantly, we did not hear *you*."

"Who do you think fired the gun? When I came upstairs, I saw the two of you lingering on the deck engaged in whatever lover's reunion dialogue reunited lovers have that should be held anywhere except on a ship being boarded by the British Royal Army. I had to get you off."

I am not about to let her logic prevail. "Someone was injured. Someone had been shot."

"Not shot."

"What?"

She slows her speech and over enunciates like she's teaching a dog to obey commands. "Not. Shot."

I blink and struggle to recall the words from last summer, in the midst of the storm, the desperate cries soldiers make when a comrade has fallen, the way Nick's body tensed, obeying the call of duty. And the words. *Resuscitate.* Someone had already stopped breathing. The smell of almonds comes back to me. And cigarettes. The dark, bitter tobacco hanging in the air. And the absence of a single cigarette in Dame Wallace's purse today.

Almost afraid to utter the words aloud, I say, "You don't smoke."

"Not as a habit." She folds her hands together, calmly waiting for my brain to connect the puzzle pieces.

"Cyanide can smell like almonds on the breath."

"Can it?" She widens her eyes as if we are engaged in small talk. Not the very opposite.

"If you've consumed a heavy dose, yes," I answer. "Your skin turns a bright cherry red because the oxygen isn't getting into your cells. You cough a great deal. May even vomit." I stare down at my lap, where my fingers twist round and round each other, exonerated and horrified.

I did not kill Carburry. Nick did not accidentally inject my potassium chloride-loaded needle into him. The cigarettes were laced with cyanide. We are both innocent. Which is worse than being guilty. Because now I understand. Nick and I are powerless.

Dame Wallace observes, "You don't look relieved."

"Nick and I were pawns."

"Enough with your self-pity and chessboards!" She drums her fingers against her forehead like I'm the cause of an irksome headache. "Carburry was part of an organization designed to destroy England. Even now, the war is over but his network lives. He wasn't even the leader. I pulled what information I could from him, but he would rather raze humanity than give up what little power he had. So I did what SIS determined was necessary to disrupt his organization. This, this is my job. The ugly side of peace and order. All you had to do"— she points at me—"was get off the goddamned boat and disappear."

"Because you planned to use me as a decoy?" I swallow hard and bite my inner cheek.

"Vera Betts is a fictional name. There are no records of her in England. The records in France are haphazard at best, loose sheets flying in the wind." Dame Wallace twirls her hand in the air. "Vera Betts wears a Red Cross uniform, but no one notices her face. She could be young. She could be old. She is listed as accompanying Major Carburry onto the ship in Calais. But she never gets off in East Sussex. She is a figment, a mystery, a nothing. She does not exist. And you, you reemerge in England—"

"—As Margaret Halladay—"

"as who you are. And all is well. The papers have their hero." She indicates Master James. "We suppress all mention of Vera Betts. Life goes on. In a few months, you reunite with my son and live happily ever after or whatever nonsense children believe."

The boldness of her plan, the simplicity of it, hollows me out. Were humans predictable and logical, were we simple equations, it would have worked. Except it didn't. Dame Wallace has focused so singularly on how to exploit people's weaknesses, she's failed to recognize their strengths. Of all the things she miscalculated, her real mistake was not understanding the depth of her son's sense of duty. Ironic, considering how deeply hers runs.

"Where were you when he returned to the ship?" I ask.

"Already off. I fired the gun and slipped away on a waiting dinghy."

"And that is when everything went to hell. Nick confesses to a murder he did not commit. He reaches out to no one except the two people who have the most to lose if the truth comes out, Mrs. Carbury and her son. He rots in an army prison."

"Until Alexander finds him and moves the Court Martial to London," she answers. "Which is when your boss"—she gestures to Master James—"makes good on a favor he owes me. And still, my plan could have worked if you did not choose to have Vera Betts reappear."

Anger, hot and piteous, flares through my belly. "Good God, Dame Wallace, do none of you, do you never as a family sit down over a roast chicken and actually talk? Does SIS not share information with the Home Secretary? You are fighting to safeguard the same ideals, are you not? Or have you forgotten you both serve the King."

She studies me, making a show of patience while waiting for me to calm myself back down.

I won't have it. "Nick will hang because you hoard your secrets and trust no one. In addition to Vera Betts, I am Margaret Halladay. Whose father is the Earl of Halsop. Who runs Blackpond Manufacturing. Which produces *picric acid*. Which he sold for weaponry."

She shifts her gaze to her feet, thinking. "Our investigation found Blackpond sold its excess picric acid to the War Office, no one else."

"Then your investigation was inadequate. Eye—Alex, that is—he must have discovered something and shared it with Nick."

I take no pleasure in watching Dame Wallace absorb this blow. Her failure is not esoteric. It does not involve the lives of strangers on the street, taxi drivers and chimney sweeps and boys playing in the park. She has failed her sons.

"Holy Hell," Master James whispers.

"No," Charles answers. "Up until the other day, we suspected Blackpond because small amounts of picric acid were unaccounted for, but we had no proof." She shifts the clutch and speeds up. "But we weren't sure. Not until we discovered some odd receipts."

"Odd?" I ask.

"The receipts were for a case of custom-made pens, aluminum plated with gold. But hollow inside, no ink well. So not intended to function as pens at all," Charles says.

"Rather to disguise a bomb." I tense my jaw. Leave it to Papa's vanity to insist on only the finest pen maker when selling out his soul. "How could Nick have figured this out on his own, before either the Home Secretary or SIS? Who was he talking to? Carburry, obviously. And Alexander. And you." I nudge Dame Wallace.

"You," she replies.

The newspaper clipping my mother held in the little white box my father gave to me. It must have been from Nick. All the stories I told him, of Old Betts and the cottage hospital, though I never named the place; of my childhood home with its park full of giant oak trees; of the kite we once made where even Gwendolyn helped; of my letters from my cousin in New York, the pages of which we chased along the beach. Besides Old Betts, I never gave away a name or a place. And yet he listened so carefully, he brought all the parts of me together.

And it will cost him his life.

CHAPTER TWENTY

Inside the motorcar, the life seems to have drained out of all of us. Charles maneuvers the motorcar through a pair of metal gates, circles around a hexagonal building, and idles in front of a low-rise brick building. Her motions are automatic, her mind seems preoccupied. Master James surreptitiously reaches his hand to the floor, searching for his missing pencil like it's his lucky talisman. Dame Wallace and I glare at each other, she finding my emotional tendencies quixotic, I finding her logic meaningless.

"Well?" she asks.

"What?"

"Are you going to get out?"

"I don't even know where we are."

She puffs with smug satisfaction.

Charles supplies the answer. "Brixton Prison."

I survey Brixton with its tiny windows squeezed into heavy brick, the barbed wire, the armed prison guards monitoring the green, and the out of place cheery vicar with his fading-to-grey red hair bustling out the infirmary door and waving happily to us.

Charles leans her head out the window. "Hello, Da."

"Hello, Dovie." He wipes his brow with a handkerchief. "Terrible influenza about. If Dr. Wallace makes me wash my hands one more time, I think my fingers will split open." His use of *doctor* over *colonel* seems deliberate. He recognizes Nick for who he truly is and I want to thank him for it.

When Charles opens her door, Rev. Charles motions for her to stay. "Won't do England any good if you fall ill." He taps his right eye, indicating that for Charles, all of England boils down to one man wearing an eyepatch. Good luck to her. No matter how human his mother describes him to be, Alexander Wallace is an impenetrable wall whose Achilles heel is a too clear moral code. He could use a touch of ambiguity.

Dame Wallace has already stepped out of the motorcar and reached the infirmary steps. She places her gloved hand on the door, leans her shoulder forward as if she's eager to push her way in, but pauses. It's a momentary stillness, fraught with some inner tension that vibrates through her, like she's struggling to suppress all the things in herself she finds disdainful about me. The things she has sacrificed in the name of the institutional pillars she values more than motherhood.

"We haven't more than fifteen minutes," Rev. Charles warns. "The governor will be returning from his meeting and will question why the actual reverend of Brixton Prison is tied up."

"Da!" Charles exclaims.

"Having tea and a chinwag with your mum. She's got a mind to start a Morris dance group for the inmates," he replies, imitating the steps. "You don't think I'd actually bind a man of the cloth in knots, do you? I say!" He looks heavenward and Charles rolls her eyes at him.

I am not the only one who envies the easy good humor binding father and daughter. Dame Wallace watches the two as if perplexed by this mythological creature, the untroubled trust between a parent and child. She and I are used to more strained relationships.

Dame Wallace shifts her attention to me as I sit in the car and pick at the tips of my gloves. She says, "It's not me Nicholas needs to see."

I catch my heart before it jumps out of my throat and leap out of the motorcar, racing up the path.

Caught off guard, Rev. Charles huffs and puffs, following behind me. "Bless my soul, you're a sprinter."

At the infirmary door, I come to a stop before Dame Wallace, who, though she may not be aware of it herself, blocks me from entering. She stands before me with her feet splayed and her arms crossed. Her composed face betrays nothing, but I'm not fooled. She has not seen her son for the nine months he was in prison. I think of Mama and what she would have given to have welcomed me home after four years apart. I regret the muted anger in most of my letters to her, how I filled the pages with reports on the weather at Bryn Mawr, a place I have never stepped foot in. How it must have pained her to realize she would never be able to speak her last words to me. Instead, she placed them in a box, locked them in a safe, and waited beyond her grave.

"There's time enough for us both," I suggest.

Dame Wallace checks her wristwatch. "You've only fourteen minutes left to persuade Nicholas to end his crusade to protect you." She shifts to the side and swoops her hand forward, indicating she will brook no argument, reminding us all she is the Deputy Chief of the SIS. Sentiment has no place in her world order.

From the corner of my eye, I catch Rev. Charles ready to salute her. He lowers his hand before completing the gesture and instead leads me into the infirmary, where the smells of metal and antiseptic and sweat mix with the sounds of sick men moaning and vomiting. My muscles tense the way a dancer's do when the orchestra strikes a familiar song, instinctively, ready to spring into action, and my brain thinks . . . *home.*

Rev. Charles tuts and directs me toward the dispensary. "You cannot dally. The governor has permitted Dr. Wallace to work in the infirmary out of desperation, but he's not so desperate he wouldn't rescind the privilege if he thinks he's being made a fool." The older man pats my shoulder and smiles at me. "Thirteen minutes."

I enter the dispensary on stolen time. Nick, who is busy grinding a powder, looks up from his work. His mouth relaxes as if he is about to smile, then tenses as if he's reminding himself that he sealed our fates with his courtroom confession.

What can I say when there is too much to say? I have a war's worth of questions and a handful of minutes. How do I berate him for sacrificing so much for me? Shake the fight back into him? Tell him I love him. Tell him I'm sorry. I should have found him sooner. I should have marched into SIS's office and made a scene and demanded his mother disclose his whereabouts, if she knew them. Even if her hands were tied with politics and her odd sense of patriotism, mine were not. I need to grab Nick by the collar and yank him out of the building and throw him over the prison wall to freedom. It's not too late. It can't be, not for us.

"Rev. Charles is nearsighted, not blind," he says. "Yet he seems to have mistaken you for my mother."

In response to Nick's flat joke, I fly to him and slam my head against his chest. He is not as strong as he once was. He stumbles backward before he rights himself and brings his arms around my shaking shoulders. Had I tears left, I would soak his thin prison uniform. Instead, I dry sob, rubbing my face into the scratchy fabric and trying not to panic at the way his bones poke out from beneath his emaciated frame.

Laying his cheek on the top of my head, he inhales, and I hear his chest rattle, the beginning of an upper respiratory infection. "Bergamot?" he asks. "Have you changed shampoos?"

Which is when I scream. How dare he notice every unimportant minutiae of my existence when he is about to disappear forever. I bear down on my diaphragm, drag air up through my lungs, rake it over my vocal cords, and scream. The sound pouring forth is feral and full, so full. Glass should shatter. Brick walls should crumble to dust. I should not be able to stand so steadily. Nick should not be able to hold me so tenderly, absorbing each note of my broken heart into his own.

I fall quiet. Not because I have ripped my vocal cords to shreds and my throat is raw, though they are, but because if Nick and I cannot change tomorrow's outcome, the Judge Advocate will bang his gavel and sentence Nick, and I will spend the rest of my life screaming.

"How many—how many days between tomorrow's sentence and the . . . your . . ." My tongue freezes, my body refusing to give voice to my brain. Nick traces the fine baby hairs on the back of my neck as if he means to coax out the terrible words. "Before they will carry out the sentence."

"Not many." He peers at my gloves, decorative, useless things. I shuck them and toss them onto the table. My fingertips tremble when they at last connect to his, skin to skin.

"It's a relief, in some ways," he says trying to sound philosophical as opposed to what he is, bone-weary. "Every day is both a gift and a torture when you know the outcome is grim."

"You designed the outcome."

"Not intentionally." He takes a lock of my hair and rubs it between his thumb and forefinger, breathing deep. "I went back into the ship because I thought someone, quite possibly my mother, had been shot. But instead it was Carburry, not shot at all, though very much dead."

"I didn't kill Carburry." The guilt of intending to still prickles. "I loaded the needle with potassium chloride, but I thought of his son, of all things. No matter how much I hated Carburry, I couldn't take a boy's father away from him."

"I never thought you did. I know my mother's signature. Karelia cigarettes have a deep, acrid scent. And cyanide has no flavor."

"If you knew it wasn't me, then why?" I tug him by the sleeves. "You could have said Vera Betts murdered him and we could be running away to Argentina instead of this clandestine meeting in a prison dispensary. You didn't need to martyr yourself."

He clasps my face and presses his forehead against mine. "Fukimoto was doomed the minute she passed Hildebrand's letter. Her innocence didn't matter, not when the letter contained the passcode for deciphering communications in Carburry's network. What would they do to Vera Betts? Who is really Lady Margaret Halladay. Whose family produced the picric acid bombs. That are designed to kill English boys."

"No one knew."

"Anyone could find out."

"How did you?" I ask. "Did someone tell you?"

"You're no spy and not particularly talented at subterfuge. I may not have had time to track down Dr. Victor Bettany, but the facts still draw a line from you to Halsop House. Even now, you're too young to be a qualified nurse. You have a cousin in New York who is wealthy enough to send cases of chewing gum to France. You grew up in the countryside, on an estate by a river. Your mother came from a manufacturing family. You purposefully adopt words from the north, but it's a hodgepodge. *Hitchy-dabbor* is from Northumberland; *fettle* is from Manchester. Your sister attended Cambridge before she stole your sweetheart, for which I am eternally grateful, by the way. You know too much about picric acid."

"You could have asked for help! For God's sake, Nick, your mother is the Deputy Chief of SIS. Your brother is second only to the Home Secretary. If anyone, *anyone* had a chance of avoiding the Army's noose, it's you."

"Between the woman I love and the country my mother loves, who do you think Dame Wallace would choose? And Alex? Those picric acid bombs killed our younger brother. Do you think he is remotely inclined to forgive the family who invented them and, in doing so, unwittingly or not, gave Carburry the means to his ends?" Nick hitches his hip against the table and tries to hide a cough.

I run my hand over his back to help relax the muscles. Neither of us is going to admit he is ill. Not when this may be our last chance to speak together. "Couldn't you have made up another story?"

"I tried to stall and divert." Nick wipes his mouth on his sleeve. "I tried to do right by Carburry's family. Like you, I thought I owed something to his son who is blameless and young. Yes, my family is powerful, but that was a hindrance, not a help. It's why the Army censored records and monitored my communications and made it so damned difficult to find me. I do not think either my mother or Alex knew where I was until a week ago."

I reach for his other hand and lay my forefinger on his pulse. It jumps beneath my touch. He smiles at me, bittersweet, and continues. "You are built on instinct. Me, I am a planner. I lay out steps. I diagram strategy. I assess. Which requires the ability to think. When Alex asked me to pretend to ally with Carburry, it was a straightforward venture. Alex, being rather Greek in his dispensation of punishment, wanted me to drug Carburry with a neurotoxin, but that's not something I can do, not as a doctor. So he shot out his knees instead. Then all I had to do was befriend Carburry, gain his trust, stand by my insistence of no deaths, learn the names in his network, and get my hands on his code. That was why Hildebrand was at our hospital. Because we thought eventually the two would trip and disclose the key."

"But instead Fukimoto mailed the key to Germany."

"The things one does for love." Nick shrugs at the irony. "But from the moment I reentered the ship in East Sussex, there wasn't so much as a second to think. Things spun so quickly, far, far out of my control." He raises my hand and inspects the knuckles, runs his thumb across the pads and creases of my palm like he's trying to memorize a map. "I didn't start out meaning to be a martyr, but if that is the price I have to pay for your safety, then you'd best believe no one can stop me." Our eyes locked, he focuses intently on me. "Do you understand? Not even you."

I jerk away, but cannot let go of his hand. "I'll stop you. I'll expose Carburry. I'll justify his murder. I will claim responsibility for it. I will out-martyr you. Why should I live when you won't?"

Nick smacks his fist on the table, causing the medicinal powder he was grinding to scatter in clouds of dust. "Look about you, Vera-not-Vera. England is gutted. They won't listen, not because they don't care, but because they need to move forward. They need their heroes, even the false ones, to stay heroes. Otherwise, they will be dragged backward into a war with no end. We need peace."

"What about truth and justice?"

"Two different things," he answers, comfortable cleaving one from the other. "I have lived for nine months in filthy cells among murderers, madmen and cutthroats. At night, some of them cry themselves to sleep. You can hear their sobs, even when they're trying to stifle them beneath a pillow, and I swear I would rather they howl. It's the quiet that keeps you awake, shivering in your own sweat. Not the rats scurrying across your toes. Not the clank of your cell door. Not the slash of sunshine you're so desperate to grasp hold of like it's a solid, tangible thing."

"Nick—" How can I speak when the only words I have are the words are the very ones sending him to the gallows? *I love you.*

His eyes crinkle, but the shadows beneath are darker than ash. A lifetime of sunlight will not erase what he's seen these past months. "The truth is you are not a nurse. And yet there is no one who triages better than you. The truth is most of my prison mates are guilty. Still, they deserve mercy. Though they'll not get much of it."

He reaches out to stroke my hair again. "Which is why you can't ask me, Vera-not-Vera, not for a single moment, to stand aside and risk you being thrust into their darkness."

"How did we get ensnared in this game?" I bury my head in my hands.

"We aren't on a chessboard." He pulls my hands from my face and clasps them in his. "We're just two people trying to do right, like so many others around us."

"Why bother when we are helpless against these institutions your mother and Lady Carburry so devoutly believe in? Even in peace, we lose."

"We don't control governments; we don't declare war or peace. We'll never shift the stars so Bootes catches Ursa Major. But you and I, Vera-not-Vera, we're type O negative blood. Universal donors. Our best matters. Men and women are alive because of us."

"But you won't be, because of me."

Nick acknowledges my bluntness by nodding once while he takes me in, ounce by ounce, like I am the horizon and he a shipwrecked sailor. All he wants is to come home. But horizons don't move. I need to be the rolling sea keeping him afloat, not a distant shore.

"There is so little time left," he says. "I don't want to argue with you. I don't have the strength." He is gaunt. His shoulders have narrowed and, were it not for his sheer force of will, I think they would cave in.

"We never have enough time," I complain. Another thing over which we have no control. I add it to my list of enemies. "What would you like to do?"

The grin he flashes is so bright and wide, so full of my Nick, the man who believes always *the trick is there is no trick*, it slices straight through me and I am split open.

"I want to dance." He takes my right hand into his, spins me around.

My left hand comes up to rest on his shoulder. I inhale the sour scent that comes from living in dank prison quarters and caring for influenza-stricken men. I hold on, tight, tight, tight. "We have no music."

"We have the moon," he answers.

Less than a year ago, we danced thus, beside a lake on a warm summer's night, where I pointed out we had no orchestra and Nick joked the moon was our music. Nonsensical then, nonsensical now.

275

Still, our bodies move to the memory of a song created by the shuffle of our feet on forest earth, the breeze through the trees, the giving over of our hearts.

His lips brush my ear, my cheek. His sigh rustles my hair. He strokes my throat, still sore for having screamed my pain. When we kiss, it is as if he is savoring me, a prisoner with his last meal.

In the distance, strolling down the hall we can hear someone whistling "Onward Christian Soldiers", a warning from Rev. Charles. Nick and I part, inch by painful inch. First our lips separate and hover, the wisp of cold air separating us as sharp as an electric shock. He releases my right hand. I drop my left from his shoulder. His arm around my back slides down my hip, pausing at my pocket, and then peels away.

Neither of us dare speak. We drink in the sight of one another. His golden hair has greyed. His skin has paled to sallow. A curved line marks the left side of his mouth, but like an open parenthesis, there is no match on the right. I want to ask him how he got the tiny white scar above his lip; why he sprinkles cinnamon in his coffee, who taught him how to sketch; what is it about the constellations that draws him; why, of all the people in the world, he chose to gift his love to me. All the details of him that have saturated my pores and entered my bloodstream, I want to hear the stories behind them.

Except we are out of time.

Our dance has ended. He smiles wistfully. "'She dances like a Bomb,'" he says, recalling the line from the Emily Dickinson poem he read me once before, when the world was at war and he and I shared a moment's peace.

Afterwards, when I've taken one last look at Nick as he returns to the medicine table and presses my discarded glove to his chest, as I stumble forward bleary-eyed, and Rev. Charles loops his arm through mine to lend me his fortitude, as I squint into the horrific light of an English day because the sun will continue to rise and set no matter what happens to Nick, I tuck my hand into my pocket and feel the round, metal edge and smooth glass of a watch face. I don't need to check. I know it bears the initials V.B.

Nick is giving me back my heart.

CHAPTER TWENTY-ONE

I pin my watch to my chest.

"Do you have a plan?" Dame Wallace flicks an imaginary speck of dust from the green velvet chair and inspects my mother's morning room, searching for its faults the way one does reassurance. "Otherwise, you are wasting my time," says Dame Wallace. "I should be arranging to smuggle Nicholas out of Brixton."

The air is so still, the astringent cleanliness burns my nostrils. I open a window. Charles leans out and pretends to be entranced by the rose garden, though from the way she cranes her neck left, right and upward, it's clear she's searching for unwanted listeners.

"You could fake his death and sneak him out in a coffin," suggests Charles.

The right corner of Dame Wallace's lip turns up.

"You're assuming," I say, "first, that Nick will let you."

"If you drug him, he can't argue," offers Charles.

Master James, who has been flipping his precious pencil between his fingers shoots a reassessing glance at the fresh-faced, daughter-of-a-vicar Charles, whose diabolical underpinnings run deep.

"And second," I say as I hold up two fingers, "you're assuming once he is disappeared, he won't insist upon returning." To Dame Wallace's silent obstinance, I add, "as he did once before in East Sussex." As long as Nick thinks I am at risk, he will take the blame.

"Live by principles, die by them," she mutters.

"Not a headline that sells," Master James answers. "People want happy endings, not tragedies."

I pace back and forth.

"Could you please sit down?" Dame Wallace asks irritably, because containment is her strength. But I can't. I think best when I am moving, which is why I made a good nurse. As Nick observed, I have only two speeds. Why should I fight who I am?

I turn to Dame Wallace. "Tell whoever owes you a favor at *The Times* to reserve the front page for Master James."

Master James near jumps, and swings his head between me and Dame Wallace, all eagerness and earnest ambition. He tempers himself, though, and warns, "I won't write a pack of lies. I heard your threat, Dame Wallace." He touches his black eye, the reminder of someone else's agenda. "I won't print national secrets. But the press isn't your toy thing. You don't get to manipulate us. We owe our readers respect."

"No one would believe you anyway," Dame Wallace replies, "especially if you publish Lady Margaret's bunk about how she killed Carburry." Oh the irony, when it's Dame Wallace who planned to pin the murder on Vera Betts, who exists within me.

Begrudgingly, Master James nods his head. "Even if it were true, readers will say you're prevaricating to save your lover." He turns pink. "Pardon the crudeness."

"And that is exactly the story you are going to tell," I say.

Master James crinkles his forehead and Charles whispers beneath her breath, "She hasn't got a plan." Her first doubts of the day.

I open up the white box I brought down earlier and remove Dame Randolph Churchill's article. Handing it to Master James, I point to the line my mother underlined: The speaker was a young girl, 'and her outlook on life had assumed a new and marvelous focus. "She is me."

To keep her curiosity in check, Dame Wallace turns her head in the opposite direction and feigns boredom. "Will you be trotting out family photos next?"

"I am a liar," I start. "I ran away from home. I lied my way into Lady Sullivan's Ambulance Hospital. I am not a qualified nurse."

"So your plan is to hang beside Nicholas?" Dame Wallace nods grimly. "Very Romeo and Juliet."

"They died apart," Charles points out, flipping through my worn copy of *The Count of Monte Cristo*. "He of poison, she stabbing herself over his body. All because of a miscommunication."

Dame Wallace sends Charles an icy expression that would make anyone else duck for cover.

In response, Charles smiles cheerily. "It's important to be accurate with analogies. Otherwise, it leads to faulty deductive judgment."

Unimpressed, Dame Wallace asks, "Learned that operating the telegraph, did you?"

"From Mr. Wallace." Charles squares her shoulders. I cannot help but grin. Who needs an army when one has Dorothea Dovie Charles by her side?

"The mistake we have been making," I say, "is we keep trying to reframe Carbury as a villain." Another insight from Nick, who even when he doesn't intend to be, is full of answers. "People don't want to read about pain and suffering. Not when they've lived it daily for years and are living it still. What they want is—"

"Stories to restore their faith," says Master James, a Jersey-born boy who understands what holds an island together.

"And what's better than a love story?" Charles shuts the book and clasps it to her heart.

"Especially when it's true," adds Master James.

"It humanizes Nicholas." Dame Wallace mulls over the idea. "I can find a way to use it."

"Sentencing is set for the morning," I remind her.

A dark narrowing of the left eye comes over Charles, who is clearly contemplating how to adulterate the Judge Advocate's coffee with a sleeping draught or worse. "Dr. Wallace will need to consult with his spiritual advisor," she says, thinking aloud. "Given he is about to be condemned, the Court Martial cannot deny him an hour with his priest."

"Priest?" The inflection in Dame Wallace's voice is half curious, half hurt. How little she knows her sons.

"My da." Charles' confidence is a thing to be envied.

"You'll need a lawyer," Master James points out.

"We have Mr. Higgenbotham, though I haven't got his number," Charles replies. "I can ring my mate at the office, but she'll have to avoid Mr. Wallace, who's rather inclined to wring Lady Margaret's neck." When Charles catches me checking my watch, she adds, "He lives at his office."

Dame Wallace interlaces her fingers, trying to hide how pleased she is that she shares something in common with her son, even if it is loneliness.

An idea, likely bad, pops into my head. "Mr. Higgenbotham will need to win two motions tomorrow."

"Two?" Charles sends me a don't-press-your luck scrunch of the eyebrows.

"We have to delay the hearing. And we have to have time in the afternoon for, what do they call it when people speak for the accused?" I snap my fingers, trying to recall the term.

"A character witness," Master James supplies.

"I need to be called as a character witness, yes."

Master James taps his pencil against his lips. "You testify last."

"Last?" I ask. I am not the only one improvising.

"I didn't learn to write at some posh school with Little Lord Fauntleroy, Lady Margaret." He pauses to let me feel the meaning of his use of my actual name. We're equals now. "I learned from sailors and shopkeepers and arguing uncles and my three-gins-to-the-wind gran.

You save the best for last. And trust me, after my front-page article is published tomorrow, there will be dozens, if not hundreds, of people clamoring to attest to the integrity of a man like Colonel Wallace."

Master James is a sly fox. It takes a healthy degree of self-control not to applaud him and kiss his cheeks like his three-gins-to-the-wind gran would likely do if she could see what a man he's grown into.

Like a queen, or at least a Deputy Chief, Dame Wallace crosses her ankles and relaxes into the velvet chair. "Good. You will write her love story." She points to me. "And have it published in the morning paper." She points to Master James. "You will have the sentencing hearing moved to the afternoon." She points to Charles. "I will work my strings and Nicholas will face hard labor, not the noose. Perhaps a few years, not more."

My jaw clicks so tightly, my teeth hurt. "How is hard labor acceptable? He didn't touch a hair on Carburry. He's already spent nine months in prison." And he is terrified of it. I could smell his fear of the dark place.

"It's better than hanging," she answers, level-headed and logical.

"It's not fair."

"It's a fair compromise." She crosses her arm, indicating our discussion is done.

To annoy her, I tread back and forth along the carpet. "Why should Nicholas pay the consequences for your actions?"

She presses her forefinger to her temple. "If it would make a difference, I would take the stand and declare my guilt." Not a shout, but her typically soft-spoken voice does rise a decibel and it takes her three breaths to steady herself. "But that is not how the world maintains its fragile order. The decisions I make effect more than one person. In eliminating Carburry, I removed a threat to England. Which is what is most important. And while it gives me no joy to see any one man suffer, it is what I have to live with."

"Nick is your son." My pace has quickened and zigzagged. My ears feel hot, my pulse drums.

"I envy you young people your naivete." She nods at Master James, at Charles, and then at me. "You have the luxury of being selfish because others have sacrificed for you."

"If I recall correctly, France is soaked in the blood of the young." I can still smell, I will always smell, the mixture of blood and gunfire and mud. And a necrotic foot detached from the body of a dying boy who loved to sing.

"We cannot make things personal," she snaps. "When you do, you get into messes like this, where my son is on trial because he is trying to protect you because of your family's folly. It makes a hash of things."

I stare at her agape and think of her husband who wrote a code to impress her and drowned himself when he succeeded. In Dame Wallace's book, institutions are to be maintained. In mine, in Nick's, people are to be saved. Which is why it didn't matter what flag a man fought under, our mission is always to preserve human life, without judgment. Type O negative blood.

I have to force myself to shove away my rising anger. I have to focus. Love isn't a game, but it is an all or nothing endeavor and I'll be damned if Nick spends another day in prison, much less a lifetime of hard labor because it suits the institutions upon which an empire is built. It's not enough.

"This is what *we* are going to do," I start. "James, how much time do we have before you need to send your story to the typesetter."

"Six, maybe seven hours. I need a typewriter."

"Peters can collect one."

"Peters?" he asks.

"The footman. Not only does he remember me from the War, he packs a healthy right hook." I gesture to Master James' bruised eye. "In case anyone tries to delay your story reaching the printer."

"Charles," I ask, "can you arrange for your father to visit Brixton tomorrow?"

"If you've a telephone, I can ring him up now."

"And make sure our barrister files his motions first thing," I tell her.

"Absolutely."

"Dame Wallace," I continue, trying to sound like I'm in command, not pretending I know what I'm doing when I don't. "Besides having the front page of *The Times* set for James' article, you'll have to thwart any competing agendas. The Army cannot learn about the story and they cannot be in a position to move Nick before the hearing, because if they do, we won't ever find him."

"I always have leverage." She catches herself about to relax and straightens her back.

"And for God's sake," I say, surprised at the firmness of my tone, "sit down with your son Alexander and actually exchange information as if you are on the same side."

"England's," she says, matter-of-fact.

I throw my hands up. "Nick's."

"You do have a plan." Charles exhales and relaxes against the window casing.

"No." I trace the edge of my watch. I don't have a plan. I have instinct and love and Nick's belief that humanity is not an institution. Hardly enough.

CHAPTER TWENTY-TWO

Armed with our hardly enough plan, the morning room bustles with purpose. Peters trots in with the typewriter. Master James rolls his fingers across the keys like it's a piano. Charles sets up command central at the round table by the window and tests the telephone to make sure it's working. With a cool eye, Dame Wallace assesses the activity, nods her approval, clasps her purse and is about to head out when my sister sweeps in.

"Blimey." Charles near drops the telephone receiver. Master James's hands freeze in midair. Peters blushes. Even I had forgotten how beautiful Gwendolyn is, how when she enters a room she steals all the light so she glows while the rest of us are cast in her shadow, dull and inadequate.

Except Dame Wallace. She recognizes a nemesis when she sees one. "Who are you," she demands in a house not her own.

Gwendolyn sucks in her cheeks, affronted. "The Countess of—"

"My sister." My nostrils are flaring, a bull with a pin stabbed in its flank to Gwendolyn's artful toreador. "What are you doing here?"

She answers my call with an arch in her voice, "Though I have heard you've taken to throwing your siblings out on the street, this remains Papa's house, does it not?"

"Auntie!" Matty pushes past Gwendolyn and rushes in to throw himself into my arms, though they are not waiting, and the force of his enthusiasm sends me stumbling backward onto the sofa. "I've missed you so. Mummy does not play pirates at all, but she promised to take me to all the toyshops in London. I'm going to get a sword and tin soldiers and a parrot and a ship . . ."

While Matty reels off his list of expected presents, Dame Wallace watches him, it seems struggling to come to some sort of conclusion. Unlike the warmth she displayed with young Lucy, she seems to have taken an immediate dislike to my nephew. Perhaps he reminds her of her own sons, particularly the toddler who drowned. Perhaps the twist of her mouth is one of regrets, of what could have been, of what she still has to lose. Still, her response leaves a cold uneasiness in my stomach.

Dame Wallace shifts her focus to me. "Are you really willing to do whatever it takes tomorrow?" There's an edge of doubt in her voice that feels deliberate, like she's found my weakness and is pressure testing it. "The receipts for those pens, for example."

I bridle at the hidden threat. "I'm not the one willing to settle for hard labor."

Satisfied, she strides out the door, elbowing Gwendolyn to the side, before anyone can so much as wish her "best of luck."

"Goodness, what an odd woman. About as social a creature as you are, Margaret." Gwendolyn rearranges the curls framing her face.

With Matty curled up next to me, awake but sucking his thumb, I take a moment to study my sister. She hasn't been to London since the family fled the influenza epidemic last year. Her skirt is unwrinkled and tidy, which means she didn't take the train. But her eyes are a touch watery. To a stranger, it makes them glisten even more brilliant a blue. To me, it's a symptom of motion sickness. Long hours in the motorcar make her nauseous. Her willingness to tolerate such discomfort raises my hackles.

"Why are you here?" I ask again.

"As Matty himself has told you, to do a little shopping and get a taste of civilization." She takes a seat beside us on the sofa and pulls him onto her lap, kissing the top of his head. From half-hooded lids, she appraises the invasion of strangers into our mother's morning room. "You said you'd be gone a day. It's been almost a week."

"I can count." I've spent the past six days barging into courtrooms, sparring with the self-righteous widow of a traitor I tried to kill, attempting and failing at blackmailing the Home Secretary's office, running and getting caught by a sleek silver motorcar, waltzing and falling deeper in love with Nick at Brixton Prison . . . How has it only been mere days since *Doctor To Hang* shocked me back to life?

"Also." Gwendolyn pauses to deliver one of her benevolent smiles onto Peters, Master James, and Charles. They blink rapidly and in unison. "Though I'm sure it's not the sort of thing to be discussed in public, Papa is worried for you."

At least Charles has the decency to turn her back and focus on dialing the telephone. Master James' fingers have reached the keyboard and he's stroking one of the keytops with something akin to lust. He smells a story.

I shrug my shoulders like the Margaret she knows, the insolent, irritating younger sister. "Why isn't he here then?"

"He has asked me to come in his place as he's in Silvertown." She wrinkles her nose at the thought of Papa amidst the stench of human labor and animal rendering factories.

Peters and I exchange meaningful looks. Papa has taken Tad to McMannis. He listened to me. Papa, of all people. To me, of all people.

My sister is sharp enough to pick up the cue. She's being left out of a secret I share about Papa with a man who to her is but a servant. Matty squirms and Gwendolyn clamps him to her with both arms so tight around his waist, I can't help but think of a crab clawing at the air while the fishmonger hawks his wares.

Gesturing to Peters in his livery, Gwendolyn says, "I'm frightfully parched. Perhaps tea? And Matty hasn't had his dinner."

"I'm afraid Peters is otherwise engaged. Mr. James Stahler of *The Times* is interviewing him.

Gwendolyn tenses.

I bite down on the tip of my tongue. Exactly as I thought. Gwendolyn has an agenda. Perhaps she's carrying out some request of Papa's to learn how much I know about his dealings. I lean over to Matty. "There's lemon cake in the kitchen."

Matty all but kicks Gwendolyn's shin to escape her hold and bounds off for the kitchen shouting, "Lemon cake! Lemon cake!"

Gwendolyn drops her façade. Her grit teeth and tight jaw say it all. I've been belligerent, displayed the poorest of manners, given a servant more respect than a Countess, and treated her like an interloper, not a member of this household. I'm petty enough to admit, it's been a moment's fun.

"Yes?" I ask sweetly. "Want to bend my ear a tic?"

Gwendolyn looks like she'd prefer to box my ears. "I have a matter of some concern. A private family matter."

"Is it your health?"

From her perch by the window, Charles clears her throat. Now is not the time to indulge in my childhood resentments, no matter how comforting I find them, some kind of reassurance that the world can splinter and tumble into chaos, but Gwendolyn and I will always snipe at each other.

I rise from the sofa. "Pardon us," I say to Charles, Peters and Master James. "Gwendolyn?" I indicate she follow me. Another breach of the ingrained-in-our-bones manners I'm supposed to follow. But I am sick of institutions and that includes the aristocratic family I was born into.

I lead my sister to Papa's office. The poor housekeeper has barely had a chance to put it to rights. The framed photographs on Papa's desk are out of order. Mama's takes center stage and Matty's do not line up by age.

"What are you playing at?" Gwendolyn snaps the door shut. "After nine months of monk-like solitude, you fly out of Halsop House with no clear reason to leave. You throw Tad out onto the street and accuse him of thievery. You've distressed Papa so badly he came home talking about emigration to Canada. Canada!"

I smirk and she grabs my chin and forces me to face her, a gesture Mama once did, when she told me my sister was to marry my sweetheart. "Even for you, Margaret, this is too much."

"I am not playing any kind of game. I am trying to save the life of the man I love."

Disbelieving, Gwendolyn asks, "What man?"

His name almost too precious to share, my throat closes over. "Nick Wallace."

"The lieutenant colonel?" she asks. "The one in the papers?"

"In *The Times*."

Gwendolyn steps away from me and demands, "How would you even know a British lieutenant colonel stationed in France?"

I bite my thumb and consider. The story will be out tomorrow for all the world to read, and yet confessing to her makes my skin prickle. In the age-old battle of sisters, I, the younger, want her respect. Or to one-up her. "I never went to Bryn Mawr."

"Margaret!" How exactly like Papa Gwendolyn sounds—powerful, in charge, utterly horrified and terribly pleased I am the source of the outrage.

"In Portsmouth, when I was supposed to board the ship to New York, I joined an ambulance hospital instead."

"What were you thinking?"

"I was angry." The stupidest thing I have ever done, it changed my destiny and brought me to Nick.

"What if you had fallen ill or been injured"?" Gwendolyn shakes a scolding finger at me, as if I'd gotten into the jam pot, not war. "How would we ever learn if you perished? Nurses died too, you know."

"I corresponded with cousin Kristina. She would have informed Mama if—"

"Oh grand, your precious heroine. Not me."

"Why would I tell you?" I ask, confused. "We barely like each other."

"We aren't supposed to be friends, Margaret. We are *sisters*."

"Exactly." I exist to annoy her and pilfer her wardrobe, not disclose the inner workings of something she's never cared for. My heart.

As if reading my mind, she twirls her finger toward the linen frock I'm wearing. "You're not tall enough for that dress, by the way."

"It's not even a dress you like."

In disapproving tones, she reminds me, "You're always letting your emotions run you off the rails. And dragging us with you." As if to prove her point, Gwendolyn rearranges the photos on Papa's desk. The one of Mama, she moves behind the row of Matty's.

"I do so apologize for inconveniencing you," I answer. "How disruptive it must be for Gwendolyn the Great, Gwendolyn the Beautiful, with her unmatched intelligence to learn her sister was triaging head injuries and irrigating sepsis wounds rather than studying something as useless as art history at a pastoral girl's college."

"How I adore your dramatics. It's a pity you didn't put your talents to use joining the circus." She imitates a tightrope walker. "Do you even know the first thing about nursing?"

"Dr. Bettany trained me."

She scoffs. "A country surgeon."

My sister can insult me. But she cannot ever, not for a single second, disparage Old Betts. That man, who delivered every baby born to a Blackpond factory family for nigh on forty years, is too dear, too good. Things she is not. "While I will admit Blackpond Cottage Hospital is no Cambridge, at least I completed my learning. You abandoned your studies and married your sister's lover. What have you achieved besides failure and deceit?"

"Oh, you and your *you stole my love* histrionics. Mama didn't think he was good enough for you. Not Margaret the Firecracker. Margaret the Brave. Oh no. But me? Why she practically thrust Jerome upon me when she learned—" Gwendolyn catches herself. Guilt steals over her milk and roses complexion.

We each hold still, boxers assessing the next strike, the only sound our heavy breathing.

"Learned what." I'm not asking. I'm extracting the truth.

"We were both at Cambridge." A thoroughly inadequate answer. Gwendolyn returns to the photographs on Papa's desk. She seems to have decided some belong on the mantel. Another on a bookshelf.

There is not a single picture in this room from her wedding. Nor is there one in her bedroom upstairs, or anywhere in this house and certainly not at Halsop House. She doesn't live at Bellingham Castle with her in-laws, though Matty will one day be the Marquis of Bellingham. She doesn't wear her gold band, and the only evidence she was ever married is her cherubic son.

Why is she here?

Papa would not have sent her. He's no fool and he understands Gwendolyn holds no sway with me. My lips feel heavy, almost numb when I ask, "Why are Matty's eyes brown?"

She tuts at me like one does at a dog who repeatedly ignores his master's commands. "I told you, Jerome's eyes were hazel."

"Yes. You *told* me." When I came home from the war too late to save Mama, I was too broken to sift fact from memory, so I let Gwendolyn's lie slide pass. "Jerome's eyes could veer toward green depending on the light and what color he was wearing. I remember now. His eyes were blue. As are yours. Which means . . ."

Frame in hand, she sets Matty's newborn photograph next to a later baby picture with the determination of a woman who thinks the proper order will right a hidden wrong. "Are you suggesting the future

Marquis of Bellingham is a changeling?"

"A changeling is a baby switched at birth." The gears of my brain work in clockwise motion, the teeth catching on my memories and moving my thoughts forward. Even before I witnessed the explosion at Blackpond factory, I understood picric acid because Gwendolyn lectured me on its volatility, how it interacted with other chemical compounds. More than that, she used to call me *picric acid. You need to control that picric acid temper of yours, or we'll all be gagging on yellow smoke.*

A face comes to me. Eyes like Matty's, whose color I keep describing as chestnut because I do not want to admit whose color they remind me of. English oak. Oh God! I want to be sick. "Carburry."

The name drains the blood from my sister's face.

"You were lovers." The headlines in *The Times.* My conversation with Papa. Gwendolyn's sudden arrival in London. Her career as a brilliant chemistry student cut short by a desperate desire to marry. The puzzle pieces, jagged and sharp, cut as they fall into place. I do not want my own sister to be capable of such treachery.

"All this time, I thought it was Papa," I whisper. "But he doesn't understand the nuances of picric acid, that it attacks common metals, which is why bullet shells loaded with it explode so easily. You would. You could find a clever way to encase picric acid in something like aluminum and then disguise the case so it looks innocuous. Like a gold-plated pen."

"You have your talents, I have mine." Despite her feigned indifference, my sister's bottom lip trembles.

"You created a weapon." I clutch my watch, rubbing the smooth circular face as Nick must have done all these months in prison. He knew it was Gwendolyn who created the bomb. It is Gwendolyn who could hang for it now. And even when he had the chance to tell me, he chose his words with precision, so I wouldn't know, so I wouldn't hate my sister.

"When did your affair start?" I ask, though her answer will serve as salt not salve to my fury.

Never one for clear moral codes, Gwendolyn spends an eternity deciding whether or not to answer. "The year before the War. He came to Cambridge."

"Likely to recruit," I say, recalling Carburry had once been Dame Wallace's mentee.

"Please don't reduce our intense connection down to a practical transaction. Guy and I —"

Hearing my sister refer to a traitor as anything other than Carburry makes my toes curl.

"—from the moment we met, something I had thought inalterable within me changed so violently, so beautifully. It was . . ."

"Terrifying." And wonderful. Though I won't admit the latter aloud, I too fell tumbling into love. But with a good man.

"Guy came in uniform. Invited a small group of us to dinner. Held court with his charm, his funny stories about his own life at Cambridge. He did imitations of some of the more ridiculous dons and talked about how studying chemistry is akin to studying love, a passion. When he delivered that last line, he was looking directly at me." Gwendolyn near smiles and beneath my glare, regrets it. "He was irresistible," she murmurs.

"I hated Carburry from the moment he entered my triage tent." His bandages were too white, his suffering self-indulgent, as if he were too important to experience pain.

"You never like anyone, Margaret."

"Whereas it took you what, one kiss and a fox trot to agree to build a bomb?"

"We weren't like that!" Gwendolyn interweaves her fingers, willing her emotions to still even as she paces the floor. "I didn't set out to create a weapon. It started out as a debate between the two of us. An intellectual spark. What chemicals reacted with other chemicals. How could one control the inevitable combustion of two."

How predictable was Carburry's seduction of my sister. He preyed on her strength and turned it into a weakness. "When did you two lovebirds" —I make a sour face — "harness your inevitable combustion."

"Before the War."

"Before you married Jerome."

"Guy was already married," she answers defensively, meaning she had created the picric acid bomb, fallen pregnant, and been abandoned by Carburry after she'd served her purpose.

Unless they carried on throughout? The accusation plays out in my narrowed eyes and pinched mouth.

"I was faithful to Jerome for the life of our short, dull marriage," she answers flatly, blaming her husband and not herself for her dissatisfaction with their union.

Poor Jerome. He died in Rouen having never been anyone's one and only love. "But you sent Carburry a package to Wimereux," I say.

"How did you—oh, yes. You were playing Florence Nightingale."

"What was in it? Picric acid from Blackpond?"

"I may not have finished my studies, but I'm not an idiot," Gwendolyn snaps. "I would never ship a volatile chemical via the post. I pinched a bit from what we sent to the War Office. But that was for my own testing, that's all."

"So where did it come from?"

Gwendolyn twists her fingers, her ring finger ironically, and a joint pops. The sound reminds me of another, the crack of bone the night Nick and I danced beneath the moon and were intercepted by a courier bearing a satchel. The Swiss-German courier. It's a small relief and offers no comfort, but the picric acid did not come from us.

Still, Gwendolyn did send a package. "You corresponded with Carburry?"

My sister does her best lady-of-the-manor, settling into an armchair and crossing her legs at the ankles. Her left knee, however, jitters and she drags her forefinger back and forth across the upholstery like she's looking for a thread to hang onto. "Guy came to see me after Jerome had died. He was still magnetic and the fire between us, especially after he'd survived being a POW and learned I had borne him a son, the fire was even fiercer. He asked me about the gold-plated pens. They're a custom order, from Papa's favorite penmaker."

"And you obliged. To win back his heart. You even sent a bottle of Creed."

She sends me a plaintive expression. "It was a second chance for us. We could become a family of our own."

"He already has a son, born on the right side of the blanket," I add, "who bears his surname and is following in his military family footsteps. He would never abandon his legacy. It meant more to him than anything else."

"Well, more fool I. Satisfied?" She holds her hands up as if she's indulged me long enough.

"Satisfied?" I should punch her perfectly sloped nose so the blood runs thick down her snowy face and stains her white silk blouse. "You enabled Carburry to sabotage hospitals."

"German hospitals."

"British," I correct. "Though it shouldn't make a difference. Hospitals are refuges, not battlefields."

She considers for a moment, seems ready to remove her mask of perfection, then pushes away remorse. "Are you the only one permitted to make mistakes? Can I not occasionally err?"

"Though I loaded a hypodermic needle intending to, I never killed anyone."

"Your lover murdered mine," comes Gwendolyn's defense.

"Nick didn't kill Carburry." To explain who did and why requires of me something I don't have – trust in Gwendolyn.

"I'm an inventor, not a murderess," Gwendolyn reasons. "Guy promised we would change the world. I didn't need a degree to prove my brilliance, that's what he said. My mind was unstoppable. Imagine, all it would take to bring our enemy to its knees was a tiny combination of two chemicals timed to explode when no one was looking."

My hands clenched in fists, I ask, "Do you know how your invention was used? It was planted in the aircraft of none other than Nick's younger brother. A pilot for the RAF. That's Royal Air Force. British, in case you're in doubt. He died in midair."

She flinches, but answers, "You're lying. We would never harm our own." Gwendolyn juts her chin.

"As far as Carburry was concerned, there was never an *our* own. He was in it for himself. I was an eyewitness. Picric acid bombs destroyed the supply marquees of Lady Sullivan's Ambulance Hospital. Where I was a nurse."

Her eyes flare, she looks at me sharply, and her hope that I am lying sets fire to my picric acid temper.

"Yes. It was Lady Sullivan I met four years ago, and it was with Lady Sullivan that I ran away to France. And on that icy cold morning when your lover arranged for the hospital to be destroyed, I ran into the explosion to pull out the medicines I feared would react with your picric acid bomb to create something far worse."

I near rip the buttons off my dress (the one I stole from Gwendolyn) and pull down my camisole. "See this scar?" It's a ragged, ugly rope of clotted flesh that sometimes still burns. "A wedge of metal from the explosion cut through my sou'wester, through my uniform, and straight into me. Nick pulled me from the explosion and stitched my skin back together."

Raising a forearm, Gwendolyn shields her eyes from the searing light that is my scar. "I didn't know," she shouts. "How could I?" She struggles to retake control of her breath and bows her head. In a quieter voice, she says, "I didn't mean to hurt you."

"Of course you didn't." I button up my dress, resenting the pity welling up behind my eyes for my proud, lonely, brilliant, stupid sister.

"You were thinking on an esoteric level, where humans are faceless and nameless. War is personal, Gwendolyn. Be they German, English, French or Egyptian, real people suffer and die. One minute they're singing. The next a rat is chewing off their necrotic foot."

Her perfectly bowed lips twist. "I'm certainly paying the price for my vanity," she answers bitterly.

Humiliated she may be, but my sister is still dressed in couture, her elegant legs crossed daintily, not a single scratch to mar her outer perfection. She's paid very little for her vanity, though acknowledging it has cost her. She looks older now, more vulnerable. She wouldn't survive a day in disagreeable weather, much less prison.

Drained, I plop gracelessly into Papa's chair. "The man I love, but more than that, a man with the integrity like no other, who has dedicated himself to repairing spines and encouraging crippled men to embrace life, is going to be sentenced to death tomorrow to protect me and our undeserving family from your mistake." It's not an accusation, and my tone reflects a dull, thudding ache, not anger.

Gwendolyn raises her bent head to meet my gaze. "It seems people are always willing to sacrifice for you."

I could laugh at how jealous she sounds.

"This lieutenant colonel," she says. "Mama," she adds wistfully.

There is only one photograph of Mama in this room, and yet it was Mama who selected and arranged the photographs. Mama, who gave me her name because she felt the least loved. Mama, who Papa realized mattered only once she died.

"Mama wasn't thinking of you or me," I say, "when she had you marry Jerome. She was thinking of the future. Of Matty. He was Mama's hope that we would somehow become a better family."

Gwendolyn cannot help herself. The mention of her son brings the pink back to her cheeks. Sinned though she has, her penance is her joy. We fall quiet thinking of Mama and I wait for Gwendolyn to once again remind me of my inadequacy and her superiority. She says,

"Matty worships you."

"What? Why?" I ask, sounding thoroughly perplexed and somewhat horrified. Which I am. I am not hero material.

"Because you're fearless."

I shake my head. "Most of the time, I'm terrified."

"Yet it doesn't stop you. You ran *toward* an exploding hospital marquee."

"It was war." I shrug my shoulders.

Gwendolyn serves me one of her sister-knows-best frowns. "Though you like to ignore the fact, I have known you since birth. It was not war that made you, Margaret. You have always been . . ." She pauses, struggling to form the word as if she fears it. "Brave."

"Stubborn. Ill-tempered," I offer her in exchange for the compliment. Neither of us are used to being kind to the other.

"That too," she agrees. "But it makes your world big. Grand. Whereas the world I have to offer Matty is so narrow. Small."

"A marquisdom is rather grand."

"Rules, structure, manners," she says. "Things that must be obeyed. Don't misunderstand me, I value Matty's position in society. I know it will make him, which is why I married Jerome and why I tolerate his awful parents. But I don't want Matty to end up"—She bites her lip and stares down at her hands. "Like me."

"Perfect?" I ask, half-joking, half-sincere.

"Trapped." To my open-mouthed, incredulous shock, Gwendolyn explains, "To be perfect, one cannot risk making a single mistake. Which is likely why the mistakes I do make tend to be the disastrous. I don't know how to be brave." She drags her hands through her hair, pulling out the pins. They fall to the floor, making a weak, tinny sound against the hardwood. "I'm sorry, Margaret. For everything."

I'm not ready to forgive Gwendolyn. I may never be. But she is not the only one who would be punished if I exposed her. Yes, her sordid story of a university girl seduced by an older man would cause enough scandal to tarnish Carburry's legacy. From there, it would take but a few steps to connect Carburry to the ring of saboteurs. Perhaps that would be enough to justify his murder and thus save Nick. But the person who would suffer the most would be Matty. He would lose his mother, the center of his world.

How is it that, once again, my choice will decide the fate of a son of Carburry? This time, my own nephew, who unlike Carburry's older son, is real to me. A chubby, spoiled, adventurous child who believes villains are nothing more than make-believe pirates.

CHAPTER TWENTY-THREE

"Pirate! Pirate!"

"What the devil!"

The sound of an enthused Matty followed by the icy tones of an adult male who does not belong to this house send Gwendolyn and I flying out the door of Papa's office and into the hallway, where Matty has attached himself to the long leg of a man who carries with him the energy of a downed electric wire trapped beneath a glacier. God help us all if the ice ever melts.

Unaware of the danger, and innocent to the world, Matty calls out, "Mummy, a pirate. Auntie, a real life pirate. Argh. Ahoy, matey! Argh."

EyePatch examines Matty, sweeps his gaze across the tiled hall to the woman Matty identified as Mummy, and then to me, Auntie. The tick in his jaw is subtle, it mirrors his mother's when she had met and assessed Matty. He's the spitting image of Carburry. Damn the Wallace family and their too quick intelligence.

"Who is that?" Gwendolyn shrinks back, her shoulder leans into mine, foolishly seeking protection in our sibling bond.

"Nick's brother." A sibling bond she should be terrified of. "From the Home Secretary's office."

"Matty, darling." Gwendolyn rearranges her posture and adds a beatific smile to match the maternal sweetness of her tone. One would never suspect she'd confessed to creating weapons of destruction not five minutes before. Beauty has always been her best defense and at this moment, any ordinary man would mistake her for a Mary Cassatt painting, an idealized vision of domesticity. Not EyePatch. He is one of the two surviving men raised by Dame Wallace. To them, maternal affection appears in the form of cyanide-laced cigarettes.

Matty remains firmly wrapped around EyePatch's leg. EyePatch lifts him by the shoulders and holds him up so they stare each other square in the face.

Matty giggles, delighted. "Aargh."

EyePatch doesn't so much as exhale. In the low light of our polished hall, EyePatch's knuckles glisten a near burning white.

Would he hurt a child? Not an innocent one. No. But do the sins of Carburry stain his offspring? I watch, mute and somewhat fascinated, as EyePatch takes all of ten seconds to connect the existence of Carburry's illegitimate child to my sister to this household to the picric acid to Nick's false confession to me. Outside, it may be a pleasant dusky evening, but inside, the silence hisses and crackles.

"Matty," Gwendolyn whispers. "Come to Mummy."

But EyePatch has my nephew dangling midair and helpless. Matty, sensing his mother's fear, if not his own, peers at his buckled shoes and seems to realize the distance between his body and the floor. His safety lies in another's hands. He quivers. "Mummy?"

Gwendolyn whimpers.

From behind me comes a voice, "Put him down, you beast. You're terrible with children."

There are only two people in this world who understand the *so icy it burns* heart of Alexander Wallace. One is his brother, which lends a new urgency to saving Nick. He is essential to more than me. The other is the delicate-faced, sharp-eyed, daughter-of-a-vicar striding toward him. Charles' soft hands tense and flex as if she's testing the snap of a lion tamer's whip.

Something plays across EyePatch. An infinitesimally small loosening of the jaw. A near imperceptible easing of his posture. He sets the boy to the floor, the motion surprisingly gentle, and crouches down to meet Matty at eye level, whispering something.

Matty nods solemnly and turns to Gwendolyn. "Bye-bye, Mummy."

Charles gasps. Gwendolyn screams. And EyePatch smiles. Wide and bright and predatory. Somewhere deep inside me, I must be panicking. But after discovering Gwendolyn's vain, selfish treachery, I am too bruised. In a just world, she deserves to be punished for her crime. Pity the world is not just.

Unless EyePatch can make it so.

Gwendolyn stumbles forward to clasp Matty, but she is blocked by EyePatch, who grips her by the arm and pulls her to stand on tiptoe before she can collapse upon her child.

"Let her go," Charles urges. "Whatever you're doing, it's not right."

He ignores her. "I wonder, Countess, whether you would do me the great honor of a favor?" He raises an inviting eyebrow that registers like a knifepoint. "I have in my possession a set of receipts from the firm of De la Rue & Sons."

"Pen makers," Gwendolyn replies with a shiver.

"Mummy?" Matty looks between Gwendolyn and EyePatch.

"I admit I mistook the flourished signature on the receipt as your father trying to disguise himself out of guilt." EyePatch inclines his head in mock humility. "I realize now, it was a feminine hand. Dainty and decorous."

He raises his head, the movement subtle, as is the electric charge he releases. The hairs on my arm stand on end. No one in the hall moves. Not even Matty. "As befitting a woman who chooses domestic bliss, however brief it was, over university."

Charles clamps her hand over her mouth, absorbing the shock of my sister's crime. But her expression is one of pity, not disgust, and it's directed at EyePatch.

Gwendolyn twists her body, trying to reach Matty. EyePatch spins her back to face him. "We'll be going now." He drags her along with him down the hall.

"Mummy!" Matty cries, grabbing a fist full of her skirt.

"Matty! Matty! Matty!" One word, two syllables. All that gives Gwendolyn meaning, all that makes her human.

Charles races after EyePatch as he pulls mother and child toward the front hall. "This isn't justice," Charles says. "Whatever you think you're doing, it isn't right."

He considers her. Even beneath the glacial planes of his sharp cheekbones and the eye that shares the same color as Nick's, I can see him mulling Charles' opinion. "There's no time," he answers. "Once my brother is sentenced, even the Home Secretary shall be helpless."

"We'll figure it out—" Charles tries.

"It will be done and out of our hands."

"Have some mercy," Charles begs. "We are working on a solution. Did Dame Wallace not explain the plan? We will intervene at sentencing. Lady Margaret will turn the tide of sentiment and prevail upon the Court Martial."

"I'll save my mercy for the innocent," EyePatch snaps.

"That's not mercy, that's revenge." Charles makes as if to grab EyePatch's arm to shake some humanity into him, but beneath his glare, she retracts her touch.

To my quivering, sobbing sister, EyePatch says, "I'm not a monster, Countess. Perhaps you aren't either," he adds with a touch of what no one would call sympathy, though he means it to be. "We might spare you the noose. You're a woman, after all. And a mother."

Matty, cake crumbs still clinging to the sides of his mouth, tears spilling out from his English Oak eyes, weeps. "I want my mummy. Please don't take Mummy."

Gwendolyn tries to yank away from EyePatch, who continues to march her down the hall, with Matty holding on to her. She strokes Matty's hair. Her hand is shaking violently. She's terrified. As was EyePatch's and Nick's younger brother, when a picric acid bomb tore his fighter plane to pieces. As were my patients at Lady Sullivan's, when the marquees exploded and fire raged through what should have been a safe place.

At the front door, he pauses long enough to say to me, "I am not beyond housing mother and son in prison. Come and get the child."

I am frozen in place.

"If you want justice, I will repeat myself only once," he warns. "Collect the child."

There it is again. That word. *Justice.* Gwendolyn committed a crime. She deserves punishment. Nick committed no crime, he deserves freedom. In between my sister's guilt and Nick's innocence sits my nephew, who is not yet four, and sobbing. And what of the good men who go to war and kill other good men? They die or come home crippled, drug-addicted, mad, burdened, broken, and neglected. Women like Lady Sullivan and Fukimoto disappear as if they've never existed. Sisters betray each other. Why do we equate justice with a woman and a balancing scale? It's a knife. It guts everyone.

I cannot speak. My throat is clogged by these charged words expanding and suffocating us all. Justice. Mercy. Revenge. Innocence. Mummy. They fall into my mouth like shovels full of dirt until I fear I will be buried alive from the inside out.

In the back of my head, I long for the crunch of tires along a pockmarked road, the cry of wounded men, the voice of Lady Sullivan. *Triage hemorrhages, chest, and head cases first.* My battle cry. My call to action.

"I do not seek justice," I say, my voice barely audible.

EyePatch's nostrils flare. He'll be dining on both daughters of the House of Halsop tonight.

"What I seek is Nick's freedom," I continue, trying to sound rational and brave.

He flips his palm toward Gwendolyn. "And here you have it."

A low moan bubbles up from Gwendolyn.

"If you believe in justice, if you serve King and Country, you will not be taking my sister anywhere." The change in my voice shocks even me. It's firm and in command, a nurse entering her triage tent.

EyePatch leans forward and lowers his head to meet my stubborn face. He could smite a wretched soul with that eye of his. I dig my toes into my shoes. Unlike my gumboots, these shoes fit. I may not know what I'm doing, but I am built on instinct, am I not? My body knows how to navigate muddy fields and enemy territory, even when the enemy shares my same goals.

I say, "Major Carburry was an important, but not the key figure in the network of saboteurs the Home Secretary is investigating, correct?"

"Correct," EyePatch answers, blandly.

"And you have not identified the leader."

"Lady Margaret, if you're about to suggest you can point us to this figure, please don't bother. You're more likely to identify Rumpelstiltskin than you are a legitimate spy."

If nursing taught me anything, it was to make do with what little equipment I had. "Carburry's network communicated through crossword puzzles."

"How the devil—"

"The patients oft complained how he answered the crossword puzzles incorrectly. Names of ships and such."

"Yes," Charles says enthusiastically. "Yes. There are rumors of a large-scale attack being planned, but we cannot stop it much less arrest anyone without the code key. I thought we might be able to use the crossword to thwart them, use it for whatever code word they have for *disband* or *surrender*."

EyePatch sends her a withering quiet-down warning, but Charles is nothing if not hopeful. She's built on it like I am on instinct. And now

I know EyePatch needs a codeword.

"Anyone who spent any amount of time with Carburry would have noted the crossword gimmick," he says.

"But not just anyone was alone with him for hours on the ship crossing the Channel to return him to England. Where he was nauseous and babbling."

"Babbling?" Charles asks eagerly.

"Nauseous." EyePatch scoffs, all too pleased at Carburry's discomfort. "If Dame Wallace couldn't wrestle an admission out of him, then I highly doubt an amateur could."

"Why would he share information with his enemy? Whereas the nurse-patient relationship is far more intimate. Patients say things meant for no one else. They say things in pain or despair or hope or delirium. And Carburry said a great many things. Many," I emphasize. "And surely if I were to relay to you the contents of our prolonged dialogue, you would be able to find within it the clues you seek."

"If you know the word, whatever ship name is the signal to attack, it's an act of treason to withhold it from me. Spit it out."

I shake my head. "I honestly don't. But you'd be able to recognize it."

"You will recount this entire conversation to me. Immediately."

"There's no time," I remind him.

"You're delaying."

"I am focusing on one goal at a time. Nick is my goal."

"You have an inclination toward blackmail," he says. "And you're not particularly good at it."

"I'm worth my salt. Once Nick is free, you will have my full and uncensored report. You can interrogate me for hours. Days, if you like. I won't leave a single detail out in case it might be of significance, not even the potassium chloride needle I loaded."

Gwendolyn shudders at the nonchalance of my useless confession.

"And if you fail?"

"Then do what you will with the House of Halsop. Daughters. Father. You can arrest Matty too." I'm flippant, but only because the consequences of this gamble are devastating. "If we lose and Nick hangs, you and I both lose. His patients lose. I think our nation loses something intrinsic in us, something bigger than words like justice."

EyePatch looms over me, the tightly wound energy crackles off his skin. "I've warned you once not to be overconfident."

"And I'll warn you in return, Mr. Wallace. Don't underestimate me."

CHAPTER TWENTY-FOUR

London, May 8, 1919

I have overestimated myself. On this, perhaps the most important day of my life, when my success or failure will determine the fate of not just myself and not just Nick, but at least three families and perhaps my country; when I am caught between exposing a traitor and saving the man I love and have no strategy in place to decipher how to do anything beyond pinning my hat in place; I rip open the telegram before me and pray with the fervor of a dying sinner that my cousin Kristina has the answer.

Instead, my cousin whose writing is nothing if not detailed, advises:

All you can do, pet, is use your voice.

My shredded from four years of screaming over gunfire voice, the one that can no longer hit the notes in a song. I stare at the slip of paper and feel like the walls of Mama's bedroom are contracting so my lungs are constricted, and then expanding to remind me I am but one human, small and insignificant in the face of the institutions I will clash with today. No sword in hand.

When Gwendolyn comes into the room, her eyes are bloodshot, evidence that she spent the night battling guilt and humility, new emotions to her. Her movements are as raw as a newborn, as if the air itself feels rough against her skin. She reaches for my lapel. Out of habit I jerk away, but stop and send her a questioning glance at the item in her hand.

She smiles ruefully. "If you are going to win over a courtroom full of hostile military men, you need to look the part." She pins the red poppy to my delicate white suit.

The suit was my mother's *good luck suit*. Betsy hemmed it last night. Watching her cut the excess linen near sent me into tears, a reminder once again that Mama is gone and will never fill the fabric that once framed her. The suit smells of starch. Even her scent has faded away.

Stepping back to assess her work, Gwendolyn tilts my hat to reveal more of my face. "You look like a bride."

"Marching to an unknown fate," I reply dryly.

She explores Mama's cosmetics table, selects a tube of lipstick, holds the color up to my face, and decides against the added flourish. Instead, she pinches my cheeks to bring the blood to the surface. "Don't forget to do the same when you're called by the Judge Advocate. You want to appear vulnerable, not wan."

"Not wan," I repeat solemnly.

Unsure of this new, awkward camaraderie, together we descend the stairs and out of the townhouse, climbing into the waiting motorcar where even the preternaturally disposed to cheer Charles is tempered. She drives smoothly, taking no risks, maintaining a good amount of space between us and the next vehicle. She even stops before turning left.

Once she has parked, we walk up the Strand and pass through the iron gates of the Royal Courts of Justice. Carved into the arch of the outer porch are the heads of judges and lawyers, their faces cold and remote, immoveable stone. Inside, the ceilings of the Main Hall seem to stretch beyond even the sky, unreachable. The Italian marble floors form an intricate mosaic pattern. On a rainy day, one might slip on the smooth surface. If this building is dedicated to render justice, justice must be cold, expensive, and ornamental.

Whereas butterflies are making a football match of my stomach and my muscles are clenched so tightly, I feel as if I'm made of crumbling brick and sinking in quicksand.

I walk between Gwendolyn and Charles while they attempt small talk. I am not allowed to know what Master James wrote in *The Times*. EyePatch insisted upon it, or else I would look rehearsed. Nor was I permitted to come to the Court Martial earlier to hear the testimony of what few character witnesses were willing to come forward to speak for Nick, the confessed murderer of a national hero. So the conversation between the two women centers on the weather. The sky is blue. The grass is green. The sun is out. The world will go on, and yet if I fail today, Nick won't.

We take the stairs to the next floor. At the heavy double doors leading to the courtroom, Charles motions for me to take a seat at a bench in the hall. "I'll check on the proceedings, shall I? See if the barrister Mr. Higgenbotham is ready for you? Or if you should wait in the witness room." She pats my shoulder and brackets her smile with determined optimism.

The bench is as hard and unforgiving as everything else in this building. Neither Gwendolyn nor I have the capacity to sit still in times of stress. After a half minute of shifting left and right, we both rise and march up and down the long hall, pausing occasionally to look down to the milieu of black-robed jurists and black-frocked men below.

"Not a single woman in the crowd," I observe.

"And yet they call it *Lady Justice*," Gwendolyn muses and the two of us share a small laugh.

Our humor is short-lived. Someone grabs my arm and spins me around. If Lady Justice had a face, it would be Mrs. Carburry's: elegantly etched, lit with fury. Her fingers dig into my arm like she means to snap my bone.

"Am I to assume you are responsible for the circus going on inside?" She juts her chin toward the closed doors of the courtroom. "Who do you think you are?"

"No one of significance," I answer.

She curls her ruby red lips. "A troublemaker. An errant, spoiled child. You've no right to upend my husband's death."

Beside me, Gwendolyn flushes, realizing that the widow before us is her ex-lover's wife.

"Whatever lies you employ to save your doctor will come to naught," she warns. "Do you hear me? *Naught*. We are military. We are the backbone of England."

"Why would I need to lie?" I wriggle my arm, but she has a death grip on it. "The truth shall set you free," I say rather grandly considering that if I were to tell the truth my sister would go to prison, my family would be split apart, and the Home Secretary's investigation into the saboteur network would be exposed, risking our nation's security.

"Is that what this morning's tripe in *The Times* was all about?" Mrs. Carburry asks. "Because all I read was a story about the indulgent misadventures of a brat playing dress up in a nurse's uniform."

"My sister saved lives," Gwendolyn tries before cowering beneath the righteous glare of Mrs. Carburry.

Mrs. Carburry flicks her focus back to me. "And now you've subverted a dignified, formal proceeding into a fishmonger's market with every Tom, Dick, and Harry your doctor slapped a bandage on clamoring to take the stand to attest to the man's character. He'll be canonized by teatime."

My heart jumps. The article! Master James' article, worked! It brought out Nick's patients. It must be filling the Court Martial with what has been missing during the proceedings, Nick's humanity. We haven't won, not yet, but we've undermined the opposition. My feet shift, ready to sprint to the witness stand, but I am pinned by Mrs.

Carburry's hold. She really is shockingly strong.

"Your husband was a traitor." I may not be able to shout it in court or print it in the papers, but at the least, I can use it against this woman in her widow's weeds. "He betrayed the military you so dearly love."

"What a smug little creature you are," Mrs. Carburry hisses. "Chip at my husband's legacy and I will destroy you. You have a brother who fought in the war, no? I read it in the paper," she adds drily. "Drug addiction is difficult to overcome when opium can be made so readily available, even in Silvertown." That, she did not read that in the papers. She's reminding me of how far her power reaches. "Your family manufactures bandages? Expect for there to be rumors of defects in the product, of bribery in the procurement. Your sweet little journalist escaped with a black eye. Next time, it will be those lovely fingers he uses to type."

My arm smarts and yet I'm perversely grateful for Mrs. Carburry's grip. It's her strength holding me up. Otherwise, I might sink to the floor. Meanwhile, Gwendolyn has gone so pale, I fear she might faint.

"Mum." From the half-opened door of the court room, a boy of thirteen or so calls out. There is no mistaking who he is. He has the military-straight posture of a soldier, the auburn curls of his mother, and the brown as English oak eyes of his father. It's the sight of this young boy that has shaken Gwendolyn. He is a vision of the future, of Matty in ten years.

Concern crisscrosses his face. He's holding the door ajar and beckons for her to return.

Mrs. Carburry places a black-gloved forefinger on the fragile petal of the red poppy pinned to my suit. "Rob my son of his future and I will eviscerate yours."

She joins her son, looping her arm through his. Before the door shuts behind them he turns back to Gwendolyn and me, curious perhaps of who we are and what role we play in his life. The weight of his youth, of his innocence in this mess of a Court Martial lances through my chest. To save a life, how many lives must I ruin?

When the door shuts behind them, Gwendolyn and I lean our elbows against the railing and exhale in unison.

"Damn," I say.

"Bloody hell," she answers. "Do you know what you're doing, Margaret? That woman. The Wallace family. The Home Secretary. These are not people to trifle with."

"Canada becomes more attractive by the minute."

She presses her fingers to her temples. "Don't joke. I can't bear it. That woman . . ." I suspect Mrs. Carburry will forever be *That Woman* to Gwendolyn for fear that to utter her name would be to reduce Gwendolyn to dust. "Her boy," she says more softly, unable to say more. Because what could my sister say? Were their positions reversed, Gwendolyn would treat me exactly as Mrs. Carburry has. They are more alike than they are different.

I wish I were a planner, that I had mapped a strategy. My instincts cannot possibly be enough.

The double doors of the courtroom swing open once again. This time Mr. Higgenbotham emerges, dabbing at his brow with a handkerchief. The butterflies in my stomach have settled like lead. In a few minutes I will be called to the witness box and despite all of the tactics, from delaying this hearing to drawing men to testify to Nick's character, I am still missing the fundamental chess piece. Is it the king? Or the queen? Rook, knight, bishop? Pawn, says the cynical voice in the back of my head. We are all but pawns on an arbitrary chessboard.

I hold up my hand in a half-wave and Mr. Higgenbotham bustles toward us.

"Who is that?" Gwendolyn asks and I cannot quite tell whether she's fascinated or horrified by the short man with his wig askew who looks like he belongs in an illegal boxing match on the docks, not the marbled halls of esoteric justice.

"The barrister," I reply.

"He reminds me of a kangaroo."

"Now who's making jokes?"

"I'm not," she answers. "It was a compliment. Kangaroos are very aggressive kickers."

"Aggressive or not, unless you've got any tricks for me, we are playing a dead draw game," I admit.

Gwendolyn widens her eyes, all sense of hope sinking.

"There will be no tricks, young lady." Mr. Higgenbotham straightens his wig and shakes my hand, then Gwendolyn's, who out of habit, tilts her head to a regal angle and delivers her *it's an honor for you to meet me* smile. What an odd man Mr. Higgenbotham is. Unimpressed by all the beauty wrapped up in Gwendolyn, he scowls until her smile falters and her expression slides from vanity to one of admiration, perhaps even a touch of lust. He does, after all, radiate intense masculinity.

He places a firm palm on my back and motions me forward, reeling off instructions as we march forward. "First, you are to remember that this is a legal proceeding and you will abide by the rules of the court. Second, I am not your attorney. I am not here to protect or defend you. I represent Colonel Wallace, who dismissed me earlier this week and is only permitting me to represent him for today's hearing as the Home Secretary's office has suggested that if he were to object, he would find himself declared mad. Which, if one were to take my advice, would not be an altogether bad outcome. An asylum is far more comfortable than an execution."

We've reached the door. My knees are shaking. Mr. Higgenbotham clamps his hand on my shoulder. My assessment of his boxing skills is not wrong. His grip is mercenary. "Finally, I have not forgotten your alleged asthmatic attack the last time I encountered you. While I have no objection to court room theatrics, I will not suborn perjury. You will not make a mockery of justice."

But what if justice makes a mockery of us?

He swings the door open. A sea of heads spins around to face me, some friendly, some curious. For a moment, I am stunned, unable to move. The courtroom is packed. With men in and out of uniform. With men whose trouser legs have been pinned up because they are missing part of their limbs, with men in wheelchairs, with men whole and hearty. And they sit not alone, but with mothers and wives. One surrounded by his sons. Another in a wheelchair has a toddler bouncing about.

Because of Master James' article.

Because of Nick.

Because of me.

Because they are here to do what's right. And I cannot fail them.

Needing to steady myself, I reach for Gwendolyn's arm. She walks me down the aisle, our pace slow. A hand reaches across to press my own—Sergeant Dawson, who came to Wimereux with seven bullets lodged in his back and now stands up to greet me. Another aisle and General Brunswick, whose face I shaved each morning in Wimereux, now sits with his five sons and winks at me. Another aisle and none other than little Lucy bobs up and down, waving and mouthing *hello, hello* while her father smiles proudly. When I pass McMannis and Gaspar, they pound their fists against their chests in unison.

As we reach the front of the courtroom, my reception cools. Dame Wallace manages to acknowledge me with a nod. EyePatch ticks his jaw. Mrs. Carburry sits surrounded by officers in full military regalia, medal upon medal upon medal pinned to their chests. She makes sure to meet my eye, to convey in her bitter smile the retribution she has promised. Her son takes her hand and squeezes it and her posture softens.

At the wooden gate dividing the gallery from the judge's bar, we stop. "Tilt your head," Gwendolyn whispers.

I give her a questioning look, but obey and before anyone can take note, she pinches both my cheeks hard. The poppy she pinned to my borrowed suit earlier, our walk down the aisle, and this gesture feels oddly significant, the equivalent of a bride on her wedding day. Gwendolyn's pinch of the cheeks the same as the father of the bride lifting his daughter's veil.

She slips into the front row, gingerly evading Dame Wallace and EyePatch, and takes a seat between Charles and Master James, who pauses from scribbling in his notebook to twirl his pencil and grin at me, cheeky as ever. The bruise on his eye shines like a badge of pride, green and mottled. He's earned his rank as a journalist.

The one person who does not acknowledge me is the person who matters most. At the defendant's table, he sits with his back to me, not turning. At first, I assume Nick is being obstinate. Irritation surges. But then I note how he's pressing his forearms hard into the wooden table to keep himself from slumping. He tries to suppress a shiver and I realize he is sick. Not mildly so. He came from Brixton Prison. Where he was elbows deep in an influenza epidemic and trying to mask his own wheezing. When I touched his skin yesterday, I sensed the beginning of a fever.

Am I already too late?

Terrified, I stand before the Judge Advocate and the board of officers. Do they realize, truly realize, the depth of their power? Who are they that they may say who will live free and who will die?

The bailiff calls my name. "Lady Margaret Adelaide Halladay." Window dressing, my name. I take the witness box. He holds a Bible before me and demands I solemnly swear to tell the truth, the whole truth, and nothing but the truth.

When the truth will save no one.

CHAPTER TWENTY-FIVE

M r. Higgenbotham and I are engaged in a gentle waltz. His
questions set a simple scene and draw a portrait of the woman I
truly am.

"You admit, Lady Margaret, that you joined Lady Sullivan's Ambulance hospital without having the requisite training."

"I do."

"And that for the four years in which you served as a nurse in
France, you did so under a false identity."

"I do."

"That you participated in surgeries though you were not qualified."

"I do."

"There are those in this courtroom today who would describe your
actions as irresponsible. Would you?"

There is some uncomfortable shifting in the seats from the gallery,
but Master James' article prepared the audience for these ignoble facts.
It may be surprising to hear them in person, but except for a tut-tut
from the Judge Advocate, there is no disapproval. Mrs. Carburry, in
fact, appears delighted.

"I would agree my choices were irresponsible. But I took my responsibilities as a nurse seriously."

A few nods from the audience. A hearty *aye* from McMannis.

"You are here today to give testimony on behalf of the defendant,

Colonel Wallace."

"I am."

"Who was your lover in Wimereux."

Lord, but Mr. Higgenbotham can be blunt. Even Nick seems embarrassed, though his too pale, sickly pallor does not color. He distracts himself by reaching for the pitcher of water at the defendant's table.

"Yes," I answer. "We were lovers."

"And with whom you are still in love," Mr. Higgenbotham presses.

Nick's upper arm is shaking, the act of pouring himself a glass of water too taxing.

"I will always love Dr. Wallace."

"Colonel Wallace," the Judge Advocate corrects.

Nick's mouth twitches in amusement.

"So you will admit that any testimony you offer is colored by your feelings for the defendant," Mr. Higgenbotham says.

"Are you suggesting love is blind?" I ask.

A smattering of giggles from the gallery. Gwendolyn sends me a *no jokes* frown.

"It is not the place of the witness to pose questions," the Judge Advocate commands.

Mr. Higgenbotham folds his arms behind his back and faces the gallery as he asks, "Is love blind, Lady Margaret?"

"If it were then would it be love?" I hold my hand up as if to interrupt the Judge Advocate before he chastises me again. The motion is not lost on my audience, at least half of whom are humored by my insouciance. "If you do love someone, you know them deeply and yet yearn to know them more. Not just their strengths and flaws, but all the shades in between. Are they quick to laugh or quick to temper? Do they prefer winter or summer? Do they snore? Like dogs? Hate peas?" All the little things Nick and I have not had time to explore.

"So would you say you are especially qualified to attest to the defendant's character?" Mr. Higgenbotham asks.

"Yes."

Mr. Higgenbotham walks over to stand behind Nick. "We have spent the better part of today hearing from witness after witness about Colonel Wallace. Obviously, everyone finds him to be a talented man of medicine." He pauses to send a speaking glance toward the prosecutor and, more subtly, to Mrs. Carburry and the rows of decorated officers supporting her. Not one can deny Nick is a brilliant doctor.

Mr. Higgenbotham continues, "We have learned how he reattached severed spines and retrained bodies to walk. That he taught crippled men to find strength and courage in their condition. We have heard from two teachers, a choir director, and a young man entering the law who, though they are bound by wheelchairs, are living full, rich lives. Each of them thanks Colonel Wallace. One brave soul admitted Colonel Wallace saved him from suicide."

Mrs. Carburry taps the prosecutor on the shoulder and whispers furtively.

"Objection," the prosecutor says.

"To what?" Mr. Higgenbotham asks. "The honoring of men who sacrificed their bodies for our country?"

"Overruled." The Judge Advocate nods to Mr. Higgenbotham. "But do speed things along."

From Mr. Higgenbotham's obsequious bow, I'm inclined to believe he and I both know *speed things along* is tied directly to a bottle of whiskey and a porterhouse steak waiting for the Judge Advocate at his club.

And bless Mr. Higgenbotham's subversive barrister's soul, he proceeds by slowing the pace of his speech. "We have heard today not only from courageous men of all ranks who came home, but from the families of those who didn't. Though it would be easy for these parents, wives, daughters and sons to blame the doctor for their loved one's death, these grieving families have done the opposite today. They have thanked Colonel Wallace for his hand-drawn sketches of the men they will never again see."

The prosecutor slaps an impatient hand against his table. "Objection. The defense is engaging in a soliloquy, not eliciting testimony."

"Sustained."

"Forgive me," Mr. Higgenbotham says though what I think he means is *stuff it*. "Lady Margaret, in light of the testimony that has come before you, is there anything you, who admits to being irresponsible, a liar, and the defendant's lover, can add that would be meaningful to this court?"

I appreciate the way Nick's nostrils flare in my defense. "Colonel Wallace is no saint." Despite the halo. "He is inclined to pride and oft refuses to accept help. He takes on more responsibility than he is capable of handling. He holds secrets when he should share them. He overthinks and is terrible at games. Even a game of jacks befuddles him."

In the distance, Lucy giggles knowingly and the anxious faces of a handful of widows and mothers soften at the sound of a child's laugh.

I look at them directly. "He takes risks believing the only one who will suffer is him, not the people around him."

People flinch. Some frown. EyePatch cracks his knuckles. Many look confused. The only person in this stuffed to the gills courtroom grinning is Nick himself. I haven't insulted him. Not a whit. I have told him in all the ways I can how truly and deeply I, an irresponsible liar who runs into fires, loves him.

"Which is why," I say, concentrating on forming my words, "I can swear before God and this Court Martial today, he is the type of man who will confess to a crime to protect the honor of another."

The courtroom erupts. There are gasps. A stomping of feet. The raising of Mrs. Carburry's black gloved fist. Shouts of objection, objection, objection. The Judge Advocate pounds his gavel, demanding order. And I sit back to survey the damage I've wrought.

"The defense is attempting to interject new evidence," the prosecutor argues. "We cannot retry a case that has already been resolved."

"This testimony shall be stricken –"

"—Your Honor," Mr. Higgenbotham says in a reasonable tone, "the witness did not state Colonel Wallace *had* submitted a false confession. She merely described him as a man who would. A testament to his character."

The Judge Advocate casts a doleful frown at Mr. Higgenbotham, but acquiesces to the barrister's trick of logic.

Mr. Higgenbotham turns to me. "Lady Margaret, forgive me when I suggest that your description of Colonel Wallace, while touching, is the kind of thing many a woman will say about the man she loves. Have you ever witnessed Colonel Wallace making the kind of sacrifice of which you speak?"

The devil himself would lose his pitchfork to Mr. Higgenbotham.

"Objection."

"To what?" Mr. Higgenbotham asks the prosecution. "A fact?"

The Judge Advocate sighs. "Tread carefully. The defendant's guilty plea has been entered and is irrevocable."

"Your Honor, I mean only to substantiate the witness's statement so the Court Martial has a full and complete record for sentencing. Full and complete," Mr. Higgenbotham repeats, this time to the gallery, implying this Court Martial has ignored the record. To me, he says, "Please answer my question, Lady Margaret."

I bite my lip. "I am not sure I can."

"Why not?"

"Because to do so would be to implicate myself." A delay strategy to give my brain time to catch up to this scene.

"In what way?"

"I was Major Carbury's nurse."

"We are not discussing Major Carbury's character," Mr. Higgenbotham warns.

"There is no question of Major Carbury's character," I say. He was a poisonous rat who betrayed his principles for power and revenge. "But his character is related to my own failings and in explaining how I know Colonel Wallace would claim guilt to save another, I incriminate myself."

I don't know why EyePatch is grimacing like I'm celebrating the discovery of fool's gold (*idiot's* gold, he'd say). I don't know why a sharp pain is pulsating above my right eye like a warning signal. I have the audience's sympathy. Can I not expose Carburry just a little? Carburry may be dead, but this lie of heroism lives on, an insult. Mrs. Carburry may literally be eating off this lie, but Nick is paying for it. Nine months in prison, shivering in the dank and rancid air, it makes me shudder. Makes me furious. Of all the men in the world, the last person who deserved Nick's mercy is Carburry.

"Continue," Mr. Higgenbotham says cautiously.

Gwendolyn, her hand encased in a lilywhite lace glove, cups her mouth. She knows me better than I give her credit for. I get so easily lost in my picric acid temper, I sometimes do damage merely for the sake of damage.

But she's the one who's shown explosions can be controlled. You can time them. I can control this situation. "I accompanied Major Carburry across the Channel on his return home to England. I was responsible for his well-being. He was exhausted, anxious, and ill. Seasick."

The cause of which sits in the front row of the gallery, behind Nick, her expression one of benign curiosity. Dame Wallace could slit my throat with a hat pin and walk away without a hair out of place.

"You are suggesting you were derelict in your duties."

"Worse."

Mr. Higgenbotham narrows his eyes at me. A warning. Ours is an alliance of convenience, not mutual goals. I am on the side of Nick, he on the side of justice.

Deep breath in. Long exhalation out. How do you bring down an institution? You blow it up. "I killed Major Carburry." I wait for my words to catch fire, for the collective gasp and a cry for justice.

The courtroom does explode. In laughter. EyePatch kicks the post in front of him. Dame Wallace looks ready to offer me a cyanide-laced cigarette out of pity. Charles and Gwendolyn both cover their faces. Master James chews on his pencil as if I've tossed all his good work into the trash bin. McMannis is frowning and shaking his head. Nick coughs heavily into a handkerchief and though he folds the white cloth quickly, I spy droplets of blood.

Mrs. Carburry is gloating.

My heart is sinking, sinking, while my face reddens to a shine. They all warned me, even Matron, no one would believe me. I am *idiot's gold*.

In this mess, it's Mr. Higgenbotham who is laughing the loudest and hardest, as if my false admission were planned between us and the mockery of the court our intended goal. He adjusts his spectacles and mutters beneath his breath for only me to hear, "I will not suborn perjury, Lady Margaret. Try again."

Stupid Vera Betts. Foolish Margaret Halladay. Who am I to be tilting at institutions? What's one person in this sea of chaos? I may be a whirlwind of energy and instinct, but my emotions, as Gwendolyn complained, do run off the rails. And for what? We are all pawns. Not one of us will win. Because we don't control fate. It has us by the throat.

And yet, Lady Sullivan was only one person and she brought a hospital to the battlefront. Nick is merely one person and yet look at the lives he has touched. Everyone in this courtroom and the dead beyond it. I am only one person, and yes I did lie when I joined Lady Sullivan's Ambulance Hospital, but not about my skills. Old Betts taught me well. All I lied about was my name and Lady Sullivan never, not once, asked for my credentials. She witnessed my safe pair of hands in action and knew where I could be best put to use.

Maybe Nick is right and there is no chessboard. Our job is to simply try. In between the truth and the lies, there's just us, trying to do right. And to do right, I will shove my hatred for Carburry aside before it erodes and consumes me.

"You misunderstand me." I have to raise my voice to be heard by the crowd, who no longer trust me. "I did not kill Major Carburry." Truth.

"But I was his nurse crossing the Channel." Truth.

"And we spoke at length." Three in a row.

The gallery quiets now. Mrs. Carburry intertwines her fingers. Though I cannot see the brush marks from this distance, I remember her gloves have been dyed more than once. Her boots too. Despite the polish, the heel is worn down.

"He spoke of his family legacy. His father is a decorated hero with a statue in Westminster." The audience nods.

"He himself is a war hero." It takes all my self-discipline not to spit bile when Mrs. Carburry turns her head so all the gallery can appreciate the Madonna-level beauty and suffering of his widow.

"And we spoke of his son." I study the boy next to Mrs. Carburry. His limbs are too long, his face red-cheeked and youthful, and yet already he sits tall and straight and with purpose. He will fill out his military uniform one day soon. He nudges his mother, reminding her to face forward, not perform for the crowd. A wonder. He isn't tainted by Carburry's selfishness, nor chained by his mother's pride. In between there are other forces molding him into the man he is becoming, better than the individual parts of his parents.

"Major Carburry was proud of his son." So very much the truth. His paternal love was what made Carburry human. It was why I dropped the potassium chloride needle.

"A fine boy indeed," Mr. Higgenbotham agrees, his tone avuncular. "But it is not the Carburry family that is at issue. Major Carburry's exploits have been well reported and celebrated."

"The stories one reads in the paper," I say, gesturing to Master James, "eloquent though they are, can never capture all the nuances of a man. On our way to England, Major Carburry lamented that he walked out of a German prison camp on two legs and wound up crippled."

"He was not crippled," Mr. Higgenbotham reminds me. "He was returning to England to recuperate."

"We did not speak of the future. He struggled to make peace with the past. Being a POW changed him." Changed his allegiance.

"Even as a prisoner, he was treated with respect," Mr. Higgenbotham says.

"He was ashamed, I think." The other side of arrogance.

"A man of Major Carburry's courage and stature?"

"His entire regiment perished under his command." I bow my head when I say this, out of respect for the men who died, not as a dig at Carburry's failure to lead.

"Hard on a soldier to carry such a burden," Mr. Higgenbotham offers, his tone soothing; it's meant for the audience. Many lost family in the Battle of St. Quentin, which was a small part of the larger, more terrible First Battles of the Somme.

From the corner of my eye, I catch two of the board members nodding, recalling their own memories. I continue, "The burden of making a man a hero, I think, is that we forget the suffering, the loss, that brought him there. Four hundred and twenty thousand casualties. One hundred and twenty-five thousand of our men dead. I didn't face battle, and yet I still wake up choking on the smell of blood and smoke."

I am not alone. Too many faces in the gallery, young and old, have fallen somber.

"He asked me for relief from his pain." The pain being physical because he was unwittingly poisoning himself with cyanide-laced cigarettes. Still, thin as the ice may be, I am at least skating along the truth.

Mr. Higgenbotham sucks in his breath. "Before you continue, Lady Margaret, I must ask, were there any witnesses to this conversation?"

I shake my head. "No."

"And so we have only your word."

"I'm afraid so."

I understand Mr. Higgenbotham's rhythm now. He is playing the Greek chorus, the voice of doubt, which sharpens rather than dulls the story unfolding between us.

Mr. Higgenbotham rubs his chin thoughtfully. "So Major Carburry was in acute pain, haunted by battle losses, ashamed, suffering from melancholia perhaps, and asked you for mercy?"

Mercy? The only mercy I know is the River Mersey which borders Blackpond Manufacturing. It runs so fast and cold, to fall into it is to drown. Carburry, for whom victory meant the butchering of women and children, deserved the River Mersey. EyePatch crosses his arms as if reading my mind and agreeing with me. But Charles holds still and looks at me with encouragement, as if mercy is the cure. She would, being the daughter of a vicar. I want to believe her. I know Nick does.

"Help," I answer.

"In what form?"

Carburry died from cyanide poisoning. I loaded a needle with potassium chloride. I promised not to commit perjury and if I'm not careful, the Court Martial can dig up his grave and perform an autopsy. But I did offer Carburry something for his nausea. "Painkillers."

"And did you oblige?"

"I loaded the needle. I intended to administer it. But . . . I am a nurse. I cannot take human life. I dropped it to the floor and ran away. Forgive me, it was a moment of weakness. I pitied him." I feel it now, the pity, perhaps for the first time. His vision of peace, that it came only from victory, no matter the innocents he slaughtered for it, such belief must have been born from a festering wound, pride mixed with humiliation.

"Are you suggesting Major Carburry managed to collect the needle and inject himself?"

"I don't know what Major Carburry did. I was not in the cabin."

"Have you forgotten, Lady Margaret, he was found with his hands tied to the bedrail?"

After he tried to choke me, smashed my head against the ship's floor, and slammed his casts into Nick's hip. "Men in his position have been known to tie themselves down so they cannot change their minds."

"I thought you said he was crippled."

"No, his legs were damaged, but his arms were strong. They would have to be. Ask anyone who operates a wheelchair."

A murmur of agreement from the audience.

"Your Honor," the prosecution starts.

"Quiet," the Judge Advocate orders. He's smart enough to gage the audience. They are the counterbalance to his otherwise unfettered power, forcing him to see beyond himself.

I focus on the gallery, these soldiers who came home battered and broken. I nursed many of them, holding their hands through the night, holding them down when they thrashed in their beds and begged to be left to die rather than face a life without the ability to walk. I think of the German soldiers who caused these injuries and how they limped home with their own wounds, their own broken hearts. I think of the nature of medicine, of how no matter what uniform a person wore, we removed the bullets and sewed up their cuts; of Nick and his chalk-board filled with medical strategy even for the patient who would likely die. I wonder if this is mercy. To see even the ugliest of humanity, and to remember we are human.

"I want to make clear, I am ashamed of my role in Major Carburry's death. Life is sacred. War has taught me so. And I should not have entertained the thought that a painkiller could bring the kind of peace Major Carburry yearned for. He was forceful and desperate, but I was wrong. I am sorry."

"If Major Carburry did indeed commit suicide, then why this ruse," Mr. Higgenbotham demands. "Why would Colonel Wallace confess?"

"To protect a person's honor."

"Yours," Mr. Higgenbotham concludes, sounding satisfied.

"No," I say, trusting my instincts. I cannot expose Major Carburry without harming the innocent. I cannot save Nick by pointing to the sins of another. But I can believe in mercy, which is not blind like justice, but the opposite. It sees everything and forgives. "Major Carburry's."

The silence that descends is palpable. EyePatch appears to be feasting on it, the slow, sly smile spreading across his face is so filled with hope, I think I might splinter beneath it. He leans his head back and mutters something to the men behind him, the way one viewing a cricket match might comment to a fellow fan. The men nod their heads in agreement and turn to share their whispered thoughts with the row behind them. I recognize the tactic for what it is, a master strategist laying down tinder.

It's the ever-loyal McMannis who strikes the match. "You cannae hang a man for protecting a hero's honor," he shouts.

"The Major kept himself to himself in Wimereux," Corporal Langdon adds.

"Could never bring himself to join us for even a smoke," says Private Greene. "We must have reminded him of the regiment he lost."

"He couldn't even do the crosswords right, he was in such despair," General Brunswick says to his sons.

"Poor man," an older woman in the back moans. "To lose all hope. Poor, poor man."

The Judge Advocate lowers his gavel. The crowd ignores him.

"The war," says someone else.

"The war," everyone agrees.

"This is preposterous." The prosecutor throws his hands up.

"No," comes the trembling voice of a woman who will cede me the win so long as she keeps the trophy. "It is true. I can see that now. Colonel Wallace wrote to us. I still have the letter. He spoke respectfully of my husband. He reminded my son that he was born from a line of heroes, but to be true to his heritage, he must act with courage and integrity."

She darts a cynical half-smile of acknowledgement toward me before turning her doe-eyed widow's gaze upon the Judge Advocate and wipes a calculated tear from her face. He furrows his brow at her and then at the gavel he holds in midair, perhaps feeling the weight of his responsibility, rather than his power, for the first time in years.

He says, "Colonel Wallace, the Court Martial wishes to address you directly. Please rise."

It's painful to watch Nick struggle to stand. His limbs must ache and he is likely burning from fever. Even the smallest movement, shifting his head to face the Judge Advocate makes him wince. He closes his eyes, a sure sign he's gathering the last reserves of his strength, and forces himself to stand without leaning against the table. His hands are curled, his face has gone from pale to white.

In a stentorian voice the Judge Advocate says, "You have been present throughout these proceedings. You have steadfastly maintained your guilt, which prevented this Court from adjudicating all the facts. There were issues the Court Martial should have been engaged to consider including statements from the ship's crew that you did not appear on deck until *after* an officer called for medical aid, casting doubt on your recitation of the facts. In so doing, you have perverted the course of justice, though as the testimony today has so proven, you are a man of the highest code of honor and worthy of the Victoria

Cross you were awarded. So I will ask you once and only once, on the thirteenth of August 1918, did you murder Major Guy Harrison Carburry?"

I bow my head and press my palms together. Dame Wallace crosses herself. We know Nick too well. How easily his integrity can trip him. How he is just as likely to take a surgeon's scalpel to the solution as he is to accept a freedom based on compromises.

"Colonel Wallace," the Judge Advocate says, sounding rather aggrieved at Nick's reluctance to give the Judge the opportunity to correct his own rush to justice. "Did you or did you not murder Major Carburry?"

Nick wavers to the left, catches himself, and locks his joints and muscles in place. He has the air of a man facing a firing squad, not one being given a second chance. Finally, he answers, "I did not."

And vomits blood across the table.

The bailiff jumps back. Gwendolyn screams. EyePatch kicks down the wooden bar dividing the galley from the defense table and catches his brother before his head hits the floor.

I fly from the witness box. I check the pulse in Nick's neck. Rapid and stressed. His skin burns to the touch. Droplets of blood and saliva dribble from his mouth. When I put my ear to his chest, his lungs rattle, damp and exhausted. "Pneumonia," I tell EyePatch.

"Hospital," he answers.

"He'll need oxygen and an antipneumococcal serum." I yank off my white jacket, dip it in the pitcher of water at the defense table, and wipe his face, trying to cool his skin. His blood stains the linen fabric beneath my wilted poppy.

"We need an ambulance," says Dame Wallace.

"We'll be faster in the motorcar." Charles collects her coat and bag.

Nick shivers.

Mr. Higgenbotham throws off his barrister's robe. I wrap Nick in it while EyePatch cradles his brother, letting him lean against his chest, supporting him upright with his forearm. "Nicky." EyePatch's voice is stripped of cynicism, all I hear is the love binding older brother to younger. "You obstinate jackass."

Gwendolyn peers over the broken railing.

"We need to clear the court room," I tell her and indicate the gathering crowd.

Gwendolyn employs her lady-of-the-manor voice to direct everyone to slowly exit the courtroom. Mrs. Carburry stands. She and Gwendolyn eye each other and whether Mrs. Carburry knows of her husband's entanglements or not, she instinctually dislikes my sister.

"Come along," she ushers her son.

But he pauses and asks me, "Colonel Wallace will be all right, won't he?"

I outraced the truth and managed not to lie. I did not expose Carburry for the traitorous wretch he is. But I did the right thing. I focused on what mattered. His sons, both of them.

"I'll do my best," I answer.

"That's all we can do," he replies.

McMannis and Gaspar have borrowed a wheelchair from one of the ex-soldiers and push it down the far aisle toward us. The two of them help EyePatch to lift and settle Nick into the chair. His head lolls to the side. His smile weak, he says, "That was quite the song, Vera-not-Vera."

"I used my voice."

With his hands, Nick imitates a small explosion. "Boom."

And collapses into unconsciousness.

CHAPTER TWENTY-SIX

Skopelos, Greece, June 13, 1919

He leaps from the turquoise waters of the Aegean Sea and turns his face up to absorb the bright sun of a June afternoon. Not like Neptune. Not like a god at all, but something far more powerful. A man who has suffered and survived and takes nothing for granted, especially the sun's rays, hot against his still too pale skin. His ribs stand out, sharp against his lean frame and when he reaches the sand, he uses the strength of his thigh muscles to compensate for the weakness in his left hip. The injury is permanent. It had no chance to heal in the dankness of prison.

Barefoot, I run down the hill, inhaling the scent of all the things Nick promised—lemon trees, sea salt, and the kermes oaks circling protectively around the secluded cove where Nick learned to swim. I cross the warm sand, tenting my hand over my eyes against the bright light. The sun glints against the gold band on my ring finger. At the edge of the water, he mirrors me with his own, and in the space between us, the light dances off our rings, sparking the air.

"My husband," I say, enfolding into his embrace and tasting afresh the sweet wonder of the word.

"My wife." He cannot stop smiling.

We were supposed to have waited until September, when St. George's Cathedral had an opening, and the banns could be read, and the aristocracy roused to attend the lavish wedding of the Earl of Halsop's scapegrace daughter to a physician cum acquitted murderer. But after nine months apart, neither of us had the patience for formalities. So we ran away to Greece and were married by a thickly bearded Greek orthodox priest who smelled of Karelia cigarettes and spoke nary a word of English. The sole witnesses to our blessed union were a neighboring farm wife and her bleating goat, a hopeless romantic.

Nick cups my face and I kiss his callused palm. His hand comes around to the back of my neck. He strokes the skin, the touch so light it teases out threads of desire. I press my head against his chest, still damp from his swim. I don't mind, not when his lungs breathe clear and strong. Lines of dried salt from the sea streak his chest and arms. I could devour him.

In our embrace, he reaches for my waist and finds the stack of letters I stuffed in my pocket. Collecting them, he steps back and says, "Alas, civilization has caught up with us."

"If by civilization you mean a churlish donkey and an overly sunny postman who wished me 'good offspring,' then yes, I'm afraid so."

"That is a wedding blessing. Good man." He holds up the first letter, its neat and efficient script not at all floral and feminine, despite EyePatch's accusation otherwise.

"Gwendolyn," I answer. "Lamenting we have robbed her of the wedding of the year, where Matty would have been a celebrated ring bearer."

Nick looks up to the sky as if searching for divine intervention, and turns a baleful face back to me. "The gods clearly are no force against Gwendolyn's act of repentance."

"Do be fair," I chide. "She is now your family as much as mine."

He makes a sour face, but it is boyish and playful.

"And," I remind him, "she gifted us Jerome's hunting box for our new hospital."

Thirty-five beds for the Lady Margaret Halladay Memorial Hospital, situated on the River Mersey, a specialized facility for spinal patients, with an indoor pool, gymnasium, paved walking paths to accommodate wheelchairs, occupation and skills training, music, art, and suites should families wish to stay. The garden shall be named for Old Dr. Bettany, because something should stand in honor of a man who treated generations of Blackpond's factory families. I, of course, am not permitted to nurse. I am trained in Nick's program of Contrology, however, and it requires no license.

Nick holds up the second letter. The print is tidy, the script large and square.

"Betsy is asking if she and Peters may have a week off to marry." Betsy and Peters will join us at the hospital. She is organizing the household side and Peters, having proven his ability to toss a man over his shoulder, is becoming an orderly.

Nick agrees to their holiday enthusiastically. "I would never deny a couple seeking *good offspring.*"

He holds up the third letter. As always, the sender is short and to the point, both stern and self-pitying.

"Papa wishes to inform us that despite our elopement, he will honor the marriage contract." Which includes a hefty endowment for the hospital and a commitment to provide medical supplies at no cost. Though, between Master James' series of front-page articles in London and my cousin Kristina's in New York, donations have flooded in and we could well afford to buy our own.

The final letter I left sealed. Nick tears it open, pulls out a single sheet and bursts out laughing. *Bursts.* I have never heard him laugh thus. The sound tumbles in waves out of him, free and untroubled. If I could, I would cup my hands to catch it.

"What?" I ask.

He holds the page up for inspection.

"Your brother writes in Greek," I say in mock exasperation. "And it's one word! He spent all that postage on a single word? The Home Secretary shall have his head."

"Shall I translate?"

I give him a one shoulder shrug, feigning indifference. What a luxury it is, to be able to stand on the beach and let the water lap at my feet and joke with this man. Not a single Sopwith Camel mars the endless blue sky. "If you're so inclined."

"Meraki," he says in a hearty Greek accent.

"Which means?" My own accent is cut glass House of Halsop English.

"To do something and everything with love and gusto." Oh, the smile on that man. Slow and wholeheartedly naughty. He narrows his eyes at the stack of letters clutched in his hand and tosses them into the air. The pages flutter and scatter, falling into the waiting waters of the Aegean. "Civilization can wait."

"Time and tide," I warn. There are some institutions even I cannot blow up.

"I am on a different clock, Vera-not-Vera." He holds out his wrist and taps an imaginary watch.

I inspect his wrist. He turns it over to show me his pulse. "A lover's timepiece," he says.

Hand in hand, we run toward the waiting shelter of a grove of kermes oaks. To explore once again the beauty of each other's bodies. To hear him laugh. For him to hear mine, which though rusty, rings true. To discover the quirk of our reflexes, the way our toes curl and our spines tense and relax. The way we fit together, whether near or far. Unhurried. For this moment, for as long as we both shall live, we have, at last, time.

The End.

Dear Reader~

A heartfelt thank you for spending your precious free time with me. Every book I write is a labor of love. I tell love stories because love inspires, challenges, and molds us into our best selves. I write because I am an avid reader—the very act of reading connects me to my family's read-aloud traditions, my grandmother's favorite books, and stories that are timeless. And when I am finished writing, my hope is that my stories resonate with you. Writing and reading are acts of love.

Blooms of War sprung from my head with a single image. A man in uniform, a woman in a nurse's outfit, a full moon, a lake, and a wooded forest. The image struck something in my heart, and I needed to know more about this couple. So, I followed them from the English countryside, to the battle fields of France, to London, to the Royal Courts of Justice, all the while noting down the tumult and passion of their head and heart. I enjoyed this journey. I hope you did too! Please consider leaving an honest review of *Blooms of War*. Reviews are greatly appreciated!

If you would like to read more love stories steeped in history, please consider pulling from the Amazon shelf my very first novel, the award-winning *The Art of the Scandal*. It is a historical romance about an impoverished English Rose with a quirky eye for spotting art forgeries, and a mysterious South African from a prominent Jewish family who is out to exact revenge on the English aristocracy. His weapon? A priceless collection of Renaissance Madonnas. Except, as our heroine points out to him when she's trying to charm back from him the deed to her house (which he won in a poker game), his collection is riddled with fakes. Let the wit, sexual chemistry, character growth, and kisses ensue! I've included the first chapter here for you!

I wish you joyous reads.

Yours,
Suzanne

The Art of the Scandal

Suzanne Tierney

CHAPTER ONE

July, 1850
Beware, darling, disaster rolls in on a whisper.

In the cavernous ballroom overflowing with thick bouquets of pink roses, Lydia rubbed her engagement ring like a rosary. She missed her mother dearly. She did *not* miss her mother's hushed warnings, uttered as prayers not to ward off danger, but rather to surrender to it.

Lydia sought relief in the sight of her fiancé, Percy. She spotted him, ensconced in his circle of identically clad, identically mustached men of politics, and caught his eye. He winked and pointed to her dance card. How handsome he looked against the backdrop of the older men, with their stooping shoulders and greying hair. A young buck today, one day Percy would be Prime Minister. And she his wife. The near miracle of her good fortune made her heart swell so she feared she might float away.

Percy held up four fingers—*Save the fourth waltz for me.* She shrugged her shoulders and gave a mock frown—*All filled up.* Percy cocked his forefinger like a gun, aimed at the dance card and mouthed "Pow." Lifting it, she inspected the imaginary bullet hole and saluted him. He bowed in return. Lydia laughed, giddy. There would be no disasters. Not tonight. Not ever.

She made her way through the throng of crinkled silks and pressed tailcoats, accepting well-wishes and congratulations. The Prime Minister raised his champagne glass to her while patting his coat pocket for his hip flask. The Chancellor of the Exchequer viewed the festivities through his pince-nez, perhaps weighing the sum of the champagne and flowers against the national debt.

No doubt tomorrow's papers would devote a column to the fete, abusing adjectives like *sumptuous* and *rarefied*. They would describe Percy as *gallant* and her as *resplendent* in a gown of pink silk with Belgian lace, and no one would know she'd haggled like a fishmonger's wife for that lace or that the modiste had huffed that she was being *cheated* by the gentry.

Mama would have died before being caught bargaining. Perhaps she had died to avoid such shame. Still, how proud she would have been tonight. How her death still hurt. Even after all these hard-luck years, the loss cut Lydia's breath short.

She waved to her friend Suzette, looking ethereal and lost amidst the roses and candlelight. Suzette was allergic to both. When she reached her, they looped arms and Suzette sighed, demure and graceful as always. "Lucky Lydia."

"I am indeed." A wonder that after a lifetime of her father squandering luck, there had been a drop left for Lydia. By all rights, it should have been Suzette who got engaged first. Not only had Suzette a dowry to make the Chancellor's eyes pop, she was the true beauty in the ballroom. Whereas Suzette was diamond-blonde and willowy, Lydia was merely blonde and properly proportioned. Where Suzette's eyes were sapphire blue, Lydia's were just bright. Where Suzette smiled rarely, Lydia was told she smiled too much, even now, as she warned her friend, "Here comes Colonel Sticky Fingers."

"Don't be subversive!" Suzette hid a giggle behind her linen handkerchief, the corner embroidered with a camellia. "He's always trying to find a new place to pinch me."

"Poor man. It's the only indulgence the old enjoy now that their lascivious schoolboy days are decades behind them. He's harmless." At least, that was what Mama had taught her. "It's his bird I find terrifying. Its eyes sit sideways on its head, always shifting."

"What an odd thing to notice." Suzette dabbed delicately at her nose.

Colonel Aethelborn, dressed in full red regalia, medals from his gruesome battles in India pinned to his chest, parrot perched on his shoulder, greeted her with a teasing, "You look so happy, you'll start a scandal." His gloved hand lingered too long on her bare shoulder. Lydia took the Colonel's hands into her own, and kept them there so he could not run roughshod over Suzette. He wrinkled his brow. "Why, you've the grip of a dock worker."

"Do I?" she asked sweetly.

"English Rose. English Rose," the parrot countered.

"Thank you, Fifi." Lydia nodded, but avoided the bird's eyes. The parrot had been a gift from the Colonel's favorite mistress, who reportedly tried to claw him to death when he suggested reducing her allowance. The mistress ran off with an Austrian general. The parrot stayed and the Colonel taught it to smoke, drink, swear, and compliment women. They were a highly compatible pair.

The Colonel, having been released from Lydia's clutch asked, "With your engagement, the Fremonts gain the honor of a marquis's daughter. But what, poor girl, do you gain besides a tory who waxes on about corn taxes?" He yawned tragically. "And guano."

What a silly question. The mere mention of Percy and her heart surged—she could more likely capture the moon than keep her smile from bursting forth. Percy was the same boy she'd pushed into a fountain when she was six, kissed behind the hedge roses when she was thirteen. "I am marrying the man I have loved all my life."

Beside her, Suzette stiffened. The Colonel blinked, as if admitting affection, much less passion for one's fiancé, was evidence of madness. The parrot cocked its head. "English Rose." Somehow, he sounded regretful. Lydia squared her shoulders. Love was never a social faux pas, not even to Mama and she'd married the disastrous Marquis of Chichester, *Charming Charlie*.

Before Lydia could break the awkward moment by asking the Colonel to retell one of his well-trodden war stories, the parrot sounded a warning, "Waterloo. Watch out. Waterloo." Even as he bowed his hasty adieu, the Colonel was retreating backward into the crowd.

The cowardly vision was replaced by the Dowager Countess of Longsharp, swathed in a sea of orange so aggressive, she could have been mistaken for a ball of fire. Waterloo, her toy poodle, sat tucked under her arm much like a rifle. The poor pup was wearing a matching gown and a tiara.

"Was that the Colonel skulking away?" The Dowager licked her top lip with the regret of a lion having lost its prey. Not to worry, in a social crush such as this, there was always fresh game. She appraised Lydia and Suzette with an auctioneer's eye, and rubbed Waterloo beneath the chin. "What a pair of docile angels you two are."

Beside her, Suzette stifled a sneeze. The Dowager's perfume, French, of course, was thick with a floral combination ending with a bite, like pepper. With her fan, the Dowager gestured to Suzette's necklace, a string of sapphires each the size of a baby's fist. "God broke the bank with you. So what shall it be? Earl, marquis, or duke?" She scanned the ballroom, marking targets. "No mere viscount for you."

Percy, of course, was a mere viscount.

The Dowager studied Lydia's neckline. Tonight, so all the world could see, instead of wearing it on her finger, Lydia wore her engagement ring, a Fremont family heirloom, on a simple gold chain. "How very right of you it was, Lady Lydia, to forego adornment. Against such a busy ballroom, you stand out like a virgin at a bacchanalia."

This said by a woman whose dog was wearing a diamond tiara! No matter, Lydia had very little jewelry besides her engagement ring. Nor would she have risked wearing any to a ball attended by her wager-mad father.

The Dowager stroked Waterloo's belly. "It's a joy to see you so well settled, dear Lady Lydia. As for that wildcat sister of yours—"

"Kitty is fifteen. Not even out of the schoolroom." Out of habit as much as instinct, Lydia curled her toes and dug her slippered feet into the polished marble floor. The hard surface gave no traction. "If half the stories of her tearing through the countryside are true, there's not a schoolroom in England that can tame her."

It was far too late to tame her sister. But Lydia would talk to Percy, and surely he would help find the answer to Kitty's...predicament. Lydia inhaled resolutely. Percy could fix anything. Though the last time they'd met, her sister had smashed a tea cup over his head. Perhaps he knew of a convent full of side-eyed nuns?

"You'd do better sending her off to the wilds of Africa," said the Dowager.

"Do you know, my lady"—Lydia doused her voice with honey—"my next waltz is promised to a man from Africa."

The Dowager half-clucked, half-trilled. "Is he *wild?*"

"No, quite gentlemanly. Percy introduced us this evening. A Mr. Simon Cohen."

"Cohen? Oh, of the banking tribe." The Dowager covered the dog's ears protectively. "Though his mother, I am told, was English." Waterloo growled. The Dowager pursed her mouth to the left, reconsidering. "Or perhaps just Christian."

"Percy tells me that although Mr. Cohen is newly arrived to London, already Prince Albert is seeking his counsel in securing financing for the Great Exhibition," Lydia said with the pride of the soon-to-be perfect wife to the already perfect politician.

Suzette leaned forward, her gloved hand tracing the outline of the sapphire necklace. "It is not quite *de rigueur* to invite bankers to our balls, but my papa says Mr. Cohen is the exception."

"Mr. Cohen was heavily involved in issuing the necessary bonds after the *Sonderbund*." Lydia pushed the clumsy word off her tongue with false breeziness. How meticulously she'd practiced it before the mirror. How mercilessly her sister had mocked her for being Percy's marionette. "Switzerland has a new constitutional regime." Lydia raised her arms in a *voilà*.

The Dowager whacked her with her fan. "Do not speak of *liberal regimes* in a ballroom, child. It invites disaster."

Disaster.

Lydia refused to shudder. The Dowager was the last person anyone would mistake for a prophet. Still, it was safer to retreat into social niceties. "Who is next on your dance card, Suzette?"

Suzette shook her head. "I think I will sit this one out. My throat is frightfully parched." She coughed like an angel experiencing a hiccup.

"See if you can rescue Percy from that pack of politicians," Lydia said. "The Colonel is right. Talk of corn and guano can only be so fascinating."

Now Suzette's ethereal face took on a human touch, the eyes crinkling, the corners of her soft red lips turning up ever so slightly.

"Ah, here comes my partner," said Lydia.

"Oh." The Dowager fanned Waterloo. "I did not expect him to be so . . ."

"Continental," Suzette tried on a breath.

"Masculine," the Dowager corrected on a purr.

Golden.

Lydia delivered a swift kick to her common sense. Honestly, had they been expecting a hunchback? Granted, when she'd met him earlier, he'd been standing in the shadows and not, well, walking. Broad shouldered and long-legged, it seemed as if he gathered the light behind him the way a storm does clouds. To define him. And if the ballroom were a metaphorical battleground for the rest of them, he strode through it as if the battle were real. Not mechanical, but as if he would defeat the enemy by staring down the bayonet. The Colonel would have enthusiastically followed him into the breach.

"Mr. Cohen." Lydia curtsied. He bowed, low and handsome as any

English courtier. Waterloo raised herself on her hind legs, panting, and held out a paw. The most she got from Mr. Cohen was a perplexed nod.

The orchestra struck the beginning notes of the waltz, an invitation to lovers, untested alliances and social climbers alike to take the floor. She let Mr. Cohen lead her across the ballroom, couples parting to create a path for her because this was, after all, her ball. When he cupped her back on the dance floor, Lydia relaxed into his hold. So many of the partners Percy sent her were nothing but thumbs and wrong-turned feet. Luckily, somewhere in the plains of Africa, Mr. Cohen had learned to waltz. And well.

"My fiancé tells me you are new to London."

"I am from Cape Town, yes. Though more lately Berlin and Zurich. Still, Cape Town at heart." His accent was near English, but it veered geographically, making the way he talked both familiar and faraway. He spoke more quickly than a Brit and he hit the last consonant of each word hard, with a firm back-of-the-throat kick. One would always hear where his passions lay. *Cape Town at heart.*

"And how do you find our English ballrooms?"

"Exotic."

"Truly? I imagined in Cape Town you would have polkas danced to tribal drums."

"Polkas yes, drums no. In comparison, tonight a parrot insulted my manhood and a poodle flirted shamelessly. It makes a man of my limited experience" –this he said with an ironic tone—"wonder, what could possibly be next."

"A unicorn, perhaps?"

"With an eye patch." The right corner of Mr. Cohen's lips quirked up. "Challenging me to a duel."

It was Lydia's turn to smirk.

Lydia spotted Suzette leaning closely to Percy, chatting animatedly. They were—all three of them—old friends and Suzette was not at ease with most men. Pity Mr. Cohen did not come with a title or the right religion. "And have you had a chance to explore our fair city?"

In the single arch of one eyebrow, Mr. Cohen indicated he thought there very little fair about London's clogged streets and soot-stained skies. Perhaps he could only catch glimpses of tree line from a cramped office filled with ledgers and numbers. At least, that's what she imagined—her understanding of banking was limited to Dickens.

Her father, Charming Charlie, unfairly handsome with his thick head of still-blond curls and long gait (*all the better to give the creditors the slip, pet*) glided in through a side door. He was greeted by a chorus of cheers and slaps on the back.

Mr. Cohen spun her and asked, "What would you recommend to the man newly arrived on England's shores?"

Such an easy question. "The National Gallery, where it is impossible to be bored." Its sunlit halls filled with masterworks had always served as her refuge from the turmoil of the peeling wallpaper and bitter arguments of home. "I have spent hours divining its secrets."

"Secrets?" Mr. Cohen's question came low and deep. He smelled of eucalyptus, a cool contrast to the natural huskiness of his voice.

"So many," she said mischievously. "There is Barocci's *The Madonna of the Cat*, which everyone says is a picture of the holy family's domestic bliss—but if you take a closer look, I think the poor Madonna is allergic to fur...the tip of her nose is miserably red." Lydia wrinkled her nose to demonstrate. "And there's Raphael's *The Madonna and Child* where it seems Raphael spent all his talent on lighting the Madonna's lovely face, only to give her deformed hands."

"Deformed?"

Was he mocking her? Percy said she sometimes could go on about things of no import. But no, Mr. Cohen had lowered his head to hear her better. She said, "The index finger is too fat and the middle is obscenely long."

He rewarded her with a chuckle.

A skinny messenger in a newsboy cap and tatty jacket raced in, a liveried footman huffing behind. The boy skidded directly into her father, handing him a crisp letter. Her father broke the seal, absorbed the contents, then crumpled it and shoved it into his pocket. He did not spare a coin for the boy.

Anxiety, that familiar bedtime story, edged round Lydia's stomach. She closed her eyes and shut out the fear. "Do you know van Eyck's *Arnolfini Portrait*? Everyone focuses on the glowing bride in her velvet green dress and her ghoulish husband, as if the imbalance in their beauty is the story. Boring stuff. If you look at the wall behind the couple, there's a Latin signature—*Jan van Eyck was here, 1434*," Lydia finished a bit breathlessly, her words necessary to outrace her worries.

"Do you not enjoy the painting as a whole, Lady Lydia?" He sounded amused. Percy would say charmed.

Those tiny details of each painting were charms, she collected them to ward off despair. "I find it's always the odd feature that makes the painting come to life."

"Then I wonder what you would see in my collection. I've several Madonna and Childs from the masters—Raphael, Sassafratto, Leonardo's *Madonna of the Stones*. All of which I intend to gift to the National Gallery at the end of the summer. Perhaps as your wedding present—I will grant you a preview."

Leonardo's *Madonna of the Stones*! It had been purchased out of a crumbling Italian church by a prominent Jewish family decades ago and not been displayed since, though Lydia had seen a poor etching once. Her head near swam at the chance to see the original. Would there be five or six petals on the daffodils? Were the stones as dark and jagged as the entrance to Hades? "Then you must love art!"

Mr. Cohen tightened his jaw. "Not particularly. Like you, my interest is not in the story everyone thinks the painting tells. It's the story I tell that matters. In this case, my collection is my calling card to London. Where other men might display what they have or who they know, I prefer to make my introduction by demonstrating what I can easily give away."

How crassly Mr. Cohen diminished the best of human achievement.

They moved in silence, obeying the pattern of the waltz. Lydia caught sight of her father, who was slipping out the door. Always the first hint of an impending disaster. How was it that when scandals fell, the axe never landed on the culprit's neck? No matter what her father's sins, he was always forgiven by the *ton*. No one lost with better humor than Charming Charlie, they said. No one shared his spoils with greater gusto. Meanwhile, Lydia sold the silver to pay the butcher and she, like Mama before her, suffered the shame.

Mr. Cohen interrupted her thoughts. "Does that orange Lilith plan on seducing the poor lad?" He indicated the Dowager who had in her clutches—dear God—the messenger boy.

"Lilith?" she asked, barely able to squeeze in a breath.

He frowned momentarily, as if he had made a social slip. "In Jewish mythology, Lilith is a female demon."

The Dowager looked ready to devour the boy. She clutched him at the collar and indicated with her fat chin the direction of where her father had snuck out. The boy shrugged and, clever urchin that he was, held out his palm. The Dowager, unable to hold on to both the boy and her jeweled dog, must have called in reinforcement for the Colonel trotted forward, looking confused and yet obedient. He pulled a handful of coins from his pocket and the boy refused to fold his palm until each one was deposited securely. Then he crooked his finger, and the Dowager, her orange battle storm of a dress flaming, leaned forward. When he was done, the boy raced from the ballroom and the Dowager looked as if she'd just dined on the most tender, succulent gazelle. She met Lydia's eye and drew open her fan as precisely as one unsheathes a dagger.

What was in the letter? *Please let it be a jilted opera singer.* The

Dowager turned to whisper in the Colonel's ear. He turned red, then white, then red again. *Please let it be pistols at dawn.* The Dowager beckoned to a trio of expensively dressed matrons, who in turn gasped and clutched their throats. *Please let it be anyone but Kitty.* No one knew about Kitty. Not even Papa. Lydia had been a vigilant guard.

Hadn't she?

Mr. Cohen steered them deeper into the crowd of dancers, away from the Dowager's view. Out of kindness or coincidence, Lydia could not be sure. Her heart was beating so hard, she almost missed that Mr. Cohen was talking. She swallowed and tried to concentrate.

"Forgive me, Lady Lydia, if I spoke too roughly before. I just find art to be sadly artificial. A poor mimic."

"You don't think the genius of a human hand can be beautiful?"

"Not when you come of age in Cape Town. I learned to swim where the currents of the Atlantic meet the Indian and climbed flat-topped mountains shrouded in clouds. My boyhood, you see, was spent running across the veld, beneath constellations."

Beneath constellations. What must it be like to race the stars under a sky that stretched with no end? The gilded cornices of this ballroom seemed cheap in contrast. Lydia straightened her spine. Hang the Dowager and her petty gossip. Whatever the contents of the letter, the Dowager would still beg for an invitation to Lydia's wedding. On hind legs no less!

"Am I wrong, Mr. Cohen, in thinking you have been in London before?"

Their dancing paused for a fraction of a second. He said nothing.

"It's just, I had a nanny from the Cape Colony. And your vowels are not quite the same. Her *i* was more of an *ee* so my sister was always *Keety* instead of *Kitty*. And we could not tell the difference between her *pig* and her *peg*. Which caused all sorts of misunderstandings." Lydia thought a moment. "In fact, your vowels are rather Londonish."

"What an interesting eye—ear—for detail you have."

"Much to my father's despair. He is forever lamenting that I can identify every leaf pattern of every tree and still not realize I'm in a forest."

At her admission, he threw his head back and laughed. His laugh—she'd never heard anything so free. Bold and full-hearted, mixed with the scent of eucalyptus, it brought to mind a cool wind across what Mr. Cohen called the veld. The laugh lingered on her skin. He was indeed golden, the favorite child of an African sun. His dark hair held glints of red where the sun had tousled his locks. Even his brown eyes made her think of wheat fields in August. He had the look of a man used to surveying vast expanses, who could see well beyond the plaster walls of this ballroom. He would know exactly where he was in a forest.

The waltz ended. The couples parted for her as before. Mr. Cohen's hand fell away from her back as he led her to Percy, who was deep in conversation with the Dowager and a set of old gossips. Suzette was pulling at the tips of her gloves. The Colonel stared transfixed by the sheen of the marble floor.

Lydia had the strangest sensation, as if a pin had pricked her spine and she was deflating. Her smile was the first thing to slip away. Then the air left her lungs. Her heart seemed to stop beating, and a knot so tight it might split her in two welled in the pit of her stomach. Her legs grew heavy and unreliable.

"Would you prefer a cup of ratafia?" Mr. Cohen asked.

It was his pity that spurred her forward. She might not have swum in oceans or outraced stars, but she'd beaten the odds to become Society's English Rose. Tonight, the Prime Minister had given a short speech in her honor. She tacked her smile back to her face, lifted her chin.

She would not be bullied. The Dowager's husband had died in a soprano's bed. *Next to a baritone.* The Colonel sometimes wet himself, and it was Lydia who shifted the blame to his parrot, Fifi, and delivered the old soldier discreetly to his valet. And there was Percy, who loved her. He looked mad as thunder, it was true, but it had to be for the Dowager and her mean-spirited little soul. A Lilith indeed. The Dowager and her circle watched Lydia approach, their eyes wide in hopes of what? Tears? A scene? Something to talk about tomorrow at tea. Lydia thought of oceans meeting and constellations stretching and quickened her stride.

Mr. Cohen and Percy shook hands. "I congratulate you, Fremont, on your excellent choice of a bride." Mr. Cohen's tone sounded so even, so balanced, it brought to mind the scales of justice.

"My fiancée is full of surprises, is she not?" Percy's smile was so thin-lipped, it veered precariously close to a sneer. Surely Percy could not be angry at *her*. She'd done nothing wrong. She was always so careful to do nothing wrong.

Lydia's stomach quavered. She reached out to remind him of the happiness between them. Percy clamped her wrist hard, the force of his grip more painful than a jailer's cuff.

Want more? Buy *The Art of the Scandal*!

Subscribe to my newsletter!

AUTHOR NOTES

One of the joys of writing historical literature are the hours one gets to spend researching. One of the frustrations is that history does not always cooperate with you. Picric acid was indeed used to treat burns. Its powder was soaked into bandages carried by the soldiers of the WWI British Royal Army Corps.

Picric Acid was also used as a weapon. It is responsible for the explosion on Black Tom Harbor in New York and the fire on Parliament Hill in Ottawa, both of which occurred in 1916. Both incidents were attributed to German acts of terrorism on North American soil.

Picric acid in the form of a pencil bomb, however, did not become truly efficient until WWII. Thus, the picric acid timed bombs created by Gwendolyn were a bit of writer's license. Readers should assume Gwendolyn's invention would have been a precursor to the fully effective pencil bombs of WWII. Her bombs would not have performed perfectly each time they were planted, but the ones that did explode would have been dangerous.

I am not a physician. And while WWI is responsible for many a medical innovation, the technical aspects of blood transfusions and wound-cleaning described in the book are near a century old. I relied on medical texts of the time including the brochure issued by Johnson and Johnson's for the Carrel-Dakin Kit.

Also, I near faint at the sight of blood. In writing this book, I developed a deep respect for the courage, ingenuity and plain gumption that medical personnel displayed in the face of a brutal and exhausting war. I think in 2020, we all have a new appreciation for healthcare workers. If you would like to learn more about the medical workers in the fields of WWI, I highly recommend:

A Doctor on the Western Front, The Diary of Henry Owens 1914-1918, Edited by John Hutton

Diary of a Nursing Sister on the Western Front, 1914-1915, Anonymous

Dorothea's War, A First World War Nurse Tells Her Story, by Dorothea Crewdson

Unknown Warriors, The Letters of Kate Luard, RRC and Bar, Nursing Sister in France 1914-1915, Edited by John Stevens

The name of Nick's barrister, Nigel Higgenbotham, was selected by the winner of my Vote on a Title contest, Dottie Lafferty. Many thanks, Dottie!

ABOUT THE AUTHOR

Writer of lush, historical happily-ever-after tales, Suzanne Tierney believes in true love. But she takes delicious pleasure in making her characters fight, flutter, and find their way to each other. Her books have won numerous awards and she has twice been a Golden Heart Finalist® with the Romance Writers of America.

Suzanne grew up in Oregon, adulted in the San Francisco Bay Area, and somehow ended up in Florida, where she is very much a cold-water fish learning to navigate humid, salty seas. She loves chatting with readers and if you subscribe to her newsletter, she will share secrets, gossip, and goodies with you. Check out her author website and subscribe to her newsletter here! www.suzannetierney.com

Connect with her here!
Amazon
Facebook
Instagram
BookBub
Goodreads

Made in the USA
Middletown, DE
18 October 2020